The Last
Nanny
In Manhattan
by K.STERLING

All illustrations by

Jayla

The Last *Nanny* In Manhattan
Soundtrack

Sweet Tooth	Cavetown
Mr. Blue Sky	Weezer
Maps	Yeah Yeah Yeahs
Pumpkin	The Regrettes
Nothing	Bruno Major
Cupid De Locke	The Smashing Pumpkins
I Would Do Anything For You	Foster The People
Something About Us	Daft Punk
Time To Pretend	MGMT
Take On Me	Weezer
Blow	Beyoncé
Somewhere Only We Know	Keane

The Last Nanny In Manhattan

K. Sterling

A Note About Content

This love story is intended to be low in angst but the characters do experience homophobia briefly in the workplace. Also, Walker is grieving the loss of his husband to a drunk driver.

Expect lots of heat and some praise kink!

Want to know more and get updates on new releases?

Sign up for my newsletter: www.ksterlingbooks.com

Want advance copies of new releases and an exclusive short story from K. Sterling every month?
Join my Patreon: www.patreon.com/ksterling

For Scott. All my love. All my life.

To Roshni. For being there from the beginning and always believing in me.

A thousand thank yous to my writing bestie, Reese Ryan. This wouldn't have happened without your support and loyalty.

And to Melissa, Sue, and Cyndi.

Finally, to Kerri Buckley for reminding me that everything happens for a reason.

Chapter One

"**W**hat does the tooth fairy do with all those teeth?" Neville asked as he stretched on his toes and put his finger painting on the bookshelf to dry. Finley Marshall was at the sink with Neville's fourteen-month-old sister, Celeste, washing her hands. The three of them had created finger-paint masterpieces but it was time for Celeste to take a nap while Fin and Neville had a snack and worked on the day's French lesson.

"That is one of life's greatest mysteries, I'm afraid," Fin murmured while he juggled the squirming infant and art supplies.

"What if I want to keep my teeth? And Celeste's?"

"Um..." Fin widened his eyes at the baby. Neville was a brilliant little boy and ravenously curious but some of his interests could be...alarming. It was hard to tell if he was a budding anthropologist or a nascent serial killer.

"Do you have to sell your teeth to the tooth fairy? What if I want to buy my friends' teeth?" Neville asked, then used his tongue to jiggle one of his front teeth.

"Oh." Fin made a note to warn the Wolfords. Neville reminded Fin of a tiny Edgar Allen Poe with his dark features, pale skin, and his morbid fascination with the human skeleton and mummies. "What are you going to do with all those teeth?" Fin asked nervously but the boy shrugged.

"Make a collection. Mama said I can't have any bones but teeth are kind of like bones, and she lets me put them under my pillow." That had been a rare moment of solid parenting on Mrs. Wolford's part. At thirty-four, she was less than half her husband's age and often too distracted by the pool boy or busy with her trainer. She'd hovered in the nursery during Fin's first week but immediately lost interest after grabbing his ass three times had failed to get a reaction out of him. They rarely spoke, but she was kind yet dismissive whenever they crossed paths. Fin pretended she was Mother of the Year for Neville and Celeste's sake.

"Yup. I need to give your parents a heads up because we don't want them to panic when they find a bag of teeth under the bed," Fin said as he pointed at Neville.

The boy wrinkled his nose and shook his head. "I was going to put them with my soccer trophies."

"Wow. Don't." Fin stifled a shiver. He reminded himself that Neville had other healthy, typical interests and easily connected with his peers, unlike most serial killers. There was a tap at the nursery door and the Wolford's housekeeper swept into the room, her nose at a perfect forty-five-degree angle.

"Hello, Astrid..." Fin said warily then frowned as she efficiently plucked Celeste from his arms and deposited her in the play yard.

"What's going on?" He asked. Astrid clasped her hands behind her back, sniffing as she kept her gaze on the ceiling. She was always sour and superior but Fin knew he was in trouble because she wouldn't make eye contact with him.

"Mr. Wolford would like a word with you in his office," she said flatly.

"I'm going with Fin!" Neville cried as he lunged at Fin but Astrid grabbed his arm.

"Hey, pal!" Fin caught his nose and gave it a wiggle. "You behave and listen to Astrid. We were going to practice our French. Why don't you grab a book and read until we figure out what's going on?" He suggested, holding onto Neville's nose until he nodded. "That's my creepy man," Fin said, holding up his palm so Neville could slap it. "And you keep the mischief to a minimum," he told Celeste as he went to her play yard and fixed her bow. He pressed a kiss to his fingers and rubbed them against her cheek before he looked around the nursery. Fin had a feeling it was the last time he'd see it. "You two be very, very good." Fin coughed when his voice broke. "Later, Astrid." He bowed his head at the older woman, then hurried from the room.

Fin didn't know *why* but he knew what was coming. Mr. Wolford never wanted to see any of his employees, save the butler and the small army of lawyers that waited on him hand and foot. Wolford demanded their obedience while the rest of the household staff leapt through doorways whenever the elderly man was wheeled into the room. Fin couldn't imagine what he could have done to deserve an audience.

He jogged down the stairs to the second floor, making his way to the suite of offices at the end of the west hallway. Fin knocked on the door and pushed it open to find the aging financier seated behind his desk. Wolford didn't even bother to look up. He just waved impatiently from where he was hunkered over a stack of documents. He was flanked by two of his lawyers and one of them sneered at Fin as he approached the oversized and ornate mahogany desk.

"You wanted to see me, sir?" He asked, his eyes stinging, only to receive a dry, wheezing chuckle in return.

"You're to sign this and take yourself off the premises," Wolford ordered as the lawyer on the left pointed at a form on the corner of the desk. Fin's brows pulled together as he looked at the page. The words "Termination of Contract" were a kick in the gut.

"What? Why? I haven't done anything wrong and the kids love me. Mrs. Wolford said I'm the best nanny the kids have ever had," Fin protested but that probably made things worse. Mr. Wolford (correctly) suspected that she'd slept with half of the household's staff. "Not that we talk all that often. Just when she visits with the kids," he added but the snottier minion on the left slapped a pen against the desktop as the one on the right pointed at the document.

"Per the contract you signed when you joined the household, Mr. Wolford has the right to terminate your employment whenever he sees fit without any explanation. Furthermore, you are prohibited from speaking about the Wolford family and anything you may have seen or heard while you were employed by them," Leftie recited swiftly and the lawyer on the right pointed again.

"But—"

"Without *any* explanation, Mr. Marshall," Mr. Left Side repeated.

"OK," Fin said tightly and glared at Wolford as he snatched the pen off the table. He scanned the two short paragraphs but there were no clues as to what Fin had done so he signed it and pushed it back at Lefty. "Thank you for allowing me to care for your children. They're both wonderful little people and the last six months have been a pleasure," he said, because it was true and because Fin was a kind and decent person. Unlike his now-former employer. Fin offered Mr.

Wolford a jaunty salute then turned on his heel and strode from the room.

From the way that all but a few of the maids avoided eye contact, Fin figured that the kitchen staff knew of his termination. Tamara, one of the newer hires, was the only person who whispered an apology, but Fin waved the young woman off as he got his messenger bag from the hook and left. It stung like hell because he adored the kids but nothing the rich did surprised him anymore. And Frederick Wolford wasn't the first heartless asshole Fin had ever worked for.

As a nanny, Fin had learned to put up with a lot of bad manners and entitled behavior. The kids were usually great, albeit a little spoiled, but the adults were often nightmares. Fin had disliked most of the adults at the homes he'd worked in but the pay was fantastic. The workload was easier than when he'd taught first grade, which had barely covered his half of the rent. So Fin had learned First Aid and had turned his skill set toward private childcare. Now, he only came home covered in sticky mystery substances if he had a little too much fun with an art or science project. He got far fewer colds and loved being in charge of the curriculum as most parents didn't care what Fin taught as long as the kids were quiet.

Fin, wanting to teach history at the college level, had been studying abroad in France when he'd realized his passion was for teaching children. He had tagged along on a field trip to the Louvre and Fin had more fun teaching six and seven-year-olds about primary colors than he had searching through manuscripts and writing papers. So he'd switched from history and got a degree in early childhood education like his older brother, Reid.

Fin had found his calling and loved his work, even if he didn't always enjoy *who* he worked for. He had fun and bonded with the kids under his care. He'd parted ways with several families because the parents were divorcing and the kids were moving out of state or the children had grown old enough to go to boarding school. And he'd been fired for dubious reasons that had nothing to do with him more times than he could count. But Fin had never been fired so abruptly and without any indication as to why.

The lack of explanation made Fin even more bitter. Was it his fault and a mark against his near-perfect record? Probably not. People like the Wolfords didn't care about the damage they did to their employees' lives and their reputations.

Fin stormed out of the Wolford's house, entertaining thoughts of applying for another teaching job, despite his vow to never go back. He had a whole list of reasons why he never wanted to teach in a school again, but he didn't have a job. And unlike his employers, Fin had bills and responsibilities. He'd have to find something else soon.

Chapter Two

Fin fumed all the way home and *almost* snarled at the old woman on the train who liked to bait him every time they rode together. She almost got a rise out of him with a remark about immigrants but Fin knew better than to feed a troll and found a book to read on his phone. Fin took a little joy in how shocked she'd be if she knew that he was reading a queer romance.

His stop came too soon and Fin had to face the city and his disappointment again as he trudged up the subway's steps at Utica Avenue and past the park. He just nodded at Lisa from the cell place and gave weak waves to the women at the nail salon. Fin didn't stop to make small talk with them or grab a burrito on the way home. His stomach had turned into a cold knot, but he was looking forward to a glass of wine and venting with his best friend since middle school, Riley Fitzgerald.

Normally the flowers in the window boxes of their shared English basement apartment in Bed-Stuy cheered Fin up, but they did nothing to help his mood as he stomped down the steps. He stuck his tongue out at the cartoon cat on the doormat ordering him to "wipe your paws right meow" and let himself in.

A Nat King Cole song crackled soothingly from the antique record player, signaling that Riley was in self-care mode. All the lights were turned off, save for the strands of fairy lights that intertwined with the vines that swagged along the bookshelves and window. The plants were Riley's babies. He rescued them the way old ladies rescued cats. Vines wound their way around every room of their apartment and a large potted Calamondin orange tree proudly flourished in the corner by the window. A tea and lemon-scented candle flickered on the spool coffee table but Fin could also detect a faint whiff of a rosemary smudge stick. He should have felt sorry for himself and Riley but Fin was soothed despite his dreadful day and was grateful to be home.

"I promise, my day was worse," Fin called out as he used his foot to kick the door shut behind him. Riley was sitting on the kitchen counter, wearing nothing but his underwear. It was never a good sign if Riley was home first and already drinking. Fin wondered if he was about to take his words back. "Did I have the worst day?" He asked as he dropped his bag on the green velvet sofa and headed for the kitchen. He was often in his underwear, but Riley was Mr. Silver Lining and had an endless supply of optimism and enthusiasm, whereas Fin was the wary, cynical one.

Fin and Riley were often mistaken for brothers because they were both tall and lean and had floppy brown hair. They'd been best friends since middle school and shared a wardrobe because both believed in the Three C's: cardigans, corduroys, and Converse. Riley even wore the same size of sneakers as Fin. It was perfect.

"Didja get fired too?" Riley asked as he poured a glass of

cheap-but-easy-to-drink Prosecco for Fin. They saluted each other and Fin thanked him as they sipped.

"Turns out, I did," Fin said, causing Riley to choke and spit into his wine.

"Seriously?"

"Yup."

"Ouch. At least I wasn't that attached yet," Riley muttered into his glass. "Penn and Reid were right about Gayle and her agency. She's a homophobe and fired me because she found out I was gay."

"She just found out?" Fin asked suspiciously, not liking the timing. Riley groaned as he scrubbed a hand through his hair.

"I'm so sorry. This is my fault. I posted the video of our performance on Facebook and Instagram," he said with a hard wince.

Fin tilted his head in confusion. "What? It was *Hamilton*! We were bad, but we weren't *that bad*," he said.

"You're the one who was pitchy," Riley said defensively.

"You picked 'Helpless' and you made me sing Eliza's part," Fin replied, then held up a hand. "I still don't understand how they found out or why that got us fired."

"Because we did it for the fundraiser," Riley said and Fin's jaw dropped. They'd performed their unfortunate act as part of the "Night of a Thousand Flops" fundraiser at the local theater. Tickets had been $20 a head for an evening of cringe-worthy yet family-friendly entertainment, benefiting a shelter for homeless LGBTQ youth.

"Just when you think people couldn't get worse..." Fin said. He felt terrible for Riley. This was the second time he'd been fired for being gay. He'd handled it well when it happened six months earlier, but he was clearly taking it harder this time. "We'll figure it out."

"I know, we always do. But I've only got enough to cover

this month's rent. I'm going to be in trouble if I can't find something soon. I burned through most of my savings the last time I was unemployed," Riley warned. Fin shook his head as he reached for the bottle to top off their glasses.

"Don't worry. I messaged Reid on the way home and he told me to swing by his place in the morning. I'll bring you with me and he'll sort us both out."

There were few people Fin could count on in the world, but he could count on Riley to be ready with wine, and he knew Reid would always have all the answers. Fin's big brother was his *first* best friend and his hero. And Fin wasn't the only one who looked up to him. The city's best nannies called Reid whenever they were stumped because he understood children and families better than anyone. Everyone trusted and respected Reid. And while Fin wasn't in a hurry to grow up, he was going to be just like his big brother one day. Sans the button-up shirts and ties, of course.

"Cool. Reid will know what to do," Riley said with a relieved chuckle. "He knows everybody and everything. How's he doing?"

"Still a little down but this should cheer him up." Fin squinted and hummed. "You know he's happiest when he's solving problems and saving the day."

"True," Riley agreed. "Maybe something good will come out of this awful mess after all," he said and held out his glass so Fin could tap it with his.

"I have a feeling that this is going to be a good thing. To Reid and to Hell with Gayle and the Wolfords."

Chapter Three

"I wonder why Reid told you to dress up." Riley snorted into his coffee but Fin ignored him as they climbed the grand steps of 42 Briarwood Terrace. There was nothing wrong with Fin's outfit.

"I did dress up. This is my best cardigan and I'm wearing your new black corduroys," he pointed out. Riley leaned back and gasped appreciatively.

"That I bought at the thrift shop!" They bumped fists and Fin sang about buying a broken keyboard before Riley cleared his throat. "Obviously, I think you look great." He gestured at his own Fair Isle cardigan before wincing at Fin. "But Reid said you were supposed to dress up."

"I am dressed up," Fin replied dismissively as he rang the buzzer. The cardigan was dark gray and Fin had paired it with a new white t-shirt and his best pair of black Converse. "It's not like I'm going to see the Pope."

"Are you even allowed to wear sneakers when you visit the Pope?" Riley wondered.

"I wouldn't know," Fin said as the intercom speaker crackled.

"Did you wear real clothes?" Reid asked.

"Nope," Fin replied. They heard a long, low groan.

"Finley." The beleaguered sound was punctuated by the click of the lock.

Fin smirked at Riley as he pulled the door open. They waved at Norman, the elderly guard, as he nodded off behind the front desk. The building had once been a mansion but had been converted into ten units. Fin loved the black and cream marble floors, the giant crystal chandelier, and the wide, curved staircase. Reid lived on the first floor, in unit #4, in what had once been the dining room, a parlor, and the conservatory.

Fin and Riley turned down the hall behind the staircase to find Reid leaning against his door waiting for them. He didn't appear to be surprised to see Riley, but he was shaking his head in disappointment at Fin.

They both had their Irish mother's green eyes and dark hair, but they couldn't have been more different. Reid's perfectly trimmed, tamed hair was already going gray at the temples. He always wore shirts with buttons and kept the sleeves neatly rolled up. When he left the house, he wore ties, but Fin felt like he was being strangled if he buttoned his collar.

"I found you the perfect job and this is how you repay me," Reid said, gesturing at Fin as he led the way to the kitchen. It still looked like a conservatory with its black and white tile and ancient wraparound windows. The counters and fixtures were all stainless steel and modern but the space was bright and overrun with vines and Reid's pampered orchids.

"I'm a nanny, not a maître d'," Fin said, then spun when he heard a clarinet from the other side of the apartment. "Morning, Gavin," he called but there was no answer as "Rhapsody in Blue" drifted into the kitchen.

Reid lived with his childhood best friend, Gavin Selby, a prickly über vanilla accountant. They were both thirty-two but Gavin kept to an octogenarian's routine and played his clarinet for an hour every weekday morning before walking to the park to play chess with the other old men. Gavin inherited the building from an uncle, but the rest of his family was a sore subject within unit #4.

"This is a…special job but I'm sure you can handle it," Reid said as he went around the island and tore an address out of his notebook. "It's twice what Wolford was paying you," he added, raising his brows. He pulled the address away when Fin reached for it.

"Rich and desperate. I like that. What's the catch?" Fin asked.

"It's Walker Cameron III," Reid replied pointedly. Fin and Riley both grimaced as they leaned back.

"No wonder he's desperate. I've heard the girls are terrors," Fin murmured but he was more concerned with Cameron. He was richer than Croesus and rumored to be a terror as well. People were certainly terrified of him on Wall Street and there were rumors on social media that Cameron was in the process of buying out a handful of smaller newspapers just so he could shut them down.

Reid clicked his teeth and shook his head. "He's desperate because he's a widower. His *husband* died a few years ago, remember?"

"Then he won't care if I don't show up in a tux and I don't have to worry about him firing me if he finds out I'm gay," Fin said with a shrug. It was a level playing field as far as Fin was concerned. Cameron might be one of the most feared men in Manhattan, but he was all out of options and Fin had encountered every variety of cold, rich dickhead over the course of his career and existence in New York City. He was ready to face the final boss and was confident he could handle Cameron.

"Right!" Riley said, snatching the piece of paper from Reid. "He's single. Maybe I should take this one. I'm out of a job too." Fin elbowed Riley and took the address from him. He checked to be sure but Fin already knew the stately Beaux-Arts mansion on East 88th Street.

"Don't be gross and I'm already dressed up."

"You look like you're burying your skateboard," Reid grumbled as he dropped onto a metal stool and flipped to the front of his notebook. "I can get you into something temporary while we find a long-term situation for you," he said to Riley, then tapped on a phone number. "Penn has to take a few weeks off because his dad is sick. He works for an amazing family with two moms and two adorable kids."

"You are a lifesaver," Riley said but Reid shrugged it off.

"*A lot* of queer parents have been turned down for childcare lately too, so I've been keeping my ear to the ground. It shouldn't take me long to find a good family for you," he predicted. Fin's lips quirked as he studied his brother.

"You know, I'm seeing an opportunity here." He hummed thoughtfully on his way to refill his to-go cup with coffee from the French press. "You've got the time and you know *everyone*." Reid was between families and doing his best to hide that he was depressed. He loved the last family he worked for and was especially attached to the twin boys. He'd been with them since they were infants but the mother took a job as an ambassador and moved to Copenhagen. She had taken the twins with her and left Reid at loose ends.

"Possibly. There're fresh bagels by the toaster," Reid said absently as Fin and Riley exchanged calculating smirks. Food was one of Reid's love languages and this was the sort of thing that he excelled at and just what he needed to lift his spirits and keep him busy. They silently agreed to machinate more later. *I'll talk to Gavin too.*

"Thanks, Mom!" Fin kissed Reid on the cheek loudly, then went to help himself. The world wasn't quite right yet but Fin could feel that something good was just around the corner as he dropped into "his" chair at an old bistro table that Reid had pushed against the window seat.

Fin had learned more at that table than in any classroom. He'd talked through his most difficult personal and professional problems in Reid and Gavin's kitchen, as the two of them were more like parents than Fin's actual parents were. Their parents were busy being renowned child psychologists and famous authors so Fin and Riley often turned to Reid and Gavin for just about everything.

Reid was the calm, cool voice of reason and Gavin was the brains behind every operation they embarked upon. Together, they helped carry Fin and Riley through every storm and picked up the pieces if Fin fell apart or someone broke his heart.

They had arrived at Briarwood Terrace hoping Reid would sort them out but Fin saw an opportunity to help a new family and save his brother. With his contacts and instincts, Reid could turn his passion for problem-solving into a profession and help a lot of people. Fin considered the address in his hands and the possibilities. He didn't have high hopes for Walker Cameron III but Fin was going to prove that he was one of the best nannies in the city. He had to. Fin was representing Reid now and this was how they were all going to turn the lemons life had handed them into lemonade.

Chapter Four

The house was silent as Walker leaned out of his study, into the hall, and cautiously checked both directions. It was clear and it was almost time for the new nanny to arrive. He looked at his watch as he strode around the corner and over the ornate marble medallion in the center of the foyer then swore when the leather sole of his Italian oxfords slipped on a small puddle. Walker scowled at it and then scanned the staircase and the gallery but he didn't see the culprit.

"Amelia?" He called but there was no answer. Walker set his hands on his hips as he backed away from the stairs. There was another puddle and his arms windmilled at his sides as he skated. "Amelia!" Walker bellowed then whipped around when he heard a titter. She waved and peeked from behind a large urn. "Come here," he said and pointed in front of him.

She batted her long black lashes at him and Walker was momentarily stunned by her giant blue eyes as she edged closer. Amelia's glossy black curls were pulled back into pigtails with Tiffany blue bows that matched her white and blue polka-dotted dress. She was an angel and Walker melted until he noticed the neon green barrel peeking from behind her shoulder.

"What did I tell you?" He said while gesturing for her to hand the weapon over. Her lower lip wobbled but Walker straightened his spine. He had to be strong. "Give it. I said no water guns inside," he scolded wearily. Amelia sniffed and pouted up at him but he remained firm.

"I thought you meant no guns in the nursery," she muttered as she handed over a plastic cannon that was almost as tall as her.

"Nice try," he said dryly. Walker passed the water gun to Pierce as he arrived with one of his footmen and a mop. The butler wordlessly left with the weapon and the floor was immaculate a few seconds later. Walker narrowed his eyes as he lowered to a knee and caught hold of her chin. "Whatever you have planned won't work. Do you know why?" He asked and her eyes narrowed back at him.

Lord, it was impossible to stay mad at her. She was so clever and she looked so much like Walker's beloved Connor. Amelia was clever like him but Walker had no idea how she turned out so devious. He often wondered if using Agnes as their egg donor was asking for trouble. Walker's ulcer twinged as Amelia shook her head. She was only six and Walker was a grown man, he reminded himself. *Be strong.* "It won't work because I won't allow Mr. Marshall to quit no matter what you and your sisters do," he vowed. Because that was how utterly and completely...cursed Walker was. He didn't have just one precious, chaotic clone of Connor. He had three. "I have already promised to pay him a brain surgeon's salary to get him through the door but I'm willing to give Mr. Marshall this house and your inheritances, if that's what it takes for him to stay." He raised his brows at Amelia but she just blinked back at him. "Do you know what that means?" He asked and her tongue protruded from the corner of her mouth as she considered his words.

"He'll be our daddy and you'll have to live at his house?" She guessed.

"God, that would be wonderful," he muttered under his breath and laughed softly when her jaw fell open. "For a few days but I'd miss you too much. Mr. Marshall is the last nanny in the city who will take my call. I'll give him every dime I've got if that's what it takes to keep him. That means no more ponies or weekends at the cottage. We'll have to move in with your grandparents," he threatened, but she didn't seem alarmed. "Your *other* grandparents," he clarified and her face pinched as if she could already smell the fertilizer. Walker's parents were in their eighties and barely noticed the girls when they visited the Cameron Estate in Connecticut. Connor's parents, on the other hand, lived in Idaho and grew barley for feed. "Want to live on the farm?" He asked. She shook her head quickly. "Then, you'd better hope Mr. Marshall isn't mean because you're stuck with him."

"What if—?"

"No. There are no other options if you scare this one off." They stared each other down until the doorbell rang. "That will be him," Walker said as he looked over his shoulder, turning back only to discover his precious little hellion had vanished. He nodded as Pierce silently sailed across the foyer. The dour older man coughed softly as two of his footmen opened the doors while Walker straightened and clasped his hands behind his back.

"Welcome to The Killian House, Mr. Marshall," Pierce said as he bowed his head and stepped aside.

The gorgeous spring morning spilled into the foyer as an unkempt but beautiful young man wandered over the threshold. He was wearing an oversized gray cardigan, droopy corduroys, and black sneakers. He swept his wild brown hair out of his face as he scanned the foyer with glowing green eyes that hardened when they landed on Walker.

"Mr. Cameron?" He asked as he approached. The sharp angles of his jaw and cheekbones grew more severe as Mr. Marshall assessed him and Walker felt unusually self-conscious. It hadn't occurred to him that *he* wouldn't pass Mr. Marshall's test. It was mortifying and bordered on obscene but Walker flashed the younger man a wide smile as he offered his hand.

"Indeed. I appreciate your coming at such short notice," he said and watched the younger man closely. His lip curled just a touch, confirming that Walker's intel was accurate: Finley Marshall had been fired simply for being gay, not for "being gay" while on the job. A little scandal at his last place of work would have given Walker more leverage but the twenty-six-year-old's background and employment history were flawless. So were his eyes and Walker was struck by the younger man's carefree confidence. He'd carried it through the front door with him like the early spring breeze that ruffled the dark brown waves curling around the hard angles of his cheeks and jaw bones.

"I heard it was an emergency and you caught me while I was between arrangements," Marshall said facetiously. He smirked back at Walker as they shook hands. *I know exactly how badly you need me, asshole,* his eyes said. Walker was about to deny it when Marshall took a large step to his left and something pink zipped past them. There was a loud *splat!* as a water balloon hit the tile, just where Marshall had been standing. It burst, the water splashing on Walker's shoes and the legs of his trousers but he kept a straight face. Marshall beamed as the vein in Walker's temple throbbed.

"I wouldn't say it's an emergency but my girls certainly need a steady hand," he said evenly and Marshall chuckled.

"A steady hand. That's cute," he said, then glanced behind Walker and jumped to his right. Walker heard a soft whistle just before he was hit between his shoulder blades. He flinched as his collar and the back of his head were soaked. Walker pulled a long, steadying breath through his nose and let it out slowly. He still wanted to howl so he pressed his lips together, his nostrils flaring as he counted down from ten. Once Walker was sure he wouldn't scream, he smiled at Marshall.

"Please. *Help me.*"

Chapter Five

"**D**o you want to farm barley?" Walker Cameron III boomed but his steel-gray eyes held Fin's as the vein by his left eyebrow pulsed. "Because that's how you become a barley farmer," he threatened loudly.

Fin was begrudgingly impressed. He had expected a soft prick in an expensive suit but Cameron was tall, broad-shouldered, and well-built beneath the bespoke tailoring. He was in his late forties or early fifties but his black hair was already liberally streaked with silver. And he was just as imperious and insufferable as Fin had predicted he'd be. He had an overwhelming urge to squirm and stick his tongue out at Cameron as the older man looked him over.

"You're the nanny Reid Marshall recommended?" He asked with obvious frustration. But Cameron had reminded Fin that he was representing his brother and *had to* exude competence and professionalism.

"I'm Finley Marshall. I believe Reid provided you with my résumé." Fin murmured as he scanned the foyer and the grand staircase behind Cameron, slightly wary. The triplets should

21

have revealed themselves by now. A single six-year-old's curiosity was a luminous, unstable force. The curiosity of *three* six-year-olds should have been rampant and combustible so Fin took the silence as a sign that more shenanigans were imminent. Cameron was stiffly unaware as he stared down his nose at Fin.

"Your résumé says you speak four languages and have a master's in early childhood education," Cameron confirmed.

Fin nodded and his lips twisted as he glanced at Cameron. "I backed out of a PhD in Psychology because I didn't want to do the extra math. I spent a year in France preparing my thesis for a master's in History before I discovered that educating children is my passion."

"That's very impressive for someone your age," Cameron said begrudgingly, earning a hard snort from Fin.

"Psychology and childhood education are a family business. My brother thinks I used the M.A. in History to con our parents into bankrolling a vacation in France but I found myself and got a firm grasp on pâtisserie while I was there."

"I see. You do seem qualified and your résumé and background check were spotless." Cameron's tongue pushed against the inside of his cheek as he studied Fin. "This is the girls' current schedule," he said as he reached into his coat. Cameron handed Fin four folded sheets that smelled rather heavenly as he opened them to read the timetable. The scent of starch, French-milled lavender-scented soap, and Cameron's cologne wafted Fin's nose as he shuffled the pages, making the schedule a little challenging to comprehend. But Fin forced his brain to focus on the words that outlined the structure of the triplets' day and their required curriculum. It wasn't unusual for children like the Cameron girls to remain in the nursery with tutors instead of attending kindergarten and elementary school. Especially if the children were well ahead of their peers and preparing for the more prestigious boarding schools. But Fin suspected the girls were also being homeschooled due to behavioral considerations.

"*This* is impressive. Ballet, horseback riding lessons, soccer, chess... They're already studying French, basic mathematics, geometry, and they're reading well above their age range."

"Indeed. The girls have three nurses who see to their personal care—hygiene, wardrobe, bedtimes, and breakfast. Nurse Lisa will brief you on their routines and care in the nursery. You will be responsible for their health, welfare, and education during the day and are to consult with Pierce if you need anything. This is his household—I merely live here—and I ask that you respect his authority and his nerves as much as is possible in the course of your duties."

"I think I can handle that," Fin said as he searched again for the triplets. The girls were definitely up to something or they would be peeking and checking out the new guy.

"Excellent," Cameron said dryly. He carried himself with a younger man's athletic grace as he turned and swept to the foot of the grand marble staircase. "Amelia, Beatrice, and Charlotte! Show yourselves now!" His voice shattered the pristine elegance of the house like thunder but three tiny, identical princesses peeked and waved from behind the banister along the gallery above. "Now!" Cameron ordered and pointed in front of him. Fin was enchanted as the girls giggled and hopped down the stairs.

"We're going to be barley farmers!" One of the triplets boasted as they lined up along the bottom step. Cameron snorted and gave a shake of his head.

"I'm going to be just fine but you three had better practice your digging," he said with a glance at Fin. "I assume there's digging."

"I have no idea," Fin admitted. Cameron humphed at him and turned his attention back to his girls.

"The taller one on the left is Amelia, the one with the slightly pointier nose in the middle is Beatrice, and the shorter one on the right is Charlotte," he said as he waved at them but Fin's brow furrowed as he bent at the waist for a closer look. Each one was an identical replica of the other and they were the most precious things Fin had ever seen with their bouncing black curls and twirly polka dot dresses. They had the biggest blue eyes and all three stared at their father with pure adoration as he glowered back at them sternly.

"It's very nice to meet you, ladies. My name's Fin and we're going to have lots of fun and learn all kinds of cool things," he told them as he braced his hands on his knees so he was closer to their level.

"We already know how to climb the big tree at the back of the garden and where the cook keeps the chocolate chips," ...Beatrice said. Fin was confident he could tell them apart as long as they kept themselves in that order.

"Do you know how to ask for an attorney in French or how to make a slime volcano with your dad's shaving cream?" Fin challenged. The "short" one named Charlotte gasped as she edged closer but the other two remained unmoved.

"You appear to have this in hand. Call for Pierce if you need anything," Cameron stated and turned on his heel.

"Daddy, wait!" Amelia called as she followed. Fin immediately lost track of which girl was which when they all hurried after him. Cameron jumped and shook his head and Fin cringed as he watched the otherwise competent and composed man run from a pack of six-year-olds like his life was in danger. The shift from aloof and severe to quaking was sudden and extreme and the girls reacted as if they had smelled blood. There was a frenzy for their father's attention and Cameron's shoulders pulled together as they tugged at his sleeve and the back of his coat.

"I'm afraid I have an important call I need to sit in on in about ten minutes," Cameron said hastily. He was literally fleeing as he checked his watch and sped around the corner.

"Excuse me?" Fin called out as he tried to see where Cameron went, but he was gone. "I guess you three will have to give me a tour of the..." But there was only one angry little angel left in the foyer. Fin caught a flash of white and blue from the other side of the staircase as the one he was almost sure was Amelia reached for the banister and set her foot on the bottom step.

"We're never going to like you and we don't want you here," she whispered. Fin puffed his cheeks as he pushed his hands into his pockets.

"You know, I'm pretty stubborn too. It would be a lot less work and more fun if we tried being friends." He smiled encouragingly but she ran up the stairs and raced around the corner. "And I'm on to you. I know every trick in the book," he warned, then crouched and covered his head at the incoming barrage of water balloons.

Chapter Six

"Which one of you put the slime in his hair?" Walker sighed heavily as he sat on the edge of Charlotte's bed. He folded his hands on his lap and raised a brow at her expectantly. Amelia was stone-cold. There was no cracking her and Beatrice was too smart to risk her sister's wrath. But Charlotte was too sweet and honest for her own good. Walker cleared his throat when Charlotte's eyes darted to Amelia's. He leaned to intercept Charlotte's attention. "How did the slime get in Mr. Marshall's hair?" He asked sternly. Charlotte bit down on her lips as she giggled.

"He crawled under the table because Amelia let Mr. Bibble out."

"Mr. Bibble?" Walker shook his head in confusion. His anxiety spiked as he was once again pulled into a rabbit hole. It was an all too familiar sensation and a regular occurrence, unfortunately. Particularly during their bedtime chats.

"Our hamster!" Amelia scolded Walker.

"Close enough," he murmured to himself. Not a hole but a wheel, then. Walker was once again exhausted, treading in no particular direction nor making any progress. "Why was Mr. Bibble out of his cage and how did that result in slime in Mr. Marshall's hair?"

Pierce had much to report during dinner when Walker had asked about the new nanny's first day. Apparently, Mr. Marshall's pants and cardigan had to be sent out for emergency dry-cleaning in the morning due to a chocolate milk-related catastrophe. He'd needed ointment and a few Band-Aids for a nasty-looking scuff on his elbow and there was a concern that he might have a concussion after an incident involving some Vaseline on the nursery stairs.

Walker hadn't been made aware of the slime until he had tucked Beatrice into her bed. Each triplet had their own side of the room and their own bed so they could see each other but still have their own space. It had seemed like a good idea when the interior designer suggested it but Walker realized that had been a tactical blunder on his part. He'd have an easier time cracking Charlotte if Amelia wasn't glaring at her and shaking her head.

"Why was Mr. Bibble out of his cage?" He repeated as he continued to pivot to his right so Charlotte couldn't see Amelia. Charlotte was his powder blue princess and too pure to be calculating. She wrinkled her tiny nose and pulled her shoulders up to her ears. There was muffled laughter from the other side of the room but Walker kept his face straight and utterly serious despite the flutter in his stomach. His stern glare wouldn't be nearly as effective if he giggled with her. But it would have been so easy to laugh if the situation wasn't so dire.

Walker had been hell as a child and wondered if his past nurses and nannies were having a good laugh at his expense. He and his sister, Agnes, had grown up at the Cameron Estate in Connecticut, their parents rarely in residence. There had been no boundaries and it was a wonder the old house was still standing. It was also a miracle that Walker and Agnes were as functional as they were. They were only content when they got their way but there was never any winning with the triplets. All they had to do was smile and he'd melt, or swarm him and he'd panic. "Whose idea was it to release the hamster?" He repeated firmly. Charlotte took a deep breath and Walker braced himself. He had a feeling he was going to owe Mr. Marshall a very sincere apology.

"Mr. Marshall said he didn't want to hold Mr. Bibble because he's allergic to hamsters so Amelia let Mr. Bibble out so Mr. Marshall would have to catch him and then he'd get sick and have to go home."

"That was a terrible thing to do." Walker threw Amelia a pointed look, appalled at her poor manners. *And terribly cunning*, he noted. "And the slime?" He asked as he turned back to Charlotte. She giggled again and it was echoed by her cohorts, making it impossible for him to stay angry. There really wasn't a more precious sound in the world and Walker wasn't equipped to discipline them. That had been Connor's responsibility. He lacked Connor's patience and creativity, and he didn't handle disruptions and disorder well. That was why he desperately needed someone like Mr. Marshall in their lives but the new nanny's first day had been a baptism by fire.

"Bea was playing with the slime but Amelia told her to drop it on his head when he was crawling on the floor. Bea wouldn't do it, so I did," Charlotte said.

"Why?" Walker asked, horrified.

"Because Bea wouldn't share and it was funny."

"It was so funny, Daddy!" Amelia said excitedly. Bea pulled the covers over her head as she became hysterical and Charlotte spluttered.

"Alright. Everyone calm down." Walker gave Charlotte a stern look as he lowered to kiss her hair. Their wild curls had been restrained in braided pigtails for bed and Walker couldn't help but tug on one of Charlotte's. "At least it wasn't premeditated," he murmured. He used the end of the braid to tickle her nose. "You will apologize to Mr. Marshall in the morning."

"Yes, Daddy," Charlotte promised. Walker repeated the ritual with Beatrice and Amelia before he turned down the light and shut the door.

Over the last three years, he'd ended nearly every night with similar reports of mischief-making and requests for the girls to apologize to the numerous nannies he'd hired. Lisa, the girls' senior nurse, had been getting quite vocal about any of the night nurses staying on if a competent and reliable nanny wasn't found soon.

Despite his relaxed, slacker appearance and demeanor, Mr. Marshall was the most promising and qualified candidate to fill the position. Walker saw an opportunity to provide the girls with more than just a head start on their education and more discipline in their daily lives. He saw Mr. Marshall's strong psychology background as a godsend. He didn't want the girls to grow up without boundaries and wind up as emotionally stunted and spoiled as he was. But they were in serious trouble, if Mr. Marshall's first day was an indication of how much Walker had blown it as a single father in the years since Connor's death. Walker would make sure the girls apologized he arrived in the morning and the ritual would begin again.

"Lord, I hope he's resilient." Walker crossed himself on the way to the nursery.

Chapter Seven

"How did they even...?" Fin spun in a circle as he unwound himself from the jump rope trap he'd found himself in. One end of the rope was tied to a doll and the other was knotted around the leg of one of the stools at the craft table. His foot had gotten tangled as he had tried to disengage from the trap, and he almost cried when he stuck his hand in an empty crayon box to find it filled with a cold, sticky brown substance. It turned out to be chocolate pudding so Fin didn't scream his resignation at Pierce, but it was a near thing.

He glanced at the closed door separating the nursery from the girls' bedroom. The girls had been collected for the night and were probably with their father. Lisa arrived after the girls' dinner dishes had been cleared from the nursery to inform Fin that Mr. Cameron would be up in two hours to tuck the girls in and would most likely be discussing their behavior with them. It had been enough time for Fin to straighten up the nursery and gather his thoughts. He had a blistering resignation speech planned for Cameron but needed to make sure Riley was ready. Finally managing to free himself, Fin wound the jump rope in a tidy knot and tossed it in one of the fabric bins on his way to the desk in the corner of the nursery.

The room was decorated in cheerful shades of pink and green with crisp white shelves and white furniture but it was a disaster. Fin dropped onto a corner of the desk, exhausted and baffled at all that had happened throughout the day. He'd been a rambunctious child and Fin had spent several wild years in college but none of that had prepared him for his first day in The Killian House. He was frazzled but mostly furious with Walker Cameron as he dialed Riley's number.

"I hope you're not calling because you need bail money. You know I'm broke," Riley said, putting a grin on Fin's face. It was his first honest smile all day and it felt better than grinding his teeth.

"We're not there yet but how long will it take you to get here? I might need help hiding a body."

"Shhh! You know we can't discuss those kinds of details over the phone. The FBI is listening." Riley was joking but Fin's eyes swept around the room and to the window. He wouldn't be surprised if the FBI had found a reason to spy on an über wealthy financier like Cameron. Fin didn't really trust the FBI or billionaires.

"You're right. I was obviously joking," Fin said with a forced laugh.

"That bad?"

"A nightmare. These girls are..." Fin trailed off, eyeing an upended ballerina jewelry box. It had been knocked off the bookshelf in the afternoon's mayhem and he sighed as he went to help the tiny doll. "They're the most precious things I've ever seen, but they're not playing around. They booby-trapped the stairs and let the hamster loose. I thought I was going to need stitches and an EpiPen today."

"Devious. They really want dad's attention," Riley guessed and Fin humphed in disgust.

"Exactly. I'm telling Cameron that I'm out. I'm not staying. I adore these little girls and wish I could help, but they'll keep escalating until they put me in the hospital."

"Which is totally fair but who's going to help them if you don't?" Riley countered, his question stabbing Fin in the gut.

"I don't know but that isn't my problem. I'm not getting invested in another situation I can't save. I might not have to worry about getting fired and the pay is great but it's not worth it. He's going to make my job so much harder than it has to be because he doesn't want to parent his kids."

"What about Reid?" Riley asked with an apologetic hiss. Fin's bravado faltered for a moment.

"There is that. I thought I could handle Cameron and make Reid look good but I'm going to have to land us another whale of a client. This is only going to end in violence or flames," Fin predicted. He'd almost needed an ambulance ride on his first day and Fin knew the triplets were just getting started. Cameron was willing to spend a fortune on nurses and nannies to avoid his daughters and the girls were going to take their frustrations out on Fin.

"Don't kill Cameron. You've almost got Reid convinced this agency is a good idea but I don't think Murder Nannies R Us has an encouraging ring to it."

"Good horror movie, though," Fin said and Riley hummed.

"Is there anything I can do?" He asked. Fin smiled, glad he'd called Riley. "Get the wine and pizza ready. I'm coming in hot."

"I can do that," Riley said.

"You're the best."

"That's right. Remember you have food and booze waiting for you at home if things get heated with Cameron."

"It can't get that heated. Neither of us would risk waking the girls."

"That is reassuring. Reid wouldn't want you to stick it out just for him so go with your gut," Riley said sincerely, reinforcing Fin's determination to end the day on a professional note.

"Thanks. I'm going to edit my resignation speech so it's a touch more diplomatic."

"That's probably a good call. See you in a bit."

"Thank goodness. Be ready for an emergency landing," Fin said and hung up.

He didn't feel good about quitting as he looked around the nursery. The girls were indeed diabolical but Fin liked that about them. It always saddened him when he entered a new home and found little ghosts haunting the nurseries and playrooms instead of curious, spirited children. Fin would much rather redirect a willful child's imagination and energy than stifle it. He could imagine having so many adventures with the girls and it broke his heart, knowing they'd continue to act out and Cameron would continue to avoid them until the triplets were old enough to go to boarding school. The girls would take all the bad behaviors they'd learned at The Killian House with them and they'd retaliate against Cameron for sending them away.

Fin sighed as he stood and went to the window. The view of Central Park and the city was phenomenal but Fin wasn't impressed. Men like Walker Cameron III thought that having all the money in the world was enough, that if they threw enough of it at their problems they'd go away. Fin's pride stung at the thought of quitting and giving up on the girls but men like Cameron didn't listen to servants, and they certainly didn't change their ways for the sake of their children's happiness. Fin's hands would be tied until he was eventually fired for something he didn't do or Cameron gave up and sent the girls to boarding school. Lisa had said the plan was for the girls to stay home and attend a boarding school when they were older but Fin couldn't see Cameron keeping a decent nanny long enough.

"It's a damn shame," Fin said under his breath as he turned away from the view. He caught sight of his reflection in the window and frowned at the white shape on his back. "I thought I felt a draft," he said and took off his cardigan to inspect the large cutout. It wasn't there and the garment had been whole when it had been returned from the one-hour dry cleaner. "Well done, ladies." He tossed it at his chair and Fin's heart sank into his stomach. "I think we could be soulmates."

Chapter Eight

Walker was encouraged to find that the light was still on in the nursery. The door swung open silently as he leaned against the jamb, expecting to find Mr. Marshall in distress. Instead, it was Walker who needed the extra support as he took in the wrecked nursery. Nearly every storage cube had been toppled and the floor was littered with crayons, markers, ribbons, cards, Legos, bows... The usual carnage and aftermath of a nanny hazing. But when Walker's focus landed on Mr. Marshall he forgot all about the arts and crafts war zone.

Fin was not the usual nanny. And while it was an absurdly sexist assumption, Walker had hoped that a young male nanny might have been a bit more equipped for the girls' particular brand of mischief. But Walker hadn't expected Mr. Marshall to be so...*hot*. And he certainly wasn't expecting to be so affected by the sight of the younger man's back and ass but there he was, leering at the nanny like a creepy cliché. Mr. Marshall's white t-shirt climbed up his back as he bent to scoop a stuffed rabbit into one of the soft bins. Walker looked away when he caught a peek of Marshall's tight, lean torso as he stretched and reached for another purple rabbit.

"You can leave this. I'll make sure it's cleaned up before you return tomorrow." The words came out with a slight waver and Walker had to tug at his collar. *Of all the times to start caring about that again, why now?* Walker forced his eyes up and winced at Mr. Marshall's hair before he was caught looking. Half of the new nanny's hair was sticky from a teal substance and plastered to the side of his head. "I am terribly sorry," Walker said with a sincere bow.

"Thanks, but I don't think I'll be returning," Marshall ground out, glaring at Walker as he scratched at what appeared to be hives on his neck and then his arm. Walker felt a flash of panic and shook his head wildly. He held up his hands as he hopped over obstacles, hoping to de-escalate the situation.

"Just a moment! Please!" He pleaded, halting when his soon-to-be-former nanny stabbed an index finger in Walker's direction in warning. "I understand why you would be furious but I can assure you, this is them at their worst. I've already had a talk with the girls and they will be apologizing to you in the morning."

"The girls aren't the problem! *You are!*" Marshall whispered angrily as he checked to make sure the door to the girls' room was still shut.

"Me?" Walker was stunned.

"Yes, *you!*" Marshall dropped the fabric bin and advanced on him. "It took me all of two minutes to figure out what was going on here. I've seen this tired movie too many times and I've decided that I won't be buying a ticket for this showing."

"What are you talking about? I'm paying you to be here. I can pay you more," Walker offered quickly but Marshall snorted in disgust.

"No thank you. I've had enough of rich, crappy dads who don't care about their kids."

"I beg your pardon!" Walker protested and reeled when Marshall laughed as he flipped the clean side of his hair out of his eyes.

"You absolutely should. Amelia is *diabolical!*" He said in a loud whisper as he pointed at the nursery. "She's the mastermind and is terrifyingly brilliant and Charlotte...!" He threw his hands up and laughed. "She's adorable but my God, she's pure chaos. And Beatrice." He shook his head. "I haven't figured her out because she's quiet and stealthy but I don't want to. Do you know why?" He asked and Walker shook his head.

"I don't understand." Walker felt like he was falling down a hole *and* on a spinning wheel again as Marshall sneered back at him.

"I prefer my kids to have a lot of character and I don't mind a challenge. What I *do* mind are parents who make my job harder than it has to be and I'm tired of getting fired *after* I've gotten attached and earned their kids' trust."

"Why would I fire you if—?" Walker started but Marshall cut him off with a hard snort.

"Who knows? Last time I was in a play for a gay charity and the time before that it was because the lady of the house couldn't keep her hands off my ass. I got fired so I could be replaced by the wife's mistress once. All I know is that it's never about me and it certainly isn't about the kids."

"That's all very unfortunate but why would you assume that I'd do something like that?" Walker asked and Marshall blinked back at him.

"I don't know. It might have been the way you pushed me at your girls and ran almost as soon as I walked through the front door."

"Hold on." Walker threw up a hand. "I might not know how

to cope with my children but there's nothing I wouldn't do to make them happy."

"Aside from the obvious?" Marshall replied testily, causing Walker's brow to furrow.

"There is nothing obvious about the way their minds work."

"Wow. You're really overthinking it, Cameron. They want more of your time," Marshall said and Walker's face fell.

"Of course, they do. They miss Connor and they think I'll do all the lovely things he used to do but I don't know how. I lock up when I can't give them what they need. That's why I hired you. I was raised by servants because I had two crappy parents who didn't know how to cope with me, I'm afraid." It humbled Walker, explaining himself to a veritable stranger but he'd bare his entire soul if that's what it took.

"I'm truly sorry but that's not the girls' fault. And I can tell that I'm going to fall madly in love with them despite you," Marshall said sadly but that sounded like the best news Walker had heard in weeks. There was still a chance if Marshall already cared about the triplets.

"What would it take to get you to stay?" He asked sincerely. This time, Marshall was the one left stunned.

"I...don't want more money. And was sure I had gone too far and was about to get thrown out," Marshall admitted sheepishly so Walker decided to return his candor.

"You have me at a disadvantage, Mr. Marshall. You're the last decent nanny who would answer the call but you also appear to be the very best person for the job. It's rare to hear that my girls are likable. You were right about Bea. She's smart like Amelia, but she picks her battles wisely. She also seems to be a little less blood-thirsty," Walker said, licking his lips nervously when Marshall chuckled.

"She sounds like my kind of girl and like we could be best friends but I'm not sticking around."

"I truly wish you would and I'll do anything for you to stay. I'd be a fool to lose you if you think you could love them," Walker said. A surprised gasp burst from Marshall and he nodded.

"They are a handful but I can tell they're acting out because they want more time with *you*," he explained.

"It's hard work, trying to buy them the moon but I'll do whatever it takes. I have to have someone who cares in this nursery because as much as I worship every hair on those girls' heads, I can't be the father they need," Walker admitted. Marshall's cheeks puffed out and he made an exasperated sound. He reached to push the hair away from his face and stopped before he touched the slimed half of his hair.

"First of all, they don't want the moon. Just you. But you make my job harder by running away from them every time they want your attention. They're just going to keep escalating until you have to give in to their demands," he warned. Walker's anxiety spiked again. He had a feeling Marshall was correct about that as well.

"What do you propose? I'm at my wits' end and at your mercy, Mr. Marshall. I love my daughters but I'm afraid I've ruined them. I never know what to say or do and it feels like I make things worse whenever I try to parent them. Connor was so good at everything and he made it all look...easy." Walker stopped, suddenly embarrassed by his rambling. He cleared his throat and sniffed hard while he studied the books on the shelf by his knee.

"Alright, I'll stay," Marshall stated and Walker became hopeful again as their eyes met. But as Marshall's reassured grin returned, Walker felt a little less hopeful and slightly more panicked. "But you owe me and I've got a few ground rules."

"I owe you?" Walker's eyes narrowed as he craned his neck. "I already told you I'd pay you and—"

"And I told you, I don't want more of your money," the other man said briskly as he glided over the battlefield, unencumbered by Legos or dolls. "I want something much more interesting," he drawled while his eyes swept over Walker from head to toe as if he was sizing up his opponent.

"What do you want?" There might have been a hitch of hope to the question and Walker knew better than to assume Marshall would suggest something inappropriate but his imagination went ahead and ran with it. *Seriously, Walker?* He hadn't had as much as an itch since Connor's death. But Walker didn't want to scare away the one nanny who actually liked his girls and *wanted* to care for them.

"You." Marshall reached out, offering his hand, and Walker's eyes were huge as he stared at it. "You're going to make an effort and give me as much of your free time as you can spare so I can teach you how to communicate with your children and nurture them," Marshall explained. Disoriented, Walker grabbed the younger man's hand, hoping for a lifeline. But it felt like he was being pulled deeper into the rabbit hole of confusion and disorder he'd found himself in after the new nanny's first day.

"Fine. But keep your expectations low. I generally avoid communicating unless I am absolutely desperate. I didn't have nurturing parents or nannies as a child," he said, even though Walker wished he could be half as good as Connor was with their girls.

"All I ask is that you try. The girls will be happy as long as they get to spend more time with you and it'll make my job easier."

"Sounds fair enough..." Walker agreed hesitantly as they shook hands. "What are your ground rules?"

"First of all, stop calling me Mr. Marshall. Save that for my older brother or someone who owns a tie. Fin is fine. Second, you're going to start having breakfast and dinner as a family unless you have something important scheduled. But do your best to avoid scheduling important things during breakfast and dinner. Trust me, you'll love starting their mornings with a pep talk, and they'll get used to sharing the highlights and the low points of their days with you over dinner. Finally, stop thinking about this like it's a battle. I have no desire to rein in the triplets' imaginations or curb their willful natures. They might be terrors but the best little girls are, and they grow up to be strong, brilliant women. They're spoiled but children should be, and we've got plenty of time to turn them into decent little people."

"I do like the sound of that... Are you going to call me Walker?" He asked and *Fin's* face twisted as he shook his head.

"We're definitely not there yet."

"No?" Walker asked as he offered Fin a wry grin. "I wasn't sure. I'm not accustomed to my employees speaking so freely or making demands."

"Well..." Marshall rubbed the back of his neck and flashed Walker a sheepish grin. "This isn't your household or your businesses we're talking about. It's your family and you're in over your head. This is an emergency."

"Indeed," Walker said as he gripped Marshall's hand more firmly. "I despise change but I need different results so I'm at your mercy, Fin. *Within reason,*" he added and there was an odd tickle in his stomach when he caught sight of Fin's quirked lips and the mischievous sparkle in his eyes.

"We've got a deal. I didn't think I'd be able to work with you but this is going to be fun."

Chapter Nine

"You can do this. It's just breakfast," Walker told himself while staring at the dining room door. He could hear the girls giggling and one of their nurses whispering urgently, begging them to return to their seats and behave.

It was Walker's habit to take his breakfast in his study. He would read the newspaper and look over his planner while he drank his coffee and ate his oatmeal and grapefruit in peace. But he'd often wondered how the girls were spending their morning and longed for the picture-perfect family breakfasts he had glimpsed before they lost Connor.

The girls had been almost three when Connor was killed by a drunk driver. They were just learning to sit at the table and getting used to their chunky plastic utensils. But the syrup-sticky fingers and toppled cups of juice had been more than Walker could manage on his own, so he started taking his breakfasts alone after Connor died.

Walker had come to regret that as time passed and had wanted to join the girls for breakfast again, but he was too proud to admit that he couldn't handle them without a few nurses and a nanny for backup. *Stop thinking about them like they're the enemy. This isn't a military campaign or a corporate takeover.* Walker had Fin to thank for his second chance at breakfast with the triplets and it seemed likely that there was some sound logic behind the rest of the new nanny's ground rules.

Had desperation turned Walker into an absolute doormat? He suspected it was much more than that while staring at the door's panels. A bead of sweat had rolled down his temple and Walker's undershirt and boxers clung to his skin like a damp film. He would have paid damn near anything to keep Fin before he walked through the door. But something had changed when Fin stepped up to him in the foyer and acknowledged that he had the upper hand on Walker. Then, Fin wielded his power in the nursery and... Walker *liked* it. Not just because Fin was hot when he was smirking at Walker like they were about to square off in an alley. No one in Walker's orbit told him no or what to do but Fin's competence and confidence were so much more than a tremendous relief. They were alluring. Walker didn't have an obedient bone in his body and he commanded every facet of his life *except* the triplets, yet he *wanted* to please the new nanny.

"Dear Lord, it isn't even 8:00 a.m. What's gotten into you, Walker?" He stretched his neck and tugged at his collar. His libido had been delightfully dormant for years so it was a terribly inconvenient time to begin noticing men again. He steeled himself as he raised his hand to open the door and remembered that he wasn't going into battle. Instead, he fixed what he hoped was an easy smile onto his face and swung into the dining room. "Good morning, girls."

He halted in the doorway as he took stock of the tableau before him. Beatrice appeared to be chasing Amelia, who had what looked like Beatrice's shoe. Charlotte was crawling across the table in an attempt to escape their morning nurse, and the poor woman was as red as the Persian rug under the table.

Walker was frozen, his anxiety and his temper skyrocketing. He instinctively recoiled but the urge to run was immediately doused by shame and regret. He always panicked and ran. Walker recalled Fin's brutally accurate assessment as he witnessed the direct consequences of his actions. *I have to do better.*

"My apologies, sir!" The nurse took advantage of the girls' shocked silence and scooped Charlotte off the table. Walker sniffed hard, plucking up his courage, and strode forward confidently.

"No need to apologize," he drawled on his way to the head of the table. "Amelia, Beatrice, Charlotte." He waved at the chairs on his left. A place had been set for Fin on Walker's right, as he was due to arrive at any moment. "I'll explain if you'll join me." Pierce had materialized and was ready to pull out Walker's chair then pushed it in as he sat. The girls were curious as they scrambled into their seats. "You look lovely this morning," he told them, recalling that Fin said that pep talks would be helpful. Although, Walker wasn't entirely sure they needed more encouragement.

Their long curls had been arranged in French braids with lavender bows that matched the purple umbrellas dotting their puffy white dresses. It was an overcast day but the room seemed brighter as they smiled and batted their big blue eyes at Walker.

"I know you usually have breakfast in the nursery but *Fin* thought it would be good for us to have breakfast and dinner together, as my schedule permits," he explained. The girls put their heads together, whispering giddily as Pierce returned with a pot of coffee. Several servants followed with platters that were arranged in the middle of the table so Walker and the girls could dine family-style. "I'd like to fool him into believing we aren't barbarians and that we have *some* manners," he said as he shook out his napkin and draped it over his lap.

Amelia nodded quickly and all three girls mimicked Walker and spread their napkins over their laps. The lids were lifted off the platters, revealing stacks of pancakes, scrambled eggs, bacon, sausages, and toast triangles but the girls stared at Walker as if he had invented Christmas. His conscience twinged as Walker recalled Fin's remark about the girls acting out because they were so hungry for his time and attention.

"Mr. Marshall," Pierce announced from the dining room door. Walker popped to his feet and caught his chair before it could fall on its back.

"He's asked that we call him Fin. Good morning, Fin," Walker said as he bowed and Fin paused as he stepped over the threshold.

"Good morning... I was told I'd find you in here. I didn't expect you to take all of my suggestions all at once," he said.

"I believe they were ground rules, not suggestions," Walker corrected and waved at the seat on his right. Pierce's eyes widened in horror but Fin didn't notice. Or care.

"I did say that, didn't I," he chuckled as he headed around the table. "The three of you are visions," Fin said to the girls but they were wary as they scooted closer to the table. Walker remained standing so he could make the girls' plates but he cringed as he reached for Amelia's. He should know if she liked eggs or wanted her pancakes on a separate plate but Walker didn't have a clue about what his girls' preferences were.

"Who likes syrup on everything?" Fin asked as he rose and Charlotte's hand shot up. "I should have guessed," he said with a wink. "Me too," he whispered to Charlotte while he passed Walker plates for Amelia and Beatrice's pancakes. Fin began making his plate and started with the eggs. He dumped a scoop onto his plate, then raised a brow at the girls. "Who wants eggs?" Amelia's nose wrinkled as Beatrice and Charlotte nodded at him. Fin offered Walker an encouraging grin and added spoonfuls of eggs to the proper plates. But it was far more than a casual gesture, as far as Walker was concerned. It was a lifeline and a peace offering. Fin smoothly covered for Walker and was helping him learn without a hint of judgment. "I bet everybody likes bacon," Fin predicted as he took the tongs and gave them a few warm-up clicks. He deftly lifted two slices and Charlotte nodded quickly as they approached her plate before Fin snatched them back and dropped them onto his plate. She gasped and narrowed her eyes at Fin. "I believe it was you who slimed me yesterday..." He said with an indecisive hum as he rolled the tongs thoughtfully. "I'm not sure if I should share my bacon with you."

"It's everybody's bacon!" Amelia complained. Fin hissed and shook his head.

"That would be true if we were all polite and followed rules around here, wouldn't it?" He asked only to receive three disgruntled pouts. Walker bit into his knuckle to keep from laughing. Fin caught him and humphed in approval as he placed two strips of bacon on Walker's plate. "You don't mind cheating and being mean but I'm *a lot* taller than you. And I'm pretty fast. I could probably eat this whole plate in like...thirty seconds and you wouldn't be able to stop me," Fin boasted. He held the platter up and inspected it. "What do you think, Cameron? Want to time me?" He asked with a wiggle of his brows.

"There's no way you can do it in less than a minute," Walker said as he pushed back his sleeve to see his watch. Pierce looked ill and like he was going to faint as he observed from his post at the door.

"I'm sorry about the slime!" Charlotte blurted. "And for the pudding in your chair and for putting glue in your soup," she added. Fin frowned but gave her two strips of bacon.

"You put glue in my soup?"

"I am so sorry," Walker whispered, his eyes watering as he fought to keep a straight face.

"I thought it tasted a little strange but I didn't want to say something and offend your cook."

"Your manners are clearly better than ours," Walker said and shook his head at the girls. "Would anyone else like some bacon?" He asked pointedly.

"I'm sorry for locking you in the bathroom and for eating your cookie while you were in there," Beatrice blurted.

Walker hadn't heard about that. "I'm...not sure you deserve any of Fin's bacon."

"No worries. Now you know that I can pick locks," Fin replied cheerfully. He gave Beatrice her bacon and smiled expectantly at Amelia who let out a belligerent breath.

"I'm sorry I made the steps slippery and put the finger paint in the hand soap and let Mr. Bibble out of his cage. And all the other stuff," she said with a grumble.

"All the other stuff," Walker sighed. He couldn't blame Fin for being furious with him. The girls had resorted to truly desperate measures to get rid of Fin despite Walker's threat to make them barley farmers.

"The good thing about today is that we get a chance to try again if we can admit that we didn't do our best yesterday." Fin smiled serenely and was pure sunshine as he finished distributing the bacon and helped himself to some toast.

"I think we all need to be reminded of that now and then," Walker said as he sat. "What do you have planned for the girls today?" He asked Fin. Walker saw Amelia perk up curiously but she pretended her pancakes were more interesting. Beatrice's brow had quirked but Charlotte was staring at Fin raptly as she munched on a piece of bacon.

"I'm sending the girls on a scavenger hunt this morning. They're going to find things like their favorite stuffy and their favorite books so we can have a great big show and tell extravaganza. I'm expecting lavish costumes and top-notch artwork," Fin said. Charlotte's and Beatrice's eyes lit up and Amelia rubbed her lips together as she planned. *Oh, he's good.*

The rest of breakfast was entertaining and informative as Fin used the meal as an opportunity to share his impressive résumé with the girls. Unlike the one that had crossed Walker's desk, Fin charmed the girls with his vast knowledge of cartoon and storybook characters and regaled them with his most epic crafting disasters. By the end of breakfast Amelia was still wary and hesitant but Charlotte was in love with Fin and Beatrice wanted to see what the new guy could do.

"I'll give you a head start," Fin told the girls as they pushed in their chairs. "We're starting with capes. You can wear your favorite cape or you can design a new one but I'm expecting drama and originality. I'll get my scrapbook and meet you upstairs," he said and Pierce quickly opened the door as the girls bolted from the dining room. Walker clapped softly and Fin bowed.

"That was very well done. You'll have them in the palm of your hand by the end of the day." He was legitimately impressed. Fin had managed what no other nanny in the city could in less than two days. But Fin shook his head as he reached and put an arm around Walker's shoulders. Walker jumped and stared at Fin confused, and heard a sharp intake of breath from Pierce. Walker could count on one hand the number of people who had touched him over the course of his forty-eight years. Not including tailors, various stylists, and servants. Fin didn't seem to notice their reactions and gave Walker an encouraging squeeze.

"I knew I could win them over with your help. You did great. I'm really proud of you," he said, further confusing Walker and eliciting another horrified gasp from Pierce. But Walker felt a tickle of hope and possibly delight as they walked into the hall together. It was a stark yet pleasant contrast to the dread and anxiety Walker felt when he opened the dining room door before breakfast.

"Did I?" He asked, not that he was fishing for more compliments. Fin nodded quickly and hummed.

"We make a good team. Keep following my lead and we'll be one happy little family," he predicted. If anyone else had said that, Walker would have thought they were being sarcastic or lying but he already trusted Fin and instinctively knew that they would be happily sorted out in no time.

"Thank you. I think you're right," Walker said, unable to hide his relief.

"We've got this!" Fin insisted when he released him so he could walk backward. "I need to run to the kitchen and grab my scrapbook from my backpack. But you were really good in there. Keep that up and we'll all have lots of fun," he said then turned and hurried down the other hallway.

"We'll talk later," Walker called after Fin who waved over his shoulder. Walker craned his neck as he watched him go. "I was good in there."

His pupils dilated and he was absurdly pleased with himself as Walker replayed their conversation. Perhaps it was because the triplets were the most important thing in Walker's universe and the situation was so critical. Or, because he rarely received compliments from sincere, honest people but Walker was genuinely flattered. He was optimistic after the success of their first breakfast together and looked forward to pleasing Fin again. Possibly a touch excited at the thought of another compliment as well. Which was a rather odd turn of events, once Walker paused and considered.

"I honestly don't know what's gotten into me," he complained and took himself off to his study.

Chapter Ten

"Is Riley with you?" Reid asked over the intercom. Fin groaned sympathetically as he put an arm around Riley and gave him a squeeze.

"Yes but he's severely hungover. Rough date last night."

Fin had treated himself to a few glasses of wine for surviving his first week at The Killian House before Riley came home with a box of chardonnay and attempted to forget the whole night had happened.

"It wasn't me, it was him," Riley muttered then rolled his eyes. Which was a mistake. He pressed his fist against his lips and begged his stomach to hang on.

Reid buzzed them in, and when Fin and Riley turned at the staircase, they found Penn Tucker slouched against the door. His real name was Pennsylvania, but he'd gone by Penn for as long as they had known him. First as Reid's roommate in college, and then as a regular at Briarwood Terrace.

"It's good to see you!" Fin said as he was pulled into a warm embrace. Penn's mossy green eyes sparkled with amusement.

"I've missed you, brother."

"How's your dad?" Fin asked. Penn was Reid and Gavin's age but he was considered the Gandalf of nannies because he was gentle and easygoing and everyone looked up to him. But he looked more like a wandering wizard than usual as Fin leaned back and looked him over. Penn's blond hair was even longer and was twisted into a bun. And he had let his beard grow wilder while he was taking time off from work.

"He's doing great. He had a rough few weeks but we'll have him back on his feet and in his workshop soon," Penn said before reaching for Riley. "How have you been?"

"Better but I'm so glad your dad's on the mend. Hug him for me." Riley clapped him on the back and the three of them headed for the kitchen. "The Parker kids are angels and they miss you," Riley told Penn. "And Alice and Liza are amazing. I'm sad it's just a temporary gig but I can already tell we're going to be friends for life."

"They're the sweetest family and I miss them," Penn said sadly. "I'm going to miss the kids even more when they go to private school next fall."

Reid was just sitting down and gestured at the food and the coffee carafe on the counter with his mug. Riley went to the table and dropped into a seat.

"They're so cool, Reid. Alice is a pastry chef and she's going to teach me how to make candy and desserts," Riley said then waved at Gavin. Gavin was seated across the table with the paper and a cup of tea. He always sat on the window seat, upright and mildly disapproving, but nodded in greeting at Penn as he sat next to him.

"Morning Gavin. No chess in the park today?" Riley asked.

"You know I never play on Saturdays. Too many people," he said, peering at the newspaper through the round lenses of his glasses. His dark waves were slicked back and he was dressed in a gray cardigan with elbow patches and darker gray trousers.

53

His shirt was buttoned all the way up. He reminded Fin of his Grandpa Marvin and he often imagined Gavin with a full bent pipe even though he never touched tobacco or drugs and only drank alcohol on special occasions. "These numbers can't be right. Who are they trying to fool?" He complained, muttering about markets and bears as he flipped the page.

Fin smirked and went to help himself to what was left in the French press. Reid and Gavin were like an old married couple because they had been best friends since middle school. But there was no sexual chemistry, despite their deep bond and easy affection. Probably because they were too alike. Gavin was just Reid to the tenth degree. They understood each other better than anyone else could but there just wasn't a spark, according to Reid. Gavin was there during that particular conversation and agreed. Being the sensible, practical souls that they were, they made a few half-assed attempts because it would have made everything so much simpler but it just didn't work. Reid said the dates were disasters and Gavin said he would rather kiss a girl. Fin was relieved if he was honest. He didn't want to think about which parent would get custody of him if they got a divorce.

"I feel like absolute poo but I should eat," Riley said. He was still a touch green, but he was eyeing the fruit salad in the middle of the table. Reid shook his head, looking mystified.

"When has that ever stopped you from eating?" He asked. They all knew the answer was never because Riley was always hungry. "I was expecting Riley but what are you doing here? Please don't tell me Cameron fired you." Reid widened his eyes at Fin warily.

"Just a day off, I'm afraid," Fin told him and Reid perked up.

"Really? I wasn't that optimistic. I was sure he was going to hate you or you'd hate him for being too rich."

"He's definitely too rich," Fin said with a nonchalant shrug.

"I heard the Cameron girls are terrors and the family's 'cursed,'" Penn said, curling his fingers. Reid chuckled as he sipped his coffee. Fin thought he already looked a lot better than he had just a week ago. He and Gavin had been busy reviewing résumés, checking references, and following up on leads but Reid hadn't "officially" committed yet. Fin caught Gavin's eye and they shared pleased nods. *It's good to have the old Reid back.*

"Did you make an appointment for your dental checkup?" Reid asked Fin.

"I forgot."

"*Finley.*"

"I'll do it." *I might have spoken too quickly...* "And the Cameron girls are *delightful*. They spend every other weekend with their aunt Agnes," Fin informed them, changing the subject but Gavin and Reid shared knowing looks. They were all too familiar with Fin's lecture-avoidance tactics.

"Without a nanny?" Reid asked dubiously and Fin grinned.

"Apparently, they adore her, and she can handle them without any help. She's an artist and lives in the family cottage in Sagaponack when she's not in Paris or staying at one of their homes in the Bahamas." Between the girls' gushing about their aunt and a little light snooping, Fin was able to learn a lot about Cameron's sister and couldn't wait to meet her.

"Is she single? I wouldn't mind the Bahamas," Reid said, earning an amused snort from Gavin.

"You're only into women when you're drunk and they look like Jamie Lee Curtis," he murmured as he turned another page.

"I don't believe that requires any explanation," Reid said, then cleared his throat as he flicked something off of his sleeve. Fin winked at Gavin. Reid was the only one amongst the five of them who was remotely bisexual. And he had a thing for older women with spiky pixie cuts when he had a few too many drinks. Reid swallowed a bite of his toast and nodded at Fin. "How are things going with Cameron?"

"He's not that bad," Fin said neutrally. Riley grinned and leaned over the table conspiratorially.

"He's super hot but Fin doesn't want to admit it." He told the group and Fin threw him a scowl as he held up his hands. *What a traitor.* Penn caught it and pointed excitedly.

"Oh, I've seen Cameron. His girls go to the same dance school as Alice and Liza's daughter, Kaitlynn. They're in a different class but Cameron goes to the recitals," Penn said and Fin got up and went to the fridge to hide until his face stopped burning.

"On a scale of one to ten," Reid requested, earning an appreciative groan from Penn.

"Easily a ten. I don't usually go for suits-and-manicures kind of guys but Cameron looks like he just gets hotter when the suit comes off."

"Most guys get hotter when the suit comes off," Fin argued and shut the fridge.

"That's not true at all. Sometimes, the suit comes off and you realize he's just a regular jerk and you got duped by good tailoring," Reid said distantly. His eyes slid to the ceiling and his teeth scraped over his lower lip. "Why can't I resist a three-piece suit and a five o'clock shadow?"

"Because you're not Superman. No one can resist that," Fin replied. Gavin hummed in agreement as he sipped his tea and read his paper.

"I can't be trusted with a man in tweed and elbow patches," he murmured. Penn made a sympathetic sound as he slouched next to Gavin.

"I can't drink tequila and avoid lederhosen for the same reason."

"Anyway..." Reid shook his head at Penn before turning back to Fin. "How did your first week go and don't tell me if you've been duped by a regular jerk in good tailoring," he said, going back to the original subject.

"*A lot* better than I thought it would." Fin was still delightfully stunned.

The situation had gone from unsalvageable to Fin's dream project within the space of a few days. He hadn't been entirely wrong about Cameron—the wealthy older man was just as stuffy and self-absorbed as Fin expected—but he loved his children. More importantly, Cameron was willing to try to change. Fin could work with that. And the idea of saving a family like a modern gay Mary Poppins had Fin grinning and humming "Supercalifragilisticexpialidocious" all the way back to Bed-Stuy after he left The Killian House every evening.

"You think you'll be able to work with him?" Reid asked with some obvious cynicism. Fin didn't doubt his brother's faith in *him* but Cameron wasn't known for being flexible. Or very patient... Reid had very good reason to be cynical but Fin would prevail.

"He actually wants what's best for the girls so I'm staying positive. He's...much more reasonable and approachable than I was expecting."

"God forbid," Gavin drawled.

"No... That's really rare," Reid agreed."You're an accountant. All you care about is the way rich people spend their money but think about how you grew up. A nanny sees how rich people live and how they treat their children. It isn't always great and Fin has a hard time accepting that it isn't his place to tell rich people how to live."

"I didn't come here to be lectured," Fin warned, his Spider-Senses tingling. Problem-solving wasn't Reid's only passion. Nothing got under Fin's skin faster and made him feel like he was six than Reid's finger-wagging. He'd rather pay for breakfast and regretted taking three trains when there was a perfectly decent burrito waiting at the bodega around the corner from his place. "I've got things under control at The Killian House and everything's fine with Cameron. He listens and he isn't too proud to ask for help with the girls. We've worked out a plan and I can already tell that the triplets are going to be a delight."

"Wow. That's the kindest thing I've ever heard you say about someone who's never seen public transit," Reid replied. Gavin humphed in agreement but Fin played it cool. He popped a raspberry into his mouth and reclined with his feet stretched and his ankles crossed.

"I let him have it but he actually listened so I'm giving him the benefit of the doubt."

"There's no way that worked," Gavin said with a wry chuckle. Everyone's focus remained fixed on Fin as he reached for another raspberry.

"He was so desperate for me to stay that he offered me even more money," Fin whispered and tossed it into the air so he could catch it with his mouth. He enjoyed Reid's stunned expression as he chewed.

"Let's circle back to the part where you told a scary billionaire off and he liked it."

"I wouldn't say he liked it. Cameron's smart and knows he needs help," Fin said and there were surprised murmurs but Reid still looked skeptical.

"Does he?"

"Yup." Fin's lips twisted as he nodded. "Isn't that wild? I was sure he was going to throw my ass right out of his pristine mansion."

"What did he say?" Penn asked and Fin's cheeks puffed out.

"He said he'd do whatever it takes, that he's willing to change."

"We've got a live one!" Riley said, earning chuckles and snorts from around the table.

"What's your plan?" Reid asked. There was still an edge of skepticism and concern.

"Breakfast and dinner, for starters. I told him he needed to be present for as many meals as possible going forward."

"That should help the girls settle down because they know they'll have his time and attention at predictable intervals," Reid said and Fin tilted his head in agreement.

"I'll start with their bedtime routine and see what I can do to make that less stressful for him and more satisfying for the girls."

"Good plan," Reid agreed. "It's probably one of the few times a day they interact with him consistently and one-on-one. Well, three-on-one." His eyes narrowed as he became distant again. Fin chuckled as he stole a piece of his brother's toast. Reid was in problem-solving mode.

"My gut tells me Cameron wants more time with his girls, he's just too proud to admit he's afraid of them," Fin said with a sad click of his teeth. There were several sympathetic moans and sighs. "I'm going to help him work on his confidence—"

"*You're* going to help Walker Cameron work on his confidence?" Gavin confirmed.

"Yeah." Fin shrugged. "It makes total sense if you think about it: Cameron is used to everyone doing exactly as he says and walking on eggshells around him. The girls don't do *any* of that and they aren't afraid of him. He has zero leverage with them and it throws him off his game. I'm going to teach him some parenting strategies and help him understand why the girls are acting out."

"Mary Poppins!" Reid coughed into his fist but Gavin shook his head.

"It's *The Sound of Music.* Cameron's a widower and the kids are trying to scare Fin off."

"I like *Mary Poppins* better because I don't want to run away with my boss," Fin argued. He elbowed Riley but kept an eye on Reid. "But I'll keep an eye out for Bert while we're in the park."

"Bert was hot," Riley said dreamily. Everyone but Reid laughed.

"I don't want to know what you do with strange men in the park," he said as he draped his arm over the back of his seat, facing Fin. "Just don't get your hopes up. Men like Walker Cameron III don't enjoy change and rarely see the need to."

"Pretty sure he's seen the need," Fin countered and Reid snorted.

"Maybe, but he might be the first of his kind to actually do something about it."

"I know. That's why I'm not playing around. I'm not risking my health and safety because he's afraid to spend time with his children."

"Good. I don't care about what's good for business. You're worth more to me than Cameron's opinion of us," Reid stated. He jumped up to fetch something from the counter and a loaded look passed around the table until all eyes were on Fin. Reid noticed and was frowning at all of them as he sat. He raised a brow at Fin. "Is this an intervention?"

"Yes. We think you should quit fooling around with this and start your own agency," Fin stated. There were nods and hums from around the table. Reid hadn't laughed at them and still looked receptive so Fin continued with his prepared pitch. "You saved me and Riley, and we think you could help a lot of people with your own agency. All the parents think you're a rockstar and everyone knows who we are because of Mom and Dad. I don't know why we haven't thought about this before. Childcare's in our blood."

Doctors Theodore and Saoirse Marshall wrote a series of books together that became a hit daytime talk show. They were transitioning to podcasts and had a docuseries in the works with Netflix.

Reid sighed as he stared out the window. He was definitely coming around to the idea. Penn reached across the table and gave him an affectionate shake.

"You've published papers on developmental disabilities and you were offered your own Montessori school. This is perfect for you and you already have all the connections," he said, as if Reid needed reminding.

"That's right. You're the world's best nanny," Fin agreed and held up his coffee in salute. "But what if you had an army of nanny terminators and you saved the city?"

"It would give me something to do..." Reid mused. Fin, Gavin, Penn, and Riley traded looks again.

"I could handle all the financial and legal paperwork," Gavin offered helpfully. Fin waited until Reid noticed they were out of coffee and got up to press his hands together and mouth a thank you. They exchanged the barest nods with Penn and Riley when Reid ducked into the pantry for the coffee beans.

"I've had a few calls from some friends who are looking for leads on positions and there are parents having a hard time finding agencies that don't discriminate." Reid tapped his fingers against the side of the coffee canister as he considered. "It would give me something to do..." He repeated as he became distracted by something on the other side of the window's ancient, murky panes and nodded. "I'll think about it," he decided. He didn't notice as they smiled at each other and exchanged silent high-fives. Reid was the glue that held their lives together, but he rarely asked for help when he was struggling.

"Riley's going to need a permanent situation once Penn's dad's recovered," Fin reminded him and Reid nodded. It would be a coup if it got out that Reid had recruited him for his new agency. Just about every nanny in the city would follow Reid and Penn, and Fin could do a lot for their reputation if he didn't blow it at The Killian House.

"Very true. And if I had you, Riley, Penn...and possibly Penny?" Reid raised his brows at Penn. Penny was his little sister and almost as legendary as her brother for being a wonder with "difficult" kids.

"Of course, I'm in," Penn said and bumped fists with Fin. "And Penny will be in as soon as she hears," he predicted. This time, Fin cheered as he held out his hand so Gavin and then Riley could slap it.

"I could get a few more solid nannies to join us and we'd have a pretty decent starting roster," Reid noted.

"Cameron could write the agency's first review." Fin pointed out.

"Really?" Reid's brows climbed up his forehead. "Already have that kind of pull within the household?" He asked and Fin shrugged casually.

"Cameron's pretty cool with his staff and I don't see why he wouldn't want to help other parents."

"People pay a lot of attention to what Cameron does and his endorsement would be huge," Penn added while stroking his beard. Reid held up a hand, signaling for them to slow down.

"Hold on... I haven't exactly committed to this yet. Fin's first assignment might end in disaster."

"Or romance," Riley argued and Fin's face twisted.

"Don't say that. Reid isn't interested in running a nanny/matchmaking service."

There were hard grunts of agreement from Reid and Gavin.

"That's a much nicer way of putting it but I see your point." Riley chewed on his lip as he considered. "What if he fell in love with your roommate?"

"What if my roommate died from a fall while drinking wine in the stairwell?" Fin replied and Reid widened his eyes at them impatiently.

"Let's see how long Fin and Cameron can get along before we commit to anything," Reid cautioned. "Something like this would be expensive to get off the ground, and I'll have a hard time attracting clients if Cameron fires Fin for overstepping. And don't get your hopes up, Fin. At the end of the day, he's still Walker Cameron III. He may be willing to change a few things, but he might not go as far as you're ready to take him. He might just be doing whatever it takes to keep you until you're too attached and invested to leave. Parents have been known to put on an act until they're comfortable enough to be themselves."

"I've been to this rodeo before, Reid," Fin sighed as he sat back and folded his arms behind his head confidently. "Cameron's got another thing coming if he thinks he can pat me on the head and send me off to fix his family for him. He's getting his hands dirty this time."

Chapter Eleven

"I think she managed to capture my rakish charm," Fin murmured as he admired the picture Charlotte had drawn before bedtime. He didn't like that they appeared to be at the circus. At least, he hoped they were at the circus because there was an alarming number of clowns surrounding them. The girls were holding hands, wearing crowns, and blue ball gowns. Fin was at one end, holding one of the triplets' hands and Cameron was at the other end in a top hat and tails. He noticed that Cameron had a sword and Fin frowned. "Huh. Maybe we aren't at the circus..."

"You're still in The Killian House but it's easy to understand why you'd be confused," Cameron said from the nursery door, causing Fin to jump. He laughed and held up the picture.

"Charlotte created a masterpiece. Or my worst nightmare, but I love the way she uses as much color as she can."

"She's my little Kahlo," Cameron said as he strolled into the room. Fin handed it to Cameron and he hummed in approval as he appraised her work. "I do believe that one should always keep a sword handy when attending a clown opera," he said, passing it back to Fin. Cameron made a contented sound as he rested against the edge of the craft table. "I've been asking the girls what their favorite part of the day was, like you suggested for bedtime, and it's done wonders. I used to ask who was responsible for the day's debacles but your way has resulted in far less bickering and fussing this week."

"It's a nice way to mentally shut the door on the day. And I often feel tired when I think back through all the things I've done since I woke up."

"Once again, the genius is in the simplicity. Bedtime has always been my favorite part of the day," Cameron began. He squeezed an eye shut and grimaced sheepishly. "'They're usually more docile because they're exhausted, and they'll sit still and listen to me while I'm reading to them."

"Six-year-olds are always a handful and their chaotic energy multiplies when you have two or more together in the same room. Encourage kids to talk about things they like and they won't have anything to bicker about. You get one to say something nice and the other two will reciprocate because we're wired that way," Fin explained. He could see that Walker was adding that to his mental list of things to try. He often did that when he checked in with Fin in the evening. It was refreshing and almost exhilarating, being respected and deferred to. Fin barely had a rapport with most of the parents he had worked for in the past but Walker was genuinely hungry to learn and improve. He'd never admit it, but Fin imagined risking it all whenever they were alone and Walker confided in him.

Fin hadn't meant to do it, but he checked out his boss's ass as Cameron thoughtfully studied Charlotte's masterpiece. Like his brother, Fin could lose his head around a handsome man in precisely-tailored charcoal wool. And Cameron wasn't just fit and handsome. He ticked all the boxes. There were fine lines at the corners of Cameron's pale gray eyes that accentuated the gray at his temples. He'd always liked older men but Cameron didn't carry himself like any of the men Fin had dated. Cameron strolled as if he owned everything his eyes touched— because he usually did—or like he was on a runway. Pierce made sure Cameron was immaculately turned out and nearly every garment was handmade just for him.

Fin had learned that Cameron had a gym in the basement and worked out with a trainer five days a week before sunrise. There was also a Peloton in the sitting room of his suite. Fin had discovered this when he'd ventured across the gallery to return a silk Hermés tie Charlotte had "borrowed" for a costume. Instead of admiring the handsomely decorated room, Fin had been mesmerized by the sight of a shirtless Cameron on the bike. He was gloriously shiny as sweat dripped down his temples, his bare arms, and gathered in the hair between his pecs. Cameron's t-shirt hung from the handlebars, leaving Fin with a view of tight, toned, hair-dusted abs. And Cameron's black compression shorts accentuated his thighs and his firm, round ass perfectly.

"Came up here to work through something," Cameron had panted, tapping on his forehead. "Leave that wherever. Pierce will be along in a few moments and will take care of it."

"Cool. Good luck with that," Fin babbled, backing through the opened double doors. *You've just ruined my entire life but I'll leave this wherever.*

"You have a way with the girls," Cameron said, snatching Fin from his thoughts and returning him to the nursery.

"I have my own, willful, chaotic streak so we get along," Fin told Walker.

"There might be something to that. The only other person they ever behave for is my sister, Agnes. Probably because she's a willful brat but she takes the girls every other weekend so I can have a chance to catch my breath. The rest of the household needs the break as well," he added with a pained expression.

"I didn't understand why I got every other weekend off and those dates were set in stone but I get it now." Fin laughed as he squatted to pick up the Memory cards from their last game. "That Beatrice might be quiet, but she mops the floor with us every time," he glanced over his shoulder at Cameron only to find his eyes locked on Fin's backside. Fin slowly rose, feeling the waist of his pants slide back up, over his ass. They might have been a touch too baggy, with a tendency to sag when he bent or squatted. His face became hot when he looked across the room to where he'd draped his cardigan over the arm of his desk chair. Fin squinted at it as he mentally scrambled to remember what he was wearing under his jeans. *Red mesh briefs.* It could have been a lot worse. Half of Fin's underwear collection was women's thongs and bikinis. Just about anything he could comfortably situate himself into. This particular pair were from the men's section but the back of his bright red briefs were practically transparent. "Every other weekend works perfectly for me because I can catch up on my sewing." Fin tried to act natural as he turned and Cameron nodded quickly.

"Perfect. You're an avid sewer?" He asked weakly, looking anywhere but at Fin as a bead of sweat rolled down Cameron's forehead. Fin spied a rather impressive bulge in the front of Cameron's trousers and his embarrassment escalated into panic.

Holy shit! What do I do? Fin coughed as he took two large steps to his desk and reached for his cardigan.

"It's more of an ADHD thing and the world's being choked to death with fast fashion, so I make warm things for those in need while I'm watching movies or listening to audiobooks. I get nervous about how much pollution and waste humans create and how we're transporting landfill-sized barges of trash across the ocean because we've run out of room here," Fin babbled. "I have to keep my hands busy and I might as well put them to good use," he added and saw Cameron flinch. Fin rewound his last statement and considered slamming his hand in the drawer.

"Oh?" Came a strained reply as Cameron tugged at his collar.

"You know what they say about idle hands," Fin said, then bit down on his lips. *That made it worse, you nerd!* He rushed to put the abacus back on the bookshelf and knocked a stack of wooden geography puzzles onto the floor. All the countries and continents spilled onto the rug, causing Cameron to mutter a pained curse. "No worries! I'll pick them up!" Fin announced as he dropped.

"I need to talk to Pierce! I'll see you tomorrow," Cameron said as he hurried for the door.

"Cool. Hope it's nothing serious." Fin blinked at the empty doorway as Walker escaped. "Have a good night," he added weakly. He backed away from the door and stopped when his butt hit his desk. "What was that?"

This wasn't the first time Fin caught Cameron checking him out. And Fin was certainly guilty of looking as well. And sniffing. Cameron always smelled incredible. He was a beautiful man and Fin was young and attractive. And as far as Fin knew, they were the only queer men in the tiny microcosm of The Killian House, so it was natural that they would notice each other.

There was absolutely nothing threatening or predatory in Cameron's glances. If anything, they were cautious, fleeting things that only sparked Fin's curiosity and imagination. And he told himself it was harmless if they looked or sniffed now and then. They weren't hurting anyone and they were both consenting adults. And it wasn't like Fin had anyone, so he wasn't being unfaithful. He didn't have time for a relationship outside of work. He was stuck inside The Killian House from 7 a.m. to 7 p.m. with only every other weekend off. It wasn't Fin's fault that his boss was incredibly hot and liked to look as well. Fin reasoned that he was just making the most of an awesome but harmless situation. Or so he thought.

"What does this mean?"

Now they *both* knew and they'd practically acknowledged it. Fin had been momentarily mortified at Cameron seeing his underwear but... *He liked it.* At least, part of Cameron liked it. And it was...interesting for Fin, knowing he'd had that kind of effect on a man like Walker Cameron III. It was also dangerous.

Fin got a high every time Cameron trusted him and just *tried.* He couldn't help but get excited at Cameron's progress and sometimes, Fin got *excited* excited. No one would believe Cameron was capable of the kind of tenderness and self-aware-ness Fin had witnessed in only a few weeks. But Cameron had shared that side of himself with Fin for his girls' sake, even though it clearly made him uncomfortable to do it. It was those flashes of vulnerability and honesty that made Cameron truly sexy.

"What am I going to do?"

Normally, Fin's instinct would be to ignore, ignore, ignore and pretend it hadn't happened, but he'd never *wanted* an employer before, let alone one he liked as much as he was beginning to like Cameron. Which was another problem in itself. Fin had already fallen in love with the Cameron girls and he finally had an opportunity to save a family. He would never jeopardize that with sex but Fin was certainly tempted.

"I'm going to call Riley and tell him to get out the big wine glasses," Fin said with a decisive nod. He'd finish straightening up the nursery in the morning.

Chapter Twelve

"**C**an we give Grandma and Grandpop our picture when we get there? I don't like waiting for you and Grandpop to talk about markets and the house," Amelia complained drowsily. Beatrice and Charlotte mumbled in agreement and stifled yawns. They had practically forgotten about Walker and nodded off during the drive to the family estate in Greenwich for a subdued early Mother's Day Celebration. It was a miracle after years of raucous interrogations. Walker had spent most of the nearly hour-long drive blessedly distracted by something other than the girls' bickering and clamoring for once.

But after an hour of relative peace, Walker still didn't know what to make of his encounter with Fin in the nursery. He wasn't the sort of man who crossed the line with his employees and Fin didn't strike him as someone who'd fool around with his employer. Fin *was* the type of man who wore see-through candy apple red briefs, apparently. Walker had spent the rest of the evening after he'd fled from the nursery imagining Fin in his bed in nothing but those briefs. And that had been startling in itself.

Because what could be more foolish than making a pass at Fin? The sudden rush of arousal was an ill-timed eruption from a long-dormant volcano and Walker was still shaken in the aftermath. He wasn't sure how he felt about it, and he damn sure wasn't ready to explain it to Fin.

It had only been three years but Walker could go as much as two weeks without crying and he no longer stared at door-ways, wishing Connor would walk into the room. If he had a therapist, they would say that he'd accepted his husband's death but it was still at the "heavy ache" stage. There were times when he got so lonely and felt so isolated because of the enor-mity of what had happened, he would yearn for someone to help him seal that part of his past and move forward. Then, Walker would worry about what that would cost—letting go of Connor.

And Walker became petrified at the thought of dating again. He'd closed himself away in The Killian House and the world left him alone for the most part because he was in mourning. But the world had changed dramatically since Walker was in college, and he'd barely understood dating then.

And even if Walker *could*, he wouldn't know what to do with someone like Fin. He was younger and far more experi-enced in ways Walker couldn't fathom. He could have anyone he wanted and Walker understood him well enough to know that Fin would never put his own desires ahead of the girls' needs.

If Fin actually wanted him.

He thought he'd caught Fin checking him out a few times but Walker told himself he'd imagined it. He assumed that Fin had someone or that he had better options. Why would someone so creative and vibrant be interested in someone as stunted and stiff as him?

But Walker jealously wondered what kind of men Fin spent his time with when he was away from The Killian House. His hands tightened around the wheel as he turned at the gate and steered past the miniature maze in the center of the small courtyard. The girls became alert as he parked in front of the Colonial-Era estate. They pointed at the horses on the paddock excitedly before they attacked the buckles on their booster seats.

"Can we give Grandpop our picture then say hi to the ponies?" Beatrice begged. Walker shut off the car and glanced at the Popsicle stick and macaroni frame on the passenger seat. The masterpiece was a team project. Fin had the girls color a picture of Walker's parents in their throne-like wheelchairs to go with the brightly painted macaroni frame.

"Remember that Grandma and Grandpop can't see all that well anymore, and they don't always understand what you're saying because they can't hear well either." Walker turned in his seat to make sure they were listening.

It was easier to pretend his parents couldn't see or hear the girls than explain that the old gargoyles had always been cold and vacant. His parents were a little hard of hearing now, but they *could* follow along when it suited them. Both were in surprisingly good health for being in their eighties, and they *could* walk but Walker's father liked being pushed around and coddled by his attractive young nurse. And his mother liked to drink cocktails with breakfast and was generally safer sitting at all times.

"They're looking forward to seeing you but they get tired easily," he added. Amelia nodded impatiently while she helped Charlotte with her boot.

"Grandpop loves us but he wants to ask you about your

money," she said and went to urge Bea along. *At least they won't be disappointed.* Walker's parents paid little attention to the girls and his father's only concern was his son's portfolio and his reputation on Wall Street. Each generation of Camerons had built an empire in their own right—with a significant head start, of course— and Walker had exceeded every generation before him.

Until he hired Fin, Walker worried that he was no better than his father and that his children were paying the same dreadful price he and Agnes had paid for their parents' coldness.

As if he'd summoned her, the massive front door of the house swung open and Agnes jogged down the front steps to greet them. She was tall like Walker but willowy. Walker would never say it out loud, but he thought she'd aged rather well and looked regal and ethereal, especially when she pulled her long salt-and-pepper hair into a stylish bun. Although, she didn't appear all that regal at the moment, dressed in a paint-spattered smock and ridiculous wooden clogs. And she was making quite the spectacle of herself, jumping and waving like a contestant on a game show.

"Money's just about the only thing Grandpop understands these days." *If that,* Walker thought with a wry grimace. His father's understanding of the markets was fading as technology left him behind but money was still the only thing Walker Cameron II cared about. "Let's go. We'll play tennis with Agnes if you behave for Grandma and Grandpop," he said. The girls cheered as he got out and went around to let Amelia out. Agnes opened the other door and caught Charlotte as she launched herself from the car.

"My flying monkeys!" Agnes laughed as she caught them and kissed Charlotte and Beatrice loudly.

"We made a painting!" Amelia announced, excited to show

Agnes. She reached between the front seats and grabbed the framed picture. Her other arm stretched for Walker and she cheered as she went to him. He hugged her close and stifled a shiver. Walker cherished these moments when his girls were calm enough to hold, though they were happening more frequently since Fin's arrival. It had taken him years but Walker could finally spend more than five minutes with his chaotic little butterflies without swearing under his breath or begging them to be silent.

"This is a work of art!" Agnes declared. She continued to gush as she corralled the girls around the car. "Thank goodness you got Connor's taste and creativity. Walker's never been good with color. Which is why he likes everything in gray and black and white," she told them. Walker rolled his eyes as he followed. Despite the jab, he was grateful for her ability to talk about Connor so easily. Walker couldn't, but she made it feel like Connor was still there and kept him present in the girls' minds. As grateful as he was for the break, part of the reason Walker sent the girls to Agnes was so they could learn more about Connor. Agnes was a terrible pain in Walker's ass but she had her uses. *She's my best friend.*

"I thought so too," Walker said as he got the girls' bags and left them on the driveway to be transferred to Agnes's Range Rover. She was taking the girls for the rest of the night, then bringing them into the city for brunch to celebrate Mother's Day with them. Walker and Agnes exchanged loaded looks. He put an arm around her and kissed her hair. "How tired are they?" He whispered. She sighed wearily as she gave Walker's chest a reassuring pat. "Tired" had long been their code word for sober and sociable. Or when in reference to the girls' visits, appropriate company for young children.

"Mom hasn't been sentient since her fourth glass of breakfast wine but Dad's ranting about cryptocurrencies," she warned.

"Damn it. Who told him about cryptocurrencies?" Walker yelled. He set Charlotte down and charged into the house to calm his father before he had a stroke. Walker interrupted his father's ranting by diverting the conversation to The Killian House garden's recent renovation. Agnes had taken the triplets upstairs to the nursery and tidied their hair and dresses before the girls bravely marched in and curtsied. Walker considered his parents as they basked obliviously in a beam of sunlight from the bow window. A fire crackled in the hearth despite the late spring day outside because his mother was always cold. The girls were charming and on their best behavior but there was no reaction from their grandparents.

"Look who's here!" Walker said enthusiastically and lowered to fix his mother's hair after it spilled over her face. His mother swatted at him while Walker's father hunted for his monocle.

"What's that?" He asked loudly.

"Walker's girls are here!" Agnes shouted at them and Walker's mother's head popped up.

"I want to see them!" She pushed off the arms of her chair and searched the room. "Is that them?" She asked as she pointed at Walker's reflection over the mantle.

"Over here, Mom," Agnes scolded and guided the girls closer. Walker's hand shot out, halting the girls. He didn't want them within touching distance because he wasn't sure the girls wanted his parents to touch them. They weren't babies anymore. And he appreciated that his parents' short tempers and abrupt, blunt remarks could be unsettling to small children. And his parents had a habit of impatiently grabbing and pinching when something they wanted was within reach.

"We made something for you," Amelia said. She stepped

forward and presented the macaroni frame and Walker was proud of her business-like attitude but regretted that she had developed that armor. She was detached and uninterested as she presented the picture. Walker's soul shriveled a little more when his father adjusted his monocle and leaned forward. He made several sharp "Huh!" sounds before he sat back in his tapestry-upholstered throne.

"You should hire them a decent art tutor," he said dismissively. The monocle dropped and swung like a pendulum in the silent sitting room.

"'This is a *masterpiece*," Agnes declared and lifted it from their father's grasp. She went to the mantle and propped the frame against the mirror. "Look at that!" She clutched her chest dramatically. "You know, I think I'll paint a life-size version of this for your anniversary," she said with a decisive nod. Walker couldn't have loved his sister more as she put her arms around the girls and led them away. "We're going to change. I ordered us matching feather boas and gloves, and they just got here. We'll meet you on the tennis court, Walker," she announced imperiously.

Agnes left with the girls and Walker did the minimum until he was excused to change into his tennis clothes.

The five of them spent the afternoon laughing as they lobbed balls at each other until it was time for the girls to head inside for supper in the nursery. The girls got to watch their favorite movies and play games while Walker and Agnes suffered downstairs.

He was dribbling with his racket and looking forward to cocktails in the sitting room—they were the perfect anesthetic to dinner with their parents—when Agnes pounced. Walker realized they had the court to themselves. And she was in a mischievous mood, judging by the knowing gleam in her eyes.

"Who's this Fin I keep hearing about?" She sang, winding

her arm around Walker's neck. "The girls say he's the best nanny in the whole world and a *very* cute boy."

"Absolutely not," Walker said as he attempted to duck out of her grasp but she snatched the back of his shirt.

"I've noticed that you're steadier with the girls and they're much calmer lately."

"Fin threatened to quit unless I got my act together and it appears that there is some wisdom behind his particular brand of madness."

"It would appear so," Agnes drawled suggestively. Walker ignored her and became absorbed as he bounced the tennis ball on the racket.

"Is it too soon for me to be interested in other men?" He swore when Agnes snatched the ball.

"It's been too *long*," she said. Her hand closed around Walker's wrist and she turned him. Walker looked away so she couldn't see his eyes as they watered. It had only been three years for Walker, but to everyone else, three years was more than long enough. "Please do it, whatever you're scared of," she urged. He shook his head but she cupped his cheek and stopped him. "I heard that you're laughing again."

"Six-year-olds are terrible sources," Walker warned. "Nothing's happening. I'm just curious."

"You're not the only one."

"The one thing this situation doesn't need is a nosy older sister."

"Are you sure?" She asked gently. "You've locked yourself away in The Killian House and you only come out for work or the girls. Who else is going to tell you to go for it? Pierce certainly won't."

"No. His advice would be far more sensible and less likely to ruin my life," Walker countered but Agnes's face scrunched.

"What life, my love?"

"Don't start with that, Aggie. I've got my hands full with the girls and work," he stated. She laughed softly as she wound her arm around his.

"Not anymore. You've got Fin now and things are already a lot smoother. You might find yourself with a lot more time on your hands."

"A little but Fin wants me to give that time back to the girls and I think he's right."

"And what about you? What do you want?" She asked and Walker didn't have to think. *Fin.*

"I don't know but it finally feels like I have some control and I'm not ruining the girls anymore. There's a chance Fin could shape me into a decent father and I have to take it. That's all that matters at the moment."

Agnes sighed and leaned, towing Walker back to the house but his feet had become heavy. He was thinking about skipping dinner and heading back to the city early.

"I can't speak on this from experience because we were raised by two cracked, empty vessels, but I believe that part of being a decent parent is being a *happy* parent. The girls see how lonely you've been and they're happiest when you smile and laugh."

"That is not fair and you know it," Walker scolded. "Mom can hold liters of alcohol and often does so without spilling a drop."

"True," Agnes conceded. "But imagine how healthy we would have been if mom and dad liked each other and laughed around us," she said gently, poking Walker's conscience.

"I'll think about it, brat."

Chapter Thirteen

"I'm sorry. Did you just tell me that I can't read that bill before it hits the floor?" Walker asked, smiling when he heard the senator splutter out an apology. He sounded like he was crying. "I'll get back to you after I've had a look at it." He hung up and laughed under his breath while he crossed the item off the list in his planner. There was a soft tap at the study's open door.

"So this is where you like to hide." Fin pursed his lips as he strolled into the room with his hands clasped behind his back. He scanned the bookshelves and walls as he slowly rotated. "Weird that I've been working in this house for almost two months but have never had a reason to take a peek in here..."

"I assure you, I'm not hiding." Walker rested his elbow on the armrest of his chair and pretended he was calm while Fin poked at his trophies and plaques. He *was* hiding but Walker thought his study was a foolproof cover because that was where he worked and usually spent most of his time. Walker was still caught between a rock and the hard place in his trousers. He didn't want to jeopardize the progress he was making with the girls but Agnes's voice kept echoing in his ear whenever Fin walked into the room.

Fin was so much more than "a very cute boy" and Walker wished he had the nerve to say or do something about his attraction but there was too much at stake.

"I'm not hiding if I'm exactly where I'm supposed to be."

"If you say so." Fin went to the decanters and pulled one of the stoppers and gave it a sniff. Walker's brows pulled together in confusion.

"If I say so?" *That's usually how it works.*

"Yes. That is what people say when they don't agree. When they have a difference of opinion," Fin explained with a vague gesture. He bent to inspect a picture of Walker with the Pope and laughed. Walker's eyes slid to the ceiling.

"A difference...? I am not hiding. This is my office, Fin. Where else would I be?" He asked.

"In the nursery, in half an hour?" Fin suggested but Walker snorted.

"I'm certain I won't be. I have a call with the secretary of defense in twenty minutes."

"No! You've got to reschedule that or cut it short!" Fin urged.

"Reschedule with the secretary of defense?" Walker confirmed and Fin nodded as if that wasn't absurd.

"Yeah. I told the girls I could get you to turn up for our pre-nap time tea party this afternoon, but they didn't believe me. They said you never accept their invitations but I told them I had extra juice."

"Extra juice?"

"You know, influence. I need you to come through so I can earn some easy street cred."

"Street cred?" Walker asked cluelessly and Fin smacked himself on the cheek.

"Come on, Cameron. Act like you've seen a movie. I'm trying to impress the girls so they'll trust me and think I'm cool. You want that, right?"

"Of course. My sanity and salvation depend upon it." Walker couldn't see how his presence at a tea party would benefit his sanity or aid in his salvation. If anything, it might hasten his descent into madness.

"Then join us for tea."

"I'm afraid I can't reschedule with the secretary of defense or cut 'it' short."

"All I'm asking for is half an hour. Work with me. I'll make it worth your while," Fin said silkily, making the hairs on the back of Walker's neck stand.

"What?"

"A half-hour in the nursery sipping invisible tea will transform your girls, I promise." Fin murmured the words as if he was inviting Walker to a soothing spa getaway.

For a moment, Walker had imagined Fin was offering a different sort of trade and was shocked with himself. Then, he recalled what his end of the bargain entailed and snorted.

"It's not that I don't want to. We've had a good run of luck but I don't think it's going to go the way you're hoping. Whenever I join the girls for an activity in the nursery or we go on an outing it descends into bedlam almost immediately. The girls become excited and shout things at me until I snap and shout back at them. One of them—usually Charlotte—will begin to sniffle and I'll feel like hell and have to leave. Either that or the fire alarm is set off and I'll ruin another suit."

"No way! Not at one of my tea parties!" Fin promised as he hurried around Walker's desk and dropped onto the edge. Walker's eyes widened and jumped to Fin's. Pierce was the only other person who *ever* touched Walker's desk. Most people were too scared to cross the study's threshold but Fin had made himself right at home. He hummed curiously, care-free as he chewed on his lip and studied Walker's calendar.

"How are your tea parties special?" Walker asked as he studied Fin's lower lip. It was full and looked so soft. Walker had noticed that Fin often scraped his teeth over it when he was plotting and calculating.

"First of all, this is a nap time tea party. Second, no beans," Fin said, adding to Walker's befuddlement.

"No beans?" He parroted.

"Yup! I put on Brubeck and we danced for half an hour so the girls could shake the beans out." He raised his arms and did the wave as he whistled the opening of "Take Five." It was one of Walker's favorite songs and he was a little sad that he'd missed out. "I've got a big bowl of strawberries and raspberries because they're full of vitamins and minerals that have been proven to aid in rest and relaxation. The girls will be nodding off before the half-hour is up."

"That sounds delightful but I can't reschedule that call." Walker was still not convinced that he wouldn't ruin the girl's tea party and make a cranky ass out of himself. But the thought of appeasing the girls *and* pleasing Fin did appeal to him, if there was some way he could pull it off without losing his temper.

"How about this?" Fin tilted toward Walker like they were negotiating something far more serious. "I can postpone it for half an hour. I'll have the girls draw their favorite part of last night's bedtime story. That will get their little brains primed for resting." Fin held out his hand like that was his best offer. Walker took it, noting how strong Fin's grip was. It was sure and assertive but his hand was warm as it held Walker's.

"I'll be there," Walker confirmed. A wide grin filled Fin's face, lighting up his eyes. Fin held onto his hand and the warmth spread from Walker's fingers and up his arm, as if Fin's confidence and optimism were seeping into him.

"Good boy!" Fin said sincerely before releasing Walker's hand, severing the warm connection. Walker almost followed when Fin hopped to his feet and made his way around the desk. Fin paused and held up two sets of crossed fingers. "We haven't had a prank or a meltdown in two days. I have a feeling you're going to find that the girls are a lot calmer now because they know they'll have time with you this evening. And they know they'll see you at breakfast tomorrow. A little time goes a long way, you'll see," he said then left Walker.

The call to the secretary of defense took nearly the full half-hour but was otherwise unremarkable, not requiring too much of Walker's attention. He was able to ponder Fin's plan and Walker found that he was optimistic as well. Fin had only been at The Killian House for a few months but the entire household had already noticed an improvement in the girls which had lifted the overall mood in the house. Pierce said he hadn't seen to any spills or sent for a repairman in days and Walker couldn't remember the last time he heard a maid crying.

When Walker reached the nursery, he found the lights turned down. A sphere-shaped lamp rested on the craft table, casting the room in pastel hues. One of the girls' floral quilts had been spread out on the floor and there were pillows for lounging. As promised, a large bowl of berries and a pink ceramic tea set waited while Louis Armstrong sang "What a Wonderful World."

"You're right on time!" Fin said as he waved from his spot on the blanket. He'd taken off his sneakers and was sitting cross-legged. The girls looked up from their drawings, clearly happy to see Walker but there was no shrieking or stampeding. They calmly patted the quilt, inviting Walker to join them. And they

K. Sterling

remained calm while Walker toed off his shoes and then lowered onto the blanket across from Fin.

"May I pour you some tea?" Beatrice picked up the pot and an empty cup when Walker nodded. The cup remained empty after she poured but Walker made an appreciative sound as he sipped and ate a real strawberry.

"This is one of my favorite songs," he told Charlotte and she nodded quickly.

"I like this one and the one about Old MacDonald."

"I'm familiar with the song..." Walker squinted as he leaned toward her. "Which version is your favorite?" He asked and she looked at Fin.

"Ella Fitzgerald but it's on our 'Get The Beans Out' playlist because it slaps a little too hard for tea time," Fin explained and Walker was once again impressed.

"An excellent choice and it does indeed *slap*," he said, causing Fin and the girls to giggle. "What's your favorite song?" Walker asked Charlotte. She was unbearably precious as she tapped her chin thoughtfully.

"I like the 'Linus and Lucy' song," she said, resulting in a delighted gasp from Walker.

"I love that song!" He said, then got a little winded when the girls scooted in closer. Amelia huddled against his side as Beatrice rested her head on his thigh while Charlotte and Fin colored and sang along with the music. Their eyes would catch from time to time and Walker found it reassuring that nothing had changed between him and Fin. It had been almost a week since Walker had seen his red briefs but Fin was as relaxed and encouraging as he always was. He made soft grunts and hums of approval as Walker and the girls bonded over music. They still felt like partners, focused on the girls' well-being, and Walker suspected that they were also becoming friends.

The afternoon turned magical when "Hit The Road To

Dreamland" by Dean Martin began and Amelia asked Walker to dance with her. It was her favorite song and Walker felt like *he* was in dreamland as he and Fin took turns dancing with the girls until it was time for their nap. Turns out, it was easy to relax when Walker put his faith in Fin and stopped over-thinking things.

As Fin predicted, the girls were drowsy and were easily bundled into the princess tent in their bedroom when tea time was over. The party had been such a soothing success, Walker did something he hadn't done since he was a child after he returned to his study. He propped his feet up on the corner of his desk, crossed his arms behind his head, and took a nap.

Chapter Fourteen

I wouldn't have invited him to our nap time tea party if I'd known he was going to be so fucking hot the whole time.

Fin was a little frustrated with himself as he stomped down the steps to his front door. He'd needled Walker into attending but the plan had backfired on Fin. He'd invited Walker so he could enjoy a soothing activity with the girls *and* prove that nothing had changed between them. But Walker had done more than bond over jazz and imaginary tea, he'd been present, vulnerable, and so openly smitten with his girls. It made Fin *weak* and he had extremely lewd ideas about how he'd like to thank Walker for making his job infinitely easier.

And it's Walker now? That isn't a good sign.

He wasn't just on a first-name basis with his employer in his head, he was also thinking about how Walker spent his time when he wasn't with Fin and the girls. And Fin imagined various ways to fill his time whenever the girls were sleeping or away from The Killian House. In his favorite fantasies, Fin locked the door to Walker's study and praised him for being such a good boy.

Which would be *bad* but what made it worse was that Fin had a strong suspicion that Walker would like that. A lot. It was hard to miss the way he got flustered and blushed whenever Fin complimented him. And there was often a hopeful, hungry look in his eyes, whenever Walker glanced at Fin for approval. *That* look went straight to Fin's pants and caused his heart to skip a few beats.

"I'm home," Fin announced and kicked the door shut behind him. He let his bag slide off his arm and drop to the floor on the way to the kitchen. Riley looked concerned from his perch on the counter. He was drinking wine and supervising a pot of pasta as it boiled.

"What happened? Your text said that the tea party was a hit."

"Too much of a hit," Fin grumbled. He got a wine glass from the cabinet and Riley was ready with the bottle. He filled it to the brim and Fin thanked him before taking several deep gulps.

"Too much of a hit with the girls or Cameron?" Riley asked dubiously and Fin shook his head.

"I might have enjoyed it a little too much," he admitted, causing Riley's face to pinch.

"Ew."

"Not that much." Fin gave Riley a disapproving scowl and shook his head at him. "But I might have had...thoughts."

"Yes! I was hoping this would happen!" Riley cheered.

"No! It's not what you think. We might be interested in each other but not like that," Fin said and Riley's face fell.

"What does that even mean? Do you two like each other or not?"

"Sure," Fin said easily. "I've gotten to know Walker a little better, and he's not as awful as I thought he was—"

"Walker?"

"I don't call him that to his face," Fin said obviously and

stopped Riley before he could say it. "I've already acknowledged that it's a problem and I might be having some unprofessional thoughts about him." He ducked his head and braced himself as Riley's face split into a huge grin.

"I knew it! Let's have a spring wedding! Everyone's into winter weddings lately but who wants to be cold and wet when they're saying their vows?"

"What? No!" Fin shook his head wildly. "I said he's not as awful as I thought he was but I don't want to date him. Not even a little," he added firmly.

Riley's lip pushed out and he was disappointed as he scratched at his scalp.

"Not even a little?"

"Nope. We're getting along well, but we don't have a lot in common or seem interested in each other, aside from one very specific thing," Fin explained. Riley's eyes were huge as he processed and sipped his wine.

"I'm assuming that thing is sex," he finally guessed. Fin held up a hand and shook his head.

"I have no idea but part of me really wants to."

"What does that mean?" Riley demanded. Fin swept a hand through his hair and made an exploding sound.

"I've noticed that he likes it when I tell him he's done something good. I may have even called him a 'good boy.'"

"Oh." Riley leaned back and blinked at Fin. "Do you think he wants to be a puppy?"

"No..." Fin's eyes narrowed as he tried to imagine Walker in a collar and on his knees. It was hot but it wouldn't suit him. "He's not that kind of sub. Walker's insecure about his parenting skills and wants to be praised for real things. I don't think he has a desire to be obedient for the sake of being obedient, you know?"

"Still hot, though." Riley sighed dreamily and Fin pointed.

"There's the problem. He's been so open about how overwhelmed he gets with the girls and *he listens* and kind of turns to goo when I tell him he did something good and *I love it*."

"Yeah. But it's really hot. Tell me again why you don't want to marry him," Riley said but Fin wasn't going to dignify that with a response.

"Something else happened about a week ago," Fin said hesitantly. Riley made a giddy sound as he slid off the counter.

"I already know this is good. Give it to me," he said and gestured impatiently. Fin looked into his glass and considered throwing it at him but decided against wasting decent-ish wine. And he had no one else to talk to. Reid would strangle Fin if he knew about what had happened in the nursery.

"I caught him checking out my ass and he saw my underwear."

"Uh oh. What kind of underwear?" Riley asked because he knew how widely Fin's taste in undergarments ranged.

"Savage Fenty but from the men's section. The thing is, he liked it. In a very obvious way. And he knows that I know," Fin explained, earning an awkward grimace from Riley.

"We have an elephant in the room."

"Not anymore," Fin said, getting frustrated with himself all over again. "He was avoiding me and hiding in his office so I invited him to the tea party to prove that everything was still cool between us. He was supposed to see that we could leave whatever happened between us outside of the nursery, as far as the girls were concerned."

"But that didn't happen?"

"Oh, it absolutely happened," Fin complained. "Everything went perfectly and Walker had the loveliest time with the girls."

"I don't see the problem," Riley said but his lips twitched as if he did. Fin scowled at him over his glass.

"Aside from my brother?"

"Who's going to find out if you're careful? Cameron's going to keep it quiet because he needs you and we both know you're going to be careful."

"Normally, I'd say you're right but I had almost two hours to myself after the party and the urge to sneak down to his office was almost unbearable!" Fin whispered in disgust. "I wanted to tell him he'd been such a good boy then beg him to wreck me."

"You totally should!" Riley urged, then clapped a hand over his mouth. "That even sounded too horny for me," he said and Fin nodded.

"Just a little, but for once I'm on the same page. What am I going to do? I've seen him checking me out and he knows I've checked him out but now he's seen my underwear and I've seen his hard-on. I came up with a great way to prove it wasn't a big deal but it made me want him even more."

They were quiet for several moments as they both pondered Fin's problem.

"He really is your type," Riley noted and Fin made a forlorn sound as his thumbs tapped against his glass.

"Older men are my catnip and I have such a thing for dominant men who turn into subs in the bedroom." His background in psychology regularly extended to his relationships and his sex life. Understanding his partner's needs turned Fin on romantically and sexually and it was rare to find a man who wanted so desperately to be understood and responded so positively to praise.

"You need an icebreaker!" Riley said as he waved excitedly. "Something low stakes with no romantic risk! Something both of you can opt into gradually with a low potential for awkwardness."

"That could work!" Fin realized. He dashed to the fridge to see if there was more wine and was in luck. "Perfect!" He snatched the bottle and smiled at Riley. "And I think I have the perfect way to keep the stakes low."

"Go on." Riley waved a hand as he held out his glass.

"I already know he likes hearing when he's been a good boy," Fin said as he poured. "I'll just ask him if he'd like to explore different sorts of rewards."

"Such as?" Riley asked with a suggestive wiggle of his brows and Fin's cheeks were warm as he raised a shoulder.

"I'm open to almost anything but I do have an impressive underwear collection that I could be putting to better use..." Fin felt a rush of arousal at the thought of unzipping his pants and rewarding Walker. "I'll start with a peek at my thong and let Walker decide how far he wants to go."

Chapter Fifteen

"Have you seen the girls or Fin?" Walker asked as he passed Pierce in the foyer.

"Not since breakfast, sir," the butler replied and hovered but Walker shooed him off.

"Thank you for your assistance," Walker said under his breath on his way up the steps. It was raining so they were probably in the nursery. He crossed the gallery and was checking the time when he heard Fin scream. "Fin!" Walker's heart raced as he hurried.

He thought he was past having to worry about Fin's safety but his screams grew louder as Walker dashed up the steps. Walker slipped on the polished floors when he reached the landing and hurled himself at the nursery's door. He threw it open and the blood drained from his face as the girls pushed, pulled, and stabbed Fin wildly. Fin sobbed and begged for mercy as he writhed between them.

"Et tu, Brute?" Fin choked out as he reached for Charlotte and she cackled and jabbed him in the heart with her dagger. The foam blade crumpled as she held it to his chest and forced Fin to his knees. He coughed dramatically and laughed as he got tangled in his purple bedsheet toga and rolled onto his back. The girls pounced on him and were hysterical as they pummeled him with their tiny fists and foam daggers.

"Thank goodness." Walker clutched his chest in relief as he leaned against the door. But a smile spread across his face as he watched the girls with Fin. He bit down on his knuckle to stifle a laugh as Fin rose on his knees and screeched like a raptor.

"There were no dinosaurs in Caesar times!" Beatrice objected, but she became insensate when Fin grabbed her ribs and tickled her.

"How do you know? Were you there?" He countered then yelped when Charlotte jumped on his back and hooked an arm around his neck.

"Easy! I'm the one who has to hide his body if you kill him," Walker called, whistling to get their attention. The girls laughed and shrieked happily as they spun and flew across the nursery to greet Walker.

"Mr. Cameron?" Fin huffed as he struggled to free himself from the toga. "Were we...? Bless it!" He spat then yanked the whole thing over his head.

His t-shirt went with it and got caught under his chin, snagging Walker's attention as well. Walker fell back against the door and hit his head when the girls crashed into his legs. He didn't care as he swiftly appraised every exposed inch of Fin's back and the side of his chest.

Walker made the appropriate sounds and nodded along as the girls babbled giddily up at him. They pulled at his sleeves but Walker was consciously unavailable as Fin bent to free himself, causing the waist of his pants to pull lower, revealing a thin strip of lavender satin. Fin cheered as he kicked the sheet away and twisted to fix his shirt. Walker followed the purple strap around Fin's back and noted that it appeared to be some sort of thong.

"Were we making too much noise?" Fin asked as he yanked his shirt down and turned to them.

"Who?" Walker asked cluelessly. He was looking at Fin's eyes, as was appropriate, but all Walker saw was lavender. The entire room and all the world was lavender while Walker tugged at the thin strip of purple satin with his teeth.

"Did we disturb you? We got a little carried away," Fin said. He looked concerned and frowned as he crossed the nursery.

"Not at all." Walker laughed it off. He smiled at Amelia and fixed one of her pigtails before giving her nose a tender pinch. "I'm relieved I won't be sending the groundskeeper and his men away for the night," he murmured and she laughed when he winked conspiratorially at her.

"Snack time, ladies. Go wash up and meet me in the kitchen. We're making banana ghosts, apple daggers, and rasp-berry blood to dip them in!" Fin said. The girls cheered and stampeded from the nursery. "Are you alright?" He asked once they were alone.

"Me? Of course," Walker said immediately. Which was a lie. He was reeling because he'd had two rather significant reve-lations.

"You hit your head."

"I did," Walker agreed.

He hit his head and realized how much easier it was to smile and laugh when he wasn't worried he was ruining his daughters' lives or turning them into spoiled monsters. And Walker learned he *really* liked women's underwear. It didn't do much for him when it was on a woman but Walker would be forever changed by the sight of Fin's purple thong.

Which was as much of a miracle as laughter because Walker didn't think he was into anything beyond the basics when it came to sex until Fin started giving him orders. Walker thought he was rather bland and predictable but his tastes had taken a surprisingly kinky turn, thanks to Fin and his lavender thong. Walker's libido had stretched like the purple elastic around Fin's waist and was far more adventurous than Walker had realized. But these were wildly inconvenient revelations to have regarding one's nanny.

"Want me to take a look?" Fin asked helpfully and reached for Walker.

"What?" Walker reared back and bumped into the door. "No!" He laughed and shook his head as he held Fin off. *You'd know exactly what was going through my head if you looked.* "I'm fine. Might have knocked a little sense into myself."

He owed Fin so much more than the extravagant salary he was paying him. Fin had only been with them for a short time but Walker's family already felt steadier, less turbulent. His girls were behaving and Walker didn't have to sleep with one eye open. Most importantly, the triplets were happy and hadn't broken anything expensive for days. Fin embraced their willful, curious personalities and charmed them as much as they charmed him.

"I'm quite well, actually. Thank you," Walker said and waved at the hallway. "May I escort you to the kitchen, my lord?" He asked. Fin fixed his imaginary laurel crown and gathered the end of his invisible toga.

"Veni, vidi, vici," Fin sighed as he swept past Walker. "And now I need a snack."

Chapter Sixteen

"What was your favorite moment of the day?" Walker asked Beatrice. She stretched and her mouth split into a big yawn.

"My favorite part...was when Fin said he would ask you if we could have our own hermit crabs because he can do anything! He's never scared and he knows everything." She nodded slowly, clearly in awe of Fin.

"He is rather clever."

"Fin said we'd go to the woods and go hiking and he's going to show me how to catch a frog!" Charlotte exclaimed.

"You already had a turn," Amelia scolded and Charlotte stuck her tongue out at her.

"I don't have to have a turn to talk about Fin."

"But you already talked about Fin when it was your turn."

"So did you," Charlotte countered.

Beatrice smiled at Walker and for a moment, they ignored her sisters and had their own quiet little conversation. Walker only had these quiet moments with Beatrice and cherished them. Charlotte was exuberant and inquisitive and Amelia was direct and open with her feelings and observations. But Walker and Beatrice were developing their own secret language as he grew more adept at communicating with each of his girls.

"Fin's the best, Daddy. We didn't want *anyone* but he loves us and you're happier now and you're here more because of Fin."

"We're lucky to have him." Walker kissed her forehead and pulled her quilt up to her chin. "Sleep well, Princess."

"Night, Daddy."

Walker kissed and tucked Amelia and Charlotte in once their argument had run out of steam. He shut the door quietly and then jumped, startled when he found Fin leaning against the wall.

"What are you doing?" Walker asked in a loud whisper. Fin grinned as he pushed away from the wall and waved for Walker to follow him.

"I got the nursery squared away and thought I'd wait and walk with you on my way out. I figured we could have our own 'favorite moment of the day' chat," he explained. Walker thought that was a good idea, assuming Fin would also want to discuss the moments that weren't his favorite and how Walker could improve.

"'That could be useful," he agreed as he followed. Fin smiled, dazzling Walker.

"I think so too. Tell me, what was your favorite part of the day?" He asked with a gentle nudge, as if it had long been their habit to stroll together at the end of the day.

"Well..." Walker stalled as he considered. There had been a number of high points. A few of them were professional but Walker's cheek still tingled when he remembered how Beatrice said she thought he looked extra handsome and kissed him. And he'd made the girls laugh when he peeked into the nursery again and found them practicing their colors in French with fruit. Walker wasn't brave enough to tell Fin about the tingle in his cheek and thought the fruit would be easier. "I enjoy it when I can make the girls laugh—it might be my favorite sound in the world—and it's always satisfying when I make a dad joke and it lands," he confided. It was still a bit more honest than Walker would have preferred, but he wouldn't have thought to take a peek at the nursery or had the courage to wade in without an invitation if it hadn't been for Fin.

And Fin had made it so easy. He encouraged Walker to join them and offered prompts so he could make those dad jokes and charm the girls. "It's less intimidating now and nice being able to sneak in for a few kisses when I miss them without creating an upheaval or getting overwhelmed," he said quietly. Fin's lips parted and he looked stunned for a moment before he unbuttoned his cardigan.

"Is it just me or is it getting hot?" He did appear a bit flushed as he slid out of the cardigan and draped it over his arm. "Would you like to know what my favorite moment was?"

"I would," Walker replied. He felt a shiver of anticipation but told himself it was just a slow amble down the hall, not the walk home after a first date, despite all the butterflies in his stomach. Fin stopped and swayed closer, his lips only inches from Walker's.

"I thought it was when you surprised us in the nursery but this is my favorite moment. I like when you're real with me and you tell me how I can help you bond with the girls. You've been a really good boy today," he whispered.

"I..." Walker's brain cut off as if Fin had yanked out the plug. The words 'a really good boy' bounced off the walls of his psyche, echoing in the hollow space as heat spilled into Walker's groin. "Thank you," he mouthed. Normally, those words would have earned a sneer or made Walker want to fight but goosebumps spread down his arms and there was the powerful urge to ask Fin to say it again.

"You're welcome," Fin said and smiled as if he knew exactly what Walker had thanked him for. "Would you like me to say it again?" He asked quietly, causing Walker's heart to stop.

"I'm sorry?" His face tingled as he became dizzy. "What?"

"It's alright, Walker." Fin stepped close so he could grip Walker's arm and gave it a reassuring shake. "I might have noticed that you have noticed...something," he said. He raised his shoulder as if it wasn't that big of a deal but Walker wanted to throw himself down the stairs or out the gallery window.

"Dear God. Fin, I'm so sorry. I didn't mean to look and I would never—"

"Shhh!" Fin laughed and patted Walker's chest soothingly but it only made his heart gallop faster. "There is absolutely nothing wrong with looking as long as we're both sure you want to see and I want to show you," he explained, stunning Walker again.

"Did you mean to?" He asked and Fin's teeth dug into his lip. It was adorable and Walker felt a little drunk, he was so enthralled. The situation was so wildly inappropriate but Walker felt a thrill every time Fin tiptoed over the line. The nearness of Fin and the promise of something new and exciting was both wonderful and terrifying for Walker after a lifetime of cold propriety and never asking for what he truly wanted.

"No, but I have been wearing certain things in case you looked," Fin admitted, scaring Walker right back into his shell.

"Fin!" Walker shook his head quickly.

"It's fine! I liked it too," Fin whispered reassuringly but Walker wished there were brakes because they were veering away from wonderful and into terrifying.

"What?" He whispered back. Fin opened his mouth to answer and Walker panicked. "Don't!" His hand clamped over

Fin's mouth. "I changed my mind. I might have accidentally looked and I...might have liked it. But I have far too much respect for you to ever entertain the idea of doing anything untoward. And I would never make improper advances toward an employee," he vowed. Fin blinked at him until Walker slowly lowered his hand.

"I know, Walker." Fin was his usual calm self as he tossed his chin at Walker's suite. "I have a proposal," he explained. Walker hurried and got the door for Fin but slipped around him to make sure they were alone.

"What kind of proposal?" He asked cautiously, feeling a giddy rush as Fin shut the door and fell back against it. They were rarely alone, and they would never close the door. It would be...

"An *untoward* one," Fin teased as he shoved his hands in his pockets. He'd crossed his ankles and was relaxed as he watched Walker unravel.

"Fin, I think you're incredibly attractive and I'd be a fool to say no if you were anyone else. But the girls would burn this house down if you left us."

"Say no to what?" Fin asked and raised a brow. "Sex will never matter more to me than this job. The girls and this family are my first priority. If I'm right, this could help you be a happier person and that will always make you a better parent. But this has absolutely nothing to do with our professional relationship."

"What is it, then?"

"This is about *you* and what you're into."

"Do you know what I'm into?" It was an honest question. Walker wasn't entirely sure himself and Fin had clearly figured him out.

"I have a few guesses." Fin slid his hand from his pocket and hooked his fingers under the waist of his corduroys. He produced a strip of plum-colored lace and Walker licked his lips nervously.

"I don't understand why I like it," he breathed and stepped behind the sofa, blocking the front of his trousers. "I barely notice pictures of women in lingerie—they're everywhere these days—but I sort of fall apart when I see just a peek of what you're wearing," he admitted. Fin hissed as he slipped the button at his waist free.

"There you go being real again and telling me what you want. You have no idea how *happy* that makes me."

"Really?" Walker asked as he squeezed his eyes shut. A question formed on his tongue and became heavy so Walker bit down on his lips to keep it from falling out.

"Really happy," Fin purred. The sound tickled the hairs on Walker's neck and made him shiver despite the sweat beading on his brow.

"That was good?" He asked. *I was good?* He couldn't breathe. Walker was afraid the question would turn into a wish and Fin would hear it.

"That was very good. You've been a really good boy, Walker," Fin said and Walker grabbed the back of the sofa.

"Dear Lord. Fin, I—" Walker blocked his face as it became hot. "How did you know? I didn't even know!"

"That you might be a sub?" Fin asked tenderly but Walker jumped as if a dish had shattered.

"Am I?"

"Seems likely."

"And are you a...?" Walker sounded like he'd recently escaped from a monastery and had never seen a pornographic film.

"I'm into all kinds of things but I'm a switch and lean a little more Dom," Fin replied with a cheeky grin.

"Not just a pushy nanny, then?" Walker joked weakly.

"Does that mean you're into whips and gags?" He tugged at his tie as his anxiety swelled.

"No. Impact play and humiliation aren't my kinks. Do you think you'd be into something like that?" Fin asked carefully. Walker shook his head quickly.

"I don't think so and Pierce would probably quit if I turned up with a bunch of welts on my back. What are your kinks?" His voice broke and Walker coughed to hide it. Fin's smile was knowing as he unzipped his fly.

"I obviously enjoy pretty underthings." He eased his white t-shirt up, giving Walker a glimpse at the panel of plum silk between the halves of the zipper. "And showing off."

"I see," Walker said and Fin hummed.

"And I enjoy how much you appreciate my pretty under-things. What if I let you have a peek whenever you share some-thing real or do something brave?" He offered. Walker's brows pinched together as he struggled to understand. *Why* would Fin waste his time with a rude, repressed older widower when there were legions of younger, more exciting men waiting for him outside of The Killian House?

"And what do you get in return?"

"Want to let me pat you on the head and whisper in your ear so we can find out?" Fin asked, then groaned when Walker swore under his breath and shielded his face again. "I don't know what you'd call it but cranky, uptight guys who melt when you pet them are definitely my kink."

"A surprisingly accurate description," Walker mumbled. "And what exactly are you proposing?" The situation already seemed like it was too good to be true and Walker was searching for a catch or a pitfall.

"I think it's really hot when you take chances with the girls and trust me. Do more of that and I'll show you what I'm wear-ing. I might even let you touch, if you think you'd be into that."

Fin traced the lace between the zippers, dragging Walker's attention lower and his own fingertips itched to touch. Then, he imagined his tongue and lips replacing his fingertips and Walker worried he wouldn't be able to stop once he started.

"I want to do all of that but this is dangerous, Fin. You heard the girls, they love you and this is the easiest it's been here in years. What if this gets out of control?"

"My definition of out of control is you doing something you don't want to do and I would never let that happen," Fin said simply but Walker's confused frown deepened.

"I wouldn't mean to but what if I went too far and forced myself on you?" He asked and Fin's lips pulled tight.

"That doesn't seem like the sort of thing you'd do."

"No. But you don't know that for certain," Walker argued and asked himself why he was trying to talk Fin out of this when he'd clearly thought it through. Fin always had a well-thought-out plan and Walker was touched, given Fin's general ambivalence toward the extremely wealthy.

"I promise, you wouldn't be forcing yourself on me."

"Fin!" Walker objected but dear God, he was tempted to see what happened if he was brave enough to call Fin's bluff.

"After what you said in the hall?" Fin asked and pointed over his shoulder. "That part about sneaking in for kisses and not getting overwhelmed was enough to get me out of my pants."

"I see." Walker didn't but he was taking detailed notes. "And how would this work? I've never done anything like this and I can't risk losing you."

"What happens between us behind closed doors stays between us and behind closed doors. I won't risk losing the girls or damaging my brother's reputation," Fin stated, his hand cutting through the air as he shook his head. Walker believed him and found himself leaning forward as Fin rubbed his chin.

"What if you set the pace? I'll ask if you're ready each step of the way and if you're not, we'll stay where we are or take a step back."

"And that would work for you?" Walker asked suspiciously but Fin groaned.

"The more vocal you are, the hotter it gets, Walker," he said as he slowly zipped up his corduroys. Goosebumps spread down Walker's chest but he was *so hot*.

"Could you, please...?" Walker shut his eyes and yanked at his tie as the air became stifling. "Please say that again," he said quickly and had to lick his lips when they became dry.

"Your name?" Fin said and Walker nodded. "Did you like it?"

"Yes," Walker breathed.

"Do you want me to call you that when we're alone?"

Walker nodded again and risked a glance at Fin. He appeared to be winded too, his chest heaving as he leaned against the door for support.

"Please."

"I can do that," Fin said with a sly smile, the anticipation winding Walker's nerves tighter and tighter. "You've been a very good boy today, Walker."

The words trickled down Walker's spine like warm honey and there was a heavy throb in his groin.

"Thank you, Fin," he whispered.

"You're welcome. I'll see you in the morning," Fin said softly but didn't wait for a response. He slipped out of the room, leaving Walker aroused and flustered.

"See you in the morning," Walker mumbled after several moments of staring at the door.

The morning. He remembered that he'd see Fin in the morning, at breakfast, and Walker already had his doubts. How the hell was he supposed to eat and behave like a competent adult after that? Walker was going to make a fool out of himself and the girls and Pierce would know that something inappropriate was going on. "Skip breakfast. I'll tell Pierce to tell Fin and the girls that I had an early call I couldn't reschedule."

It was the coward's way out but Walker needed to get his bearings, and he probably needed to talk to Agnes before he made a mess of this.

"I'm in serious trouble if I'm turning to Agnes for help."

Chapter Seventeen

"They look like insects," Walker murmured as he hovered over the tank on the craft table.

"Maybe a little but they're not. The girls are going to be so stoked when they return from dance class," Fin said. He checked his watch and made an anxious sound. "I can't do cats and small animals because I'm allergic and kids are never excited about fish. But who doesn't love hermit crabs?"

"Are you sure they aren't insects?"

"Phylum: arthropoda, subphylum: crustacea, class: malacostraca, order: decapoda. I promise, they're not insects. That one with the clownfish shell is mine and I'm naming him Fini. Because he's my mini," Fin informed Walker. "The one with the Batman shell is yours."

"Mine?" Walker chuckled and shook his head but Fin stopped him.

"He's the largest, but he's also the strong, silent type. He's our hero," he explained. Walker's brow furrowed as he stared at the crabs in the tank. It was clear that Walker still didn't understand how much the girls looked up to him and how brave he'd been since Fin had arrived. "You're our hero," Fin insisted and gave Walker's arm an affectionate punch.

"That's ridiculous. I can barely handle three little girls."

"I doubt that Batman could handle your girls without help."

"You and Agnes can," Walker argued but Fin waved dismissively.

"You're already light years ahead of where we started a few months ago. And it's easier for Agnes because it's just every other weekend. Little girls always behave when they're away on sleepovers, or they can't go to sleepovers anymore. I have degrees in this and I'm only on the clock for twelve hours a day, thank goodness. Don't forget that Bruce had Alfred and a Bat Cave."

"True..." Walker became distant and drifted away from the craft table. "I'm pleased with this if you are. I need to get back downstairs."

"Do you?" Fin asked as he trailed Walker across the nursery. Walker had skipped breakfast and Fin had to track him down in his study to invite him to see the new hermit crabs. Then, Walker had tried to get out of that too but Fin was adamant that he approve of the new additions to The Killian House before the girls returned from their ballet lessons. Fin worried that he had overwhelmed Walker the night before, and didn't like that he was distancing himself from the nursery as a result. That wasn't going to work because the last thing Fin wanted was to come between Walker and the girls.

"I should. I have a few calls scheduled for later. Nothing I care about but I have responsibilities," Walker said and began to bow but Fin stopped him.

"It's going to be a beautiful day. I was thinking we'd go to the park or have a picnic in the garden instead of a party since it's so lovely out. The girls go down for naps easier, and they're generally more cooperative if I let them run amuck for an hour or so in the sun."

"That sounds like a good plan," Walker murmured.

"It usually is. You should join us. The girls would be over the moon." And Fin could sniff Walker and learn what had sent him retreating into his old habits.

"Probably not. I've never been much fun at picnics and I don't enjoy the park."

"Come on! It's the perfect day!" Fin urged. Walker opened his mouth to decline again but the girls came crashing into the nursery in their leotards and tutus. "There're my prima ballerinas! Check out what your dad let me order! They were just delivered!" The girls oohed and aahed as they climbed onto their stools for a closer look.

"Oh! I want Batman!" Amelia cried and Charlotte immediately reached for the crab with the Batman shell.

"Not so fast! I've already decided who gets which crab so there's no fighting and that one's your father's," Fin informed them. The girls were delighted that Walker would have his own pet in the nursery and nodded along as Fin assigned the remaining hermit crabs. "Now, thank your father then change your clothes. We're going outside."

"Outside!" The girls cheered and clambered off their stools so they could rush Walker and hug his legs.

"You're very welcome. Go change and be good for Fin," he told them after he'd picked up each girl and received a kiss on his cheek. Nurse Lisa was at the door and waiting for them and would have their play dresses ready. Fin laughed as he watched them go in a precious tornado of tutus and tights then raised his brows at Walker.

"Are you sure you want to miss out on a trip to the park or a picnic with those little angels?" He asked. Fin was fairly sure Walker would say yes, judging by the way his eyes were glowing as he watched them leave. Walker was happiest when he was in the palm of the girls' hands so Fin was all too happy to facilitate that. "What could be better than a stroll in the park or a quilt in a shady garden?" Fin edged closer to whisper something encouraging but Walker backed away.

"That sounds lovely but..." Walker hesitated, spinning when his heel bumped against a beanbag chair.

"Is something wrong?" Fin asked but Walker shook his head.

"That would all be lovely but I have to go." Walker ducked and made a beeline for the door.

"Nope. That won't work at all." Fin wasn't going to let Walker miss out on two opportunities to bond with his daughters in one day. "We need to have another talk," he said and went to buy them a little time.

Chapter Eighteen

I t truly was a lovely day and Walker's thoughts wandered to Fin and the girls as he turned his chair toward the garden. He wondered if they'd choose to spend the afternoon in the park or if they'd stay home and have a picnic. Walker could peek at them from the window if they stayed. A voice whispered that it was his own fault that he was missing out but Walker didn't trust himself not to get flustered and blush like a schoolboy every time Fin smiled at him.

"I need to call Agnes." He'd said it a dozen times but Walker chickened out every time he reached for his phone.

She was the only person he could talk to but Walker suspected that she'd only add to his confusion. Agnes would always choose mayhem.

There was a brisk tap at the door and Walker knew it was Fin before he turned his chair. "We've decided: we're having a picnic. The girls are changing then supervising while the cook packs us a basket," he said, beckoning Walker to follow him with a jerk of his chin.

"Have fun. Don't forget the sunscreen," he murmured while

he pretended he had something important to find in the planner in front of him.

"Come on! The girls are so excited!" Fin urged in a loud whisper but Walker shook his head.

"You'll have more fun without me and I have work to do."

"You do not! You just said you didn't care about any of that," Fin countered. He peeked down the hall before he stepped into Walker's office and shut the door and fell back against it.

"What are you doing?" Walker asked warily and his nerves flared as Fin bit his lip coyly and shrugged a shoulder.

"Want to talk about why you're avoiding me and the girls?" He raised his brows at Walker.

"I'm not I had a call this morning—"

"We both know that isn't true. This is about last night. Do you want to forget it ever happened? We can do that if this doesn't feel right," Fin offered but Walker shook his head.

"No! I don't want to forget about it. *I can't.* That's the problem. I'm afraid I'm going to do something that will give us away, or we'll get caught," he said and Fin hummed sympathetically.

"We didn't talk enough about boundaries last night, did we? But I know we need to take a step back and lay down some rules so you feel safer because you told me. I'm proud of you, Walker," he said softly. The words were both a balm for Walker's nerves and an intoxicant.

"Are you?" He asked nervously as his eyes flicked to the door. Fin noticed and shushed soothingly.

"I told the girls we're playing soccer before our picnic so they're changing. Then, Lisa's delivering the girls to the kitchen so the cook can teach them how to make finger sandwiches while I check in with you about our field trip to the Children's Museum next week. I'm taking the girls to the Children's Museum next week. Got it?" Fin confirmed briskly and Walker nodded.

"I remember the email you sent me with your itinerary."

"Good. That's how this works. We communicate and no fooling around unless the girls are away, sleeping, or under another adult's supervision. And we can engage in a little light flirting but no fooling around during the day because that's the girls' time," Fin said.

"That makes sense," Walker said and gestured for Fin to continue.

"Remember what I said last night: it stays between us and behind closed doors. We keep the flirting to a minimum when I'm on the clock but I'll be keeping track throughout the day and I'll share my favorite moments with you after bedtime," he said then cleared his throat. "They're from Savage Fenty," he drawled as he unbuttoned his cardigan.

"Excuse me?" Walker asked weakly. He tugged at his collar as he became warm. Fin laughed as he pushed away from the door. It was a low, silky sound that caused Walker to shiver despite the sweat gathering under his collar and making it tighter.

"My underwear. Half of the money you give me goes straight to Robyn Fenty and you deserve a peek for telling me you needed more boundaries," Fin explained with a cocky wink. He made his way around Walker's desk and sat on the edge. Walker pulled his eyes from Fin's waist to his face and swallowed loudly. "We just agreed that there would be no fooling around but I think we can make an exception since we're still negotiating. Communication is important when you're setting boundaries and I know how uncomfortable uncertainty makes you. Do you want to look?"

"I do," Walker rasped and Fin moaned in approval.

"Good boy, Walker," he whispered, causing Walker to shudder with delight. "That's also how you'll know this is personal and not professional. I'll call you Walker when we're alone or after bedtime and you'll be Cameron when I'm on the clock.

"I like that. And I like hearing you say my name," Walker said, earning another sultry moan from Fin.

"This one's called a Cheeky and it has black lace. In case you were wondering," he added casually.

"I might have been." Walker's voice broke as he began to sweat in earnest. "Do you prefer women's underthings?" He asked.

"I do and it seems like you might too." Fin flicked the halves of his cardigan open and Walker jumped. *Dear God, he hasn't even taken it off.* Walker gave up all hope of maintaining his dignity.

"Fin, you know I would never expect anything from you—" He started but Fin tapped one of his fingers against his lips.

"Shhh..." He winked and Walker was helpless. "I know you'd never. And I have no expectations of you, beyond whatever you want to share. If this gets to be too much for either of us at any point, we're both free to tap out and resume our friendly professional relationship. This isn't sexy or satisfying for me if you don't trust me and want this as much as I do."

"I do." This time, Walker was sure of it. He had clearer rules and Fin had taken all the guesswork out and made their arrangement foolproof. *Of course, he did. That was Fin.* "I trust you, Fin."

"Excellent. Would you like to take a look? And maybe touch?" Fin added in a whisper. Walker licked his lips and prayed they'd work.

"I might. Maybe," he agreed. He would have sold his soul, actually.

"Before I show you, we have one more rule," Fin warned sheepishly and Walker's head canted.

"Did you save the best for last?" He slid Fin a wary glance

but relaxed when his lips curved. Well. Mostly relaxed. Walker really *liked* Fin's lips and he got a little restless when they curved like that.

"You are cordially invited to an afternoon of culinary delights and outdoor frivolity," Fin purred as he raised the front of his t-shirt, exposing nothing save the waist of his corduroys but Walker's eyes became huge. Fin's thumb teased the button on his fly and a startled laugh burst from Walker.

"Right. The picnic. I think I can handle that now. I'd love to go," he said, falling back in his seat when Fin pushed against his chest.

"Thank you. I don't want anything that happens between us to keep you from spending time with the girls. I'm always going to be at my happiest when you and the girls are at your happiest so put them first and leave whatever's going on between us until bedtime, alright?"

"I can do that," Walker said with a relieved laugh. "I generally don't like when I'm told I have to follow someone else's rules but this feels easier for some reason."

"Rules help us manage our expectations and understand what's expected of us. You're less likely to mess up when the directions are laid out in front of you," Fin explained. He gave the zipper a slow tug and widened his eyes at Walker expectantly. "More?"

"Please," Walker croaked as he nodded.

"Good boy," Fin said and Walker was melting again.

"Please show me. I have to see," he begged then whimpered when Fin used his knee to part Walker's thighs and stepped between them.

"*Good boy,*" he repeated pointedly before he pushed the button at his waist free. He slowly pulled the halves apart, revealing the wide-petaled black lace stretched across his pelvis. Walker could see a peek of dark curls beneath the lace and his head fell to the side as his mouth watered. "Would you like to touch me?" Fin offered, dragging his fingers over the lace. Walker's eyes followed but he shook his head.

"I don't think that's a good idea," he confessed, in self-defense. Walker's hands were shaking. He wasn't sure if he could trust himself. Fin shrugged, stunning Walker again with another soft, sly smile.

"I've already accomplished what I came here to do," he confided as he turned. "The back's strappy." Fin swung his leg over Walker's right thigh and sat. He shimmied as he pushed his pants a little lower, then held up the back of his cardigan so Walker could see. His t-shirt was in the way. Walker's hand reached and pushed it up before he could stop himself. Fin arched as he sucked in a breath but held still while Walker's gaze slid lower. The lace dipped into a deep V, drawing Walker's eyes down to the cleft of Fin's ass.

"That looks…" He was dizzy as Fin looked at him over his shoulder, so tempted to touch the lace and trace the soft curves of Fin's asscheeks. *Delicious. I will lose my mind if I don't taste him soon.* That was why Walker didn't trust himself to stop. "That looks really good on you."

"I ordered these cute crotchless ones in a black floral print but I might have to save those for home. I think we're going to end up with a commando situation," Fin mused and went to stand but Walker locked his hand around his hip. Fin gave him a questioning look but Walker didn't know what to say. All he knew was he didn't want Fin to go. He extended his thumb and brushed the very tip against the lace. Walker closed his eyes as warmth shot down his arm, and he shuddered as goosebumps washed down his back.

"You have no idea how amazing it is to feel this again," he whispered. He didn't think he'd ever experience that kind of charge or yearning after he lost Connor.

"What?" Fin asked. His hand wrapped around Walker's other thigh and squeezed gently. Walker was smiling, relaxed as he shook his head.

"You'd better make sure the kitchen's still standing," he said. He helped Fin up and shooed him. "I'm going to run upstairs and change into something lighter."

"Something lighter?" Fin asked suggestively. He was smirking, taunting Walker as he fixed his fly and backed toward the door. Walker held up his hands, deciding that two could play at this game.

"I might take a quick shower and change into a lighter wool blend. It would be pretty brutal if I had to hide this all afternoon. Could make a picnic hell, I'd imagine," he said as he stood. He didn't bother to button his coat or hide the bulge in his trousers as he came around his desk. Fin was staring and missed a button on his cardigan but Walker would let one of the girls tell him. "If you'll excuse me." Walker reached around Fin for the door, tapping his temple in salute as he left.

"That wasn't cool," he heard Fin grumble.

"You started it," Walker replied over his shoulder. He'd planned to keep a safe distance until he'd talked to Agnes and was sure he wouldn't screw it up but Fin had taken the fear out of it and made everything easy, as usual. And while Walker's common sense warned that the situation was bound to end in disaster, he knew Fin would make the process fun and beautiful if he took the chance.

Chapter Nineteen

"See? This wasn't so bad. You did great." Fin stretched out on his side and propped himself up on an elbow. Walker sat up when Charlotte stomped her feet and yelled at Amelia for scaring the neighbor's cat out of the yard. "Relax. They're learning conflict resolution, and they'll lose interest and forget in two minutes. I'll jump in and break them up if it escalates and the hair starts flying," Fin teased. Walker humphed, but he smiled as he looked around then reclined on the quilt with Fin. They were hidden from the house by the large oak tree and the garden's rose bushes. The rest of the world was obscured by the tall privacy fence surrounding the garden.

Fin had brought the soccer ball and got Walker to join them for some passing and everyone had taken turns with the bubble wand. They'd dined on the girls' finger sandwiches, string cheese, fresh cut fruits and vegetables but Fin had plans for the plate of cupcakes on the quilt between them. Plans that were put on hold when Walker pushed out a hard breath.

"You were right, it's less frightening when I understand

what the rules are and what's expected of me. It still feels like a dream, though," he admitted in a low, soft tone that created a warm tickle in the front of Fin's pants.

"Is it a dream you aren't enjoying?" Fin asked carefully but had his answer when Walker's eyes snapped to his. They were large and full of doubt but Fin saw a spark of curiosity and he wanted to fan it into a flame.

"I am but what if I can't..."

"Can't what, Cameron?" Fin whispered. He licked his lips as he considered the best way to soothe the last of Walker's fears. "There's no expectation on my end. You're the one who decides how far this goes. If looking and touching is enough to help you open up and express your needs, then that's enough for me. That does a hell of a lot more for me than just getting off, if that's all I'm after."

"I guess that makes sense. But I worry that I'll *want* to but I won't be *able* to. Not because I lack the desire or the physical ability. Although, it's been years and I could be wrong, but because I'd lose my nerve or my...heart wouldn't let me do it," Walker explained carefully, once again taking Fin's breath away with his vulnerability.

"Remember what I said about keeping track and sharing after bedtime?" Fin said and Walker nodded. "We're going to circle back to this moment later and I'm going to show you how proud I am of you." He saw Walker's pupils dilate and heard his sharp intake of breath. "You don't have to do a damn thing until you're ready. Maybe this helps you see how far you've come and shows you where you need a little more healing. If so, that's amazing and enough."

"This whole thing is absurd, that's what it is," Walker said with a bewildered laugh. "It's wonderful but absurd and I'm tempted to ask you to pinch me but I'm afraid of what that could lead to."

"Why is it absurd?" Fin asked. Walker sighed as he scanned the garden and watched the girls for a moment.

"I didn't ask for all of this. I prayed for a miracle to save the girls from me, but I didn't think I deserved any magic for myself or a second chance."

"I'm going to have to come up with something extra special for later," Fin replied shakily. "You're killing me," he said but it was worth it when Walker blushed and grumbled at Fin.

Amelia and Beatrice shrieked as they went after Charlotte, startling Walker. Fin took advantage of the distraction and grinned wickedly as he selected a vanilla cupcake. He was so uptight and proper but Fin loved the way Walker blushed and squirmed whenever their hands brushed and their eyes touched. And he'd taken a chance and owned up to his weakness for Fin's underthings and was honest about his grief and how long it had been. It was refreshing to see such a powerful man reveal his tenderest spots and unhealed wounds.

"I think you deserve one of these."

"A cupcake?" Walker's eyes lifted from the cupcake and were full of heat and hunger when they met Fin's. "Thank you, but I probably shouldn't." His voice had gone soft and gravelly, and they both knew Walker wasn't talking about the sweet resting on Fin's palm.

"Do you know why cupcakes are my favorite?" Fin asked. He kept it low, and just for Walker. Like the cupcake. Walker shook his head, but he couldn't pull his eyes away from Fin's. Fin swiped the pad of his pinkie through the pale butter-colored frosting and purred as he sucked it clean. "It's small and it's sweet and it's just for you. Instead of a whole slice on a plate, it's just a few bites and you can save it for whenever you're ready. And you don't have to share it with anyone."

"That is...very interesting." Walker's voice was nearly gone and there was a slight tremor as he took it from Fin. "It's been a long time since I've...had a cupcake but I think I might try one." He held it up and turned the pastry, as if he was admiring something much more complex and tempting. He found the streak in the frosting from Fin's finger and dragged his tongue through it. Walker's eyelids fell and he moaned softly as he savored it. His gaze was heavier when it returned to Fin's.

"I really think you should," Fin panted as he leaned closer. He would swear he felt Walker's tongue drag over his lips. He wanted to suck on it and cover himself in frosting. Fin imagined ordering Walker to lick him clean and stifled a groan.

"I had it first!" Amelia cried as Charlotte dashed past the picnic blanket with the soccer ball. Fin and Walker parted as Amelia and Beatrice ran past them in pursuit.

"I should probably settle that before it descends into violence," Fin said but Walker shook his head as he peeled the paper away from his cupcake.

"As you said, they're learning conflict resolution and they'll lose interest and move on in a few minutes. Take a break, Fin, they can't do too much damage out here." He took a bite and nodded as he chewed and licked his lips. "I forgot how good these can be," he murmured in a deep rumble that tickled the parts in Fin's pants.

"Careful, Cameron," Fin said under his breath as he reclined again and crossed his ankles. "You might just earn yourself another cupcake." He shut his eyes as if he was enjoying the sun on his face and wondered whose was warmer as Walker choked on a bite of cake.

Chapter Twenty

"Let me guess, your favorite moment of the day was our picnic." Walker pulled the covers up to Amelia's chin and tapped the end of her nose. It had been her sisters' favorite moment as well. She nodded as she tucked her hands under her cheek.

"I liked when you played soccer in your suit. We didn't know you knew how to play but you're really good at it." There were giggles from the other beds as Walker lowered to kiss Amelia's hair.

"I played a lot of soccer when I was in school. We'll play some more and next time I'll wear the right shoes," he said, unleashing another wave of giggles. Walker was lucky he hadn't fallen on his ass, sliding around on the grass in his Italian oxfords.

"Fin is OK but you're much better at soccer than he is," Charlotte boasted and Walker shushed her and held out a hand when she began to untuck herself so she could get up.

"That's enough for tonight," he told the girls as he rose. "We had a lovely day but it's time for my little bed bugs to get some sleep. I love you very much and I'll see you in the morning." He waited until Charlotte was settled back under her covers and her head was firmly on the pillow to turn down the light and ease the door shut.

"She was being kind. I'm terrible at soccer but it's great for developing coordination and teaches kids about teamwork and communication." Fin was waiting by the door and pushed away from the wall. "I need to take off now because I'm meeting Riley at the movies but I have something very special for you," he said as he walked backward and Walker followed.

"I hope you have a good time," Walker murmured but he was disappointed. He'd spent the afternoon nervous and curious about what Fin had planned for after bedtime.

"I can't remember what we're seeing but I won't be paying attention," Fin said airily and stopped when they reached the stairs.

"You won't?"

"No. I'll be thinking about this." He looked around to make sure the foyer below was clear before reaching into his cardigan. He pulled out a Manila envelope and handed it to Walker.

"What's this?" Walker turned it in his hands and found the metal clasp but Fin stopped him.

"Wait until you're alone," he said out of the side of his mouth and Walker's entire body locked. Except for his eyes. They widened as he stared at the envelope in his hands. Fin cleared his throat and stepped closer. "You already got to see and touch but I don't think you're ready to do much more than that, so I thought I'd let you keep them."

"Keep them?" Walker mouthed. His eyes grew larger and burned as they grew dry. Fin hummed silkily.

"If you want to. You don't even have to look if you're not ready and you like where we're at. Or, you can take all the time you want with them. You don't have to tell me or you can tell me all about it." Fin gave Walker a playful wink before he skipped down the steps. "Have a good night." Fin waved when he reached the bottom and turned toward the kitchen.

"Goodnight," Walker said but no one heard him. He wasn't even sure if his lips had moved.

It was a perfectly ordinary medium-sized Manila envelope but it grew and became heavier when Walker realized he was holding something very, very big. This was possibly the biggest thing he'd ever held, after his children, as far as life-changing moments went. Walker's life pivoted around him as he weighed his options and the consequences. Not looking wasn't one of the options but chickening out and saving it for later was an immediate favorite. Until Walker imagined Fin's underwear in *his* underwear drawer, pulsing like a heart under the floorboards. He shook his head. He wouldn't be able to sleep. He'd be a nervous wreck until he looked inside. Then, Walker remembered where he was and that he was holding a pair of Fin's underwear and ran.

He crashed into his suite, dashing past the sitting area and into his bathroom. Walker locked the door behind him and hurried to the closet to close it. He fell against the door and his heart slammed and his hands were shaking as he flipped the clasp with sweaty fingers. Walker ripped it open then slapped it closed at the first glimpse of black lace. He glanced at the mirror over the sink to be sure it was still *him* holding the nanny's panties.

This was without a doubt the most scandalous thing that had ever happened to Walker. He was shocked to his core, but he was also thrilled and enthralled as he carefully parted the halves of the envelope, slowly revealing a satin and lace miracle.

Instead of feeling like he was cheating or taking something he shouldn't, Walker's fingers trembled with awe as he freed the thong from the paper and let the envelope fall to the bathroom floor. This wasn't another body—another man—but a beautiful souvenir from a fantasy. This was an object Walker could explore and cherish without anyone to witness his wonder.

He closed his eyes and raised the thong so he could rub his cheek against the wide front panel. He enjoyed the soft abrading of the lace against his skin. The fabric grew warmer next to his cheek and Walker imagined taking the thong off of Fin himself. He rubbed his face against the lace as he knelt in front of Fin and gasped at the burst of heat and yearning in his core. It rolled through him like a hot tide and Walker cried as he mashed his nose into the fabric and inhaled deeply, seeking every whiff of Fin's scent. There was mostly fabric softener and Fin's soap but there was also a faint hint of sweat.

Walker was euphoric as he yanked his belt off, attacking the fly of his trousers with one hand. He shoved his pants down, groaning into the thong as he gripped his shaft. Walker was so hard, he ached to taste Fin. He sucked on the strip of satin that had parted Fin's asscheeks and Walker sobbed. Every nerve in his body wound tight, tight, tight before combusting. He was engulfed in heat as cum rushed from his cock and spilled over his fist.

A delighted, breathless laugh burst from him as he surveyed the damage. He was standing on the ripped, rumpled envelope and his trousers and briefs were down around his knees. Walker glanced at the mirror and smirked at the dazed man holding a black thong and his semi-flaccid cock. A string of cum hung from the end of his fingers and Walker's hair, coat, shirt, and tie were a disaster.

"Well done, I suppose," he muttered at the mirror and shuffled to the sink. Walker carefully laid the thong on the counter and turned on the water. He watched his face as he washed his hands and waited for it to change. Walker listened for any rumblings from his conscience but there was no guilt or regret. He didn't feel dirty or confused but...*better* and happy. "Why don't I feel guilty?"

That did it. The smile slid off his face.

He hadn't thought of Connor once. It was a miracle that Walker hadn't worried about how wrong it was that Fin was his employee or what he could be taking from the girls, but he should have thought about Connor, at least.

"What's happening to me?"

He fixed his trousers and folded the thong before putting it in his pocket. Walker gave it a reverent pat and went to call his sister. He'd put it off because he had no idea what he was going to say or if her advice would even be helpful. Agnes would always be an agent of chaos, but she was all Walker had unless he wanted to confide in Pierce.

"I don't pay him enough for that and he'd probably quit," Walker said as he swiped at his phone and found Agnes's number. He pinched the bridge of his nose and prayed for patience.

"Are the girls alright?" She asked immediately and he smiled.

"They're sleeping."

"Thank goodness. Why are you calling me at 9:30 on a Friday night? It's your weekend," she teased. Walker heard a snicker in the background.

"You've got company."

"I do, but they can entertain themselves if this is important." She was being sincere but Walker wondered what *they* meant. It was so ambiguous. Walker decided he didn't need to know.

"I need your help, Aggie. I think I might be in trouble."

"Give me a moment. I'll go into the other room." The line went quiet and Walker lowered onto the sofa before popping up to go pace by the window. "What happened? Are you alright?"

"I'm fine." He scrubbed a hand through his hair and searched for a good place to start. Nothing came to him. That was why he hadn't called Agnes yet. "I'm fine but something's happened with Fin."

"Oh, God. Has this turned into an extortion situation? Because I know someone," she whispered.

"Jesus, no! Aggie!" Walker decided he was going to find a few friends once he got a handle on things with Fin and the girls. "This is why I was afraid to call you. Fin doesn't care about money."

"You said you were in trouble and you called me so I just assumed it was something illegal."

"It's not something illegal but it is wrong. Or, it should be wrong and I'm worried about why it isn't."

"Do you have to be vague and speak in riddles, though?" She asked, sounding bored. Walker could picture her checking her manicure or flipping through a catalog.

"I might be sabotaging the thing holding my life together but I can't seem to stop myself."

"Now, this sounds interesting. Please tell me you went for it with that adorable nanny. The girls can't stop talking about him and he sounds yummy."

"That was disgusting and inappropriate."

"So you didn't go for it with the nanny?"

"No. I kind of did but it sounds disgusting and inappropriate when you say it like that," he explained as he ground his palm into his eye socket. Agnes squealed and there were muffled cheers as she danced or jumped up and down. "I'm finally regretting something," he noted. He'd give her to the count of ten then hang up. Walker got to seven.

"This is *excellent*. I couldn't be happier."

"And there's a red flag."

"Stop it. Tell me what happened."

"I've wanted to but I'm afraid you're going to tell me to dive in and go all the way," he worried and she pouted sympathetically.

"Maybe that's exactly why you called me. You might be looking for a nudge, darling."

"I don't need a nudge. Fin already gave me one but I need a flashlight or a map so I don't get lost."

"He didn't give you one of those?" She sounded concerned. "Is this more than a nudge? He isn't pushing you, is he?"

"No. That isn't the sort of thing Fin would do. He noticed that there was...a mutual interest and made it known that he'd be open to exploring that since we already spend so much time together in The Killian House."

"You're a fool to say no if he's half as hot as he sounds," Agnes replied a little too quickly.

"Why are you an animal? And we're not even addressing why I don't feel half as awful about this as I should."

"According to whom? Who are you hurting? The only person I'd worry about is Fin but I know you'd never force yourself on anyone, especially an employee."

"What about the girls?"

"Your need is greater than theirs at the moment, I'm afraid, and I doubt you or Fin would allow any harm to come to them."

She was right, of course. Fin had created boundaries to protect the girls and guard their professional relationship. Walker was dancing around his real concern.

"What about Connor? It's only been three years."

"Don't say *only* like you haven't been through hell or built yourself a new heart from scratch. You've worked so hard to be strong for the girls and Connor. You deserve to be happy again. Have you asked the girls how they feel about you dating again?

I have a feeling you'd be surprised at how much they want that for you," she suggested. Walker laughed softly and gave his head a shake.

"I'm definitely not dating our nanny and Fin isn't interested in dating me. This isn't that kind of arrangement. It's barely even a physical or sexual arrangement at the moment."

"What do you mean?"

"There are boundaries. I get to set the pace and he rewards me for expressing my feelings," Walker said then braced himself. There was more giddy squealing.

"Oh, Walker! This is *exactly* what you need and I couldn't be happier for you."

"How do I set the pace when I don't even know what that means or what I'm supposed to do? I haven't decided if I'm ready to have sex with other men again and I'm already confused because I'm getting excited about things I didn't even know I liked."

"'That's wonderful!" She laughed. "Start fresh and do things you've never tried and you won't feel like you're replacing all the memories you made with Connor."

"Hold on. You might have said something rational," he said and she snorted.

"It has been known to happen."

"It wouldn't hurt to try a few new things and make a fresh start. And I like the part about not replacing all of Connor's memories," he said.

"As long as you're making room for new ones. You were right: I want you to dive in and go all the way. I have high hopes for you and Fin and you're off to a promising start."

"And now you're back to being ridiculous. Goodnight, brat," he grumbled but he was smiling as he stood and headed back to the bathroom to start the shower.

"Goodnight and love you."

"Love you too," he said, then ended the call. It was a mostly ridiculous conversation because that's what happened whenever he talked to Agnes but Walker felt better and she had actually helped. "No one's getting hurt and it's good to start fresh and try new things," he told himself, then went to hide Fin's thong from Pierce.

Chapter Twenty-One

"Time for a story, ladies!" Fin announced. He was seated under the nursery window and his hand was stuffed inside a dinosaur puppet hidden behind his back. The girls dropped their crayons and foam swords and hurried to join him. "Once upon a time, on a continent known as Pangaea—"

"Fin!" Amelia whispered loudly and he shushed her.

"Dinosaurs roamed across a giant supercontinent—"

"Fin!"

"I didn't even explain what a supercontinent is!" He complained as he threw up his arms in exasperation. Charlotte gasped and snatched the dinosaur off Fin's hand and hugged it.

"Doug!" She exclaimed as she squeezed him.

"We need your help!" Amelia whispered urgently and Fin frowned.

"Of course. What's going on?"

"We want to have a big party for Daddy's birthday, but we don't have any money, and we're not supposed to use the phone," Beatrice explained. Amelia nodded and slapped Charlotte's arm to get her attention. She nodded too.

"We want a big cake and lots of people in fancy clothes," Charlotte said with an enthusiastic squeal.

"I see," Fin said as he rubbed his chin. "I don't have the budget for something like that either but I could talk to Pierce and he could make that happen..."

"A really big cake!" Charlotte insisted. Fin clapped excitedly.

"Definitely. And I assume you want this to be a surprise and you want all the credit?" He asked and the girls nodded in unison. "I love it," he said and they pushed their little fists into the air as they cheered. "Now that that's settled." He plucked Doug from Charlotte's grasp and shoved his hand back up the dinosaur's neck. "The dinosaurs roamed across the supercontinent..." Fin made loud sounds as Doug hopped and crashed from Charlotte's shoulder to Beatrice's head and then to Amelia's knee. He screeched and twisted as Doug dove at a plastic Brontosaurus on a stack of books.

"Why are your fingernails pink, Fin?" Charlotte asked and Fin froze.

"I...was running a little late this morning and forgot to take the paint off," he stated as he anxiously glanced at the hand planted on the floor. Fin had painted them while listening to a podcast before bed. His face was on fire as he wondered how he was going to explain this to Pierce.

"But they're pink!" She laughed.

"So? I love pink. Why can't I wear pink?" He asked and all three of the girls looked puzzled. "You wear blue and green, don't you?" The triplets nodded. "Girls can wear blue and green and like things with race cars and dinosaurs on them. And boys can wear pink and purple and things with ruffles and bows if they want, too."

"But that's for girls! Boys don't wear nail polish," Charlotte said. Fin's head tilted before he gave it a shake.

"I'm...pretty sure I know all the rules and that isn't one of them."

"Daddy never wears pink except on his ties. Why don't you ever wear pink?" Amelia asked as she tugged at the corner of his cardigan.

"All your father wears is suits," he said and tucked Doug under his arm so they'd focus. "People can wear any color they want, regardless of whether they're a boy or a girl." Fin checked to make sure that all three girls were listening. It was too early to talk to them about how oppressive traditional gender roles could be but colors and clothes were an easy way to start. "Why do you like dresses with lots of poofy layers?" He asked them.

"Because they make me feel like a princess and twirly?" Beatrice guessed.

"Exactly," Fin said with a firm nod. "Wearing things that makes us feel special is fun. That's it and it's no one else's business. Did you know that pink is my favorite color and that I wear it all the time when I'm off?" He asked, hoping that would be much more interesting than his nails.

"Pink is my third favorite color! Why can't you wear pink when you're with us?" Charlotte asked.

"I want to paint your nails!" Amelia said but Fin shook his head.

"No. I don't think your dad or Pierce would approve. The household's staff has a dress code," he said and the girls groaned.

"I wouldn't mind," a deep voice rumbled and Fin gasped when he found Walker leaning against the nursery door. Fin kicked himself for forgetting the polish remover before he hurried out of his apartment. For once, Walker was composed and enjoying himself and Fin was fumbling in front of the kids.

"I am so sorry!" Fin hopped over a stack of books and tossed the puppet at the basket. "I was starting to nod off while I was listening to a podcast so I painted my nails..." He cringed but Walker swatted dismissively.

"I heard enough to get the gist. You're right. It's nobody's business and I like pink and painted fingernails too," he said.

"OK," Fin replied weakly, holding onto the craft table as the nursery swayed around him. "I thought I was toast!" He whispered. Walker waved it off and chuckled.

"It would take *a lot* more than that after what we've put you through."

"Can I paint your fingernails, Daddy?" Amelia asked. Walker pulled his eyes from Fin's to smile at her.

"I don't see why not but I'll have to take it off before I go out or people will think I'm silly because I'm not as cool as Fin."

"Sure you are," Fin said. *Am I swooning? I think I'm swooning.* Fin had read a hundred romance novels but didn't think that anyone actually swooned until he met Walker Cameron III. "I'm in so much trouble," he mumbled and rubbed the back of his hand along his forehead.

"Are you alright?" Walker asked and Fin nodded.

"I'm fine! It's just a little warm in here."

"Girls, I believe it's time for you to meet Nurse Lisa so you can dress for your riding lessons," Walker said, rescuing him. The girls cheered as they scrambled to their feet and hurried from the room, leaving them alone. "They're going to be gone for a few hours and I've got the afternoon free. I was wondering if there was anything you needed to discuss with me." Walker smiled at Fin keenly.

"Actually, I was thinking we might continue this conversation. There's something I'd like to show you." Fin toyed with the button on his cardigan and raised a brow at Walker. He nodded and blushed.

"That sounds like it might be important. I'll make sure we

aren't disturbed," Walker said, excusing himself as he bowed and backed out of the nursery. Fin thought so too and was glad he wouldn't have much to do until the girls returned from their riding lessons. He had been anticipating a slow day but Walker had made it special by giving Fin something to look forward to.

"Someone's adding a lacy pink bikini to their collection tonight."

Chapter Twenty-Two

Walker should have known something was afoot when Fin requested that he bring flip-flops to the nursery after breakfast. Pierce looked concerned as well as they stood in the shoe closet and he passed Walker his flip-flops.

"Perhaps we're going on an imaginary trip to the beach," Walker guessed.

"Should I get you some swim trunks as well, sir?"

"Not unless Fin says so and I'm certain he would have specified if swimwear was necessary. Lord, I hope swimwear isn't necessary." Walker was willing to humor Fin and the girls but bearing his legs to the rest of the household would be highly irregular and undignified.

"As do I, sir," Pierce replied before he disappeared, leaving Walker to carry his flip-flops and face the nursery on his own.

At first, Walker thought it was story time. One of the pink armchairs from the girls' sitting room had been relocated to the middle of the nursery. Then, Walker noted the pink tub at the foot of the armchair, and several brushes and numerous little bottles were arranged on the craft table.

"What's going on in here?" Walker asked as he leaned over the threshold cautiously.

"Ah! There you are! You must be our 9 o'clock!" Fin announced, hurrying into the nursery. He had one of the girls' pink feather boas around his neck and was carrying a pink clipboard.

"Your 9 o'clock?" Walker parroted and jumped when Fin swept around the armchair and gave the seat a pat.

"Right this way! Here's your seat, Mr. Cameron." Fin's hand rolled dramatically as he bowed.

"I'm not sure if it's safe," Walker said under his breath. He looked around apprehensively as he crossed the room and lowered into the chair.

"Of course, it's safe! Take off your shoes."

"I was afraid of that."

"Don't be!" Fin gave him a pointed look. "My team of master

stylists will have you sorted out in no time. You're in good hands," he reassured Walker.

"Sorted out?" Walker grumbled as he bent to unlace his oxfords and slide them off. Fin clapped briskly and Walker bit back a laugh as the girls marched into the room in a swift formation. They were wearing their swim robes over their dresses and they circled around Walker as they murmured to each other about dead ends and roots. Amelia clicked her teeth at Beatrice then shook her head at Charlotte. "I just saw my stylist two days ago." Walker patted his hair self-consciously.

"Well, they've made a mess of it," Amelia informed Walker.

"I can fix it!" Charlotte declared and pulled a chunky pair of purple scissors from the pocket of her robe.

"No!" Walker tried to escape but Fin's hand locked around his shoulder.

"I told you, we're just brushing his hair today," Fin told her calmly. Charlotte just shrugged and stuffed the scissors back in her pocket. Walker relaxed and was treated to a half hour of pampering and entertainment.

He found he liked having his hair brushed and twisted into little pigtails. It was soothing as Beatrice and Charlotte held his hands, pretending to file his fingernails. And he didn't mind their little hands patting his cheeks and the feather-soft brushes dusting his eyelids. The makeup might have been pretend but the bottles of nail polish were real, Walker discovered.

"Pick a color, Daddy!" Charlotte ordered. Walker's lips twisted as he perused the row of glass bottles. Most of them were in shades of pinks, reds, and oranges but there were a few blues and greens as well as black and silver.

"Where did these come from?" He asked.

"They're Fin's!" Amelia told him and sat at Walker's feet. "Pick a color!"

"Well..." Walker slowly shook his head. It didn't matter to

him; they'd be hidden inside his shoes as soon as Walker could put his socks back on. "Why don't you go ahead and pick, Bea."

"This one!" She plucked a hot pink from one of the rows in the back. "Fin said that this one's his favorite!" Beatrice beamed at Walker as she handed it to him.

"Alright..." Walker thanked her and passed it to Amelia. She and Charlotte took turns painting his toenails and they did an exceptional job, to Walker's delight. "You know, I didn't think I'd be able to pull this color off but I do like it." He took out his wallet and saw Fin clutch his chest out of the corner of his eye. "I believe Fin mentioned something about a trip to the bookstore later today." He gave each of the girls a $20 bill before standing and easing his feet into his flip-flops. He glanced at his watch. "Same time next week?" He asked them and checked with Fin whose eyes glittered as he nodded. "Excellent." Walker bowed and headed for the door.

"Don't forget your socks and shoes!" Fin said and swiped them off the floor as he hurried after Walker. They met at the door and Fin cleared his throat as he stepped close and passed them to him.

"You've been a very good boy. I'll be waiting for you after bedtime," he whispered.

"I'll look forward to it," Walker replied. It came out smoothly but Walker wanted to skip and sing as he turned for the stairs. He was smiling as he jogged down the steps and checked his watch again. "Shit!" He remembered that he was expecting a call from a prime minister in ten minutes.

Walker tossed his shoes and socks on the sofa as he passed through his study and was still smiling when he sank into his chair. He reclined behind his desk and stretched his legs as he waited. Walker's imagination went to bedtime—well, after bedtime—and his heart beat a little faster and he became warmer.

It had become their ritual for Fin to wait outside the girls' room so they could share the stroll to Walker's suite. Once they were alone, Fin praised Walker for all the ways he had pleased him. He would reward Walker with soothing words, a glimpse of something pretty and soft, and possibly a new addition to his growing collection if he had been an extra good boy. Walker felt a hitch of arousal and swore when he checked the time again. He only had two minutes until the call and hours until bedtime.

"I thought you might like a cup of tea during your call," Pierce announced as he appeared with a tray and set it on the sideboard. Walker nodded absently and reached for the phone when it rang.

"Cameron," he said and crossed his ankles while Pierce prepared his tea. The prime minister was calling because he wanted to move most of his money before his wife and the public learned about his affair. Walker already had a plan and was going to buy the girls ponies with the commission he'd make on the deal. There was a loud gasp as Pierce came around the desk and saw Walker's painted toenails. There was a dull thud and a clatter as the teacup and saucer bounced on the thick rug. Walker acted as if he didn't notice the tea dripping down the fronts of the desk's drawers. "I am looking to fund a program in East Harlem. Would be good for the community and provide a decent return if you're able to give it a few years," Walker said. He handled the prime minister like the deal was child's play, because that was the sort of thing Walker did just about every day. Walker turned his seat and tuned Pierce out as he silently prepared another cup of tea and quickly cleaned up the mess he'd made. Walker's mind was free to wander back to bedtime and his newfound obsession.

It was madness, falling under Fin's spell, but they were all so happy and the house was so much more peaceful thanks to him. Fin's brand of magic was a bit unorthodox at times, but he seemed to know exactly what the girls and Walker needed. Sex with him seemed inevitable and didn't scare Walker nearly as much as he thought it would, but the last rational voice in his head reminded him of how much he'd lose if he made a mess of things.

Chapter Twenty-Three

P_lease don't be late!_ Fin shut the nursery door and silently rushed to the other end of the hall. He pressed his back against the wall next to the door to the girls' room and listened. It had taken him several extra minutes to clean up all the confetti and the glob of purple slime they'd managed to stick to the ceiling.

"And what was your favorite moment of the day?" Walker asked and Fin silently cheered as he waited. _His_ favorite moment of the day was when Walker asked the girls that question. It was part progress report and part signal that Fin was officially off duty and no longer in nanny mode.

"My favorite moment was when Amelia didn't want her strawberries and she gave them to me," Charlotte said, making Fin melt a little. He could tell their voices apart without looking and there was no way he'd confused them now.

"It was very nice of her to share," Walker replied in his gentle rumble. "What about you, Amelia? What was your favorite moment of the day?"

"My favorite was when Fin took us for a walk to drop off our postcards and we got to see Abigail and Annabel."

"The Delaney girls?" Walker confirmed. Fin heard a soft hum and one of the girls clapped.

"Annabel says their mommy has a new boyfriend and they help her pick out dresses and jewelry when she goes on dates!" Amelia whispered excitedly.

"I'm happy for Judith. It's been a few years since she lost her husband," Walker replied.

"You should go on dates with Fin!" Charlotte said. Fin's mouth stretched into an appalled gasp and he held onto the wall in case his legs gave out. Fin wasn't at all surprised that the girls would suggest it but it was embarrassing and he felt terrible for Walker.

"What? No! Why? What?" Walker sounded equally stunned. "Why would you...?"

"Because Fin's awesome and he likes boys too!" Amelia declared and Fin recovered with a grin, popping his imaginary collar. She wasn't wrong.

"Sometimes you look like you want to go on a date with Fin," Beatrice chimed in. Fin winced at his sneakers and didn't like the awkward grunts and Walker's groan. He was struggling.

"I don't know what you're talking about," he said. Fin kind of had an idea and felt bad for him.

"You look at him like Charlotte looks at puppies," Beatrice said.

"Like he's made of ice cream and you want to eat him!" Charlotte snickered and it spread around the room. Fin cringed and any thoughts he had of rescuing Walker faded as he edged away from the door. *You're on your own, pal.* Walker didn't pay Fin enough to walk into *that*.

"I'm sorry but you're mistaken and that would be absolutely inappropriate. I could never go on a date with Fin because he's my employee," Walker explained. *And because it would just be plain weird,* Fin added with a firm nod. There were disappointed moans from the girls' room and someone might have punched a pillow. "Enough," Walker stated firmly and the girls settled. "Fin is a wonderful *young* man. But I'm more than twenty years older than him and he has too much of his life ahead of him."

Fin didn't like that. There weren't a lot of men his age who were as hot as Walker, as far as he was concerned. And men in their mid-to-late-twenties were often unreliable and kind of obnoxious. Fin rarely had anything in common with them. Not that he had a lot in common with Walker either, but he was incredibly hot and smelled *amazing*.

"But we want you to have a new husband and Fin is perfect."

"Correct me if I'm wrong, but weren't you trying to assassinate him just a few months ago?" Walker made a judgmental sound and there were snorts and snickers.

"We love him now. He makes you spend time with us and he makes everything better," Amelia declared and Fin pressed his hand against his chest. He loved the triplets and felt awful because he had wanted Walker to lie to them until he heard how disappointed they were.

"We're very lucky to have him with us, which is another reason why I would never date Fin. Would you want him to quit and leave us because we went on a bad date?" There was a pause before Walker chuckled. "I didn't think so. Goodnight, Amelia." He kissed her hair and Fin listened as Walker made his way around the room. Walker shut the door behind him and sighed at Fin. "I suppose you caught all of that."

"I missed story time and Amelia's and Beatrice's favorite things but I caught the rest," he said. Fin made an exploding sound as he pushed his hands into his pockets and walked with Walker. "That was rough but you handled it well."

"Thank you. I considered jumping out the window but asked myself how you would have handled it," Walker murmured, causing Fin to trip.

"Um. Thank you?"

"Why are you surprised? You're always rescuing me and you were bound to rub off on me." Walker raised a shoulder, clearly unaware that he'd made one of Fin's dreams come true.

"It's finally happening!" Fin bounced excitedly as he pumped his fists.

"What's happening?" Walker asked warily when they had reached Walker's suite. He held up a hand, gesturing for Fin to wait as he hurried through the sitting room and leaned into his bedroom. It was empty so he jogged to the bathroom and peeked around the doors. "All clear. What's happening?" He asked again. Fin shut the suite's doors and unbuttoned his cardigan as he turned.

"This is my holy grail, my Moby Dick," he said, then cackled when Walker stumbled.

"I suppose I've been blessed with a—" He began clumsily and stopped when Fin laughed.

"Not you specifically!" Fin said and wiped his eyes. "Although, *yay!*" He wiggled his brows at Walker, causing him to blush. But sternly. It was pretty sexy. "Part of the reason I got out of teaching and became a nanny was so I could work with *families*. I thought I'd be like Maria or Mary Poppins and that I'd be helping them, instead of cooped up in a classroom with kids I could never connect with. But those families weren't like the movies and the parents didn't want to know their children, and they didn't want to listen when I tried to help. I was talked down to and told to mind my own business until I came here."

"I'm not sure who told you that wealth was an indicator of intelligence, but they were woefully misinformed," Walker said with a dismissive snort. His teeth scraped over his lip and he was unsure as he approached Fin. "I did well, though?" He asked. His brows rose, causing Fin's stomach to flip. It was an aphrodisiac, the way this impervious man softened and hung onto Fin's every word. There was a tenderness and fascination that Walker only reserved for his girls—as far as Fin knew—and it was heady having that effect on a man like him. And when said man looked like *that*...

"I heard what you told the girls and I'm very happy with you, Walker." He tossed his cardigan onto one of the armchairs and raised a hand, beckoning Walker closer. There was a heady rush as Walker's shoulders dropped and his lips curved into a loopy, bashful grin. *That's it. Let it all go and let's have a little fun.* It was getting easier for Walker to leave his cares at the door and trust Fin. Their fingers interlocked and there was that current of warmth again as Fin pulled him closer and guided his hand to the fly of his corduroys. "You've been such a good boy. Would you like to see what I wore for you?" Fin watched as Walker slid the button free then shuddered. Not because Walker was relinquishing his power or control of the situation. This wasn't a shudder of weakness but of release. He had taken off the restraints and given himself permission to play and explore.

"Yes. Please." Walker curled his fingers under the waist of Fin's pants and slowly dragged them back and forth, as if he was testing the textures against his knuckle. He shut his eyes and licked his lips. "Is it lace? It feels like lace but I also feel...*laces*." Walker gave it a few more heartbeats before he took hold of the zipper and Fin moaned encouragingly as he pulled it down. "Good Lord, Fin." Walker's voice crumbled, along with his control.

He captured Fin's cheek and Walker swore as he pulled

him closer. He mashed his lips against Fin's and Walker gave up. He lapped and sucked wildly as he mumbled incoherent pleas and apologies. Fin threw an arm around Walker's neck, inviting him to take as much as he needed. There was a growl as Walker's head tilted and he took their kiss deeper. Walker slid his hand around and under Fin's pants to caress the thin triangle of fabric there before cautiously cupping Fin's ass. He squeezed and Fin couldn't help the strangled, pleading whimper that slipped from him as he clung to Walker.

"This is getting really hot but I think we should pause and check in." Fin was shaking as he leaned back in Walker's arms so he could catch his breath. "How are you doing?" He asked Walker. He looked dazed but starved as he panted and stared at Fin's lips.

"Fine. I think. Do you um...want to go back to my place?" He said and tipped his head at the bedroom door. There was a hopeful hitch to his voice that went straight to Fin's groin. His heart and his body ordered him to say yes but Fin recalled why they were going slow and how much hotter it was when Walker felt safe and trusted him.

"More than you could possibly understand but I think we should stop." Fin sighed heavily so Walker knew just how deeply he regretted it. "Tonight's been an emotional roller coaster and I think we should hang out right here," Fin said and waved between them. "Let's see how this feels before we try something else."

"That might be a good idea," Walker said with a grimace, scrubbing his hand across his mouth as he muffled a curse. "Was that too much? Did I go too far?"

"No!" Fin whispered and waved wildly. "We would be naked and trying to break things right now if I thought you were ready for that, but we both know you're not."

"Break things?"

"Mainly me," Fin said as he squinted over Walker's shoulder and imagined it. "I do like it rough now and then," Fin said as he petted Walker's tie. "I'm really proud of you and I think you and the girls are going to be just fine."

"Because we've got you. We have to be careful, I can't lose you, Fin"

"Maybe you haven't noticed, but I'm pretty stubborn. I'm not going anywhere," Fin stated and pressed a hard kiss to Walker's lips before releasing him. "Except home. But I'll be back tomorrow and we'll have another amazing day."

"We will if you say so." Walker smiled and waved as Fin picked up his cardigan and silently slipped out of the room.

Fin's feet didn't touch the ground as he left the house and took the train back to Brooklyn and Bed-Stuy. He was still on autopilot as he let himself into his apartment and was glad Riley wasn't home for once. Fin planned to open a bottle of wine, draw himself a hot bath and finish what Walker had started.

Chapter Twenty-Four

"Right this way, ladies!" Fin looked down the servants' hall as he got the door for the girls. He held them back and his neck shifted from left to right dramatically as he pretended to make sure the coast was clear. The girls tittered as they huddled behind him. "We're going to duck and run for that door on the other side of the old kitchen," he said as he pointed. The Killian House's original kitchen had been restored but was no longer in regular use. The lights were low but a warm glow peeked from under the door to the butler's quarters. "Looks like he's in there," Fin whispered and signaled for his little commandos to follow as he made a run for it. They were able to cross the kitchen without being detected and Fin tapped his lips and straightened his shoulders so the girls knew it was time to behave. He gave the door a quick knock then tilted his nose back as he waited. The door was thrown open a second later and Pierce was baffled but he offered them a stiff bow.

"Sir. Miss Amelia, Miss Beatrice, and Miss Charlotte. How may I be of assistance?" He said with his usual placidness. Fin considered asking if they could move their meeting inside for more privacy but a quick scan revealed a spartan sitting room with a small round table and a single chair. There was a record player on an old stand and dozens of records were meticulously organized on the shelves but that appeared to be Pierce's only indulgence. The rest of the room was bare and Fin could see a twin-sized bed through the opened bedroom door. There was a single flat pillow and the bed was perfectly made with hospital corners.

"Mr. Cameron's birthday is in three weeks and the girls and I need help throwing a surprise party for him. We were hoping you could give us a hand with a few of the items on our list or point us in the right direction," Fin said, handing the list to Pierce. It was extensive so Fin crossed his arms over his chest and the girls mimicked him as they waited. Pierce glanced at it then raised a brow at Fin and cleared his throat.

"A big, big cake, lots of people in fancy clothes, guys carrying trays with tiny food with toothpicks, a big band..." Pierce read then stared at Fin over the list. "There will not be a bounce castle, a water balloon fight, or fireworks but the rest should be easy enough." He folded the list and tucked it inside his coat.

"Oh... Awesome!" Fin gave Pierce's shoulder a grateful punch. "We obviously don't have any money to contribute to the budget, but we've got plenty of elbow grease," he said, indicating his little minions.

"That won't be necessary," Pierce stated. "Mr. Cameron has allotted a generous allowance in the household budget for holidays and special events such as birthday parties. I'm allowed to use those funds at my discretion so that will be of no concern," he informed them.

"That's even more awesome!" Fin said and raised a thumb so the girls knew that Pierce was The Man.

"It is indeed. I believe I understand the young ladies' preferences in regard to decorations and types of cake but I will confer with them *in the nursery* before finalizing any decisions."

"Gotcha," Fin said with a salute. "Anything else we might have missed?" He whispered to Pierce. The butler was still for a moment before his focus flicked to the girls and then back to Fin.

"I will also arrange for fittings in the nursery while Mr. Cameron is away from The Killian House. One cannot attend a fancy birthday party unless they are properly attired."

"Yes!" The girls all shouted and Fin beamed at Pierce.

"You're a genius. I knew we could count on you." He held up his hand so Pierce could slap it. Pierce's face pinched with disapproval but he raised his hand and *almost* pressed it against Fin's.

"This is a commendable idea and I'm happy to assist. Mr. Cameron's birthday party should be treated as a special event. I just ask that you please keep yourselves upstairs and out of the kitchens unless you have permission from myself or Ms. Lester," he reminded Fin sternly. Fin held his hands up apologetically.

"I'm sorry! We were having fun with the sneaking around part and I might have gotten a little carried away because of the rain," he said and Pierce cleared his throat again.

"We can make an exception now and then but it would be far more sensible for me to report to you in the nursery if our goal is to avoid detection."

"You have my word. From now on, I'll clear it with you or the cook first. In the meantime, give us something to do. We can't sit on our hands while you do all the hard work."

"That is very nearly the definition of a butler, sir," the other man replied flatly.

"Right..." Fin cleared his throat and rubbed under his nose

so he could point at the girls discreetly. "We can't let you have all the fun," he added slowly, hoping Pierce would play along. He blinked at Fin for a moment then bowed his head.

"I see." He glanced at the girls then back at Fin. "I'm afraid that I am not permitted to spend any household funds on gifts so it will be up to the four of you to procure those."

Fin mouthed a "Perfect!" and held up his thumb so only Pierce could see it.

"What else?" Fin asked. Pierce's eyes hardened and his lips pulled tight as he stared back at Fin. Probably in frustration. Fin flashed him a sheepish smile. "I will owe you big time," he vowed. Pierce's lips pursed and he made a thoughtful sound.

"It would be helpful if Mr. Cameron was distracted when the planner and the caterer come to the house."

"Yes! We can definitely handle that!" Fin pumped his fists and there were similar cheers behind him. He thought he saw Pierce's lips twitch.

"I have the utmost confidence. There is the matter of the lights," he added, his tone becoming serious and somewhat ominous.

"The lights?" Fin asked and looked back at the girls. Amelia and Beatrice shrugged at him while Charlotte was crouched on the floor. She was pretending to tie her sneakers but had her sisters' laces in her hands and was winding them into a tight knot. "Charlotte!" Fin waited until he had her attention and wagged a finger. He refused to proceed until Charlotte began untangling the laces then turned back to Pierce, grinning proudly. "I love that little menace. Now, what was that about the lights?"

Pierce didn't miss a beat and acted as if Charlotte hadn't attempted to assault her sisters right in front of him. "I'm certain I can coordinate everything on the afternoon of the party without Mr. Cameron suspecting anything out of the ordinary for his birthday *except* the lights. The landscaper installs them for a nighttime event and that's usually an all-day job and needs to be done *before* the decorators and the caterer's team arrives. Under normal circumstances, I would arrange that for the day prior but I'm afraid I can't hide a team of landscapers from Mr. Cameron for that long."

"Leave that up to me!" Fin rubbed his hands together as he planned and was even more excited about Walker's party. "I'm a theater nerd and lighting is my passion. I can make magic on a shoestring budget and I've got plenty of help."

"We do not operate on a shoestring budget at The Killian House," Pierce replied briskly, as if Fin had offended his honor. "You will have *whatever* you need. Simply provide me with a list," he added and Fin had to bite his knuckle. He wanted to scream, he was so happy. The girls and Walker were going to be blown away when they saw all the lights.

"Wait until I tell my brother and my friends that we're breaking into Cameron's backyard and turning it into a wonderland."

"That won't be necessary. Your passcode will work at the back gate."

"But that wouldn't be nearly as much fun," Fin explained distantly as he calculated. Rarely did Fin get the opportunity to display his flair for dramatic theatrical lighting and commit a little light trespassing and vandalism. "This just got even more awesome."

"I'll be sure to notify security and close the curtains in Mr. Cameron's room," Pierce, then extended his hand, signaling that it was time for them to go back the way they came. "That is *all* the help I could possibly need but if I think of anything else, I know where to find you, sir. Ladies," he added with a bow for the girls. They giggled and curtsied as they thanked him, making Fin's heart swell. He couldn't imagine anything more precious, and they could be so sweet when they weren't plotting.

"Thanks, Pierce." Fin wanted to hug him for coming through in such a big way. The four of them had bombarded Pierce in his sanctum but the starchy older man had patiently listened. Fin suspected it was because Pierce loved the Camerons and would do anything in his power to make them happy. But Fin also knew that Pierce would not appreciate a hug so he tapped his temple in salute before he turned and crouched. "Let's be as silent and invisible as we were on the way down here," he whispered to the girls they were all business as they nodded and tapped their lips like proper little super spies. "OK! Follow me!"

Chapter Twenty-Five

"I 'll worry about the funding. You make sure the research and the estimate are ready in time and you've got all your ducks in a row. I'll call you at the same time next week and I want the projections for the next two quarters, at a minimum." Walker hung up and made a note in his planner. Pierce came in with the tea tray and left it on the sideboard.

"Ms. Lester and the rest of the kitchen staff are enthusiastic about Fin's proposal for the 'chef's table' in the kitchen for the girls," Pierce said. He gathered the loose papers from Walker's last call and swept them into the appropriate folder. The planner was closed and set off to Walker's right side for later, leaving the desk cleared for his tea.

"Are they?" Walker asked, surprised. "I didn't think they'd want the girls eating in there and being underfoot," Walker admitted. He considered his household to be much more relaxed—there wasn't the severe separation between the "upstairs" and "downstairs"—than the one he was raised in, but Walker assumed his staff still preferred the children remain confined to the nursery as much as possible. It would have been unheard-of for Walker to eat a meal in the dining room when he was a child, but the kitchen? That was always off-limits and Walker was scared of the cook and the pastry chef when he was the girls' age. "I was a thoroughly rotten child, though..."

"Yes, sir." Pierce set a cup and saucer in front of Walker. "The kitchen is quieter in the afternoons, as long as the cook and her staff aren't preparing for an event. Ms. Lester said that she wouldn't mind seeing more of the girls now that they're more content and manageable," Pierce said, gently chiding Walker for his past parenting sins. A plate of shortbread took out some of the sting, comforting Walker as he dunked a cookie in his tea.

"No thanks to me," Walker chuckled and Pierce offered him the barest nod.

"I did believe that there could have been a bit more...intervention on your part but I also understood that you were in a great deal of pain and doing your best." He spoke in his low, utterly even tone but it was the most revealing and unnerving moment of their very long and supremely professional relationship. Pierce had been in his late thirties when he started working for Walker, tending to his personal needs and laying out his clothes for the day. Walker was twenty-two and lived in The Killian House but it still belonged to his father, then. Walker bought the place over on Fifth Avenue and promoted Pierce, giving him command of his own household. And Pierce followed when Walker Cameron II retired to Connecticut, taking responsibility of The Killian House in addition to his duties as Walker's butler

"I'm getting better at intervention, thanks to Fin," Walker conceded.

"You are indeed, sir."

"Speaking of... What the girls are up to at the moment?"

"Mathematics, I believe. I passed by the nursery a few

minutes ago and the girls were learning their fractions and decimals with a pizza game and a worksheet," Pierce said and Walker became alert.

"I might see if I can be of assistance. I'm rather good at fractions and decimals."

"Excellent idea, sir."

It *was* a particularly excellent idea because he could never be out of his depth with mathematics! Walker was practically a savant when it came to money and numbers which meant that this was his time to shine. He was whistling happily as he jogged up the stairs, recalling math tricks and sequences he'd learned so he would have them ready to impress the girls but slowed as he approached the nursery. He wasn't sure if it was even occupied when he eased the door open a little wider and leaned inside. Walker stared, perplexed as Amelia passed Charlotte a blue crayon and calmly whispered about quarters. Beatrice was nodding along, her tongue clamped between her teeth as she colored studiously. It was a dream come true and Walker wasn't sure if he was in the right nursery, but he was concerned because Fin was nowhere to be seen.

"Knock, knock," Walker called as he tapped his knuckle on the door jamb. The girls turned and waved excitedly but there was no shrieking or swarming. "Where's Fin?" It wasn't like him to leave the girls unattended for any amount of time.

"He had to go to the bathroom because Charlotte stuck a crayon up his nose and it started bleeding," Amelia announced but none of the girls thought the matter was worthy of interrupting their work.

"It was an accident," Charlotte stated simply and leaned toward Beatrice. "Can I have the purple when you're done?"

"Why did you stick a crayon up Fin's nose?" Walker asked as he went to get a closer look.

"I asked Fin if grownup noses were bigger inside and if a

K. Sterling

crayon would fit and he said no but I wanted to see if he was right," Charlotte explained. Beatrice gave Walker a suffering look as she shook her head.

"Fin is always right but she never listens. He told her it wouldn't fit, but she tried anyway."

"I do too!" Charlotte protested while she colored a slice of pizza. "But I had to hide the red because you both keep taking it."

"I should probably check on Fin," Walker said, cringing in the direction of the bathroom. He could hear the water faintly through the door and decided he'd give Fin a few more minutes.

"Can you check my work, Daddy?" Beatrice asked as she pushed her worksheet across the table.

"Of course," Walker replied. He held his tie against his chest as he leaned over the table, then pointed at Charlotte. "Don't even think about it," he said sternly and she dropped a yellow crayon. He clicked his teeth at her but went ahead and smiled because her face scrunched adorably as she pouted at being thwarted. Walker hummed thoughtfully as he examined Beatrice's worksheet. There were colorful stuffed felt pizza slices on the table that the girls could Velcro together to assemble in various fraction denominations. They were aids to help the girls color pizza fractions on their worksheets and Beatrice had done hers correctly. "This is remarkable," Walker began as he held it up. "I particularly appreciate your choice of color for the mushrooms. Most people wouldn't think to use blue but it really makes this pop. And the work itself is flawless. Not a single error. Very well done."

"Can you look at mine?" Charlotte asked and Walker went around the table. He lowered and braced his hand on the back of her chair. One of her pigtails was within reach so he gave it a playful tug.

"This is excellent, Charlotte." It truly was. The colors were even more psychedelic than Beatrice's. "You have a remarkable sense of balance and your choice of colors is inspired. I really like what you did with this three-fourths pizza."

"It has a horn because it's a unicorn!" She boasted.

"Remarkable." Walker kissed her cheek then stood. He stepped around and Amelia held up her worksheet. "Now, this looks like a menu from a fine establishment. All of your fractions are correct and I would eat any of these pizzas," he declared, making her swell with pride. Unlike her sisters, Amelia had rendered her pizza fractions in traditional pizza hues and did her best to make them realistic. "Isn't it fascinating? Each of you can be given the same worksheets and the same box of crayons and yet you create three incredibly unique masterpieces. And look at how brilliant you are, my little mathematicians."

"They're already so far ahead in math. You're going to need to hire a real tutor because they'll be doing algebra soon and I specifically told Reid to put an algebra clause in the contract because I'm allergic to it," Fin teased. He was watching from the bathroom door with his arms crossed over his chest.

"Allergic to algebra?" Walker said and Fin hummed and nodded solemnly.

"My whole face and tongue swell right up. You wouldn't like it."

"No. We wouldn't want that." They exchanged easy, laughing grins and there was a sparkle in Fin's eyes that Walker could easily translate now. *I'm so proud of you.* Walker raised a shoulder, denying that he'd done anything special. Although, he was surprised that he hadn't panicked and turned back as soon as he noticed that Fin wasn't there. Walker had done a decent job of covering for Fin and had a lovely time with the girls. He hadn't raised his voice once and there were no tears or wobbly lips.

"Time to put everything away, girls. I have good news: I got permission from the cook to use the brick oven. We're making pizzas for lunch!" Fin announced. This time there was pandemonium and some stampeding. The girls jumped and shouted orders at each other. Walker darted out of their way, choosing to check on Fin while they scrambled to tidy up. He spotted a few drops of blood on Fin's gray v-neck and mouthed a curse. Fin looked down and gasped. "I have an extra shirt in my backpack downstairs and will totally change before I step foot in the kitchen. And I swear, I'm *very* careful and I get tested every three months."

"I'm not worried, Fin," Walker promised and gave Fin's arm a gentle nudge.

"Good," Fin said, then cleared his throat as he looked over Walker's shoulder. "Because I always keep my latest labs in my backpack in case I do get a bloody nose or crack my head open on some slippery stairs. I'm on PrEP, too," he added quietly. Walker's brows pulled together and he shook his head.

"I don't know what that means but...good. I'm sorry about your nose."

"No worries!" Fin laughed. "It would have been an amazing paper towel commercial. It all happened in slow motion. Charlotte, shooting out of her seat, wielding a red crayon. Me, trying to stop her. Charlotte, jamming it straight up my nose. My nose, gushing because I get nose bleeds if I walk into the wind, which is why I keep my labs on me. Me, stumbling and tripping like a clown to the bathroom while attempting to catch all the blood gushing from my face."

"I'm always impressed at your ability to laugh regardless of the situation, no matter how tragic or messy."

"Can we go now, Fin?" Amelia demanded. The girls had

put away their crayons, Velcro pizza slices, and their worksheets.

"We can go. Want to join us?" Fin asked. Walker nodded as he checked his watch and held up a finger.

"You might have to start without me. I need to make a quick call to one of my attorneys but it shouldn't take more than ten minutes."

"Great! And you should look up that other thing," Fin said while he corralled the girls and herded them toward the door.

"I'll do that," Walker said. Content to watch them go, he sighed happily as he strode from the room in their wake. Fin and the girls were singing a made-up song about making pizzas and it bounced around the foyer as they calamitied down the stairs.

Walker couldn't have asked for better lunch dates and was humming along with them as he took his phone out of his pocket and searched for 'Taking prep'. Walker's eyes flared and he tripped on the runner when he saw the results. Walker had never heard of PrEP and wasn't aware that there was a drug for preventing HIV. "Oh. ... I see." Once again, Fin was handing Walker another envelope and allowing him to decide if he was ready to open it. He suspected he might be but Walker trusted Fin to slow things down if they started going too fast. "It might not hurt to take a look," he said and was delighted at the beautiful turn his day had taken.

Chapter Twenty-Six

"I'm glad you came home early, Daddy. I miss you when you don't kiss us goodnight." Amelia kissed his cheek loudly and Walker treasured her scrawny arms around his neck. He missed the dimples on the elbows, the full, round cheeks, and how tiny the girls' chubby hands and fingers were when they were toddlers. But Walker was seeing little glimpses of the people his girls were becoming as they lost their baby fat and got taller, and he was already so proud of how smart and strong they were. That wasn't the only reason Walker left the benefit early, but he greedily basked in the girls' delight when he swept into the room in his tuxedo and overcoat to surprise them.

"I always miss you when I can't say goodnight but tonight I missed my girls even more, so I told them I had something much more important to do and came home immediately."

"You did?" Charlotte gasped and Walker hummed.

"I have a few more events on my schedule that I can't do anything about but I've told my assistants that I won't be available in the evenings anymore, once those are done."

"No more fundraisers and galas and benefits?" Beatrice asked excitedly as she untucked herself and stood on her knees.

"I have a few more on my calendar that I've already RSVP'd to but no more after that unless you're going with me. You'll be old enough to have homework and you'll have later bedtimes as you get older. I'm sure we'll want to watch movies and play games... I'd rather be here for that instead of going to boring parties and giving boring speeches," he explained. All three girls kicked, squealed, bounced, and cheered wildly. "Alright!" He laughed as he stood. "I'm glad you're all so happy and I'm looking forward to all of that too but this is still your bedtime. Calm down and go to sleep so we can see each other in the morning," he told them then made his way around the room, kissing each girl's hair and tucking them in again. "I love you all so very much," he whispered as he turned down the light.

He was struck again by a profound sense of gratitude and joy. He had longed for a way to tame his daughters just enough to have an even footing with them, instead of feeling like he was constantly stumbling into quicksand. Though it wasn't the girls who had been transformed, Walker realized. They might have been tiny hellions but Walker had made them desperate and ravenous for his attention. He'd run from the little things when they were toddlers because *he* was scared. He'd been afraid to face them and learn and he had turned them into adorable monsters. But they were Walker's monsters and he was learning how to be the parent they needed, with Fin's help.

The girls weren't the only ones who were happy with Walker's change of plans. Fin was waiting and breathless when Walker shut the girls' door.

"I didn't think I'd see you again tonight!" There was a waver in his voice and Fin's eyes shimmered. *Oh, you've been a very, very good boy.*

Pure joy. And pride. Walker was so *happy* and certain that

he'd made the right decision. He was exactly where he was supposed to be and he wanted to pull Fin into his arms and tell him how much better his life was and thank him for all the beautiful ways he'd changed him. And Walker wanted so much more that it terrified him. He wanted to worship Fin and whatever beautifully wicked undergarment he was wearing. And Walker wanted Fin to tell him how *good* he was while he was doing it.

"Let's go!" Fin whispered, pushing Walker to get him moving. They hurried until they reached Walker's room then paused to make sure they were alone. The bathroom and closet were clear so Walker waved for Fin to come in as he removed his overcoat and tossed it at one of the armchairs.

"I meant what I said, I missed my girls and I didn't want to go without saying goodnight to you." Walker had said it matter-of-factly but his heart fluttered and his hands were sweating as he shrugged out of his coat and tugged his tie loose. He offered Fin a hungry look as he went to him.

"You've been a *very* good boy today. Would you like to see?" Fin let his cardigan drop and swiftly untucked his shirt. Walker nodded quickly as he drew closer and chased Fin's lips. They moaned as their tongues swirled and thrust hungrily.

"Please!" Walker's hands hovered around Fin's face, waiting for permission and guidance. Fin moaned raggedly in approval and was hard as he bucked against Walker, spurring him on, tempting him to let go. And Walker found that he could. It was so easy and he was safe. Walker was lighter and looser and there was vibrant lust and joy, just at the thought of pleasing Fin. "Again," Walker whispered.

"You've been such a good boy!" Fin's voice had gone higher and he was shaking as he reached between them and flicked his fly open. "Would you like to touch?" He whispered and guided Walker's hand to his waist.

"May I?" Walker breathed. It was as reverent and tender as a prayer and Fin drank it from Walker's lips.

"God, yes."

Walker's knuckles trailed around the waistband of Fin's pants before his fingers slipped along the zipper. A shiver passed between them as Walker caressed the red lace with his thumb. He leaned back so he could see and Walker licked his lips, parched and aching when he finally looked. Fin's erection was restrained by a red lace thong and Walker was mesmerized as a wet spot spread around the head. Walker dragged his knuckle along his shaft and Fin let out a sharp gasp as another burst of pre-cum saturated the lace.

"Christ, Fin!" Walker growled as his control went up in flames. He was demanding and rough as he kissed Fin. Walker's hand twisted in Fin's hair as the other pushed deeper into the front of his corduroys and cupped his sac. He released Fin and Walker groaned as he traced the side of the thong around and into the cleft of his ass.

"Fuck!" Fin pressed against Walker and ground against his hard-on, urging him to touch as much as he wanted. Walker twisted the back of the thong, pulling the panel in the front tighter around Fin's cock. They became wild as they lapped and sucked and bucked against each other.

"I can't do this! I'm your boss!" Walker swore as he wrenched his lips free but he dove into the corner of Fin's neck. He tasted so good, Walker's mouth watered as he licked Fin's jaw and sucked on an earlobe.

"I think we both know who's really in charge," Fin panted. The words had an immediate effect and Walker shuddered in delight at the thought of Fin taking control of *him*. "What do you think? Should I touch you?" Fin whispered as his hands dragged down the front of Walker's shirt.

"I... Please, Fin." His chest heaved as he floundered,

wondering if he had ever wanted to be touched as badly as he did when Fin touched him. Fin shushed gently and pecked at Walker's lips.

"It's alright, Walker. We're only touching. We can stop whenever you want."

"I know and it doesn't hurt to try something new," Walker said, nudging his lips against Fin's. He couldn't get enough of him, the way his tongue tasted like apples, mint, and a hint of tea. The delicious tingles his puffed breaths caused when he nuzzled against Walker's skin. Most of all, he cherished how new he felt when Fin touched him. Walker was setting himself up for more heartache because he could never truly have Fin and it would have to end. But until then, Walker would greedily touch and lick every part of him.

Fin needed to touch too, apparently. His fingers twisted and clawed frantically at Walker's shirt. Walker was in agony as Fin's hands slid around and gripped his ass. *Fuck, yes! Please, please touch me!* As if he read his thoughts, Fin dug his fingertips into his ass before he went to work on his belt and the fly of Walker's trousers. Fin unzipped and Walker arched, gasping at the flaring of his nerves.

"I can slow down if you need a moment, or we can stop here," Fin said softly but Walker shook his head.

"Don't stop yet! Please! I just—"

"Shhhh... I know." Fin shushed soothingly as he reached into Walker's trousers. The pads of his fingers slid over the fine cotton of Walker's boxers and they both swore as Fin's hand curled around straining heat.

"Oh God, Fin." Walker's legs were shaking so he stumbled forward a few steps, clumsily dancing Fin into the nearest wall for support.

"Mmmmm... Does that feel good?" Fin watched for any sign of distress but Walker's lips parted on a silent cry and his head bobbled loosely. "And you'll tell me if it's too much and you need to stop?" Fin confirmed.

"Yes!"

"Good boy." Fin tightened his grip and stroked. The heat between them rose and Walker was dizzy as he planted his hand on the wall next to Fin's shoulder.

"How do you always know?" He was reverent again as he pecked at Fin's lips. How did he know how to soothe Walker's pain and make telling the truth feel so good?

"Because I see you, Walker, and I can feel how much you need someone to touch you. And how good it feels when someone else is in charge for once."

"Yes." It was barely a breath, as if Walker was afraid someone other than Fin might hear. He didn't want anyone but Fin to have that kind of control or to know him like this. *No one but Fin.*

"Everyone tells you yes and that you know best but you can never tell if they mean it, can you?" Fin said and Walker swallowed hard before he shook his head. *Only Fin.* "That's why you love it when I tell you no. That's why you get harder every time I tell you you're a good boy."

"I've never cared before. But I feel like I'm coming undone when you say it, like I'd do anything to hear you say it again."

"Good. I want to tell you and I want you to come undone when you're ready." Fin guided Walker's hand back to the waistband of his thong and purred, encouraging and tempting. "I like it when you're honest with me and you trust me. You've been so good, Walker. Do you want to touch me?" Fin panted shakily.

"May I?" Walker's fingers skimmed along the edge of the lace.

"Yes. Yes, you may."

Walker slipped his hand into the front of Fin's thong and

ever so gently cupped his hard-on. His fingers stretched and pushed lower and Fin moaned as he rose on his toes so Walker could reach his sac.

"Fuck! Fin!" Walker was crying as his mouth covered Fin's and he kneaded and stroked. Fin moaned loudly and shoved his hand into Walker's boxers. "Yes!" Walker sobbed and they became frantic. Their teeth clicked and their hands became slick as they writhed against each other. Fin sucked on Walker's tongue as he pumped his cock and it was hard to tell who popped first. A bright swell of pleasure and pressure crashed into Walker as Fin cried his name. "God, yes!" Walker jammed his fingers into his mouth so he could lick Fin's cum off of them. He tasted crisp and tart and Walker made a blissfully contented sound as he licked them clean, surprising Fin.

"Wow!" Fin gave his head a shake, looking dazed. "You were a very, very good boy." He raised his fingers to his lips so he could taste Walker. He licked the cum off his palm and hummed. "Mmmm... A very good boy."

"I'm so glad I came home early." Walker gathered Fin in his arms before he gave himself a chance to overthink it. "My day isn't complete if I don't get to say goodnight to you."

"It's my favorite part of the day too." Fin sighed as he leaned into Walker and kissed him. They were heavier as they let the kiss draw out and Walker didn't want to let go as Fin eased out of his arms to retrieve his cardigan.

I wish you didn't have to leave.

But Walker didn't share that because Fin would say that was definitely too far and that there wasn't anything they could do about it.

"Goodnight, Fin, and thank you."

"That was all you and you made my night." Fin lingered at the door as if he didn't want to go either. "I'll see you in the morning." It sounded wistful and echoed the longing Walker felt as they parted. Fin waved before he stepped around the door and took all the warmth with him.

"I think I might be in trouble," Walker murmured. He didn't need to call his sister to know what her advice would be, though. "This is what happens when I listen to Agnes," he said, smiling as he finished shedding his wrecked and wrinkled tux.

Chapter Twenty-Seven

"You had better slow down or your French is going to be better than mine," Fin told Beatrice. She bounced happily and pointed at the picture of him. "You're a prince!"

"I love it. Finally, someone appreciates me," he said with a cheeky grin then bent to kiss her hair. "It's a beautiful story and I love the picture. I'm going to hang it on my fridge at home so Riley can be jealous." He checked the clock and hissed as he stood. "Time for my little cowgirls to put on their boots and grab their lassos," he said and the girls laughed. They were off to riding lessons, but they wouldn't be practicing for a rodeo.

"I wish it was a dance day," Charlotte pouted. "Are you coming to our recital, Fin?"

"I wouldn't miss it for anything! I'm going to be in front so I can record every moment! But you all need to get going or you'll be late."

The girls cheered as they jumped up and scattered. They put their work and art supplies away and hurried from the room, leaving him alone. He wasn't exaggerating. Fin was excited to see the girls perform after weeks of helping them practice in the nursery. And he was also looking forward to an evening out with the Camerons. Walker had invited Fin and the five of them had plans to celebrate with ice cream afterward. He'd already picked out a pink cardigan and matching Converse so he could surprise the girls by coordinating with their costumes. The girls would be tickled.

"You're up to something," Walker said, making Fin jump. He laughed and went to turn off the music while Walker propped himself against the door, looking dashing and immaculate.

"Planning my ensemble for the recital. It's going to be lots of pink!" He whispered loudly from behind his hand and Walker grinned.

"Then I'll have something else to look forward to. You look good in pink," Walker said as he strolled into the room. Fin threw him a scandalized look, legitimately blushing. "I passed the girls on the stairs. We're alone," Walker added quietly.

"You know we're only supposed to flirt in the middle of the day if it's very important and the door is locked. That door is open," Fin said and pointed behind Walker.

"My apologies," Walker murmured but Fin knew it wasn't sincere. He was getting bolder but Fin liked it. "The girls are going to be gone for a few hours and I've got the afternoon free. I was wondering if you'd join me for lunch on the back terrace." Walker looked around before he stepped closer and traced the top button on Fin's cardigan. "I told Pierce I wanted to go over any improvements or additions you might want to make to the nursery and I thought that might be more comfortable than my office."

"Improvements?" Fin asked and his face became hot. Walker was asking him on a date! Not a real date because that was impossible but the back terrace off Walker's study was far more private than the dining room. Pierce might appear once or twice but it was as close to a date as they could get. Fin was touched that Walker had arranged it. And a little wary. They had made out a little while the girls were napping and out of the house but Walker was proposing something more personal and intimate, in a way. "I would love to, although I don't know what I'd change. Everything's pretty perfect."

"I'm sure we can come up with something if we put our heads together." Walker caught Fin's hand and pulled it to his lips. "It would be perfect if I didn't have to wait until tonight to kiss you."

"Cameron..." Fin looked at the door and resisted the urge to stomp his foot. He didn't want to be on the clock and he didn't want to worry about boundaries. "I really want to kiss you too, but we should save this for after bedtime."

"Just one. Please," Walker whispered. Fin was helpless as their lips brushed. He licked Walker's tongue, delighting at the taste of crisp mint and a hint of scotch and a cigar. He couldn't get enough of the smell and taste of Walker's breath and the hot huff of it against his skin. Fin knew he was in trouble but Walker was impossible to resist when he begged. "Have lunch with me."

"Don't you think that's a little risky? What if we slip around Pierce?"

"I think he already knows," Walker said and Fin gasped in horror.

"No!" He cried. Walker laughed but it was soothing and sympathetic as he rubbed Fin's shoulder.

"I don't think you appreciate the state of my suits lately. Some curious event befalls them between the nursery and my suite nearly every evening. I doubt he suspects that I'm being attacked by ninjas," Walker mused.

"Awesome. How bad would it be if I had to kill him?" Fin

asked very quietly. Pierce was a little like a ninja. He was stealthy and Fin didn't know why he'd thought they could sneak anything past him.

"I can assure you, Pierce prefers to mind his business and stay out of ours. That might be why he's been so scarce in the evenings and doesn't wait to help me undress."

"That's not the point," Fin argued, then opened his mouth to ask why a grown man needed help undressing but decided against it. He still needed Reid's help whenever he had to wear a necktie. "He's essentially my manager and his opinion of me matters. I respect Pierce," he said, giving Walker's arm a swat. He caught Fin's hand and nodded.

"You're absolutely right. No flirting and we'll spend at least half of the meal talking about the girls and the nursery."

"And what do you want to talk about the other half of the time?" Fin asked and didn't hide that he was suspicious. Walker's brow furrowed curiously.

"Nothing in particular. You? What you like to read and watch when you're not entertaining six-year-olds? Where you grew up?" He shrugged and laughed. "We talk about me all the time and you know everything about me. But I only hear the little anecdotes you tell the girls."

"That's risky too, Walker," Fin warned softly. The problem was, Fin didn't mean it. He wanted Walker to know everything.

"I know but that doesn't stop me from wondering what you're doing when you're not here or thinking about where I'd take you if I wasn't limited to my sitting room or the terrace," Walker said. Fin had to gulp for air before he swatted Walker again.

"You can't say things like that! It's really lovely and I think about you too but you can't make this romantic by saying things like that."

"My apologies," Walker said solemnly but Fin scowled.

"You say that but you don't mean it."

"Sometimes. Please have lunch with me, Fin. I promise I'll behave. No flirting."

"There could be *some* flirting, if we're careful," Fin said, despite his better judgment.

Fate conspired against Fin. Lunch with Walker had been terribly romantic. Someone had set their plates next to each other, causing their hands to brush far too many times for no reason at all. And Walker's fingers kept tangling with Fin's under the table. After their plates were taken, Walker propped his chin on his palm and peppered Fin with questions. He was attentive and engaged, hanging on Fin's every word. Before they parted, Walker asked if they could have lunch together every Thursday.

Fin couldn't say no. The afternoon had already been perfect before Walker pulled Fin into the alcove under the stairs, stealing a kiss before sending him up to the nursery. Three tired and fussy little cowgirls moseyed in half an hour later, which worked out perfectly for Fin. He turned down the lights, put on a gentle nature documentary, and gave them some popcorn, allowing him time to plan while they were snacking and nodding off. Thanks to their quiet afternoon, Fin didn't have much to do after he turned the girls over to their nurse. He snuck into the bathroom while Walker was tucking them in and changed into a lace jockstrap. Pink. Because that was Walker's favorite color.

The jockstrap was a hit. Walker babbled and stared and he loved to wind his hands in the elastic straps around Fin's asscheeks as they kissed. They ground against each other like teenagers until they came in their underwear and Fin made Walker keep his eyes closed while he quickly shimmied out of his pants, then hopped back into them.

"Thank you for today." Fin whispered the words as he

placed the jockstrap on Walker's palm. "You can open your eyes now." Fin watched as Walker's thick black lashes lifted and saw his eyes widen when they dropped to the jockstrap. "Have a good night," Fin said and felt like a god as he left Walker on the sofa, stunned and aroused all over again.

Chapter Twenty-Eight

"I'll have one of the new tuxedos laid out for you. It's going to be windy this evening and there's a chance it could rain overnight. Your overcoat and scarf will be waiting at the door."

"Thank you," Walker replied distantly as he turned and Pierce helped him into his coat. The butler rattled on about the day's agenda but Walker wasn't listening. He couldn't hear Pierce over the sound of Fin's seductive purrs and frantic gasps. He heard their stifled but still primal cries as they were getting off in the other room the night before. They were careful to keep their clothes on in case someone walked in on them and it was driving Walker out of his mind. He'd only seen peeks of Fin's skin and his undergarments. But what Walker had seen... And all that he'd touched...

"Is everything alright, sir?" Pierce asked as he stared over Walker's shoulder at their reflection in the mirror.

"As far as I know. Why?"

"No reason at all." Pierce cleared his throat softly and smoothed the fabric over Walker's shoulders and leaned to check for any wrinkles on his back. He stepped around Walker to make sure he was pleased with the pocket square's arrangement. He was frowning and his gaze flicked repeatedly to Walker's face.

"What is it?" Walker insisted but Pierce shook his head.

"It's nothing, sir."

"Nonetheless."

"It's just that you keep smiling and that's not the sort of thing...you do. Is there something off about my appearance or is there something special about today that I've forgotten?" Pierce asked carefully. Walker stared at him for a moment before he laughed. Pierce flinched and blinked back at Walker as if he'd grown an extra set of ears.

"Everything's fine!" He said, clapping Pierce on the shoulder. "And you look just as dour and unremarkable as ever."

"Very good, sir," Pierce said with a relieved exhale and bowed his head.

"Although... It is a hell of a thing, not being worried about the girls every waking moment of the day," Walker confided in a whisper.

"I concur," Pierce said with a faint nod. "I might not approve of Mr. Marshall's...bearing or his appearance but I cannot deny that he has had a soothing effect on the girls that the entire house has benefited from."

"I'm glad you approve," Walker said while he gave his tie one last tug, then quit the mirror and headed for the door. "Frankly, I'd fire *you* before I let Mr. Marshall go. And he prefers to be called Fin," he reminded Pierce with a playful wink. Pierce jumped and shrank back, causing Walker to laugh again as he left the room.

If Walker was smiling more, it was certainly Fin's fault and Pierce was right, Fin had a soothing effect on the girls but it wasn't just them. Walker was soothed by the younger man's confident, competent presence as well. For the first time since Connor's death, Walker wasn't failing every time he faced his girls. It was a bit like having training wheels or water wings, but for a father who was afraid of crashing or drowning. Walker somehow knew what to say or how to react when Fin was in the room but when words or his temper failed, Fin gently steered every encounter back on track and brought them to a smooth landing.

Instead of dreading each day and all the perils awaiting him, Walker was confident and reassured that everything would go smoothly. Which was rare for Walker while at home. He was fierce and feared as soon as he stepped foot outside his front door but the entire city would laugh if they knew how Walker had cowered and hid in his study before Fin had come into their lives.

Daughters.

Not just one but three who were the light in their father's world but also Walker's Achilles heel and his greatest fear. Not in that he was afraid of Amelia, Beatrice, and Charlotte—although he was—but in that he paced for hours and lost sleep at night over his fear that he was ruining his and Connor's perfect little girls. Walker wanted them to be spoiled and assured that the world was theirs, but he wanted them to be good and kind as well. He wanted the girls to be as fearsome as he was so they could dominate in whatever they set out to do, but he wanted them to have Connor's generous, curious heart as well. Unfortunately, Walker didn't possess those softer instincts, and he was failing miserably at everything but spoiling the girls until he hired Fin.

The whole household seemed to breathe easier and Walker could almost sense a collective sigh of relief when Fin arrived each morning. Walker felt the same gentle euphoria when he woke up but this morning's smile was due to an entirely different sort of soothing effect.

Thanks to Fin, Walker had conquered another much more personal fear. He'd touched another man and let another man touch him without having a nervous breakdown or curling up into a weeping ball of guilt. And Walker didn't feel as if he was betraying himself or Connor like he thought he would, whenever he imagined asking an attractive man out for drinks. It was still wrong because Fin was Walker's employee but it also felt like the most natural thing in the world and safe when they were alone.

Somehow, Fin saw right through Walker and understood exactly what he was afraid of and how to soothe the things that were loudest and hurt the most. He made it fun and he made it OK for Walker to get turned on again and crave another man's lips and body. And that was *tremendous*. It was huge and Walker was using more of his newfound confidence to express those cravings with Fin.

Walker hovered by the top of the stairs and waited until he heard Fin greeting one of the maids to jog down the steps.

"Good morning, Fin. I trust you had a pleasant evening," he murmured dryly as he checked his watch. The nurse would just be delivering the girls to the dining room.

"Just a normal night. Nothing special," Fin replied with a teasing wink.

"That's too bad. But there's always tonight. Could I have a moment? I'd like to run a few things by you," Walker asked and gestured at the sitting room.

"Sure!" Fin followed Walker through the foyer and around the wall. He stifled a laugh as he was yanked across the room and behind a Chinese screen.

"God, I've missed you!" Walker hauled Fin into his arms and attacked his lips. Fin chuckled softly as he wound his arms around Walker's neck and leaned into him. It was magic and Walker felt like a new man as their lips clung and curved into secret smiles. Walker tightened his arms around Fin so he could spin him.

"Careful!" Fin urged but it turned into a muffled yet gleeful shriek as he pushed his face into Walker's shoulder. "No one will believe we're talking about the girls if they catch you doing that," he whispered in Walker's ear, causing him to shiver as the hairs on his neck stood. Walker forgot what it was like to shiver in delight or how good it felt to wake up turned on and excited to see someone. Even though he couldn't do a thing about it until later.

"I have to attend a fundraiser tonight, but I was thinking I'd sneak in and say goodbye to you and the girls before I leave. I was hoping we'd find a moment alone as well..." Walker couldn't think of anything at the fundraiser that would be more enjoyable or rewarding than a hug or a kiss on the cheek from one of his girls. And nothing would hold his interest the way Fin in a thong could. Fin growled softly as his lips dragged along Walker's cheek until he found his mouth.

"That's rather fortuitous because I have a plan that you're going to love. We're going to have the best day ever and I intend to reward you for being a very good boy later."

"I do like the sound of that. You have my undivided attention."

Fin had a lot more than that, judging by the hard-on pressing against the front of Walker's trousers. *I don't know what's gotten into me but I'll die if I don't have sex with him soon.*

Although, it was far more likely they'd get caught. He was having a harder time maintaining his control and found himself flouting the rules Fin had created for them. They were designed to help Walker ease back into intimacy and protect their professional relationship but it was hard, sticking to Fin's rules and boundaries. Walker was getting bolder and he was infinitely happier. Sometimes, it was easy to forget what was at stake and much more fun to get carried away for a moment.

"Something tells me we're both going to have a really big day." Fin sucked on Walker's lip and made everything brighter. But also a little more painful in the pants region.

"You should tell me about this plan before I do something disgraceful."

"Oh! Disgraceful?" Fin teased with a waggle of his brows.

"Stop it. What's your plan?"

"I was thinking that since the girls were so brave at their check-ups yesterday, we would take them to the park before the weather turns. But I thought you'd look like a superhero if it was your idea because you were so proud of them for getting four shots without biting anyone or breaking anything."

"They were very brave, indeed," Walker agreed. "Even though the last thing in the world I'd ever want to do would be to venture out for a stroll amongst the unwashed and mediocre masses we're bound to encounter in a public park..."

"Pretend you're a young child with a pure, imaginative soul, and not a jaded asshole," Fin suggested as he squinted at Walker in disapproval.

"I beg your pardon."

"You should. 'Unwashed and mediocre masses?'" Fin repeated and shook his head. "Don't say things like that around the girls. I want them to have friends," he added, tugging Walker's arm to get him moving. "They're waiting on us."

"All I'm saying is that it doesn't sound like the sort of thing I'd suggest," Walker mused as he followed Fin through the foyer and down the hall. Fin rolled his eyes but his lips twitched and Walker caught a hint of a smile.

"It doesn't but the girls won't be excited about a trip to the bank or your accountant's office."

"I don't go to the bank and my accountant comes to me," Walker said and wondered why Fin glared. "I take it, it isn't a lot of fun at the bank."

"No. Most of us can't swim in the money or make it rain in the vault." Fin nodded at Pierce as he got the dining room door for him. The butler was once again baffled as he blinked at Fin.

"Daddy! Fin!" Amelia was on her knees in her seat, waving over the back of the chair excitedly. "Me and Bea lost two teeth!" She spread her lips in a wide smile and pointed at the new gap. Beatrice popped up onto her knees so she could show them as well.

"Excellent!" Walker said but noticed that Charlotte had her hands in her lap and her lip was trembling. Fin noticed too and winced. "Pretty soon all three of you will have big, toothless, silly smiles. I cannot wait," Walker declared as he went to his seat and relaxed when Charlotte brightened. "I heard that you were especially brave yesterday," he told her and truly felt like a superhero as Charlotte's eyes lit up and she nodded quickly.

"I had to get four shots!" She informed him. Walker gasped and held his tie against his chest as he leaned toward her.

"Do you know, I think I would have cried. You were very brave, indeed."

"I had to get four shots too!" Amelia said and Beatrice pushed out four fingers belligerently. Walker made a sympathetic sound as he sat back and let Pierce fill his coffee cup.

"You're turning into the bravest young ladies," Walker said proudly. Fin hummed in agreement so it seemed like the perfect time to suggest the outing. "Since you've been so good and brave, I was thinking we'd take the morning off and go to the park."

"The park?" All three girls gasped in unison and Walker

wondered if there was something he didn't know about the park.

"Yes... After breakfast, we'll change into our park clothes and Fin can lead us on an adventure." He reared back when the girls squealed and clapped loudly. Fin waited until their gazes caught to offer Walker a nod of approval. Which blew Walker's attention to bits. Thankfully, the girls were babbling amongst themselves about what they were going to wear and what they wanted to see at the park. The rest of breakfast was a pleasant blur until Fin gathered the girls and bundled them off with their nurse to go change.

"A word, please, Cameron," Fin said and waved for Walker to remain behind as the last of the breakfast dishes were whisked out of the dining room, leaving them alone. "You handled that well," he said as he prowled closer and backed Walker into the door. "Did I?" He smiled to cover the waver in his voice. Fin purred as he leaned into Walker.

"You were a very good boy."

"Was I?" Walker was generally an eloquent person but sentences were beyond him when Fin was this close.

"I'll have to find a special way to reward you later," Fin whispered. He dialed up Walker's agony with a playful flick of his tongue. It swept along his lips and Walker swallowed a groan.

"Oh?" *See? Pathetic.* But Walker chased after Fin's tongue as he leaned back. Fin bit his lip while he pulled the front of his t-shirt loose and pushed down the waist of his corduroys, revealing a hint of hot pink mesh. "Oh." Walker tugged at his collar as the room grew warmer. "What did you have in mind?"

"Just about anything, honestly. But I have a few ideas to get us started," Fin said silkily. He raised a brow at Walker as he pulled him off the door by his lapels and turned them. "Now, go put on your 'park clothes' and meet us in the foyer." He pressed a quick kiss to Walker's lips then left him staring at the dining room door for several moments.

"Please don't lose your nerve," he begged himself. He sniffed hard and shook his head. "Stop it. You're going to have a lovely outing with the girls and Fin. And who knows, you might make him even happier and give him more reasons to reward you..." He said and a dreamy smile spread across his face at the thought.

Chapter Twenty-Nine

Walker was actually quite dashing in his "park clothes." He turned up in the foyer wearing a fitted black cashmere sweater, jeans, and leather loafers. The girls had traded their dresses for overalls and glossy black rain boots with rubber bows on the toes. Their cardigans were red with black dots and antennae on the hoods. Walker pardoned himself for just a moment so he could run back upstairs and Fin nearly fainted when he returned.

"Thought I'd match my little ladybugs." He said, winding a red scarf around his neck as he jogged down the steps. He was more relaxed than Fin had ever seen him and it made him even sexier. "Ready?" Walker asked as he gestured at the door.

"I'm so ready," Fin sighed. He enjoyed the way Walker's jeans hugged his ass. He made a note to tell Walker that he needed to dress down more often.

They gathered on the sidewalk, waiting for the driver to bring the limo around, and Fin took pictures of Walker and his girls. The shots were heartbreakingly adorable, the triplets twirling, Walker searching for their car. And for a moment, Fin pretended they were his perfect little family, and a sharp pang of pride and longing filled his chest.

"Let's take a picture for the scrapbook and to put on the fridge in the nursery," he called. There was another rush of pride as the girls crowded around Walker's legs. Walker looked so happy and the girls were practically angels compared to Fin's first day. He told himself he could only take half the credit as he climbed into the back of the limo and sat next to Walker.

"Seat Belts!" Fin ordered. The girls obediently squirmed into their booster seats on the other bench and hunted for belts and buckles. The limo wouldn't get above a crawl through traffic to the East 66 and 66th Street entrance to the park so Fin and Walker didn't bother. They settled in next to each other in the darkened cabin and enjoyed the girls' elated chatter as they pointed at sights and pedestrians outside the car.

"You were right. This morning already feels like the best day ever. Thank you," Walker said quietly. His hand closed around Fin's as they rested on the seat between them. Their eyes met and Fin shrugged despite the way his cheeks warmed.

"It was nothing," he said breathlessly.

"Daddy!" Amelia's focus swung back to them so their hands slid apart and they leaned away. "Can we ride the carousel?"

"I don't see why not."

The girls went back to being giddy spectators and forgot about them again. Fin coughed as he stretched his arm, discreetly strumming Walker's hair at the back of his neck. Walker shifted in his seat and Fin heard a faint, pained groan. *You just want to be petted. No wonder you're so cranky all the time.* Fin risked a glance and felt a whiff of sadness as he wondered how lonely Walker's evenings were once the girls went to bed and the day staff went home. He hoped it was better now that Fin had gotten in the habit of "saying good-night" but it must have been lonely before. Walker's habit of lingering with the girls at bedtime was even more touching. Fin had seen it as the one glimmer of hope for Walker as a parent and the reason he'd given his new employer a second chance. But it was so much more than that, Fin realized. Walker, like his girls, had been clinging to those last few moments of attention and companionship before facing another long, lonely night.

"It really is a beautiful day. Can't believe it's supposed to rain later," Walker mused. Fin murmured something in agreement but he was too distracted by all the premium dad porn.

Dad Porn was an extremely niche genre. Fin hadn't been aware that he was susceptible to leather loafers, bedtime stories, and dads who were proper picnic guests but apparently, that floated his boat.

Sure. Blame it on the dad porn.

Walker was Fin's version of catnip. And he might have been a breath of fresh air compared to the other fathers Fin had encountered as a nanny but that didn't explain all the pictures on his phone. There was a special secret album where Fin stashed all his favorite shots and the one of Walker and the girls waiting for the limo was already in it. Fin would stare at it later, when he was alone. He would imagine they were his and that he'd kissed Walker the way he wanted to before they all climbed into the car.

Fin's well-laid plan and all his ground rules had backfired spectacularly. But he didn't have many regrets as he admired Walker's profile. Walker was distracted by a pair of arguing pedestrians waiting for the crosswalk. His brow furrowed and his lips tightened with disgruntled confusion, an alien watching humans interact. But he was so damn handsome and he made Fin's tummy flip, even when he grumbled about the unwashed masses.

He was clearly in love with Walker. Fin couldn't say no or

stop thinking about being alone with him. And they were getting reckless with their private lunches and stolen kisses. He was mortified at the thought of embarrassing Reid and hurting the new agency so Fin made a mental note to talk to Walker. Sex was imminent and Fin wasn't going to do a damn thing to stop it as long as Walker was ready and the girls and Reid weren't being hurt. In fact...

"This fundraiser tonight..." Fin said quietly.

"What about it?"

"Will you be having dinner there?"

"Unfortunately. Agnes is in town for an appointment and is taking the girls out for dinner and back to Sagaponack since I'll be out late," Walker said, distracted by another altercation between a bike messenger and a bus driver as they waited for the light. Fin made a thoughtful sound as he stretched his neck and pretended to check the view. He could tell they were close to the park by the number of joggers and strollers on the sidewalk.

"I'll hand the girls off to Nurse Lisa to get ready for their date with Agnes then head home," Fin decided. "I'll probably drink a few glasses of wine and try on some new...*things* I ordered. In case I have a guest."

"That sounds like...an interesting evening. Tomorrow's your day off. Don't you have other plans for the long weekend? Walker asked, keeping his focus fixed on his window. Fin checked to make sure the girls were adequately distracted before curling his hand around Walker's again and giving it a quick, affectionate squeeze.

"You know, *it is* a holiday weekend! But I don't have a thing planned. Just another reason I should drink a little too much and do something disgraceful."

"Oh?"

"Mmmmm... I can sleep in since the girls are spending the

weekend with your sister in the Hamptons," Fin said then bit
down on his lips. He wasn't planning to invite Walker to his
place and to possibly stay the night but the words just tumbled
right out of his mouth as a loose plan formed in his brain. *But
we both have the night and tomorrow off, and he looks so hot in
jeans and loafers.*

"Are you sure?" Walker whispered as he looked at the girls.
Fin couldn't resist.

"Am I sure that your sister lives in the Hamptons?" He
asked and stuck his tongue out at Walker. He laughed. It was
lovely, the way Walker's eyes crinkled at the corners and he got
a little embarrassed because he was supposed to be Mr. Seri-
ous-And-Cranky. Fin would have kissed him if they were alone.
He sighed and told himself he'd kiss Walker twice later.

"We're here!" Charlotte announced, sending the car into
chaos as everyone scrambled out.

"Alright! We have four hours until we have to be back here,"
Fin told Walker and the girls.

The morning turned out to be pure dad porn. They'd
wandered through the park, starting at the Delacorte Clock and
the Children's Zoo. The girls had dragged Walker and Fin to
their favorite animals and activities until they made their way
to the Lake and had burgers, fries, and ice cream at the Loeb
Boathouse. Fin's heart skipped as he watched Walker dote on
the girls and awkwardly bask in their attention. He was so
clearly starved for affection, melting each time they grabbed his
hand or kissed his cheek.

And Fin loved every minute of it. He hadn't been thinking
when he'd invited Walker to spend the night but it felt right as
they made their way to the carousel. He and Walker didn't
make sense and it wouldn't work but Fin was proud of the little
family he had rescued, and he was proud of how far Walker
had come.

There wasn't a long line for the carousel and the girls bee-lined for their favorite horses as Fin led Walker around to the exit.

"You've been *so good* today," he said while Walker aimed his phone's camera at the carousel. Walker glanced at Fin and fumbled his phone. He saved it before he dropped it and laughed nervously.

"You planned everything. All I had to do was tag along," Walker replied. Fin wished he could shake Walker and kiss him.

"But you're here!" He whispered. "Do you have any idea how many children I've seen on this carousel, wishing mom or dad were here to take pictures and get ice cream with them?" Fin looked around them before he rubbed his shoulder against Walker's and let their knuckles brush. "Today's been really special and something tells me tonight could be special too," he said softly.

"Are you sure?" Walker threw him a quick glance and their eyes caught. He was vulnerable again and Fin ached to throw his arms around Walker and tell him how much he wanted him.

"Just about anything, Walker," Fin repeated. "It's a little like this trip to the park. All you have to do is show up." He wandered away to get better shots of the girls when an older woman in a massive fur coat and a gold turban pushed through the children and parents gathered around the carousel.

"Walker Cameron, it can't be you! What in the world are you doing here?" She demanded. Fin raised a brow, hoping for an explanation but Walker was frozen and pale. His eyelids fluttered as she barreled toward him. "Don't just stand there, give me a hug!" The top of her head barely scraped his chin but Walker looked terrified as he bent and dutifully greeted her.

"Muriel," he rumbled as he kissed her cheek. "I'm here with

the girls, of course. What brings you to the park? I wouldn't have expected you to venture this far away from your martinis and your poodle."

"Nonsense. Jonathon's walking Calista over there, somewhere," she said with a vague wave of her handkerchief. "And he's got a thermos of martinis in his bag for me. He wants to be one of those Insta celebrities, so I thought we'd take some pictures of him and Calista by the carousel. Doesn't that sound darling?"

"I'm sure it will be," Walker replied dismissively, pointedly focused on the girls and the carousel. But Muriel was not to be deterred

"Am I to take it that you're no longer in mourning?" She asked. There was a slight purr to her words and her nostrils flared as if she smelled a fresh carcass. Walker's eyes widened and Fin discreetly edged away. He wanted to help but Fin had a feeling the last thing the situation needed was a mouthy nanny.

"I think..." Walker began, but his retreat was halted when Muriel's talon snatched his wrist just above his Patek Philippe. "I think I'll always mourn Connor but I might be ready to go out more—socially," he added awkwardly. It was a rather noncommittal and minimal admission but Muriel's eyes lit up and she crowed in delight.

"How lovely and lucky for us! Jonathon!" She called loudly and spun around. "Jonathon!" Muriel rose on her toes and searched the crowd. "Where is that boy?"

"No. That won't be—" Walker began but Muriel ignored him and bellowed Jonathon's name. Fin searched with her, dying to get a look at this Jonathon.

"Over here, Aunt Muriel," a young man called back. He took his time and all Fin could make out were long blond waves and a bland, bored expression. A tall, angry apricot poodle growled as it pushed its way through the crowd to get to Muriel.

"There's my sweet Calista!" Muriel said ecstatically. Fin clapped a hand over his mouth to hold back a yelp of laughter at Jonathon's bright floral suit and Tiffany blue tie. His boots were in the same shade of blue and he was carrying a matching blue tote bag. "Jonathon, say hello to Walker Cameron," she drawled suggestively. She rolled a hand at Walker as if they were at a ball and she was Jonathon's fairy godmother. Walker looked horrified and Jonathon looked only mildly interested.

"Cameron," Jonathon said as he held out his hand with all the urgency of a yawn.

"A pleasure," Walker replied flatly while giving Jonathon's hand a quick shake. Fin was enjoying himself a little too much until the carousel stopped. He became alert and scanned the line as people came out of the carousel, searching for the girls.

"Fin!" Charlotte spotted him first and grabbed Beatrice. She grabbed Amelia and all three squeezed around legs so they could run to Fin.

"Did you get a picture of me on my unicorn?" Amelia asked. The girls began to hop around Fin excitedly while he herded them back to Walker.

"I got lots and lots of pictures! We'll make a collage when we return to The Killian House," he promised them.

"What's this?" Muriel demanded and Fin found her calculating scowl locked firmly on him.

"You remember my girls. Amelia, Beatrice, and Charlotte," Walker said as he waved at them but Muriel snorted.

"Knock it off, Cameron. Who's this?" She asked with a nod at Fin.

"Ah. You mean Mr. Marshall. He's our nanny," Walker informed her as if he'd forgotten that Fin was there. Fin thought Walker had done an excellent job of downplaying his presence but Muriel's jaw fell and her eyes took on a feral glow.

"*I see!*" She whispered as she clutched the collar of her coat.

"No, you don't," Walker replied and shook his head. But it was too late. Muriel's gaze swept Fin from his head to his Converse before she laughed.

"Oh, I certainly do..." She drawled. Her smirk grew wider and Fin could practically hear the lewd thoughts churning in that garish gold turban. She probably wasn't that far off but Fin still wanted to shout that it wasn't like that, that *they* weren't like that. "And I don't blame you at all. He looks delicious but you've still got to move on. You know what they say, a single man in possession of a good fortune, must be in want of a wife. Think about how striking you and Jonathon would be as a pair. He's even younger than your Mr. Marshall," she boasted. Fin's face twisted, he couldn't help himself.

"It isn't like that! I have a master's degree in early childhood education and I speak four languages," Fin stated, but he had a feeling he'd only made things worse.

"Mr. Marshall is the finest nanny in the city and his first priority is the girls' welfare and education," Walker said smoothly but Muriel guffawed.

"And I assure you, not a single soul will give a damn as long as you're discreet but you've got to marry someone respectable."

"I don't have to marry anyone at all and is your nephew even old enough to drink?" Walker countered.

"Barely and you do if you're going to carry on with your servants. You don't want people wondering what's going on over at The Killian House. Or if you're getting reckless and unreliable," she reminded him.

Fin's eyes widened in shock. It was possible that Walker could lose clients and opportunities if banks and investors were no longer confident in him but to suggest it out loud, to Walker's face, in the middle of Central Park was...bold. There were a few coughs and strangled gasps amongst the families around the carousel. Muriel had shouted Walker's name like a fishwife so just about everyone in the park knew one of the city's wealthiest and most powerful bachelors was in their midst. And Jonathon.

"I am never reckless nor unreliable, Muriel," Walker stated tightly. She finally sensed that she'd overstepped and shrank back.

"I would never suggest such a thing but you know how people talk and how important it is to maintain an aura of stability when you're the face of an empire as large as yours," she said. She had a point but Fin didn't see how marrying a twenty-one-year-old man-shaped Pokémon was going to help Walker's reputation. Then again, nothing about being that rich made sense to Fin. Or seemed all that ethical, honestly.

"I appreciate your concern. It's time we were leaving." Walker offered Muriel a stiff bow.

"But...! What about Jonathan?" She said as she tried to follow. Walker's head canted and his brow furrowed.

"I'm sure I couldn't tell you. Have you considered a new stylist?" He offered. Fin's lips pursed as he spread his arms and corralled the girls away from the carousel.

"That's our cue to make our way back to the entrance. The car should be on its way," he told the girls quietly and did his best to be invisible. He could feel Muriel's stare but kept his head down as he bundled them toward the exit. Walker took Amelia's hand and his expression was relaxed but there was a hardness in his eyes as he steered them toward the path back to 5th Avenue. And he hadn't looked at Fin or even acknowledged him.

"I don't like that woman," Amelia said as she looked up at

Walker. He chuckled but it was low and there was a wry edge to it.

"Neither do I, Sweetheart, but we have to tolerate people like Muriel Hormsby, unfortunately. Daddy wouldn't have any money if it weren't for their money, but they're a good reminder that you can have lots and lots of money but lack anything resembling manners."

"Why do we have to tolerate them?" She asked, earning a sincere laugh from Walker. They made their way out of the park just as the limo pulled up.

"Practice, I suppose," Walker replied and held the door for the girls as they climbed into the back. "And I'd like the three of you to do well in society and marry successfully when you're adults if you so choose."

Once again, Walker didn't look at Fin as they got into the car and he was quiet during the drive home. Fin was concerned but he made small talk with the girls until the car came to a stop in front of The Killian House. Once inside, Fin sent the girls ahead with their nurse to change out of their overalls and boots. He waited until they were alone in the foyer to catch Walker by the elbow.

"Hey. About what happened in the park—" He started but Walker held up a hand, halting him.

"I handled that poorly. I should have seen that coming when I hired you," he said. Walker's eyes narrowed thoughtfully but they darted around the foyer, avoiding Fin.

"Wow. I'm not sure how I should take that."

"My apologies. I'm afraid I won't be able to leave the fundraiser early. I've remembered that someone important will be there and it would be better if I stayed," Walker said under his breath as he lowered into another stiff, proper bow.

"Alright..." Fin said, even though he wasn't sure it was. "You know where to find me if you need me." He attempted a smile but it failed when Walker shook his head. It stung and Fin's heart plummeted. Everything had been completely perfect right up until Motormouth Muriel came along. Fin's dreams for a whole night alone with Walker had been dashed. To make matters worse, he had been far more excited about all the ways they could fill the hours around sex than the idea of getting off with Walker. He wanted to have sex, obviously, but Fin was looking forward to the time and privacy so he could spoil Walker with affection and intimacy. "Cameron?" Fin urged under his breath.

"Thank you for this morning. I'll talk to you later," Walker said and escaped around the stairs to his office, much like the day they met. Fin blinked at the tiles and wondered what he'd done to upset Walker.

"Or maybe it was just Muriel. She was awful enough to ruin anyone's day," he said absently but shook his head. She was a piece of work but her behavior wasn't at all surprising, given everything Fin had experienced. He suspected that she had embarrassed Walker and made him feel guilty. "Looks like we need to have a talk." Fin wanted to explore more with Walker behind closed doors and lavish him with praise and affection, but he liked their professional and public relationship just the way it was. He didn't want things to change between them outside of the bedroom. And the sooner Walker understood that, the better.

Chapter Thirty

The dream bubble had burst in Central Park's Children's District and Walker realized he wasn't in the midst of his own personal fairy tale. Instead of a happily ever after, his life was rapidly escalating into a nightmare. He'd fallen in love with his nanny and turned himself into the worst sort of Manhattan cliché imaginable.

How did I miss this too?

He'd foolishly overlooked the possibility of being tempted by Fin and reality had slapped Walker in the face almost immediately. Why didn't he foresee what would happen if it got out that there was a gorgeous young nanny getting cozy with Cameron at The Killian House? Walker had been so desperate to find someone competent to take the job, he hadn't looked past Fin's amazing résumé and the fact that he was available immediately.

Walker had felt guilty and gross after his confrontation with Muriel and fled from Fin as soon as they'd returned home. He had no one to blame but himself for what had happened in the park and the blurring of the boundaries between him and

Fin. Walker was the one who'd rearranged all his Thursday afternoons to have time alone with Fin and stole kisses while he was on the clock. He got carried away and fell in love with his nanny and it bit Walker in the ass the first time they ventured out of The Killian House as a family.

Ashamed and sick with himself, Walker had avoided Fin and the girls for the rest of the afternoon then snuck into the nursery in his tuxedo to wish the girls an early goodnight. Walker still couldn't look Fin in the eye and mumbled excuses to escape him whenever he could. But Walker's guilt and embarrassment weren't Fin's fault.

Walker kept seeing the concerned look on Fin's face as he had hurried from the foyer after they returned from the park. And he felt like hell. Fin was probably afraid he was getting fired again, not that Walker would or that he'd have any reason to do so beyond Fin being too beautiful and too tempting.

So, Walker quit pretending he gave a damn about the fundraiser and had left without shaking a single hand. It took him over an hour to reach Fin's address in Brooklyn, but Walker still hadn't figured out what he was going to say. He just knew he had to apologize and let Fin know he still had a job, at least.

"This is rather nice," Walker murmured as he signaled for the driver to go ahead and leave him. The three-story row house was tidy and rather charming with its brownstone facade and window boxes. He pushed out a hard breath to ease the fluttering in his stomach then climbed the front steps. He pressed the buzzer by the door and gave his bow tie a tug to make sure it was straight. The door swung open and Walker rocked back as a tall, glaring elderly gentleman stepped out.

"What do you want?" The older man asked suspiciously. Walker blinked back, confused and a touch offended.

"Hello... I'm looking for Mr. Marshall."

"Fin? Wrong door," the man said, jerking his thumb to his right, over the side of the stoop. Walker looked and frowned at the steps leading to the basement.

"Ah." Walker jumped when the door slammed shut. He gave his head a shake as he made his way down and around. The little stairwell was hidden by a rose bush hedge and Walker smiled at the bossy cat on the doormat ordering him to wipe his paws right meow. An iron sconce filled the doorway with a welcoming glow and Dean Martin's velvety voice crooned invitingly. Walker pressed the buzzer and hummed along as he waited. He spotted a woven basket at the top of the stairs, filled with what appeared to be several folded scarves, hats, and mittens. A sign was propped against the basket and Walker recognized Fin's neat, confident handwriting.

Free if you're in need: warm things made from recycled warm things.

The door opened and a young man who wasn't Fin stared back at Walker expectantly. He was adorable, with dark brown waves like Fin, but his eyes were a soft, clear blue and sparkled with laughter. He was wearing a vintage Sesame Street t-shirt and boxers with a tyrannosaurus rex print. Walker would have been concerned if he hadn't recalled that Fin lived with his childhood best friend, Riley.

"This isn't a dream so you can't be here for me," he said, without any of Fin's cynicism or suspicion. Walker chuckled softly and shook his head.

"I apologize for calling so late in the evening, but I was hoping Mr. Marshall was in and available." He bowed his head and the younger man's hand clapped over his mouth.

"Oh, my God. You're..." He whispered, then turned. "Fin! You've got company!"

"Is it Reid? I told him I'd bring his kitchen torch back next weekend. I still need it for a science project," Fin grumbled from somewhere behind the other young man. Walker tried to look over Riley's shoulder. He stepped aside and grinned widely at Walker.

"I think it's your boss."

"What?" Fin replied from what appeared to be the kitchen. It was just on the other side of the counter and Walker was bemused. He could see into two bedrooms and a bathroom as well. He wasn't used to being able to see so many rooms at once. Fin rushed around the counter holding a glass of wine, eating a cupcake. "Walker?" He was shirtless and Walker would have stared at his tattoos had his attention not been snagged by the pair of tattered gray sweatpants that hung from Fin's hips. It wasn't immediately clear what he'd interrupted but Fin looked like Walker's wettest dream.

"I..." He took a few cautious steps over the threshold. Walker scanned, noting the vines that crept along the walls and the shelves lined with books and framed photos. There was a green velvet sofa and fringed rugs in jewel tones that drew Walker's attention because it was all so Fin. He hadn't thought it through but now that he was there, Walker wanted to see and catalog every detail of Fin's life away from The Killian House. "I didn't say goodnight to you and I don't like the way we left things," Walker murmured. He glanced at Fin and grinned apologetically. "I couldn't get out of dinner but once I was there, I wanted to be with you so I did the minimum and slipped out as soon as I could."

"You wanted to be with me?" Fin asked faintly, then pulled in a shaky breath and tossed his head at the young man smiling knowingly at Walker. "Walker, this is Riley. Riley, this is Walker Cameron."

"A pleasure but I can tell when I'm not needed," Riley said with a jaunty salute as he slipped past Walker and into the room on the left. The door slammed and Walker smiled at Fin as he took off his gloves and tucked them into the pocket of his overcoat.

"I hope I wasn't interrupting," Walker said.

"You're not interrupting anything. We were finishing off a box of wine and about to throw some chicken nuggets and random frozen things into the air fryer," Fin replied as he clung to his glass and hugged his chest self-consciously.

"That sounds..." Walker squinted at the intricate pattern on the rug between them. "I have no idea what an air fryer is or what it does but I'm sure it's much more interesting than the evening my assistant had planned."

"Poor Nancy. I'm sure it was all really important, though," Fin scolded but Walker waved it off.

"I pay Nancy a CEO's wage because she doesn't need me. This is more important."

"This is more important?" Fin asked and shuffled closer. Walker nodded.

"I wish I was...someone else and not your boss. I don't think you're beneath me in any way—God knows it's the opposite, actually—but I felt like a bit of a dirtbag after we ran into Muriel at the park," Walker explained. Fin slouched and groaned.

"Don't! I promise, I understand. The last thing I want is to be *that kind of nanny*. And I don't want to do that to Reid. He's just getting this agency off the ground and he doesn't want to be associated with *that*."

"You're not upset with me?" Walker asked warily.

"Not at all. I thought today was a success. We were celebrating," Fin said as he held up his glass. "The girls had a wonderful time and you did too until Muriel happened. My expectations were exceeded."

"Mine as well. I'm relieved but I didn't want to end my night without seeing you." Walker edged closer, wrapping his hand around Fin's so he could sniff at the wine in the glass. It smelled too sweet and acidic.

"Oh?" Fin asked shakily. He swallowed hard and licked his lips. "That's really... Did you want some?" He offered but Walker shook his head.

"Probably not." He took the glass and set it on the table and raised Fin's hand to his lips. "I don't know what to do about this —about us—but I can't stop thinking about you." He rubbed his lips against Fin's knuckles and savored the tremor that passed between them. "I didn't think I'd feel *anything* again and it scares me. Sometimes, it feels miraculous and like I'm getting a second chance or trying something new. Other times, it feels terrible. Like I'm starting over and leaving Connor behind. There are times when I tell myself he'd want this for me and I can almost talk myself into it. But then I think about how this would look and what we might go through and that scares me."

"What happens between us is no one else's business but I don't like that I make you feel terrible," Fin said as he slid an arm around Walker's shoulders. Walker shook his head.

"You make me happier than I've been in years. I didn't think I'd ever feel anything good again but I feel alive and there's so much joy when I'm with you."

"Why is that terrible?" Fin asked gently. Walker hooked a finger under his chin and brushed his lips against Fin's.

"Because I was supposed to love *him* forever and I'm afraid I'll lose him if I share the things I promised would always be his. I haven't been able to be with another man since Connor died. I'm afraid of how much it'll hurt if I lose what little I have left of him." He winced apologetically and Fin leaned back and shook his head.

"Don't let him go. Cherish his memory and honor him by being happy. He wouldn't want you to be alone."

"Tell that to my heart. I know that Connor would want me to love again but it still hurts."

"Don't think about it like you're losing Connor. You're just making a little more room for me. There's no reason you can't love both of us," Fin said softly and Walker grinned.

"That's what he would say. His heart was so big and he could always find a little more room if someone needed him."

"Connor was a wonderful man and I wouldn't want you to stop loving him. You should remember him and honor his memory by being happy. It's what he would want."

"He wouldn't approve of me sneaking around with the nanny. Not because you're a nanny. He wouldn't like the sneaking around part," Walker said before a soft laugh trickled out of his throat. "He'd love you but he'd think this was a disaster."

"We don't have a choice and I'm going to make this even easier for you," Fin declared. He gave Walker's chest a firm, confident pat. "I want you, Walker, but I don't want *any* drama. Taking care of your girls is my first priority and I love my job because I love them. I might love you too but I won't let that interfere with my commitment to the triplets. They need me more than you do so whatever happens between us stays between us." He nodded, punctuating the statement with a humph. Walker sighed as he gathered Fin in his arms.

"I might need you a little more than they do but I would never forgive myself if I made a mess of this and caused you to leave us."

"I'm not going anywhere," Fin vowed.

"You *might* love me?" Walker felt a rush of hope and there was a deep yearning for it to be true.

"I do," Fin whispered, breathing the words against Walker's lips. "But we can leave that in an envelope so no one knows but us. We don't have to take it out until we're ready."

"Oh, Fin... I..." Walker was lightheaded and so happy. "I do too," he said but it was strained and hoarse. "But I don't know how long I can hide something this big and this beautiful. All it took was a trip to the park for Muriel Hormsby to figure out what was going on between us."

Fin made a slow, soft shushing sound, blowing Walker's concerns right out of the room. He rested his forehead against Walker's and sank into him.

"We'll be more careful in the future and people will forget everything Muriel said in a week. I belong with you and the girls but nobody needs to know just how much I belong *to you*."

"Good lord. You have no idea how much I need you, Fin." Walker groaned into Fin's mouth. They became frantic and their fingers fumbled with Walker's buttons and his belt buckle. Walker pulled his lips free and whimpered when they bumped into the sofa. Fin's eyes were heavy with lust and his lips were swollen. He was so beautiful and Walker was suddenly nervous.

"What's wrong?" Fin cradled Walker's jaw and searched his face. "Talk to me," he ordered gently. Walker shut his eyes as he rubbed his cheek against Fin's palm. He felt safe and like he could trust Fin with his fears.

"What if I can't go through with it? I want to scream, you have no idea how much I want you. But I'm afraid I'll lose my nerve, or start crying, or I'll finish too soon, or I won't be able to finish... What if I—?" He started. Fin's lips crushed Walker's, halting his rambling.

"What if we went back to my room and just let it happen? I

don't care if you change your mind or if you finish in under a minute. This is a huge step and I think you've been brave enough for one night. Anything after this is just icing, Walker."

"Just icing," Walker agreed. And Fin was so sweet as he tipped his head to the side and kissed him thoroughly, making Walker's toes curl. He stopped worrying about what everything meant or if they were going too fast. Fin towed Walker with him as he backed around the sofa and across the living room. He bumped into his door and Fin laughed against Walker's lips and tongue. It tasted sweet and bright and Walker was intoxicated. He slid out of his coat and tossed it at a chair.

"I need, like, two minutes to bribe Riley into giving us the place for a few hours. Take off your tie and get comfortable," Fin whispered as he slipped out of Walker's arms.

"OK." Walker nodded and obediently tugged off his bow tie as Fin backed into the bathroom and shut the door behind him.

As Walker expected, Fin's room was filled with books and photos. The walls were lined with shelves and Walker was captivated as he explored. There were books on just about every topic and so many photos of Fin on adventures with numerous beaming kids. The bed was under the window and rested on pallets that Fin had stuffed with even more books. Like the rest of the apartment, lights and leaves framed the window and crawled along the higher shelves. Walker smiled at the tall ceramic Dalmatian in the corner and relaxed as he reclined on Fin's bed. There were far too many pillows and a quilt made out of old flannels and t-shirts topped the thick duvet. It was soft and warm and it reminded Walker of Fin. Everything smelled like Fin—like fabric softener and cookies.

He recalled that Fin had tattoos and Walker shook his head. He'd been so distracted by the soft trail of hair that drew his eyes down the tight, flat plane of Fin's lower abdomen and beneath the waist of his sweatpants. Walker was aware of the mystique associated with the gray sweatpant and had rarely encountered them, but he finally understood and appreciated their allure. The bathroom door opened, casting the room in a soft glow as Fin casually propped his shoulder against the jamb.

"Are you sure I can't get you a drink? The girls are spending the night with Agnes and no one's expecting you at The Killian House for hours," Fin said. Walker shook his head as he sat up and reached for Fin.

"I won't get in trouble as long as I ask Pierce for permission to stay up past my bedtime," Walker replied. Fin laughed as he pushed away from the door and went to Walker.

"I'm sure your driver is discreet and Pierce won't say anything but it's a big deal when you deviate from your routine and you never do anything spontaneously." Fin slid an arm around Walker's neck as he lowered onto his lap.

"I do when I'm with you. I don't normally go on picnics, or to the park, or have breakfast in the dining room but I do those things with you and the girls now."

"Because I make you," Fin countered and cocked his brow, daring Walker to deny it.

"I promise you, I wouldn't if I didn't want to. But you make it a lot easier and I'm not as scared because I know you'll make everything perfect."

"That's my job, but what you're afraid of? They're just little girls and they worship you." Fin tilted his face back and traced Walker's brows with his thumbs, smoothing away the last of his doubt. Fin was as calm and confident as ever and that aroused Walker just as much as the brightly colored designs scattered across his torso and upper arms.

"I'm realizing that now, thanks to you. I didn't know you had tattoos," Walker murmured, letting his head tip sideways. A rainbow cuff circled Fin's bicep and a colorful bouquet of flowers spilled over his shoulder.

"Bet you didn't know I had a wild and dangerous side," Fin drawled.

"Wild and dangerous?" Walker teased, tracing the cupcake on Fin's pec with his thumb. "What's the name of this gang you roll with?" He asked. Fin's eyes narrowed and his lips pulled tight.

"Are you doubting that I have a wild side?" He pushed Walker onto his back, planting his hands on the bed as he loomed over him. Fin bit into his lip mischievously. "Are you daring me?"

"I know you can be an absolute menace and give the girls a run for their money. Are these ponies?" Walker's fingers swept along the waist of Fin's sweatpants. Walker had spied some sort of stuffed animal with rustic stitching peeking beneath the gray band earlier as well.

"They're the unicorns from *Where the Sidewalk Ends.*"

"I see."

"Would you like to?" Fin asked and pulled Walker with him as he rolled. He untied the strings at his waist and gave it a tug, loosening his sweats and offering Walker a glimpse of black lace. Fin took Walker's hand and pressed it against his stomach.

"Christ, Fin..." Walker's voice cracked as lust and the overwhelming desire to claim swelled. "I came to apologize for being a privileged asshole but you've gone and turned this into my hottest fantasy," he scolded weakly. His fingertips tingled as they feathered along the lace and Walker's cock throbbed. Fin's teeth dug into his lip as he moaned and bucked his hips invitingly.

"Surprise! No apology needed." Fin announced, clearing away the last of the tension and allowing Walker to simply enjoy...*them.*

Fin couldn't comprehend how enthralled Walker was or how surreal it was, finding paradise in a modest basement apartment in Brooklyn. There was no pressure, no stress, or insecurity. Fin's room was soft and quiet and there were no servants to walk in on them and nowhere for either of them to be. Walker was turned on but there were no expectations, just an invitation to explore.

"I really like it here. It feels like a dream," he whispered and lowered so he could kiss Fin.

"I've dreamt about finding you in my bed but I never thought it would actually happen," Fin admitted breathlessly. He sucked on Walker's lip and bucked again. "I'm trying so damned hard not to rush this but I really need you to touch me."

"Like this?" Walker reached beneath the thick gray cotton so he could caress Fin through the lace but there was a slit in the fabric.

"They're crotchless," Fin panted as Walker's fingers curled around hot, hard flesh. Fin's shaft and sac spilled from the slit and filled Walker's palm. Walker groaned in delight as he squeezed and stroked. "Yes!" Fin cried and kissed Walker frantically, urging him on. Walker's fingers reached lower and trailed into the cleft of Fin's ass. "Yes, yes, yes!" Goosebumps spread across Fin's stomach but Walker shivered and his mouth watered. "We can do whatever you want. I'm vers but I usually prefer to bottom unless I've had a lot to drink and I'm in a wild mood," he said. A whiff of anxiety rolled through Walker at the thought of disappointing Fin. He licked his lips and swallowed hard. He didn't know the names of any positions other than missionary and doggy style. He still had no idea what a savage Fenty was or what they were going to do if Fin didn't have condoms because Walker sure as hell didn't have any.

"That's...perfect but it's been a long time and I've never been really creative when it comes to sex. I know I liked using my mouth a lot," Walker rasped.

"I can work with that," Fin replied quickly. "And I'm creative enough for both of us. Stop worrying." Fin's fingers twisted in his hair and Walker's lips were guided back to his for a demanding kiss. "We can take this one step at a time and you can take all the time you need."

"I'd really like to taste you," Walker said as his fingers strummed Fin's hole. He raised a brow at Fin hopefully. Walker wasn't sure if rimming was still "cool" or if it had gone out of style, like body hair had in the 90s.

"Excellent!" Fin nodded, biting down on his lips. "I'd like that too," he said calmly but Walker caught the slight waver in his voice. "And anything else you want, not that that wouldn't be enough. I'm just about there, actually," he added. Fin lifted his hips and shoved his sweatpants down his thighs, allowing Walker to see what he was doing to him. A thread of pre-cum stretched from the head of Fin's erection as he swore and undulated beneath Walker.

"Fuck, that's beautiful." Walker's mouth watered as the last bits of his restraint crumbled. Black lace wrapped around Fin's pelvis and his firm, round ass. His cock was long and hard and his sac was tight and hairless. "I want you to tell me how you like to be eaten out and then I think I'd like to Fuck you. If I don't lose control and get off while I'm eating you out."

"That sounds *great* too. All of that sounds great."

"Great. Do you have any...condoms? I don't."

"I don't but I still have my labs in my bag and they're all clear and negative. You can take a look." Fin pointed at the backpack by the closet. "I know you're in perfect health and I haven't been with anyone since...way before my last labs, so I'm cool with not using one. As long as you're comfortable with it," Fin added. *Comfortable with going bareback?* Walker kept his face straight and nodded calmly despite the fireworks in his psyche. Fin was so delightfully confusing. He was adorable, with his basket of recycled mittens and scarves and his cupcake and unicorn tattoos. But he also wanted to make all of Walker's sexual fantasies come true and he wanted to do it *bareback*. There was a very good chance that Walker was madly in love and well on his way to a romantic catastrophe.

"I think I can work with that," Walker said with a nervous laugh and a wink. "You'll tell me what to do and when I do something right?" Walker asked quietly and held his breath.

"Would you like that?" Fin tightened his grip on Walker's hair.

"Very much."

"Then show me what that mouth can do. Start with my ass and work your way up." He pushed Walker's head down as he spread his thighs and there was no doubt that Fin knew exactly what to do. The terrible tension evaporated and Walker was left with giddy wonder and insatiable hunger. He rubbed his face all over Fin's stomach, licking and breathing him in as he made his way lower. "That's good. Like that." Fin nodded as he fell back on the bed. He held onto Walker's head and gently guided him, allowing him to explore as he made his way down Fin's body.

And Fin's body... He was lithe, lean, and electric as he hummed with a vibrant, restless energy and encouraged Walker to touch and taste anything he wanted. Walker's tongue swirled around Fin's navel, lapped along the inside of his hip, and swept around the head of his cock, stealing a drop of bright, crisp pre-cum. It had been so long since he had been completely naked and alone with another man, Walker hadn't realized how much he had missed the taste and the feel of another body. And it was all the more miraculous and reaffirming because this was *Fin*. Walker became ravenous as he dragged his tongue over the taut flesh beneath Fin's sac and into the cleft of his ass.

"That's it! Right there!" Fin begged ecstatically. He rested his feet on Walker's shoulders like they were stirrups and they were truly in fantasy territory. Walker held Fin open and dove in. He licked and sucked and reveled in the taste of Fin's hole and his ragged, desperate moans. "Oh, you're so, so good, Walker... More of that, please," he babbled as his head lolled. Walker was so hard, he was afraid he was going to destroy his boxers. He drilled with his tongue and was rewarded with a strained yelp. Fin's grip was so tight, there was a good chance Walker was going to be bald. But he was having the time of his life as Fin rode his tongue. "Fuck! I'm so close! Finger me and suck my cock!"

Walker shuddered at the rush of lust and joy at the thought of pleasing Fin and tasting his release. A bottle of lube was pushed at Walker and it was thrilling, sliding two fingers past the tight ring of Fin's ass and hearing him gasp and moan. He was direct and demanding and Walker *loved it*. Fin got even louder when Walker took him deep into his throat before sucking on the slit in the head of his cock. He was enthusiastic and made Walker feel like a god as he praised and begged for more.

"Ohhhhhh... *Walker*." Fin's body jerked and his back arched. "I'm about to come!" He squeaked in warning. Fin's heels dug into the bed as he held on but there was no way Walker was letting go. He rubbed the pads of his fingers against Fin's prostate and sucked harder. "Walker!" Fin shouted just as a burst of cum flooded Walker's mouth. There was a euphoric groan but, this time, it was Walker's. His head bounced slowly as he sucked and coaxed every drop from Fin. "Holy shit. That was incredible," Fin huffed and laughed drunkenly.

"Mmmmm..." Fin tasted incredible. Walker licked his way up his body, savoring the sweat between his pecs and on the sides of his neck. He sucked on Fin's chin, giving him a moment to catch his breath. "You taste like heaven. Can I...?" He whispered, tentatively rubbing his erection against the inside of Fin's thigh.

"I was hoping you would but only if you're sure you're ready," Fin whispered back. He reached between them and gripped Walker's shaft. "I think you might be," he said as he coated it with lube.

"I'm ready. You're so beautiful and I need to feel you." He wasn't going to last long but Walker still felt like he was a god and no longer on earth as he lined up the head of his cock and eased into Fin. He took his time and slid forward inch by inch until he was fully seated. "Are you alright?" Walker asked once he could speak. Fin was so slick, hot, and tight.

"So much better than alright." He curled a leg around Walker's hip and Fin purred as he got comfortable beneath him. "Now, start out slow but keep it hard and really deep," he breathed in Walker's ear. The hairs on his neck stood as he rolled his hips.

"I can do that," he mumbled, then lost himself in the slide of his cock as it plunged into Fin's hole. *Keep it hard and really deep.* Walker did just that. He kept every stroke deep and grinding until Fin was mindless and clawing at Walker's back.

"You're so good. So, so good, Walker!" Fin screamed. "Now! Faster! More!"

"More?" How could there be more? This was everything and Walker was delirious as he crashed into Fin and lapped at his lips. They were so close, as if they were melding and fusing. Something in the recesses of Walker's brain joyfully noted that this wasn't letting go or severing a piece of himself. He was whole for the first time in years and it was so good, not being alone. He felt incredible and Fin's body felt beyond incredible but it was the ease and the safety of trusting Fin and knowing everything would be perfect, that did it for Walker.

And Walker gave him everything. He flipped Fin onto his knees and the sound of their curses and his groin slapping against Fin's ass filled the room. Fin was insatiable and demanding. He clawed at the bedding and begged for more until his head snapped back and his eyes rolled. Fin's passage squeezed brutally tight and Walker was pulled into his release. All the pressure and heat rushed from Walker's body as he came with a hoarse sob. Cum pumped from his cock, deep in Fin's ass, and Walker bucked hard as he jerked and shuddered.

"Jesus, Fin! That was... You're so..." Walker shook his head. He couldn't find the words. He fell forward, bracing his hand on the bed, and nuzzled the back of Fin's neck and his hair. It was damp with sweat but smelled clean, like Fin's shampoo. "I didn't think I'd be able to feel like this. I didn't think I'd feel anything ever again."

They crashed onto the bed and Fin twisted until they were facing each other. He wound an arm and a leg around Walker, locking them together. Both seemed content to wallow in the slick warmth of their bodies, sated and intertwined. Fin traced Walker's jaw and pecked at his lips.

"I've never felt anything like this. I've been in a few relationships but they didn't last long. Usually, because the guy didn't like how much I worked or because I couldn't see myself giving up work to make more room in my life for him. But this already feels so much bigger, like I'd give up everything for you if I had to."

"You don't have to give up anything for me," Walker said, making Fin chuckle.

"I know. I get to have the dream job *and* the dream guy."

"That's not what I meant but thank you."

"I know. But it's amazing, feeling something this big without it conflicting with my professional life. This time, the guy won't complain when I spend too many hours a week at work or talk about my kids too much."

"No, I don't think he will." Walker couldn't think of anything better, actually. He tried to imagine what it might be like, dating Fin from the outside. While Walker might pity anyone who tried to come between Fin and the kids he cared for, he didn't like the idea of sharing Fin and was startled at the flash of possessiveness and jealousy. It was so rare for Walker to be jealous, he was both humbled and grateful that Fin was his. "I would guess that he feels absurdly blessed."

"We've got a really good thing going here," Fin told Walker. "All I'm focused on is you and the girls. I don't care about anything else." He did his best to melt Walker's brain with a long, lingering kiss. Walker considered asking Fin to pinch him again but that would definitely lead to trouble, and he needed a little more time to recover and for his head to stop spinning. "I'm afraid you've finally got something wrong, Fin. I'm the one who gets the dream guy."

Chapter Thirty-One

"Looks like I did catch a whale," Fin drawled. But he felt like a cat that had just had a very big bowl of...

"Come here." Walker's fingers swept through Fin's hair and curved around his head. He pulled gently and Fin purred like a sated cat as he crawled up Walker's body. He rubbed his face in the dark hair dusting Walker's stomach and chest. He flicked at a nipple with his tongue and treasured Walker's strained grunt. Fin added it to his collection. Every tight little "Oh, fuck!" was precious and they were the highest, squeakiest sounds Fin had ever heard come out of Walker.

And Fin had heard a chorus of curses as he woke Walker up with his mouth. Sore from being murdered the night before, Fin had made himself at home between Walker's thighs. The man truly had the largest set on Wall Street. Fin had nuzzled and sucked on Walker's sac, then tried to swallow every inch of his shaft. He'd sucked and stroked until Walker came with a delirious sob. Then, Fin let him watch as he jerked off and came all over Walker's stomach and his semi-flaccid cock. He'd made loud, greedy sounds as he licked Walker clean and basked in their shared afterglow. It was going to take some hard work and practice but Fin was dedicated to hearing Walker scream.

"I didn't think it was possible but you're even sexier in the morning," Fin said. He dragged his lips along Walker's jaw and whimpered. He loved the way they stung as he rubbed them against Walker's stubble.

"You see me nearly every morning and I'm almost forty-eight, Fin. I'm going to need a few hours." He cradled the back of Fin's head and there was a deep groan of delight as their tongues tangled. Waking up with Walker was so much better than anything Fin had conjured in his dreams and his fantasies. He wanted to stop time and keep Walker in his bedroom all for himself.

"Not like this, though." He brushed his thumb over Walker's jaw, abrading the pad and making Fin shiver. "You're always immaculate and composed when you come downstairs. I like you like this." Fin cataloged the fine lines around Walker's eyes, his wild hair, his morning beard, and the smell of his warm, aroused body. "I like being with you like this."

"Me too." Walker swept the hair away from Fin's eyes and traced his cheek. "It's beautiful, being this close to you and finally being able to touch you."

"You can touch me as much as you want. Whenever you want. As long as the girls can't see us, and we're alone," Fin added with a playful scrunch of his nose.

"You know, I never thought I'd be able to do this with anyone and I definitely didn't think I'd do something like this," Walker mused. Fin didn't like the furrow in Walker's brow or the way he sighed.

"What are you talking about?"

"I usually roll my eyes when I hear about someone carrying on with their employees. I thought I was better than that."

216

"Of course, you are! We both are," Fin protested as he pushed off Walker's chest to straddle his waist. "This isn't that kind of affair. We have serious reasons for keeping this to ourselves."

"I'm sure most people who have affairs feel the same way."

"Fair. But why? Are you changing your mind?" Fin asked warily, an alarm going off in the foggy recesses of his brain. Had he broken his contract with Walker? What if Fin was acting in bad faith because *he* wouldn't be able to face Walker or The Killian House if this didn't work out? How could Fin be near Walker and not ache to touch and smell him? "Do you think this was a mistake?" He asked. Walker laughed as he wrapped his arms around Fin and rolled them. His eyes glittered with joy and adoration as he stared down at Fin, erasing *most* of his doubts.

"Absolutely not but it feels gross, asking you to hide this. And this doesn't feel like the kind of thing you hide. I think you're incredible and you've already made an amazing difference in my life, in just a handful of months."

"But this is all I need," Fin said. He was on his back but he was breathless and a little dizzy. Fin cupped Walker's cheek and kissed him. "All I want is you and I don't want anything to change. We have no idea how bonkers it could get if everyone found out. Let's take this one step at a time and see how *we* feel first," he suggested.

"This is rather perfect," Walker said and lowered so he could rest his forehead on Fin's. "It's just us and this is the quietest my life's been in a long time. What do we do now?" He rubbed his nose against Fin's, making him warmer and drowsy.

"How about breakfast in bed and a long nap before you have to drive out to Sagaponack to pick up my girls?" He offered and Walker smiled. It was so easy and content, and a smile he saved just for Fin.

"I think this might be a dream but I'm not in a hurry to wake up. Do you need my help?"

"Do you know how to cook?" Fin asked and Walker shook his head.

"I know the basics of making coffee and I have a solid repertoire of cocktails."

"Why don't you hang out? You can come out and meet Riley or you can hang out in here," Fin said. Walker's nose wrinkled as he looked toward the kitchen.

"He seemed like a charming young man but I wouldn't mind skipping what's bound to be an awkward exchange, if that's alright. I'd like to wallow in..." He winced as he considered. "This peace for a bit longer," he explained.

"I think that's a lovely idea." Fin rolled them back over so he could pin Walker. "Relax and make yourself at home."

"Is it alright if I use your bathroom to freshen up?"

"Yes!" Fin dropped a kiss on Walker's lips, then rolled off the bed. "I should have an extra toothbrush in one of the baskets under the sink." He jogged to the bathroom and leaned against the door. "You can leave it next to mine, for when you stay over the nights the girls are away." He raised his brows at Walker, hoping that wasn't too presumptuous.

"I'll do that." He nodded.

"Great. I won't be long," Fin promised and turned on his heel. He quickly brushed his teeth and washed his face before pulling on a robe. Fin left the new toothbrush on a clean hand towel but felt self-conscious as he looked around. Walker's shower was bigger than Fin's entire bathroom. Fin had a normal-sized claw foot tub and a glass stall shower. All the white subway tile was spotless and the nightlight/wax burner made the room smell like clean laundry. He decided it would have to do and went to see about breakfast. Riley was waiting with an assortment of pastries from the bakery around the corner. "You're my MVP of the morning," Fin told him.

"From the sounds of it, you were the MVP," Riley replied and held up his hand so Fin could slap it.

"I definitely scored." He wasn't sure why two theater nerds were trading sports puns.

"I'm proud of you. I waited until the sex sounds stopped to start the coffee maker. We have juice, cut melon, and some really nice cheeses in the fridge that Alice brought back from her trip to Vermont," Riley said. Fin threw his arms wide and tackled him.

"You're the best and I'm going to look like a for real domestic goddess when I sweep back into the bedroom with the perfect breakfast!" Fin gave him another high five and ducked to hunt for a tray.

"You're going to look like husband material!" Riley predicted.

"No!" Fin popped back up and shook his head as he pointed. "Neither of us wants to deal with the kind of drama that would unleash. The girls need stability and they need Walker. They don't need the new nanny stealing their daddy when they just got him back."

"Or, they could be gaining a new daddy!"

"That's not the plan."

"But it could be!" Riley countered.

"Stability is the plan. A whole...debacle with me and Walker wouldn't be cool right now. And what happens if this doesn't work out? What would that do to them? What would it do to them if Reid murdered me for making his new agency a laughingstock before he's even printed business cards?"

"You may be overthinking this."

"I'm doing my best just to *think* at this point. I kind of panicked yesterday and looked into a teaching position because

I thought I'd made a mess of things with Walker. But everything's back on track and we've got it all figured out. I think," Fin admitted. His cheeks puffed out and he shook his head. "This agency could be a great thing for Reid and a lot of people. And this arrangement I have with Walker has been great for them as a family. Why would I blow all of that up if I'm happy too?"

"Are you, though? How long before hiding and lying gets too complicated?" Riley asked. Fin held up his hands.

"It's already complicated, but we're going to take it one step at a time and let this sink in first." He went back to hunting for the lap tray Reid had bought when Fin sprained his ankle "There it is!" Fin ducked and practically climbed into the cabinet to reach the tray. Neither he nor Riley were the breakfast-in-bed type, and they rarely had company in the mornings.

"I'm going to make a prediction," Riley began as he hopped and sat on the counter in his pajama pants.

"Do you have to?"

"I can't say I was right if I don't."

"Fine. Get it over with." Fin glared at Riley. He would probably be right. He usually was because he knew Fin better than anyone, even Reid.

"I'm giving you a week, tops before you're tired of keeping secrets. You're not cut out for being a mistress... Manstress?" He asked and Fin's face twisted.

"No. It's not like that and I can live with this because we're not hurting anyone. Neither of us are married, and he's only paying me to take care of his children. We're keeping this separate and very, very private," Fin said with a firm nod.

"A week. Tops." Riley handed Fin a plate of neatly arranged cheeses.

"We've already agreed that we like things the way they are. We're keeping our relationship private and taking it slow." Fin thanked Riley for the bowl of cut fruit, then went to fill the coffee carafe.

"I really like him and I'm happy for you, for what it's worth," Riley said softly, reminding Fin that this was still huge, even if they were keeping it quiet.

"Thanks. I wasn't expecting this. I didn't think that I could love someone who wasn't you or Reid this much. It's almost the same with Walker except I always want to be naked with him and put his penis in my mouth."

"Wow. That's really beautiful. I can't wait to find something like that," Riley said as he slapped Fin's hand and held onto it.

"You will. And I'll owe you," Fin said and gave Riley's hand a tight squeeze before putting the finishing touches on their breakfast. "I'm back!" Fin announced as he returned with an overloaded tray. Walker leaned out of the bathroom and looked impressed. He tossed the hand towel at the counter and turned off the light.

"You didn't have to go through all that trouble," he said.

"I didn't. Riley got carried away." Fin didn't want any of the credit now. It was tainted by Riley's ridiculous agenda.

"That was thoughtful of him."

"Trust me, you don't want to know what he was thinking."

Fin set the tray on his bed and took the mugs out of the pockets of his robe. He handed one to Walker and filled them from the insulated carafe. Fin busied himself with preparing his coffee and was frowning at it as he shook a packet of raw sugar. Walker drank his black and looked amused as he sat on the bed and reclined against the pillows.

"Why are you scowling at that mug like you want to fight it?"

"It wasn't very thoughtful of him at all. He put something in my head that I didn't need." Fin didn't want to daydream about marrying Walker and telling everyone the girls were his, that he was their daddy too. It would start to feel tragic because Fin wanted to fall in love and he wanted a family. And Walker needed a husband. He was lonely and craved companionship and the girls craved another parent to love them and offer the kind of security they couldn't get from a nanny or a nurse.

Fin didn't want to dwell on how tragic it was that he was *right there* and ready to give Walker and the girls all the love and commitment they needed but couldn't. It also seemed likely that Walker wanted that from Fin as well but his hands were tied because it could be devastating for his reputation. *Musk and Bezos haven't been exactly stable lately...* Fin scoffed. Neither man had the reputation of having an iron fist and impeccable self-control.

Walker was feared for his rigid, demanding temperament—his girls withstanding—and would never do anything as reckless as have an affair with his children's nanny. It would be shocking and investors and shareholders would question Walker's judgment and reliability. Unlike Bezos and Musk, Walker didn't own one company. He was a financier in the ambiguous way many super-rich financiers were in that he made his wealth in various ways that often involved brokering deals with other people's money. His judgment was the bedrock of his reputation and a relationship with Fin could put everything in jeopardy. Fin hadn't uploaded his résumé to the public school system's website yet but it was suddenly looking like it might be a break-the-glass option if both of their reputations were at risk.

"I thought we were going to take it one step at a time and feel our way through this together," Walker said, pulling Fin from his thoughts. He nodded and laughed, hoping it would chase away the doubt and disappointment.

"We wouldn't be this great together if either of us were the kind of person who didn't care about how many lies we told or who we hurt," Fin mused.

"This wouldn't feel half as awful if you weren't too good for me. But then, I wouldn't find you all that tempting either," Walker concurred and smiled at Fin over the rim of his cup as he sipped his coffee. Fin snorted as if he wasn't melting.

"Don't say things like that unless you're trying to seduce me."

"My apologies."

Chapter Thirty-Two

Once again, Walker was struck by how dramatically the drive up to the family home in Sagaponack had changed in the few months since Fin's arrival. He was still basking in the afterglow of his morning with Fin and Walker was a little giddy because he was nearly there and would see the girls soon. And he was looking forward to the coming week's tea parties, picnics, and even another trip to the park. Walker usually spent the solo stretches mired in guilt and wishing he knew how to do those things because he'd always wanted to.

But Fin knew how to do all of those things, and he was teaching Walker how to be the father the girls had craved since they lost Connor. Now, Walker sang Dean Martin at the top of his lungs and daydreamed about cupcakes and unicorns. He cringed now and then when he recalled Pierce's knowing smirk when Walker returned to The Killian House in a rumpled tuxedo but even that wasn't enough to truly dampen the mood.

Walker was floating as he drove through the teak gates and

around the curved driveway and parked in front of the gambrel-roofed "cottage." It had been built in 1899 and had only changed hands twice before Walker's ancestor purchased it. The cottage had been expanded to nine bedrooms and had a newly remodeled chef's kitchen but it had always been Walker's and Agnes's hideout, whenever they needed to get away from the city. The honey-colored hardwood floors and the oversized, brightly upholstered couches and armchairs evoked memories of laughter and tears.

In many ways, the cottage in Sagaponack was Walker's true home. His favorite memories of Connor were there and Walker was glad the girls had someplace they could run wild. The property sat on four-and-half lush green acres.

As usual, he found Agnes on the back deck, sitting in one of the Adirondack chairs as she watched over the girls playing in the garden. The triplets were achingly precious in their sundresses and miniature sun hats, distracting Walker until Agnes called to him. She was wearing an oversized blouse as a tunic, a wide-brimmed hat, and sunglasses. Her long legs stretched and crossed as she hugged a bottle of champagne.

"It's so beautiful out, let them play a little longer." She patted the chair next to hers and held up the champagne. She rarely bothered with a glass because she said it was harder to misplace a whole bottle.

"Thanks, Aggie." Walker sighed as he lowered into his usual chair. She offered him a drink but he shook his head.

"You look like you've got a lot on your mind. Why don't you grab another bottle and stay the night? I've got a few joints for after the girls go to bed."

"Not this time. I have to get the girls back to the city tonight." So they could see Fin in the morning.

"Out with it. What's wrong?"

"Nothing's wrong. I've just got a lot on my mind at the moment," he said, then reconsidered. "I spent the night with Fin. It was amazing and I couldn't be happier but it's rather complicated." He kept his expression relaxed and watched the girls and the butterflies despite the wild slamming of his heart.

"Walker! That's...! I think that's wonderful!" She sat forward so she could snatch his hand and leaned to see his face. "Why is it complicated?"

"Come on, Aggie. He isn't someone most people would consider appropriate for me."

"In what way? His age? His occupation? His social standing?" Her other hand rolled as she watched Walker's eyes, waiting to lecture him for being shallow.

"All the above, I believe," he replied.

"*Wonderful.*" She said sincerely and gave his hand a firm squeeze. "Why do you care what people think? And who's going to say something to you, honestly?" Agnes asked.

"Muriel Hormsby, maybe..." Walker said with a nonchalant shrug. Agnes's head fell back as she laughed.

"That old bat! I hear she's trying to marry off that awful nephew of hers because she's sick of his expenses. The boy's mother married a banker, but he ran off with his mistress after doing time for embezzling. Heard he's in Ibiza acting like he's twenty-five. Can you imagine? No wonder that boy turned out the way he did."

"He really is awful and he's got more hair than brain cells," Walker murmured, then shuddered. "I don't know what Muriel's thinking, throwing that boy at me."

"She's thinking you can afford his coke habit better than she can, probably," Agnes guessed. "I'd disown you if you married that boy."

"That settles it, then," Walker replied. She raised a brow at him archly but Walker was more disturbed by the possibility that he was just a trip to Ibiza away from being as ridiculous as Jonathon's father. *At least I'm not a deadbeat.* Walker might stoop to having a tawdry affair, but he would never turn his back on his girls.

"I'm giving you time to prepare him but I can't wait to finally meet Fin. Hiring him was the smartest thing you've done in years. Look at you, you're happy and I can tell that you're sleeping better." A knowing grin stretched across her face. "The girls can't stop talking about Fin, and we know how determined they were to slay every nanny in the city. Seems like everyone's a lot happier since you hired him," she mused. He threw her a hard glare, but she ducked coyly and chewed on her lip.

"I don't know what the girls have told you but—"

"They've told me nothing but lovely things about Fin."

"He's done wonders with the girls."

"And you, judging by the way you're blushing. May I assume that you've embraced your wilder side and found peace?" She gasped when Walker's face became even hotter.

"Enough, Aggie. And you make it sound impersonal when you say it like that. We were supposed to be friends with benefits but...with boundaries. Now it's complicated because I don't want any boundaries. I want it all," he complained.

"This is everything I've ever wanted for you!" She whispered as she hugged the bottle and clapped. "My little brother's in love!"

"Shhhh!" Walker sat up and made sure the girls couldn't hear them. They weren't paying any attention to the deck so he sat back. "I don't want the girls to hear! They've already got their hopes up but I told them there was no way I'd ever date Fin."

"It's safe to say they don't believe you. I may have overheard

227

a plot to get their daddy to propose to their new nanny. They know dad doth protest too much," Agnes warned.

"Oh, no, no, no, no, no..." Walker shook his head. That was the last thing he needed.

"I think it's delightful. Charlotte says you stare at Fin like you want to eat him."

"For the love of...! We need to go," Walker said, jumping to his feet but Agnes grabbed his wrist and yanked him back down. "This is officially a nightmare."

"It's wonderful," Agnes insisted. "And a little 'How do you solve a problem like Maria' but only it's Fin."

"You're not making this better."

"It's such a shame you can't sing or this would be perfect," she said and hummed the line as she took a pull from the bottle.

"How do you solve a problem like murder in broad daylight?" Walker asked as he straightened and scanned the gardens and the hedges to see if anyone else could see them. The girls were distracted with their buckets and shovels and wouldn't notice anything short of a giant unicorn until Walker went to collect them.

"Stop it. I don't understand why you're getting upset. It's time you put yourself back out there and found someone."

"I didn't realize you were that drunk. It's only four in the afternoon, Aggie," he muttered and she laughed. "He's the nanny."

"And? Do you know how many people have affairs with their nannies? I'd be more concerned if you didn't, from the way the girls describe Fin."

"It's not at all like that," Walker objected but his face pinched. It absolutely was. "He's twenty-six."

"Even better."

"The girls need him. I need him," Walker admitted softly.

Agnes reached over their armrests and grabbed Walker's hand again.

"Then you'd better not blow it."

"He's the *nanny*," he repeated heavily but her shoulder bounced.

"So? He's good for them and more importantly, he's good for you. The girls only need a nanny for a few more years but you need a partner for the next thirty or forty years," she said, earning a hard snort from Walker.

"That's rather optimistic."

"Nonsense. Dad and Uncle Hamish are in their eighties and you're their spitting image. All the men in our family live into their nineties so you'd better find someone good while everything still works. I assume everything still works." She ducked her head and looked over her sunglasses at him. Walker grimaced as he pulled back.

"Everything still works but I'd prefer we didn't discuss that. And I did find someone good. I found someone who was too good but I lost him," he reminded her. She sighed as she squeezed his hand.

"Grief is the price we pay for love. It costs you everything but the memories are one of the few treasures we keep for a lifetime," she said, tossing her chin at the girls. Walker pushed out the breath that had caught in his chest and it loosened.

"I don't know if I could survive anything that painful again but at least I have them. They make it better and it feels like I still have the best of Connor when I'm with our girls."

"Because you do," Agnes said with a firm nod. "We certainly can't take any credit for that. They're all Connor, thank goodness. They only resemble you when they're being beasts."

"Thank goodness," Walker agreed with a chuckle. He had been a terror as a child and there was no doubt in his mind that the girls were his penance for those past sins. He became serious again and sniffed hard to stop the tingle in his nose as it threatened to run. "What if I'm not as ready as I think I am? What if I'm caught up in the moment and all the amazing new things? Every now and then, I panic when I'm touching him. What if I'm letting go of Connor when I reach for Fin?"

"Oh, Walker..." She held on tight to his hand and they were quiet for several moments. He knew she was holding steady against her own wave of pain. She had loved Connor too. The three of them were inseparable until the girls were born and Connor and Walker settled into domestic bliss at The Killian House. Agnes kept the girls every other weekend to give Walker and the house a break, but she also kept them because she missed her best friend. "More than anything, he would want you to be happy and for the four of you to be a family again. Imagine how heartbroken he'd be if he knew how miserable you've been the last few years. And think of how *thrilled* he'd be about Fin. He would want someone who keeps that ego of yours in check but also loves you and the girls as much as he did. The girls think Fin's amazing and they say you have fun with him. He gets my vote, for whatever that's worth," she added cheekily.

"It's worth a lot. Thank you. It's a comfort knowing you won't laugh at me if I should decide to make an ass out of myself and date my nanny, like every other entitled asshole in Manhattan."

"As you said, it isn't like that. You've never been the kind of man who sleeps around and chases after younger men. Dating Fin isn't going to change that just because he happens to be younger than you. Let people think you're one of those entitled assholes, then prove them wrong by living happily ever after with your adorable boy toy," she teased. Walker rolled his eyes but his lips wanted to curve into a grin. He might not have meant to do it, but Walker had certainly picked the most adorable boy toy possible. Fin excelled in every way as a nanny *and* he was incredibly sexy. He kept all of that seductive charm hidden beneath his cardigans and corduroys but Fin was even more irresistible and enthralling when it was just the two of them.

"Thankfully, Fin isn't interested in dating publicly and would prefer that we kept things between us as quiet as possible. His primary focus is the girls and I like that. *A lot.* He doesn't want to hurt his or his brother's reputations either but Fin is adamant that things remain as stable and steady as possible for the girls." Walker recalled how their lives were before Fin and gave his head a shake. "He was right, they've been acting out because they need me. And they've been craving emotional stability. We're more like a family now and the girls are doing so well, I can't jeopardize that."

Agnes slanted her eyes at Walker. She was going in for the kill. "What if you lose him because you didn't take a chance? What if someone else sees Fin for what he's worth and sweeps him off his feet while you're twiddling your thumbs? Imagine how that will feel, seeing Fin with the girls every day after he's been stolen out from under you. *Literally.*"

Walker's head pulled back and a befuddled frown clouded his expression. He hadn't thought about what it would be like if things between them fizzled and Fin moved on. Walker would have to grin and bear it, knowing Fin could have been his.

What if he falls in love with someone else and decides he's ready to start his own family?

Of course, Fin would want a family of his own one day. And he only had so many years... Walker had dragged his feet until Connor threatened to fill The Killian House with cats and *he* regretted waiting so long. He would have had more energy for the girls' antics if he was younger and Connor would have had more time with them. He didn't want Fin to wait, now that Walker thought about it. Fin would be an incredible husband and father and Walker *ached* at the thought of someone else having him.

"You have given me a lot to think about," Walker conceded, then rose to gather the girls and shake the dirt out of their hair and sundresses before he loaded them into his Range Rover. "Perhaps I won't murder you."

Chapter Thirty-Three

"I don't understand why this is necessary," Fin complained. He twisted to check at his backside in the mirror and the fussy little Italian tailor Pierce had hired slapped at Fin until he straightened. "Why do they have to be that tight?"

"Because you're twenty-six and you look like that," Vincenzo said around the pins clamped between his lips. Fin widened his eyes at him scoldingly before he frowned at the girls.

"I'm not planning for anyone to see me. I thought I'd hover in the shadows and give your dad and your Aunt Agnes a hand if they needed me but I don't have to wear a tux. I've got my good work outfit." Fin preferred his practically invisible cardigan and corduroys, actually. Muriel Hormsby was on the guest list and her suspicions were only going to be confirmed if Fin turned up in a tuxedo he couldn't afford and started mingling with the guests. None of Walker's other employees would dare. Fin was always opposed to wearing a tuxedo but it felt like an even worse idea this time. But Pierce, the cunning

233

old fox, was using Fin's passion for dramatic birthday lighting against him. He refused to approve Fin's plans for the back terrace unless he cooperated during the fitting.

"It's going to be a fancy birthday party, Fin! You have to dress up so you don't embarrass us," Amelia said. Fin's head drew back and his jaw fell.

"Embarrass you? What's wrong with my good work outfit?"

"You can't wear that to Daddy's party! You have to dress like a grownup," she said. Beatrice and Charlotte nodded in agreement. Charlotte held up a swatch of hot pink fabric.

"You should wear something pink like this underneath your suit! You like pink!"

"I do..." Fin said weakly. Vincenzo raised a brow at him dubiously.

"Perhaps a cummerbund and a tie?"

"Black is fine. Pierce suggested black and it's my second-favorite color," Fin said, giving Charlotte a pointed look. Vincenzo would get the wrong idea if the girls weren't careful. *Technically not wrong, though...* "I still don't understand why everything has to be so tight." He squirmed and picked at the boxers he'd worn for the fitting and Vincenzo flicked the back of his hand. "Ouch!"

"You had better not wear boxers with these trousers," he threatened under his breath. Fin knew exactly what he was going to wear under his trousers. Nothing said "Happy Birthday, Walker!" quite like a black Versace jockstrap.

"I've got it covered," he said, then flashed Vincenzo a hard smile. "How much longer is this going to take? We have cookie dough resting in the fridge."

"It can rest for another fifteen minutes. Do you have any idea how much my time is worth?" Vincenzo asked haughtily. Fin's eyes flicked to the nursery's rafters.

"No, but I don't think you want to make this a competition.

Mr. Cameron pays me an obscene salary. I mean, how many private fittings have you done for a nanny?" He asked, then cringed. "Don't answer that. This is different," Fin lied and smiled nervously at the girls. They were one stray comment away from proving just how much of a liar he was. He thought he'd have a light morning and that the appointment was for the girls' party dresses, only to be blindsided by Vincenzo after Walker left for a meeting on the other side of Manhattan.

The rest of the fitting was uneventful, thankfully, but Fin was still a bit shell-shocked when he escorted the girls downstairs to finish making cookies. There was a sink, refrigerator, and a microwave for crafts and snacks in the nursery. But there wasn't an oven, so Fin got permission from the cook and the housekeeper to use a corner of The Killian House's kitchen. There were several ovens so they wouldn't be in the way as long as the girls behaved. The girls promised to be angels in the kitchen if Fin cooperated during his appointment with Vincenzo. Fin suspected the girls and Pierce had teamed up against him and he did not like it one bit.

"You're finally putting the girls to work, I see," Walker said when he returned and peeked in on them. The girls smiled and waved sticky fingers at him. They were icing state-shaped sugar cookies. "I think a quiz might be in order..." He was all business as he inspected the cookies on the racks and hummed. "I would like to try a...California, Bea."

She cheered and slid off her stool, then sped around the work table. Beatrice held up her arms and Walker picked her up and set her on his hip, allowing her to see the racks. Fin leaned forward and held his breath as she pointed her finger. She hesitated over Florida but wasn't fooled. She found the proper cookie and Fin's arms shot into the air.

"That's my girl!" Fin said as he bounced on his toes. Walker nodded in approval as he chewed.

"And California tastes yummy. Well done, Sweetheart." He set her down and tapped his chin as he inspected the racks. He picked up one of the square states and held it up. "Who decorated this Texas?" He asked and Amelia shook her head. She stretched and pointed at the largest cookie with the orange frosting. "This one?" Walker confirmed. She nodded and he sounded pleased as he took a bite out of Texas. He set it next to California and his fingers danced over the rest of the states, momentarily captivating Fin. "Which state is my favorite, Charlotte?" Walker asked, then picked one up.

"New York!" She declared and there were claps and cheers from the staff around the kitchen. Walker grinned as he took a bite and winked at Fin as he gathered his states.

"You are the smartest cookies," Walker declared. He strolled around the work table and kissed each girl's hair and Walker slowed as he passed Fin. Their eyes locked for one heated moment and Fin longed to offer his lips. The muscle in Walker's jaw twitched and Fin knew he'd read his mind.

"Later," Fin breathed, just so Walker could hear. There was a soft answering hum as Walker bowed and left them.

Thankfully, the rest of the afternoon passed quickly and the nursery was blessedly disaster-free after a day of fittings and baking in the kitchen. But instead of hurrying, Fin took his time as he rounded up all the stuffed animals and hung up all the costumes. He didn't want to miss the evening's bedtime story or each girl's favorite moment of the day but Fin needed the time to take stock of *his* day and his feelings.

It was hard to tell if he was still irritable about having to wear a tuxedo or if it was his misgivings about drawing more attention to himself. But the tuxedo and the girls' and Pierce's scheming had only made Fin feel worse about the lies *he* was telling to hide his relationship with Walker. As Riley had predicted. Except Fin hadn't even lasted a week. All it took to break Fin's conscience was one fitting with Vincenzo.

"There you are."

And there he was. Walker smiled at Fin from the nursery door, looking dashing as usual. His tie had been loosened and his hair was in disarray. Probably thanks to the girls. They often ruffled their fingers through his hair and yanked on his tie when Walker was kissing them goodnight and it was one more reason why this was Fin's favorite part of the day.

But it was getting harder to listen at the door. Fin wished he didn't have to let go when the nurses came to collect the girls. He wanted to help braid their hair, tuck the girls in, and snuggle with them during their bedtime story. Fin wanted to kiss them goodnight too but it wasn't his place. His responsibilities stopped at the nursery door once they were taken away for bedtime.

"I had a few things to take care of." Another lie. Fin smiled and did his best to shove his concerns and his feelings aside for later. He must not have done very well because Walker was frowning at Fin as they turned into the hall to take their nightly stroll. "What?" Fin hugged his cardigan against his chest and acted clueless.

"Something's wrong."

"No." Fin shook his head. "Everything's fine. I've just been overthinking."

Walker hummed thoughtfully and opened the suite's door for Fin. There was a serious edge to it, though, and Walker's frown returned as he went to check for Pierce. They were alone so Fin shut the door and left his cardigan on the knob. Walker waved for Fin to follow him.

"What is it that you're overthinking?" Walker was tossing his coat at the work table when Fin leaned into the closet. He'd never been inside and was stunned at the long rows of coats, shirts, and trousers. And there were so many shoes.

"It looks like The Men's Warehouse in here."

"I have never been inside a warehouse but I should hope not." Walker had removed his tie and his cufflinks. He rolled up his sleeves as he paced toward Fin.

"You know, you're really hot when you—"

"Stop changing the subject," Walker said briskly, startling Fin. "I noticed you do that whenever it's time to talk about you." He caught Fin by the wrist and towed him from the closet.

"It's one of my superpowers. My Spider-Sense always starts tingling when my mom or Reid want to lecture me about something." Fin followed Walker to the sofa and dropped onto the cushion next to him.

"I don't want to lecture you."

"I know but I don't know if I want to talk about it," Fin admitted. He held up his hands apologetically. "I'd rather help with where your head is at than worry about what's going on in mine. My dad says it's a manifestation of unresolved little brother/competitive/competency issues. I'm not as good as my brother or as smart if I've got problems and I don't like appearing unprepared or inexperienced," he summarized. "It's not that deep." He added a cheeky grin, hoping that would pacify Walker. It didn't. Walker's mouth opened and closed several times before he snorted.

"Was I good today?" He asked, disorienting Fin. His Spider-Sense was definitely tingling.

"Yes... You were great. In fact, I was hoping you'd help me with some ideas for your birthday present," he said and tried to put his arms around Walker but was turned.

"We can talk about that later." Walker pulled Fin back so he was resting against his chest. "You know how sometimes you reward me with a thong or a jockstrap?" He whispered the words against Fin's ear, causing him to shiver as he was wrapped in Walker's arms. There was a tender brush of Walker's lips against Fin's neck before teeth grazed his skin.

"Sometimes I blow you. I love that I can do that now," Fin huffed. He had to grab Walker's thigh when he licked under Fin's ear. "Do you want me to do that now?" His voice had gotten a little higher.

"No."

"Do you want to see my underwear?" Fin guessed shakily.

"No." It was a low rumble and punctuated with a kiss to Fin's nape. He should have warned Fin instead. "I want you to open up to me so I can help you, the way you help me." Large, strong hands spread around Fin's shoulders and all the tension in his body immediately melted as Walker began to knead. Fin felt like he was made of wax and let his head drop and bobble limply.

"Oh, God... This is not helping," Fin slurred.

"What?" Walker's hands froze and he became alert behind Fin.

"Not that. Don't stop."

Walker's magic hands really weren't helping, though. He went back to squeezing and rubbing and Fin sort of resented Walker for being so wonderful. Fin's feelings were getting messy enough without falling *harder* for Walker. He was right, though. It had taken a lot of hard work and bravery, opening up to Fin. Walker deserved the truth. Or at least, most of it. Fin couldn't tell Walker about his misgivings over the tux or about Vincenzo.

"Remember how I said that nothing had to change and that what happened between us stayed between us?"

Walker's hands stopped again. "Has something changed?"

Fin glanced at the Peloton in the corner by the window.

Life was a lot simpler when Walker was just a smoking hot rich guy Fin barely liked.

"I did. I thought I could keep everything compartmentalized but I messed up. My feelings for you and the girls are already all over the place.

"The girls love you, Fin."

"I know. Which makes this harder." All the pieces for the perfect family were right there, and he wanted Walker and the girls *badly* but Fin was the one who didn't fit. He was out of place. "Your birthday is in a few days. I can't give anything away but the girls and I are having a lot of fun so I'd like to focus on that for now, if that's alright." Fin had to make sure Walker's birthday was perfect. The girls were counting on him.

"Of course, that's alright. Is there anything I can do to help?" Walker asked and Fin shook his head. Riley, Reid, and Penn had been briefed and were prepared to scale the back wall of the courtyard at 8:00 PM to help with the lights.

"Want to help with a gift idea? I bought something I'm sure you're going to enjoy but I want to give you something...fun that only I can give to you."

"I'm assuming you mean a sex thing," Walker guessed hesitantly.

"Yes!"

"I told you, my imagination is severely lacking. Especially when it comes to sex. I think everything we do is fun."

"Thank you!" Fin was pleased with the turn the conversation had taken. "Come on. *Anything.* Or give me someplace to start," he prompted but Walker's brow furrowed.

"I can't think of anything but even if I could, I doubt I'd be able to tell you without expiring from mortification."

"Nonsense. You've already come a long way. Let's keep it simple. It doesn't even have to be kinky. Is there something you've thought about doing recently that you would never have considered before? Or something you tried and want to try again? Just something fun like..." Fin tapped on the end of his chin, rummaging through his recent fantasies. "I imagined covering myself in frosting like a cupcake so you could lick it off of me."

"I like that," Walker said quickly. Fin shook his head and kissed him.

"I'm saving it for my birthday."

There was another pause and Walker looked confused before he flinched and his face became red. Fin gave him an expectant look but Walker shook his head, obviously not ready.

"Oh." He shielded his eyes as he became embarrassed. Fin leaned forward and held his breath, anticipating something naughty, given the way Walker was squirming. "I've thought about doing...things...in the middle of the day."

"Things?" Fin was careful and pronounced the word evenly, without a hint of amusement. Walker nodded quickly and averted his eyes. Fin was about to ride Walker like that Peloton, he couldn't take how adorably proper and uptight this man was. "What kind of things?"

"I don't know. Very...rough, dirty things," Walker added under his breath. "In a place that isn't here or a bedroom." Walker pushed out a loud breath, as if he'd set down something heavy.

"Alright. A rough, dirty nooner." Fin looked at Walker to make sure that was right and he nodded.

"That would be... Yes."

"Awesome!" Fin cheered and rose on a knee, preparing to pounce. "And well done. You've been a very good boy, Walker."

Chapter Thirty-Four

"Thank you, Mr. Silverstein!" Fin whispered as he shut the door to the girls' room and ran through the nursery. He hurdled over the basket of puppets and slipped out of the door. They'd had a particularly vigorous morning, starting with a walk to the library to drop off their books and ending with puppets and poems from *Where The Sidewalk Ends*. It was always a hit when Fin curled up his finger and pretended the snail inside his nose had bitten the end off. Exhausted from acting out their favorite poems and hysterical giggling, the girls happily crawled into their tent and curled up together. "I've got at least an hour!" He predicted. He passed a maid on the stairs and managed a casual, friendly smile despite the wild fizzing of his nerves. "How's it going, Steph?"

"Can't complain. How's your day, Fin?" She asked. Fin shrugged like he wasn't about to shock Walker's pants off. Fin's as well if he was lucky. This was one of many surprises he had planned for the big birthday weekend, including birthday breakfasts and a movie in the nursery. But this was the "fun" surprise that Walker had picked.

"So far so good," he replied as he jogged down the steps. "And about to be better," he said under his breath. Turning at the bottom of the stairs, he hummed "The Birthday Song" as he headed down the hall. The door to Walker's study was open and Fin glanced behind him to make sure he was alone before creeping closer and listening. There was just the soft tapping of the keyboard so he went ahead and peeked around the door. Walker was alone and raised a hand, gesturing for Fin to come in.

"Did you need something?" He asked as he sat back in his seat. Fin purred silkily as he closed the door and locked it.

"As a matter of fact, I do." Fin unbuttoned his cardigan, then pulled a packet of lube out of his pocket. "The girls are out cold and Nurse Jasmine's covering for me while I run an errand on my lunch break. Want to get off with me, birthday boy?" He asked as he held up the lube.

"Here?" Walker sounded slightly scandalized.

"*In a place that isn't here or a bedroom,*" Fin quoted. Walker processed for a moment before he jumped and grabbed his tie.

"But my birthday isn't until tomorrow."

"Do you really want to have this conversation again? We can go round and round like we did about the birthday cake pancakes this morning, or we can have sex. Want to have a nasty nooner?" Fin asked lewdly. Walker's eyes lowered to his planner and he scratched something off before he nodded.

"Yes, I would." He stood and went to slide out of his coat as he came around his desk but Fin held out his hands as he hurried to stop him.

"Stay there. Just like that!" He ordered. Walker froze and raised a brow at Fin.

"Wouldn't the sofa be more comfortable?"

"Probably but it'll be nastier at your desk and in your perfect suit. I want you to wreck me without getting a wrinkle on your trousers or messing up your hair," Fin explained as he made his way around Walker's desk and pushed him back into his seat. He dropped his cardigan and pulled his shirt over his head. There was a soft tap at the door and their heads swung toward it.

"I'm busy. Do not bother me again for an hour," Walker called, then gestured for Fin to continue. Fin grabbed Walker's face and kissed him hard.

"I'm going to make this so worth your while," he vowed.

"You always do," Walker rumbled, making Fin's knees weak. Fin dropped between his legs and hissed appreciatively as he pushed his hands up Walker's thighs.

"Take it out for me," Fin ordered with a sultry grin.

"Take it...?" Walker's hands shook as he obeyed Fin and quickly jerked his belt and his fly open.

"I'm not here to service you, Walker. I want to see what you can do to me without messing up that suit."

"I see." The words were ragged as Walker reached into his boxers and pulled out his cock. He was already hard and Fin's mouth watered as he scooted closer on his knees.

"Good boy," Fin whispered and Walker's cock jumped. "Now, fuck my throat, Walker, and don't be afraid to be *rough*." He swung his hands behind his back, grabbed his wrists, and opened wide.

"Fin!" This time, Walker was scandalized but a string of pre-cum dripped from the head of his erection as he nervously licked his lips.

"Go ahead, don't be shy. I want you to mess up my hair and choke me with your—"

"OK!" Walker hesitantly extended his hand and set it on Fin's head.

"Moby Dick," Fin whispered. Walker rolled his eyes and brushed his fingers through Fin's hair. He cradled his head but Walker's grip was still tentative, almost supportive as he eased Fin closer. "Come on. This is my first nooner. I want this to be really hot and raunchy," Fin informed him.

"Oh, fuck! Fin!" Walker's chest heaved for a moment before his grip tightened and Fin laughed as his face was smashed against hard, twitching heat. His head was raised and tilted before Walker's cock pushed into Fin's mouth. Fin moaned ecstatically as he opened wider. He wrapped his lips around Walker's shaft and gagged as the head rammed against the back of his throat. Walker gasped and spit curses and words of praise as Fin slurped and sucked loudly. Fin's lips burned as they stretched around Walker and his jaw ached but it was *heaven*. He could hear Walker struggling and straining to hang onto his composure. Walker's other hand clawed at the armrest and the knuckles were white. "Fin!" He growled and pulled Fin's lips free.

"That was so good!" Fin panted up at Walker as he gathered the drool on his chin. "I want you to bend me over your desk and fuck me just like that." He barely got the words out before Fin was scooped up by his armpits and kissed savagely. Walker ripped Fin's fly open and shoved his pants down his legs.

"How am I supposed to work in here without thinking about this?" He complained. His fingers swept into the cleft of Fin's ass and tightened in the back of Fin's thong.

"That's going to be a real problem *for you*, isn't it?" Fin pouted, then gasped as he was spun and his chest hit the desk. He bit his lip and hummed happily as Walker's slick fingers swirled around his hole and slowly pressed past the tight ring of his ass. "Don't you dare be gentle," he said. Fin laughed when Walker slid the thong aside and held him open before driving in hard and deep. He grabbed on tight to Fin's hair, setting a brutal pace that hammered Fin's prostate with each swift stroke. "I'm about to come all over your desk and make you feed it to me."

"Fin!" Walker rose on his toes, filling Fin to the hilt and lifting him off his feet as wet heat flooded his core.

"Yes!" Fin's eyes crossed as every nerve in his body twisted tighter, and tighter, and tighter, then snapped. He jammed his fist into his mouth to muffle a scream as cum pumped from his cock, splattering onto the cover of Walker's planner and the glass top of his desk.

"Fin," Walker sighed into his hair. He held Fin locked against his chest as they fought to catch their breath. He carefully pulled out and kissed Fin's temple. "That was incredible but I feel deeply conflicted."

"Why?" Fin leaned back and searched Walker's face.

"Because that was incredibly filthy and I enjoyed that far more than I should have."

"You have no idea how many times I imagined you punishing me just like that. It was perfect!" Fin reached behind him to catch the cum before it leaked down his thigh. He moaned as he licked his fingers clean and found Walker staring in awe and confusion. "What?"

Walker laughed in disbelief. "You're *a nanny!*"

"Mmmm..." Fin agreed as he sucked on his thumb. "Nannies can be really naughty when they're off duty."

"I had no idea."

"Neither do I," Fin confessed with a wink. "I made that up. I'm going to run by the kitchen and grab a sandwich before the girls wake up. Love you," he added.

"Wait!" Walker captured Fin's jaw for another kiss. "That's it?"

"What?" Fin's left eye slowly twitched shut as his brain finally caught up with what he'd said. He hadn't meant to say it out loud. Fin thought about taking it back and laughing it off, but he didn't want to. "I meant it but that doesn't mean we have to do anything with it yet. We can stick that in the envelope with the other one." He silently prayed and was mad at himself for getting carried away again when it was meant to be a fun surprise. Walker chuckled softly, but it turned into a contented sigh as his arms tightened around Fin.

"I love you too," Walker said tenderly. "Shouldn't we...talk?" He asked with a wince. Fin shook his head and gave Walker's chest a pat. That was a lot to unpack in thirty minutes or less and Fin wanted Walker to take a little time to process those two big emotional developments. First I love yous and first nooners were important steps in any new relationship but Walker was still grieving as he navigated those milestones.

"Not after a nasty nooner. We can do that after bedtime." And Fin had to keep his own emotional mess contained until he'd given Walker the birthday party of the girls' dreams. He ducked and yanked up his corduroys. "This was absolutely perfect and we're going to do it again but I need to eat. I starved myself all morning so we could do this."

"Oh, God. Go!" Walker insisted and helped Fin gather his clothes and pull himself together. He checked the hall to make sure it was clear, then pressed a quick kiss to Fin's lips before pushing him out of the study.

"That could not have gone better," Fin said to himself as he stuffed his hands in his pockets and strutted down the hallway. He attempted a jaunty skip before he turned at the stairs and swallowed a curse at the twinge of soreness in his ass. "But I will not be up for more than cuddling tonight."

Chapter Thirty-Five

Walker had "nooners" in the past and they had been naughty and exhilarating, but they had never been like that. He didn't know who Fin had conjured when he slipped into the study and ordered Walker to "take it out." But it couldn't have been him. Walker did not throatfuck nannies and breed them in his study.

Except, he had and Walker *loved it*. He was utterly spent and weightless as he sank into his chair with a scotch. Walker rescheduled a call with one of his financial advisors and spent the hour alone with his thoughts. They all revolved around Fin as Walker replayed their latest encounter over and over again.

I'm having sex again, Walker noted. He waited for his psyche to give some sort of indication as to how it felt about that but Walker's inner monologue remained quiet. He was definitely enjoying it and Walker loved everything about who he was having sex with, but Walker didn't know how he felt about himself and the things he'd done.

He was expecting there to be some guilt and a lot of doubt but there wasn't any. Somehow, the things Walker did with Fin didn't involve the parts of his heart and his soul that he'd used with Connor. They felt like entirely different acts that occupied entirely different places within Walker. Perhaps it was because he'd been changed so much by grief and then by Fin that Walker felt like *he* was different.

Sex certainly felt different. It had been incredible with Connor and Walker had enjoyed a good run of luck before they met. But Walker had an entirely new appreciation for the feel of another body, naked and intertwined with his. The taste of skin, sweat, saliva, and cum were so much more vibrant and intoxicating after years spent alone. Walker had turned it all off and locked it all up but now his nerves hummed with anticipation and there was a simmering need for Fin. It didn't matter that Walker had just had Fin and could still taste him. The echoes of their strangled cries still rang in his ears but Walker longed to touch Fin and hear him come again. The nasty nooner wasn't the first thing that had come to Walker's mind when Fin asked for "fun" ideas but it was far less intimidating.

Despite a very healthy libido and an abundant eagerness to please Connor, there were several things that Walker had yet to experience. It was entirely due to a lack of imagination on Walker's part. And he'd thought he would have time to work up the nerve to tell Connor that he wanted to try new things.

He didn't how to explain that he wanted to learn more about himself and what else he might be into because sex with Connor was great, not because Walker wasn't satisfied. Walker hadn't given much thought to sex or experimenting until he fell in love with Connor. Then, Walker had wanted to try *everything* but it had all stayed in his head because he had to overthink when it came to sex and expressing himself.

Now, Walker was older and wiser. He knew how much overthinking and procrastination had cost him. That didn't mean he was braver. The sky was the limit with Fin, all he had to do was ask, as Walker had just learned. Fin had already introduced Walker to a new lingerie obsession. And apparently, he was into being praised and liked being submissive as well. But Walker had yet to tell Fin he wanted to bottom.

He never got the chance to try it with Connor because he lost the nerve to tell him but Walker was going to ask Fin soon. Unfortunately, that was a conversation that would have to wait until they had more time because Walker suspected that this was the calm before the birthday storm. Fin and the girls were obviously in charge of keeping him distracted so Walker spent the last few days pretending he wasn't aware of the parade of visitors sneaking in and out of the house.

It was a shame Walker couldn't ask for what he truly wanted for his birthday. But then, adults rarely got what they wanted because they were usually too polite or too afraid to admit that they just wanted to get drunk and watch *The Lord of the Rings* by themselves or get plowed by the nanny.

If anyone had asked Walker last year or the year before, he would have told them he wanted to spend the evening with his girls, cuddling on the sofa with a giant bowl of popcorn and their favorite movies. He would never have asked for that because Walker would have needed at least a nanny and possibly a nurse for backup. Now, Walker wanted pretty much the same thing. Except after the girls were asleep, Walker wanted to ply Fin with champagne until he was in a wild mood and see what happened.

The thought of trying *that* with Fin was both thrilling and nerve-wracking. Mostly thrilling because Walker didn't worry about whether it would be good or not. Fin would know what to do and he'd teach Walker.

And Walker already knew it *could* feel good because he'd gotten himself off in the shower with his fingers several times after Fin had told him he was vers. He hadn't been gentle with himself. Whenever he thought about Fin being that close, sliding deep into his ass, Walker lost control. His hot, soapy fingers became Fin's cock, plunging into Walker's hole as sweat and cum dripped down his thighs. He imagined licking Fin clean after he finished and being told he was a good boy. Walker had chanted the words over and over again, hearing Fin's voice in his ear before coming all over the shower wall.

But how did one ask for *that* for their birthday? That was the nerve-wracking part for Walker. He could barely ask for sex. Asking Fin to hold him down and fuck him the way Walker had fucked Fin in the study was impossible. Walker got dizzy just thinking about it. He'd faint before the words came out of his mouth. He wasn't a hedonist and his boarding school manners and fear of fun didn't allow him to use that kind of language or ask for that kind of attention.

"You're not that man anymore. You're different now and you've got Fin," Walker said, nodding as he propped his feet on the corner of his desk and went back to imagining Fin's filthy commands and breathy moans. "It's your birthday. You're supposed to make a wish."

Chapter Thirty-Six

I t was quiet. Too quiet for nap time so Fin peeked around the door to the triplets' bedroom. The girls were still in their princess tent and hugging their stuffies, but they were sitting cross-legged and whispering.

This could be bad...

Fin tiptoed into the room and drifted around the side, making sure they wouldn't see him if they glanced at the tent's open door. The lights were turned down low so they wouldn't see his shadow through the soft pink cotton. There were fairy lights inside the tent and Fin could make out the girls' shapes. They were like fireflies in a pale pink jar and he was enchanted as he listened to them whisper and scheme.

"What if we told them that Charlotte was hiding and we couldn't find her and then we locked them in a closet?" Beatrice suggested. Fin pitied whomever they'd chosen as their target. He was suddenly glad he'd listened to his instincts and had gone to check on the girls. A little light eavesdropping might help head off a catastrophe...

"Fin knows how to pick locks," Amelia pointed out. Fin's senses tingled and his eyes widened.

"We could stuff the lock with cheese!" Charlotte said and Fin assumed it was her clapping. It was definitely Amelia who had shushed her.

"Be quiet or he'll hear us! How do we know they'll kiss?"

"Maybe Daddy will kiss Fin if he unlocks the door in time for the party and frees them," Charlotte said. The color drained from Fin's face. *He* was their target.

"But he can't do that if you stuff it with cheese, silly," Beatrice countered, resulting in a hard sigh from Amelia.

"How do we get them in the closet at the same time?" She asked wearily. Fin decided he'd rather sneak away and pretend he hadn't heard them.

He crept back into the hallway and dashed to the nursery. Fin did his best to ignore the pang of guilt as he headed to the craft table to tidy and restock the supplies. He found a folded note among the scraps of construction paper and his heart sank when he unfolded it. He and Walker had been rendered in bright crayon colors and tears flooded Fin's eyes as he traced Walker's boxy gray suit and the heart encircling them.

"Oh, no..." Fin dropped onto the edge of the table. They wouldn't understand how impossible it was but Fin wished he could give the girls what they wanted. He had a feeling they would be tickled to see him and Walker holding hands or kissing. They would adore how tender and attentive Walker was and the way he laughed when Fin teased him. *Damn it, Riley. Why do you always have to be right?* There was a tap at the door and the happy family fantasy faded and Fin was in the nursery again.

"Have they been down for long?" Walker asked. Fin shook his head and sniffed to clear his vision while Walker silently shut the door behind him.

"They haven't fallen asleep yet. You should see this." He held up the drawing as Walker pulled him into his arms. Walker made a knowing sound but he smiled as he admired it.

"I think that's Beatrice's work. That's how she usually draws my suits," he said.

"It's sweet that you can tell the girls' art apart," Fin groaned as he sank against Walker's chest and kissed his cheek. "But this is really sad, Walker."

"Why? I think your cardigan looks rather cheerful. It's pink and it has a heart on it," Walker said and pointed at the little heart on the pocket.

"The picture's perfect. But this situation is really sad. I felt bad about the lying but didn't think we were hurting anyone. I'm starting to feel selfish. We're hiding *this* because we're afraid of the social ramifications but imagine how happy they'd be! They'd be so thrilled but we're keeping it to ourselves."

"I thought you didn't want anyone to know. You said..." Walker frowned as he drew back and Fin nodded quickly.

"I don't! I still think it would bring too much attention and you should be more focused on the girls. Not us," he said. "I just feel terrible because we can't share this with them."

"We could if we wanted to, we'd just have to find some way to ensure they don't tell another living soul," Walker offered but he looked as sick as Fin felt at the idea. Fin shook his head.

"Absolutely not. They wouldn't be able to help themselves and I would never expect them to lie or hide anything for us." He'd leave The Killian House before he allowed the girls to lie for him and Walker.

Fin hadn't submitted his application to the school system yet, but he'd made a few calls and was told he had his choice of a number of positions. That hadn't moved Fin because none of those positions spoke to him, but he was thinking about a job teaching second grade. He wouldn't be happy but Fin would stick it out for Walker and the girls. He just didn't know how to tell Walker he was thinking about going back to teaching.

"Good. I wouldn't either and there isn't a chance it would work." Walker was distant as he folded the picture and tucked it into his coat's inner pocket.

"I'm sorry. I didn't mean to bring you down on your birthday." Fin stretched toward his lips but Walker held him off.

"You and I have different definitions of sad and our family has survived worse," Walker replied tightly.

"Wait. I didn't mean—"

"I need to go." Walker raised a hand, signaling that he was done. Fin knew when it was his place to push or stand his ground but this wasn't it.

"I'm sorry. Please don't forget, you're supposed to meet me downstairs at seven."

"I won't. And I'll be dressed in a tux," Walker said and bowed as he smoothly backed out of the room and left Fin. The door shut softly behind him and Fin groaned as he sat back down on the edge of the craft table.

"Way to go, Fin. You made him feel guilty *and* sad on his birthday." He rubbed his temple as his head began to ache. "I'll figure out how to make this right," he vowed but Fin knew it was time to break the glass as he scanned the nursery. "I have to leave them."

Chapter Thirty-Seven

Pierce looked like he was going to have an aneurysm as he mumbled an excuse about a delivery mix-up and a dinner delay. But Walker truly didn't mind the hassle of dressing himself in a tuxedo on this particular evening. He usually preferred for Pierce to oversee all the little details like the waistcoat, the cufflinks, and the arrangement of the bow tie and the pocket square. It allowed Walker's mind time to wander. He often practiced speeches or made last-minute mental checklists of whom to flatter and whom to avoid before an important formal event.

But Walker didn't want his mind to wander as he dressed for what was most likely his surprise birthday party. He had caught little wisps of whispered conversations and spotted tell-tale signs of preparations throughout the afternoon. Walker was secretly looking forward to whatever Fin and the girls had planned, so he was happy to feign ignorance and play along. But after his retreat from the nursery, Walker was happy to have something tedious like donning a tuxedo to distract him.

He'd been short with Fin and had run away because

Walker *wanted* to tell the girls. He'd gotten excited at the thought of not giving a damn about the consequences and giving in to the joy of the moment. Because that's what it was like, loving Fin. Walker wanted to squeal and cheer and sometimes, he felt like twirling like his girls, he was so happy when Fin walked into the room. Then, Fin had gone and brought reality back into it and popped Walker's happy imaginary bubble.

It would have made the night truly special and the girls would have been so happy but Fin was right. They'd turn all of their lives upside down in ways neither of them could predict. Walker wondered if there was a chance it wouldn't be a disaster and remembered his conversation with Agnes. She was right too. Connor wouldn't want him to hold back if there was a chance Walker could be happy.

Connor had never given a damn about society or keeping up appearances. He fell in platonic love with Agnes when they met at Tisch and then fell in love with her uptight little brother when she brought Connor to the cottage one winter break. Walker objected to sharing his sister and his favorite holiday tradition until she shoved Connor through the front door of the cottage. It had been love at first sight but Connor had loved Walker *despite* his wealth and good breeding.

Walker had run away from Fin because he realized he was letting the girls and Connor down again. He was disappointed in himself for how easy it was to agree with Fin and do what was the safest and most comfortable.

"What the hell am I doing?" He asked the mirror. "I'm letting down everyone who matters," he said and accepted that the people who didn't matter were just going to have to mind their own damn business or go to Hell. Walker stepped back and gave his reflection one last inspection, then nodded. He already felt lighter and was smiling as he hurried from his room and went to meet Fin in the foyer. "I have to tell him before I shake a single hand or kiss a single cheek," he decided. He was grinning when he reached the gallery and the stairs but froze when he spotted Agnes. "What are you doing here?" His brows rose as he admired her ice blue lace gown. It was a sleek one-shoulder design with a tastefully dramatic train. Her salt-and-pepper hair was swept into a loose bun and Walker thought she looked like a princess.

"I was told to turn up right before seven in something *fancy*," she informed him.

"You look stunning," he said as he kissed her cheek.

"Happy birthday, baby brother. You look as dashing as ever."

"You used to tease me and you told me I looked like a bellhop once," he recalled and her eyes lit up as she remembered how gawky he looked as a teenager in his first tuxedo. "You were all feet and you had the longest neck, you poor thing!"

"Bold of you to bring up feet," he drawled. Agnes's jaw fell and she swatted him.

"Don't you dare! I can't help that I got Daddy's big feet."

"You certainly did," Walker murmured and tilted, then whistled at Agnes's silver kitten heels.

"Knock it off or this will be your last birthday," she growled before grabbing Walker's arm. She looked around and stepped closer. "I finally met Fin and *wow*! I came early to check on the girls and walked in on the sweetest little dancing lesson in the nursery. He was teaching Beatrice how to waltz and I wanted to eat him right up. He's perfect and I'll make the rest of your life miserable if you don't marry him."

"Calm down." Walker checked the halls and the opened dining room and sitting room to make sure it was still safe. "I've already decided that we can't keep this a secret any longer. I want to tell the girls and go about my life in peace with Fin. I can't worry about what people think of me anymore. Not if it means I can't be with Fin," he told her. Agnes pressed her hand to her heart and sighed.

"I am so glad. I didn't think he'd live up to the girls' descriptions, but he's even lovelier. And hotter. He had me reconsidering motherhood so I could hire him..."

"Wonderful. I would appreciate it if you kept that to yourself until I've had a chance to work this out with Fin."

Walker looked behind Agnes and nearly fainted when he spotted Fin at the end of the hall. He was coming in from the terrace and everything slowed around them as Fin smiled at Walker. Fin had traded his cardigan and corduroys for a fitted tuxedo and Walker's brain was utterly broken.

"Uhhh..." He couldn't remember what they were talking about or where they were going. All he understood was that Fin looked incredible. There was a powerful urge to rub himself all over Fin in that tux. He wanted to start by licking Fin's patent leather loafers. They had a liquid-shine finish and Fin had worn them sans socks.

"There's the man of the night!" Fin clapped his hands together as he hurried toward them, snapping Walker out of the filthy fantasy and back to reality. Agnes laughed as she pointed at Walker.

"Keep it to myself? Darling, you've got about fifteen minutes before everyone with decent vision figures it out. It's all over your face. And the front of your trousers," she added suggestively and Walker pushed her away.

"You look incredible, Fin," Walker said. He reached for Fin's hands and wished they were headed somewhere private. Soundproof would be helpful as well. Fin took Walker's hands and searched his face.

"About earlier—" He started but Walker shook his head.

"That wasn't your fault. You were right about us—me—being selfish and I panicked and left before you said something else I didn't want to hear."

"I get it..." Fin said slowly and widened his eyes at Walker before he tossed his head at Agnes. "And there's something I would like to tell you but it's kind of private," he said, mouthing an apology at Agnes.

"Oh! That's my cue! I'll be out back and good luck!" She pressed a loud kiss to Walker's cheek, then picked up the skirt of her dress and ran for the terrace doors. Fin laughed as he watched her go.

"Your sister is as wonderful as I imagined she'd be," he said.

"She said the same thing about you. She thinks you're perfect and that I'd be a fool if I let you slip through my fingers," Walker told Fin as he gathered his hands in his. "She's right and I know it's going to be complicated and that it could even get a little gross once people know but I don't want to worry about that anymore."

"We don't have to!" Fin raised Walker's hands to his lips so he could kiss them. "It's not going to be complicated because I'm going to quit!" He was so excited about it and bit his lip to hold back a shriek.

"What? No!" Walker shouldn't have yelled, but he was panicking and could already hear the girls' wailing.

"Just from my position!" Fin reassured him but Walker's hand slapped across his forehead.

"I don't understand but everyone's going to kill me!"

"Only for a little while. Then, I'll be back forever! Or until you decide you've had enough of me," Fin added sheepishly.

"I'll never have enough but what are you talking about?" Walker's hand hovered in front of his forehead in case he needed to slap it again.

"I was offered a job as a second-grade teacher at a public

school a few blocks from here. I figured that if we were quiet for like six months or so, nobody would make too much of a fuss if you decided to start dating a hot young teacher. If you don't mind dating a simple elementary school teacher," he qualified.

"Mind?" Walker was lightheaded again. There was no way he was going to let Fin take that job but Walker was profoundly touched. "You said you didn't like teaching in a classroom and it would be a tremendous pay cut."

"I don't care. I'll have you and the girls and I'll still be working with kids."

"For about 90% less than you make now," Walker argued.

"You're missing the part where I get the man of my dreams and the triplets," Fin said smugly. He patted Walker's chest soothingly, distracting him for a moment.

"What about the girls? They'll be without a nanny if you quit."

"I won't have a problem finding a replacement. Reid knows the girls have turned over a new leaf and will cooperate because you'll be here to help them with the transition. We'll explain to the girls that it's temporary and I'll still sneak in on the weekends to see them. That way, it won't be a big deal if they tell their friends because you'll be dating some school teacher, instead of their nanny."

"I love you but I can't let you do this," Walker said as he lowered his head and kissed Fin.

"I love you too and it's the perfect solution. I was waiting until tomorrow to tell the girls and everyone else because tonight's your night," Fin said and stepped back so he could offer Walker his arm. "I'll walk you to the door, but then we have to pretend we aren't waiting to rip these tuxedos off each other. I won't be able to flirt with you once we step outside but just remember that you owe me a dance later." Fin's teeth scraped over his lip as his eyes held Walker's, telegraphing his intentions. Walker groaned at the door.

"I take it there are a lot of people out there and we have to stay."

"Everyone is out there. Pierce turned the back garden into a birthday gala while you were getting dressed. You'd better act like you're blown away and give the girls all the credit. It was all their idea. I was just the middleman and relayed their wishes to Pierce. He gave them everything but the bounce castle and the water balloon fight. Even though I did insist that you would have loved a bounce castle."

"I wouldn't but I appreciate everything you've done and Pierce's better judgment," Walker said. He hooked a finger under Fin's chin and kissed him. "This is already the best birthday I've had in a long time. We're going to pick up this conversation later, when we're alone again, because I don't want to wait months to celebrate how amazing this feels."

"You don't?" Fin whimpered. "We have to go! Can you pretend for a few more hours, and then we'll figure it out?"

"I don't know if I can make any promises, Fin. This is the first time I've seen you in a tailored garment and it's hard for me to think straight right now."

"Really?" Fin asked breathlessly as he swayed toward Walker's lips. The door opened and they jumped apart.

"Are you two coming?" Agnes urged, stomping her foot impatiently. "The girls are seconds away from storming in here and demanding you present yourselves. How dare you keep us waiting when there's cake?"

"We'll be right there!" Fin laughed and shooed her off. "She's pretty great, and we'll figure this out as soon as we have a moment to ourselves." He kissed Walker's cheek, scattering his wits. "Remember to act surprised," he said before he threw the door open.

"OK..." Walker replied but it faded as he took in the sea of guests in formalwear, the explosion of string lights and paper lanterns decorating the trees, the six-tiered birthday cake, and the band on the other side of the pool. "How did you all do this in an hour?"

"We snuck in last night while you were sleeping to do the lights and Pierce has been staging everything in the kitchen until the last minute," Fin explained out of the corner of his mouth. "The girls were behind all of this," he said loudly. Walker clapped as he jogged down the steps and looked for them. They were with Agnes by the cake and ran to Walker when he kneeled and opened his arms. They looked like angels in their pastel purple gowns.

"Happy birthday, Daddy!" They cheered as they crashed into him. Walker's heart swelled with joy as he was squeezed by three sets of tiny arms. He buried his face in shiny black ringlets and kissed each girl's cheek.

"Thank you. You've outdone yourselves." Walker smiled at Fin who was hovering behind the girls, then gave Amelia's nose a flick. "Let's take a look at this cake."

"Yes! Yes! Yes!" Charlotte's arms shot up as she spun.

"Can I help you cut it?" Amelia asked.

"You're going to have to. I've never cut a cake that big," Walker said as he stood and steered them closer to the table. A cake knife was handed to him and Walker was momentarily overwhelmed as the crowd drew in around them. He couldn't see Fin or Agnes but his entire Rolodex was there, including his accountants, what looked like most of Walker's New York workforce, his personal trainer, and numerous socialites he barely knew... Even Muriel Hormsby was there. Which meant her awful nephew was close by. "This is a lot of people," he noted.

"Can we get a little help from the band?" Fin asked loudly

as he scooted in behind Walker and the girls. "Happy birthday to you..." Fin began and the crowd and the band joined in. Everyone was singing and the girls were elated so Walker put on a brave face and smiled despite an awful sense of foreboding. He had a feeling things were about to go terribly awry.

Chapter Thirty-Eight

Perhaps inviting every single person in Walker's Rolodex wasn't the best idea, judging by the bewildered expression on his face, but he was handling it well. The girls were thrilled because everyone had turned out and dressed in their snotty rich person best to wish Walker a happy birthday.

Walker pretended the cake knife was too heavy for him to hold on his own and allowed the girls to help him cut the first slice. He let each girl have a taste before he took a bite, then handed his plate over to Agnes.

"Let me make a toast so you all can go back to enjoying your evening," Walker announced.

Pierce materialized with a glass of champagne for Walker as footmen made their way around the back terrace and the garden with glasses for the guests. Fin was handed a glass and raised it to Walker. Their eyes clung for a moment before Walker cleared his throat and looked around.

"Thank you for coming and making this a very special celebration for our family. I was expecting something a little more low-key but my girls went all out. They did an amazing job planning this and I want to thank them and everyone who helped make all of this possible." Walker's gaze touched Fin's before he scanned the crowd and found Pierce by the cake. He bowed his head at Pierce and Fin, then held up his glass. "To another year and another trip around the sun. Let's hope I get it right this time," he said. Everyone laughed and raised their glasses.

The music resumed and Walker was swallowed by party-goers eager to shake his hand and congratulate him. Walker endured it all with a bright smile and Fin made a mental note to add that to the list of reasons why Walker had been a very good boy. He felt a tickle of arousal and Fin hummed along with the music and waited for the crowd around Walker to thin enough to get another peek at him in his tuxedo. No one wore a tux like Walker Cameron III.

"You'd better get in there and rescue my brother," Agnes said, appearing at Fin's side. She had another slice of cake but Fin shook his head.

"I'll have some later," he said, resulting in a dry snort from Agnes.

"I didn't bring this for you." She shoveled a large bite into her mouth and her eyes narrowed as she watched over her brother. Fin had only a few brief exchanges with her, but he was already madly in love with Walker's older sister. She was almost fifty and Fin was drawn to the sparkle of mischief in her pale gray eyes. Agnes was Walker's opposite in just about every way, but they could have been twins and they had all the same mannerisms. She was free-spirited, outspoken, and fiercely protective of her "little brother." "You can't dance if you're eating cake."

"Neither can you." Fin winked and held out a hand.

"Not me!" She snapped, but she punctuated it with a

266

mischievous grin and tipped her chin at Walker. "Go and rescue my brother."

"What if I'd rather dance with you?" Fin said smoothly and gave her a nudge. As much as he would have loved to, Agnes's plan was terrible.

"What if I was secretly a Romanov? Since we're telling tall tales!" She whispered excitedly, then threw a hand at Fin. "Hurry up and ask him to dance before someone else does. I've spotted four very single gay men in need of a rich husband already, including that awful Jonathon. Do you know his Aunt Muriel's been telling everyone that Walker's back on the market now that his children are all sorted out?"

"That's..." Fin winced as he rose on his toes and tried to find Walker. "I'm sure he can handle them." He wasn't going to be pleased with Fin for turning his birthday into a speed-dating mixer.

"Huh. I was hoping you'd be jealous and make this party interesting."

"Hey! I planned most of this!" Fin said.

"And you pulled it off flawlessly. But you didn't plan any fireworks and my brother's life has been too quiet for far too long."

"No. You've got the wrong man." Fin pushed his hand out defiantly. "I won't have any scenes. I promised the girls that tonight would be perfect and all about them and Walker."

"You might be a brilliant nanny but you clearly don't under-stand those girls' devious little minds as well as you think you do. They weren't planning a birthday party. You're Cinderella and Walker's Prince Charming."

"What?" Fin shook his head quickly. "On, no..." His face burned as he looked around, then down at his new tuxedo. "What happened to my Spider-Sense? I should have seen this coming. I was so distracted with the party and Walker," he mumbled to himself, then looked at Agnes. "The last thing I want to do is disappoint them but your brother can't turn his life upside down for me. That would make everything so...*messy!*"

"Why do you say that like it's a bad thing? What about you? What do you want?" She asked. She handed what was left of her cake to a passing footman and took Fin's hand. "Pretend Walker doesn't care about whether his world is right-side-up or if it's messy. Pretend you don't care about what anyone else thinks. What do you want, Fin?" Agnes pulled him into her arms and made him laugh when she led. Walker told Fin that Agnes would have been the black sheep of the family if the Camerons were the sort of family that acknowledged bad behavior. Fin wished that Walker could be as free as her but he had different responsibilities. Fin had responsibilities as well.

"If this was a romance novel or a movie, I'd go after him. I *am* going after him. Just...sensibly," he said but frowned as a dashing older gentleman sidled up to Walker. He gestured as if he was asking Walker to dance but Walker declined and lifted Charlotte up and onto his hip so he could spin her around with the other dancers. Fin hadn't realized he was holding his breath. "I love Walker and the girls," he continued and gave his head a shake. "I have a plan and I've already offered my resignation," he added with a loaded look.

"Oh, Fin. You really are too perfect," Agnes sighed. The song came to a close and she wound her arm around Fin's. "Let's see what we can do to help him," she whispered. Fin would have preferred to stay as far away as possible but she wouldn't release his arm. "Walker! Over here!" She waved as she dragged Fin along. He was happy to see the triplets again but they were quickly surrounded.

"Stop moving, Cameron!" Muriel Hormsby shouted and they turned. She pushed through the crowd, looking like a giant flamingo in her bright fuchsia gown and turban. One of her knotted, jewel-encrusted fists was wrapped around Jonathon's wrist. Fin felt a whiff of sympathy. "Happy birthday, my boy. Kiss me." She offered her cheek and Walker bent and dutifully kissed it.

"Thank you for coming," he said blandly.

"I wouldn't have missed it. Gorgeous party and so good of you to open up the house again now that you're out of mourning."

"Muriel!" Agnes barked, then bit down on her lips. "You look lovely. Is that a new nose?" She recovered as she leaned in to kiss Muriel's cheek.

"Where are your manners, Agnes? You remember Jonathon."

"Of course," Agnes murmured and glanced at the young man. Her nails dug into Fin's arm as they both smiled at Jonathon. His hair had been styled to look like it was still wet and his black tuxedo had a glossy satin finish. He'd also decided to skip a shirt and everyone was treated to a view of his pierced nipples adorned by a chain of black diamonds. "Don't you look...like a lot," Agnes choked out.

"He's famous on Instagram," Muriel said haughtily. Her focus swung back to Walker and she smiled sweetly at him. "You two should dance. Jonathon was just telling me that he thought you looked very fit for a man your age. Isn't that right?" She asked him, but he was making eyes at one of the footmen if Fin was correct. Fin leaned to look around Muriel and guessed it was the larger one with the beefy ass and thighs. "Jonathon!" Muriel demanded and he jumped and nodded.

"Mmmhmm!" He rolled his eyes and held up a hand as if he didn't know what else to do with her. No one did and they all shook their heads.

"Jonathon would love to dance with you, Cameron," Muriel

declared. Walker grimaced but Muriel didn't notice or seem to care that Jonathon wasn't paying attention. She elbowed him and pushed him at Walker.

"I sure would!" Jonathon said with another roll of his eyes.

"I'm afraid I've already promised this dance to Beatrice," Walker said as he swooped her into his arms and escaped.

"Will you dance with me, Fin?" Amelia asked. She rose on her toes and reached for Fin, but he felt like he was being saved as he picked her up and settled her on his hip.

"Next year, we don't invite this many people," he told her. She giggled as she hugged his neck and held onto his hand. Fin led her through a turn and risked a glance at Walker. He was laughing as he swayed with Beatrice and Fin couldn't wait until they were alone and it was his turn. Walker looked so handsome and happy as he charmed Bea.

"We should have a party at the cottage next year and make it just for us. But we still get the big cake."

"This was all your idea," Fin reminded her and Amelia looked smug as she smiled.

"We just wanted you and Daddy to see each other in your tuxedos and dance with us. And we wanted a big cake."

"Played us like a fiddle. How's the cake?" He asked her.

"Pretty good. I don't think there's going to be very much left, though." She sounded sad so Fin gave her temple a kiss as he chuckled.

"Next year, we'll have a whole cake to ourselves!" He promised. The song slowed and Fin was disappointed when it ended and he had to return Amelia to her family.

"We don't want a big party next year," Amelia informed them.

"Hear hear," Agnes said, then groaned. "Lord, here comes Muriel again."

"Is that Dean Martin? This is Jonathon's favorite!" Muriel

insisted as the band played "You're Nobody 'Til Somebody Loves You" but Jonathon shrugged.

"I prefer Lana and Kendrick Lamar. I honestly have no clue who this is."

"You know how sarcastic kids are these days," Muriel said with a dismissive wave.

"No... I'm afraid I'm a bit too old and out of touch." Walker picked Amelia up and she cut her eyes at Muriel.

"It's my turn," she stated with an imperious tilt of her nose. She wound an arm around Walker's neck and pointed at the other dancing couples.

"If you'll excuse us," he said before hurrying off with Amelia.

"My turn!" Charlotte's arms flailed as she hopped in front of Fin.

"I would be honored, madam." He bowed dramatically before whisking her off her feet and onto his hip. "Are you happy with the way your party turned out?" He asked her. Charlotte nodded, distracted by the gowns and jewelry for several moments. Fin predicted that she was about to jump tracks and head in a different direction so he had to stay on his toes.

"We should have an even bigger party when you marry Daddy," she declared.

"*No!*" Fin cried and offered the people around them a hard, wide smile. "Sorry. That was crazy. She's joking." He shook his head and steered them closer to the band. The crowd was thinner there and the music would make it harder for anyone to overhear them. "I know it sounds fun for me and your dad to get married but that could be really complicated." He didn't want to say anything until he and Walker had a chance to talk and make a decision together.

"Is complicated bad?"

"Not always... But you have no idea how much chaos we'd be asking for. People are going to want to know everything about us and there could even be a lot of people taking pictures of you," he explained but Charlotte brightened.

"Daddy said I love chaos and I love taking pictures!"

"I know *you* wouldn't mind the chaos... Neither would your sisters, now that I think about it. The three of you like watching us suffer," he realized.

"We like it when Daddy's happy. He used to be happy all the time but our other daddy died and Daddy was really sad for a long time. Daddy wouldn't make a lot of sound but he would cry a lot. Then, he didn't cry but he was really grumpy. He stopped being grumpy when you came to take care of us. He's happy again and I like the way he stares at you all the time," Charlotte rambled. Fin shushed her and kissed her hair. He had to put her down because he didn't feel steady.

"Oh, Charlotte..." Fin brushed his thumb against her cheek. "I love you so much, Sweetheart. I promise, we're going to figure this out and we're all going to be happy."

The song ended so Charlotte decided that was her cue. She gave Fin's hand a hard jerk before he was pulled through the crowd.

"I see Daddy and Agnes!" She said and pointed.

"Slow down!"

"It's your turn to dance with Daddy!" She announced. Fin shook his head wildly and silently pleaded with Walker to do something.

"Maybe your dad could ask Agnes to dance," Fin suggested. Walker smiled as if he was going to say something teasing, but became irritated when Muriel reappeared.

"You've run out of daughters, Cameron. Be a good host and dance with one of your guests," she pouted.

"It's *our* party. We planned it," Amelia informed her and

dared the older dragon to say otherwise. Muriel drew back for a moment and Fin secretly hoped she had the nerve to contradict Amelia Grace Maxwell Cameron. Walker pinned the woman with a hard stare, warning Muriel not to upset his little girl.

"Of course, you did!" Muriel said dismissively as she recovered. "I was just telling Jonathon that this has to be the party of the year. Wasn't I, Jonathon?"

"I don't know. It's fine, I guess." Jonathon said before giving Fin an appraising glance and a nod. "What's up?"

"Don't." Fin shook his head and threw him a disgusted glare. Muriel gave Jonathon a hard swat with her beaded clutch.

"If you don't ask that man to dance, I will cancel your credit cards," she threatened him. Jonathon groaned and slouched as he turned to Walker.

"That won't be necessary," Walker said, attempting to cut him off.

"I insist!" Muriel cried, shoving Jonathon. He stumbled into Walker and gave his hair a dramatic sweep. Walker grunted and threw a hand up, clearly ready to end the discussion. Fin slid Agnes a nervous glance. She was chewing on her thumbnail with what he guessed was a mixture of dread and delight.

"I'd rather not," Walker ground out.

"She isn't going to shut up unless we dance," Jonathon muttered.

"You really should dance with someone," Muriel said. Agnes and Fin caught the twitching of Walker's jaw as his temper boiled over and they both braced themselves.

"For the love of—! No! I don't want to dance with Jonathon!" Walker bellowed, bringing everything to a halt around them. "There's only one man I want to dance with and that's Fin," Walker said and tossed his hand at Fin with a wry laugh. "It's my birthday but I can't dance with the man I love because he happens to be my nanny."

"Walker!" Fin gasped and jumped when Agnes jabbed him in the ribs.

"Don't interrupt him!"

"But he's talking about me!" Fin whispered back.

"I knew it!" Muriel announced and looked around to make sure everyone made note.

"I can't help it, Fin." Walker held up his hands and shrugged. "It's my birthday. I've already danced with my little girls. All I want to do now is dance with you."

"Are you sure?" Fin asked quietly. He was afraid to see how many people had heard and were watching them. Walker reached for Fin and he smiled in that secret, just-for-Fin way. Fin's tummy flipped as he bit down on his lips and fought back tears.

"I can't waste any more time worrying about what people think. Dance with me, Fin." He grinned and Fin thought his knees might buckle. There was so much love and heat in Walker's eyes as they stared into Fin's.

"OK," Fin mouthed and took Walker's hand. He pulled Fin into his arms and the party faded around them.

"Next year, I'm spending my birthday with you and my girls. Agnes, Amelia, Beatrice, Charlotte, and you. That's it," Walker stated, then chuckled. "And probably Pierce," he added. Fin laughed and it was watery as he nodded.

"That sounds perfect." He cautiously slid an arm around Walker's shoulder and risked a quick scan of the faces around them. The girls were hopping and hugging while Agnes dabbed at her eyes with a handkerchief. Muriel was pouting and Jonathon was nowhere in sight. Fin noticed a few curious stares and some knowing smiles, but he found that he didn't care about them as he watched the triplets. Their joy was infectious and Fin laughed as he pushed his face into Walker's chest. "What are we doing?" He looked at Walker and he shrugged.

"I don't know about you but I'm dancing with the man I love and thinking about how I'll spend the rest of my birthday, once this party's over."

"I have some ideas," Fin said, his voice wavering with emotion. He didn't know what tomorrow would be like, once the news got out that Walker Cameron III was dating his nanny but Fin was so proud of Walker. He had chosen his own happiness over society's and Muriel's expectations. And Fin was surprisingly proud that Walker was his and everyone knew it. "I'm still extremely worried but this is unbelievable. I can't believe we're dancing and...dating now!"

"Dating?" Walker asked and Fin swatted his arm playfully.

"Stop it! I don't know what we're doing but everyone knows now. Or, they will by tomorrow afternoon."

"Perfect. That means we can go out to dinner tomorrow night or take the girls to brunch next weekend without worrying about who might see us. From now on, all I care about is you and the girls. We live in the greatest city in the world and I want to *live* in it with my family. You're mine and you're part of my family, and we're done hiding in The Killian House."

"I love you and I love your crazy family." Fin felt like he was dreaming as he rested his chin on Walker's shoulder. Walker sighed happily as his hand spread across Fin's back. He was holding Fin so close—so possessively and affectionately—that there would be no question as to the nature of their relationship or Walker's feelings.

"I'm so glad, you might be the only other person in the borough willing to put up with us."

The song ended but Walker refused to release Fin. He kept them swaying for several songs and ignored the rest of the partygoers until Agnes tapped him on the back.

"It's getting late. I'm going to help get the girls ready for bed but you should thank your guests before they leave."

275

"I suppose," Walker sighed. He raised Fin's hand to his lips and kissed it.

"Walker!" Fin whispered. Walker grinned and rubbed his lips against Fin's knuckles.

"It's my birthday. I'm allowed. Will you wait for me upstairs?" He asked and Fin nodded. "Good. I'd be really happy if you were naked but I'll leave that up to you," Walker whispered, then pressed a kiss to Fin's cheek before he left him.

"Oh, I'm definitely going to be naked. You've been a *very* good boy tonight," Fin said with a decisive nod, then dashed through the crowd to help Agnes and say goodnight to the girls.

Chapter Thirty-Nine

"They really are precious and I don't know what I'll do when they don't want to spend their weekends with me anymore," Agnes said as she wound her arm around Walker's and rested her head on his shoulder. He had done his duty and thanked all his guests but Walker couldn't wait to kiss the girls goodnight and tuck them in. They were nodding off and Walker felt extremely blessed and *proud* of his little family. It was the best gift he could have been given after years of getting just about everything wrong.

"What are you talking about? They'll always want to stay with you."

"No, they won't. They'll have more games on the weekends and want to spend more time with their friends as they start to have little lives of their own. And that's OK!" She said but Agnes sniffled. Walker frowned at his slumbering princesses. They had already grown so fast and almost left him behind. He was finally catching up and getting the hang of things but Walker knew they would keep on growing and changing on him.

"It isn't fair, is it? Just when you think you have everything you want, time starts taking it away from you."

"I might have been wrong about not having children of my own," Agnes said softly. Walker was thoroughly stunned but the possibility warmed his heart and he smiled, enamored with the thought of being a doting uncle.

"You know, it's never too late to adopt. There's always a child waiting for a home and someone to love them," he told her and kissed her hair.

"Don't encourage me, Walker. I'm almost fifty," she said, but he could already hear the wheels turning in Agnes's head. There wasn't any doubt in Walker's mind that she'd be a wonderful mother. She was a phenomenal aunt and devoted to the triplets, despite her impetuous, rebellious nature. The girls had been good for Agnes too.

"We're always here and I'm sure we could find you an excellent nanny, if you're worried about how you'll manage on your own."

"Maybe... But you already snagged the best nanny in the city."

"I did but I owe Reid Marshall an apology and a very big favor, after the damage I've done to his new agency this evening."

"It won't be that bad. Tonight was incredibly romantic and it won't take long for everyone to see how perfect you two are together," Agnes predicted as she shut the door and wound her arm around Walker's. She was staying in her old room and would take the girls back to the cottage with her after breakfast.

"I hope you're right. He will have to find a replacement for Fin, though."

"I have a feeling he won't mind. In fact, I suspect he'll be happy for his little brother." She hugged his arm and they were content to stand in front of the picture window in the gallery.

One of Pierce's footmen was zipping back and forth across the terrace, barking orders. All traces of Walker's birthday party would be cleared away before the last of the partygoers picked up their coats and got in their cars. "Will you ask Fin to marry you?"

There was an immediate, resounding *Yes.*

"I have to marry him." He loved Fin and they were a family now. The world would know what Fin meant to Walker and the girls. And Fin would be respected as Walker's husband and have all the protection that afforded. "I didn't think if I'd ever be ready for this, or ever want to again, but I can do it with Fin."

"I'm so proud of you and I know he is too."

"I think so. I was afraid of letting him go or replacing him but I can feel that this is what he wants for me."

"As if we could ever let him go." She pulled a face but a tear slipped from the corner of her eye and rolled down her cheek. "Every time Charlotte pulls a stunt or makes me laugh I see him and know he's laughing with us. And the way Amelia's nose scrunches when she's being stubborn is pure Connor," she said, making Walker laugh.

"Everyone thinks she got her evil streak from the two of us, but Connor was a mastermind. Do you remember that year we nearly killed each other?"

"Lord, I thought the pranks would never end and I don't know how neither of you ended up in jail or the hospital. It was like living in a frat house." Agnes shook her head. "Do you remember when we were in Val-d'Isère and he filled your ski helmet with shaving cream?" Her hand clapped over her mouth and Walker tossed his head back as he cackled. Agnes grabbed his cheeks and did her best to shush him. "You'll wake the girls!" She whispered and laughed softly as they went back in time together. "Your reaction was priceless."

"I spent the whole day with sticky hair and smelling like I'd bathed in cheap cologne, like some sort of gigolo," he grumbled, but he couldn't keep a straight face. He pressed a kiss to Agnes's lips and they both sighed.

Walker laughed softly. "Beatrice has his big, beautiful brain and I'll always blame him when she asks questions I can't answer."

"I'm so happy for you. I've been worried but it never goes well when I tell you that you need help. You never would have accepted help from Fin if it weren't for the girls."

"You might be right," Walker conceded. "What about you? You can't keep having flings with your trainers and banging lonely trophy wives."

"I don't believe I asked you."

"I want you to be happy, Agnes."

"I fell in love with a man once and it was the worst mistake I've ever made," she replied and Walker hummed thoughtfully.

"Try falling in love with a woman. It was a long time ago and you're a different person."

"I am and I can tell you that women can be just as unscrupulous. You'd disown me if you knew how many trophy wives I've banged. They're easy-picking at the country club because they're already drunk and looking for a reason to piss off their husbands."

"Seriously, Agnes."

"I know. I'm terrible, Walker. Sometimes, I can bag two at once if they're best friends and one of them's just found out about a new mistress."

"Are you trying to ruin my birthday?" Walker asked and Agnes pursed her lips thoughtfully.

"Probably shouldn't tell you about what happened in the caterer's van, then..."

"This is a good time to say goodnight, I think." Walker kissed her firmly on the forehead. She stuck her tongue out before she kissed him again. "Goodnight, brat," he said and turned her so she could head upstairs.

"Goodnight. I'm very proud of you."

He waited until she was gone and went back to the window. Walker recalled his declaration at the party and everything that had happened since Fin's arrival and was proud of himself too. None of it would have happened without Fin but Walker had taken a risk, a leap, and put himself and his family first. All in one night. And now, Fin was waiting for Walker in his suite. *Their suite.*

"Soon," Walker promised himself and went to say goodnight to Fin.

Chapter Forty

"I've taken the liberty of sending your tuxedo to the dry cleaners and your...other clothes are on the work table in the closet," Pierce informed Fin in his low, dry tone. Fin had found him waiting in Walker's suite, robe in hand, with instructions to "see to his every comfort."

"Thank you..." Fin said hesitantly and threw his hands up. "Do *we* have to do this? It's weird and I don't like it. You're still kind of my boss and I don't want you doing things for me."

"I'm sorry, sir, but I'm afraid it would make me very uncomfortable and make my job unnecessarily complicated. I appreciate traditional, predictable boundaries, myself," Pierce explained, then cleared his throat. "Not that I haven't seen the wisdom in your methods. I'm grateful for all that you've done for Mr. Cameron and the girls. In fact, I'm rather pleased with how things have turned out. I'm very happy for you...Fin."

"Thank you, Pierce. That means a lot. I know how much you care for this family," Fin said. He smiled at Pierce but the butler merely blinked back at him. Fin assumed that was as close to smiling as Pierce was capable. "I guess I'll wait here,"

Fin ducked his head, excusing Pierce so he could hurry from the room.

Fin laughed softly but it faded as he finally took stock of his surroundings. He'd peeked from the sitting room a few times but Fin had never gone past the door to Walker's bedroom. Like, the rest of the suite, the massive, antique mahogany four-poster and the upholstery were swathed in pewter velvet. Large leather armchairs flanked the fireplace and a fire cracked and popped invitingly. There were matching pewter-colored marble floors and counters in the cavernous bathroom. The decor reminded Fin of Walker's suits.

"We can redecorate if this is too dark for you," Walker said, sneaking up on Fin while he was admiring a black and white Jackson Pollack over the mantle in the bedroom.

"I love it." Fin turned in Walker's arms. "How are you doing?"

"I'm happier than I thought was possible. How about you?" Walker asked. His head canted as he returned the favor and searched Fin's face.

"I'm a little numb but in a good way. Mostly concerned about you. A lot happened for you tonight," Fin worried. Walker nodded slowly in agreement.

"True...but I feel much better now that we're not a secret. I can go about my life and focus on the things I truly care about without worrying about what the world will think."

"That is pretty amazing," Fin agreed with a sly grin. "I can't wait to tell my parents and my friends. I have an insanely *hot* boyfriend now!"

"Do you think they'll approve?" Walker asked. Fin rubbed his lips together as he considered.

"My friends will think it's great because you're you. My parents won't be thrilled at first, but they'll be fine once they've met you. Mom and Dad will *love* the girls and might be too excited to get their hands on them. They've been after me and Reid to have kids sooner than later because 'they're not getting any younger.' But their schedules are ridiculous so Reid and I usually ride out to Park Slope together and have brunch with them on the first Sunday of every month."

"Oh." Walker grimaced as he calculated and realized Fin would have missed the last two Sundays because the girls weren't with Agnes. "Why didn't you tell me?"

"I planned to once things were settled enough here that it wouldn't be a big deal. My parents understand that kids need more time and attention during major transitions."

"I think we can spare you for a few hours on Sunday but I'd like to meet your parents and I'd like to have a talk with your brother," Walker said. Fin shrugged and nodded.

"I have to introduce you to Reid soon and Mom and Dad will want to meet you once they hear about tonight. I usually go to Reid's on my mornings off. Want to go with me tomorrow? I want to see how bad he thinks this is going to be and apologize."

"I should definitely go with you, seeing as I'm the one who told everyone. I did think of some ways I can help and I've got some leads for him," Walker said, surprising Fin.

"That's great. Maybe Reid can turn this around if people think the two of you are friends too..."

"We will be after tomorrow and I'll make this right," Walker vowed but Fin threw him an impatient look.

"Make this right? Don't say that like you didn't do the most amazing thing tonight. Reid is going to be pissed at me for sleeping with his client, but he loves cleaning up messes. Nothing makes him happier than solving problems. That's why this agency is perfect; he's helping families by pairing them up with the perfect nanny for their needs *and* helping queer nannies find homes they can truly fit into."

"It sounds like a worthy undertaking and I'm happy to put

my support behind it. What about you? What do you want to do?" Walker asked and Fin frowned in confusion.

"What do you mean? Everything's perfect here. I don't want to change a thing."

"I was hoping a lot would change, actually," Walker said carefully as he loosened his tie and headed for the closet. Fin shook his head as he went after him.

"Why? Everyone knows now and it'll blow over."

"It will but you can't work for me anymore, Fin."

"No! This is the best job I've ever had and no one else is going to hire me when they find out that I'm dating my last boss."

"I was hoping you'd stay...in an unofficial capacity."

"What?" Fin held up a hand. "This is not going where I was hoping it would go and I'm starting to get a headache."

"Did you seriously think you'd still be the girls' nanny on Monday and take them to the library as usual?" Walker asked delicately. Fin actually had and nodded quickly.

"Yes! I thought that we would do exactly that! People will lose interest if there's nothing to see except us getting on with our lives," he explained, widening his eyes at Walker hopefully. "But I could do a little rearranging of our routine so the girls won't notice that we're lying low for a few weeks."

"I was hoping you'd live with us from now on and move in here with me." Walker took off his coat and left it on the work table for Pierce. "That will require a lot more than rearranging our routine. I want you to be a part of our family, not an employee."

"Oh..." Fin stumbled back. "You really want to get serious," he murmured and Walker laughed.

"Fin! I told everyone on my contacts list and my employee roster that I'm in love with you and that you're the only man I want to dance with."

"I guess it would be weird if I didn't move in... It's not like you and the girls could move in with me and Riley," Fin mused.

"No. But we'd still be lost without you to look after us," Walker reminded him, making Fin feel a lot better. Instead of being employed by Walker to look after the girls, they would be Fin's too. "Is there something else you'd like to do? Perhaps you could do something like Reid and work from home," Walker suggested. Fin's head cocked and he hummed as he considered.

"I have always wondered how long it would take to give away enough warm things to save a landfill... Maybe I could turn it into a real operation." While Fin had never considered what he'd do once he had his own family, he was deeply concerned with how fast fashion was contributing to pollution and filling landfills. And he was passionate about repurposing discarded clothes into warm garments for those in need.

"I think that's a wonderful idea and I'd be happy to invest in that so you can hire more people to help you," Walker offered. Fin cheered and grabbed his shoulders.

"One of the shelters I send warm things to helps women learn to read, get their GED, get into job training programs, apply to colleges... Whatever they need for a second chance. I could start there!"

"Go big and hire as many people as you want. I'm happy to invest in this," Walker said. He bent at the waist to slide off his shoes and socks and Fin shivered as Walker straightened and padded toward him. "You've given me my life back. It's my turn to make some of your dreams come true."

"I just did my job," Fin argued but leaned into Walker when he pulled him close.

"We had twelve nannies in three years, Fin. I knew you were different the moment you walked through the front door."

"I was so mad at how hot you were because I was sure I was going to hate you," Fin admitted. His teeth dug into his lip as he unbuttoned Walker's shirt. "You've been such a good boy tonight."

"I have, haven't I?" Walker asked and this time, *his* voice wavered and crumbled. Fin nodded as he moved to his trousers.

"So good." He unzipped, then groaned when he reached inside and found Walker's erection. "You deserve a very special birthday wish."

"Oh?" Walker croaked.

"Mmmhmm..." Fin sucked on Walker's chin as he stroked him. "Anything you want, Walker. *Anything.*" He felt Walker's cock throb against his palm. "Whatever that was! Tell me about that!" Fin begged. Walker nodded, his eyes heavy as he lowered his head and brushed his lips against Fin's.

"I had planned to ask..." He licked his lips nervously and Fin enjoyed the way Walker's tongue flicked his. Walker was getting hotter and he was trembling as he kissed Fin. He could feel Walker mustering his courage and it made Fin anxious but hungry.

"Please do."

"I was wondering if you might... If you could..." Walker squeezed his eyes shut and swore at himself. "Have you had very much to drink tonight?" He blurted out and Fin's brow furrowed in confusion.

"Not as much at the party but I did help myself to some of your scotch while I was waiting. I really wanted to be naked but Pierce was hovering. Why?"

"Would you say you've had enough to put you in a wild mood?" Walker asked. There was a rise in his voice that Fin wasn't sure what to make of.

"Possibly... Why?" Fin asked carefully. He didn't want to say anything that might discourage him. Walker pulled in a deep breath.

"Because if you were and you were in the mood to...take me, I wouldn't mind that," he said in a quick rush.

"Take you...?" Fin echoed, then finally caught up. "Oh! You want me to...!" He said and Walker shut his eyes again as he nodded.

"If you think you'd be interested in doing that," he said through clenched teeth.

"Interested?" Fin laughed as he gathered Walker's face in his hands. "I had no idea but I am *so* interested." He was hard as he guided Walker's hand to the belt at his waist. Fin helped him tug it loose and opened the robe so Walker could see how interested he was. "Why didn't you tell me?"

"Because I'm me. I've never...before because I was too scared to ask."

"Wow. You're really going for it," Fin said. He towed Walker with him as he backed out of the closet. "I'm so proud of you. You've been an especially good boy tonight." He slid out of the robe and let it fall as they made their way to the bed. Walker's eyes dropped to Fin's jockstrap and he groaned appreciatively.

"*Very* nice but those are rather understated for you," he teased.

"Pierce hired some snotty Italian tailor to make my tux and he said he'd murder me if I wore the wrong underwear. He was adamant that I be mindful of my panty line," Fin explained and earned a thoughtful snort from Walker.

"I assume that was Vincenzo."

"You know him?"

"I do. He's *my* tailor. I'll probably receive a bill for that tuxedo next week."

"Happy birthday!" Fin cheered apologetically.

"It truly was and the highlight was seeing you in that tux."

"Really? I might have to order a few more... How much does something like that run?" Fin asked.

"For something like that? Around $12k," Walker guessed, causing Fin's jaw to stretch as wide as it would go.

"*What?!*" He shook his head. "I should have had him put some elastic in the waist and add more pockets for snacks because I'm going to have to hang onto that tux until I'm ninety to get your money's worth."

"Don't worry about it. We'll have you fitted for a few more tuxedos and suits. You can't wear a tux like that to everything. You'll need something more conservative for business-related and political events. Possibly something more informal for entertainment-related parties..."

"What are you talking about? I don't need to go to all of that and I don't need more tuxedos," Fin said, hoping to put the matter to rest but Walker nodded.

"I've missed having someone to keep me company and to commiserate with when I have to go to those things. And I intend to show you off, now that I've told the whole world about you," he warned as he shrugged out of his shirt. Fin's ears popped, and he was a little nauseous at the thought of more tuxedos and suits.

"So many buttons and so tight and itchy," he whispered as he held onto Walker's shoulders. Walker groaned sympathetically and stopped so Fin could push his trousers and black briefs down his legs.

"You looked incredibly sexy if that helps."

"A little," Fin admitted. At least he didn't look like a miserable tool, he only felt like one. "I should have been nicer to Vincenzo."

"Why? He isn't paid in kindness. I don't find him particularly pleasant either, but he can cut a suit that would make angels weep, as you displayed for us so marvelously this evening."

"You don't have to keep flattering me, I'm going home with you tonight," Fin replied. He turned them so he could ease Walker back onto the bed. Fin felt like it was his birthday as he stepped out of his jockstrap and crawled over Walker.

"This is your home now, too." Walker captured Fin's lips for a deep, lingering kiss. Fin hummed as he rested his forehead on Walker's.

"I'm so excited about living with you and the girls but the rest of it scares me and kind of makes me want to pee in my pants."

"We can have Vincenzo fit you for a diaper," Walker offered.

"Alright, if that's what you're into," Fin countered, causing Walker to howl. He held onto Fin as he laughed and it was arousing in a new way. It was better than sex, seeing Walker's joy as he wiped his eyes and caught his breath. This was a whole different type of intimacy for Fin, holding someone and laughing while naked. Walker's body vibrated against his and the way his chest hair abraded Fin's skin and nipples was delicious. Walker's hands spread across Fin's back and he was pulled closer.

"Not as far as I know but I'll give just about anything a try with you," he said. Fin laughed softly and it turned into a purr.

"That's so sexy." He angled his head so he could suck on Walker's earlobe and gave it a nip. "It's really hot when you tell me what you like and what you're curious about."

"Everything, Fin," Walker breathed. His hand reached and swatted at the bedside table until he found the drawer. Fin growled encouragingly as he licked and bit his way down Walker's neck and shoulder.

"Toys?" Fin whispered as he hovered over Walker's nipple.

"Yes," he whispered back. A tube of lube fell onto the mattress and Walker's fingers slid through Fin's hair. Fin hummed in approval as his tongue swirled, making Walker gasp and buck beneath him.

"I've got a set of clamps at my place." Fin was rewarded with a pained whimper when he nibbled on the pebbled peak.

"Yes!"

"Such a good boy," Fin crooned as he slid to the other pec and flicked with his tongue.

"Fin!" Walker's cock jumped between them and he was restless as he writhed beneath Fin.

"Shhhh!" Fin drifted lower, nuzzling, sucking, and licking. Walker swore, moaned, and twisted as he chanted Fin's name. This was all the power Fin needed. There was nothing more thrilling than being the man who could make Walker Cameron shiver with delight and beg. Fin cherished Walker's secret vulnerability and his trust. "You're so good, Walker." Fin lapped at the head of Walker's cock, pleased that he'd shared the things that had scared him in the past. He wasn't rewarding Walker for being one of the most powerful men in Manhattan or for his vast wealth. Everyone else did that. Fin encouraged and praised Walker for the things he was most insecure about and the things that mattered most to him.

"Thank you!" Walker panted and undulated on the bed as Fin took him deep into his throat. He touched the man at Walker's core and soothed him. Fin used words, his lips, his tongue, and his fingers to stoke Walker's confidence and his lust. Fin worshiped Walker's sac and greedily sucked and licked at his hole until he was hoarse and shaking. Then, he asked Walker if he'd like to try swings, plugs, cages, restraints... And Fin rewarded Walker for each gasped admission.

"And you're into ass play?" Fin drawled as he gently slid two slick fingers past the tight, clenching ring of Walker's ass.

Walker nodded frantically and his head tossed on the pillow as Fin reached deep and twisted. "Oh, you're so good and so, so tight." Fin's voice was a thready rasp. His cock ached and he worried that he wouldn't be able to last long as Walker began to ride his fingers.

"Please! Fin!" He cried and reached for him. *Not helpful!* Fin gripped the base of his shaft and breathed through a swell of pressure. His nerves flickered and fizzed wildly, he was already so close.

"Just a moment," Fin said calmly despite his slamming heart. He carefully coated his cock with lube as he scooted forward on his knees and lined up the head with Walker's hole. He nudged forward and they both groaned as Fin slowly slid deep. "Oh God, that's tight," Fin choked out. Walker nodded jerkily and his toes curled as Fin flexed his hips.

"It's really good, though!" He said shakily. Walker swore and clutched at the velvet duvet.

"So, so good!" Fin agreed. His hands spread around Walker's thighs as Fin bucked his hips, setting a steady pace. He kept his strokes shallow because he could only handle so much friction. Fin was hanging on by the skin of his teeth as he kneaded Walker's sac and tugged at his shaft with slick, shaking fingers.

"Christ, Fin... I can't!" Walker's head thrashed and slammed against the pillow. Fin silently thanked the sex gods and thrust faster. He tightened his grip around Walker's cock as they cried and begged each other's names. "Fin!" Walker screamed as his back came off the bed and cum shot from his cock and spilled over Fin's fist.

"Thank God!" *Finally made him scream.* Fin let go and shattered. Cum rushed from his cock, flooding Walker's passage. He shivered and bit back a string of ecstatically filthy curses, then laughed as he fell forward. Walker caught him and gathered Fin in his arms as he rolled them.

"You always know." He kissed Fin and there was so much gratitude and satisfaction in Walker's lips and his touch.

"Because you trust me enough to show me and tell me. You have no idea how much I love that and how much it turns me on."

"Only with you, Fin. You make it easy and you make it feel safe."

"That's my job now," Fin said with a yawn. "I love you and all I want to do is make you happy."

"I love you too, Fin. You make me happier than I ever thought was possible." Walker wrapped his arms tight around him and they whispered plans and kissed until they drifted off to sleep.

Chapter Forty-One

"**W**hy are you here this early? I thought you'd be sleeping in after last night," Reid Marshall asked through the intercom.

Fin winked at Walker and gave his hand a squeeze, dousing a little of his anxiety. He was determined to make a good impression because Walker understood how much Fin loved and looked up to his older brother. But he worried they weren't off to a great start with his outburst at the party. Fin said he was waiting until he talked to Reid before deciding they were a scandal. He looked surprisingly relaxed, beaming at Walker as they waited on the stoop. Fin sighed dreamily at him as he leaned toward the intercom.

"I didn't get to tell you everything and Walker's with me. We thought it was time you two met," he explained and the lock clicked half a second later. Fin got the door for Walker and waved him in. "Morning, Norman!" Fin told the elderly man behind the desk. He nodded in greeting but his chin sagged to his chest and a loud snore echoed around the lobby of the converted mansion.

Walker was charmed by the original black and white marble tiles and the ornate wrought iron banister. He peered up at the massive crystal chandelier but followed when Fin gave his hand a tug. They headed around the left-hand side of the staircase and took a left down the long hall.

He was enjoying the view of the postage-stamp-sized garden when he spotted an older, more strait-laced version of Fin waiting for them. He was leaning against his door and had his arms crossed as he studied Walker with shrewd, piercing curiosity. The sleeves of his shirt were rolled up, he was wearing a tie, and his hair was neatly trimmed. But he was clearly Fin's big brother.

"You've got room at your table for one more, right?" Fin gripped his brother's shoulder. "Reid, this is Walker. Walker, that's Reid. I need more coffee," he stated as he passed. Reid gave Walker a suffering look.

"It's good to finally meet you," Walker said as he held out his hand.

"I'd like to say he's told me a lot about you but he hasn't," Reid replied wearily. "Come on in. There's plenty of room and plenty of food as long as Riley doesn't show up. He eats enough for three people." He smiled and waved him in but Walker could feel Reid's eyes on his back. *That's why you're here,* Walker reminded himself.

He admired the quirky comfort of the converted dining room and conservatory as he made his way past a well-worn leather sofa and armchairs and into the kitchen. Vines and orchids surrounded them and soft light spilled through the conservatory's original paned windows. A clarinet played from somewhere in the apartment, impressing Walker as Fin helped himself to a raspberry from a bowl on the counter on his way to the French press.

"Fin tells me your party was a success," Reid said with a

wry smirk. They both caught the pink that tinted Fin's cheeks as he poured.

"It was going brilliantly and just as I planned until Walker went and made it romantic," he pouted playfully. He handed Walker a mug of black coffee and slid him a conspiratorial grin. He was having fun but Walker was getting more anxious by the moment.

"I heard," Reid said with an impatient gesture. "That's why I didn't think you'd turn up this weekend. Why are you really here?" He got the sugar bowl from the shelf by the fridge and stared at Fin expectantly as he passed it to him. Fin hunted in a drawer for a spoon and winced.

"We've decided that there's no reason for me to take that teaching job since I don't need a cover anymore but I won't be returning as the girls' nanny either."

"So... You won't have a job or any income?" Reid asked, unable to hide his concern. Fin gave him a hard look and shook his head.

"I'd be climbing the walls by the end of the day. I'm going to take care of the girls and work from The Killian House. Walker's helping me expand my warm things recycling, so I can sell recycled warm things with matched donations. You know, one of those buy-one, donate-one companies. That way I can source bigger hauls of used clothes and provide even more free warm things and blankets to shelters and nursing homes," he explained.

"That's great!" Reid said as he looked between them. "Why did you need to come all the way from Manhattan to tell me that? Not that I'm not thrilled for the both of you," he added. Fin pointed at Walker as he stirred his coffee.

"Walker felt that we owed you an apology and wanted to be formally introduced. Sorry I blew my first and only assignment. I hope I haven't tanked your new agency's reputation," he said with a pained grimace. Reid fell against the counter and crossed his arms over his chest. He blinked at Fin as he navigated his exasperation and Walker knew everything he needed to know about Reid: his brother was his heart, but he lived on Reid's last nerve. Walker had never related to another human being more as they traded bemused glances. He couldn't wait to introduce Reid to Agnes so they could commiserate.

"The agency will be fine. All I care about is whether you're happy and doing what's right for you."

"I agree," Walker interrupted. "Fin was only looking at that teaching job for me so I asked him to find something he'd be passionate about and that he'd find fulfilling instead."

"You're off to a strong start, Cameron," Reid murmured and was nodding as he went to one of the chairs around the little table in the corner. "I've already got the perfect long-term job lined up for Riley. We've got Penn and Penny on board too. And I have two new guys with excellent résumés coming in for interviews later as well so I'm not at all worried. Turns out, there are a lot more queer nannies in the city than we thought."

"That's excellent news but I'd like to help as much as I can, since I'm partly responsible," Walker said and Reid looked surprised.

"I appreciate that but I don't think your relationship is going to be as bad for the agency as you're expecting. If anything, it could help, being connected to Walker and Agnes Cameron. You're both pretty influential," he said. Walker nodded as he reached into his coat and pulled out two business cards.

"I thought so as well. If it's alright, I've hired an advertising firm and a team to handle PR for you. I've also found two prospective clients and you should hear from them shortly."

"Wow," Reid said.

"Wow," Fin agreed as he hurried around the stainless steel island to look at the cards. "You said you had leads but when did you do all of this?" He asked as he lowered into the seat next to Reid's. Walker shrugged dismissively as he sat across from Fin.

"I did a little damage control last night, while I had everyone there and in the mood to kiss my ass."

"This is..." Reid pushed out a loud breath as he scrubbed the back of his neck. "Huge. I guess this is actually happening. I officially have my own agency," he said in disbelief. Fin smiled at Walker as he rubbed his brother's back. There was so much gratitude in that smile but it was full of promise as well. *You have been such a good boy.*

"This is exactly what you need and you're going to help so many people," Fin told Reid.

"I don't know why I didn't think about having my own agency before but it feels right and things keep falling into place." Reid sounded a little overcome but Walker was hoping that would work in his favor.

"I was also hoping you would give me your blessing," Walker said slowly and leaned forward so he could take Fin's hand. "I can't officially ask him until the girls have helped me pick out a ring but I'd like your permission first."

"What?" Fin squeaked. His lip wobbled and he sniffed hard.

"Hell, I'll marry you," Reid said, then gasped when Fin elbowed him.

"You've gone and made this even more romantic," Fin scolded but his eyes shimmered and he sniffled again as he blinked at Walker.

"My apologies. Is that a yes?" Walker asked as he ducked his head and Fin nodded.

"Of course, I'll marry you."

A tall, conservatively dressed younger man wandered into the kitchen with a newspaper under his arm. "I think I've missed something." He was handsome, with dark hair and bright blue eyes behind the round lenses of his wire-framed glasses.

"This is my roommate and business partner, Gavin Selby. Gavin, this is Walker Cameron," Reid announced.

Walker stood to shake the younger man's hand and squinted at him.

"Selby? You look familiar. Is your fath—?" Walker stopped when Fin and Reid coughed and shook their heads, ending the conversation but momentarily piquing Walker's interest. The Scarsdale Selbys were rather influential as well. He did recall something about a grandson who had left the family over a falling out with the aging patriarch, Randolph Selby Sr.

Gavin's expression remained distant. He was uninterested as he went to prepare his coffee before returning to take the seat next to Walker's.

"I am estranged from my family and haven't had any contact with them for years. What's this about Fin getting married?"

"Cameron's asked me for his blessing," Reid told Gavin.

"A questionable decision on Cameron's part but I assume he knows what he's getting into," Gavin said as he perused his paper.

"Shhhh!" Fin tapped a finger against his lips. "He's also done some generous things to help the agency," he added. That got a reaction out of Gavin. He flipped the paper down so he could stare at Reid.

"How generous? Do I need to draw up contracts? What's this going to do to our taxes?" He asked.

"I'll make sure all the necessary contracts get to you by the end of the day," Walker reassured him. Reid swatted dismissively as he got up.

"Let's celebrate before he comes to his senses. Fin's found

someone who's willing to overlook his many, many flaws and we have everything we need to get this agency off the ground. It looks like we're officially in business." He returned with a bottle of Prosecco and champagne flutes to accompany the carafe of juice on the table. The buzzer peeled through the apartment and Reid's cheeks puffed out as he looked at the refrigerator. "That's probably Riley. We might have enough food if I make a few omelets..." He hurried from the kitchen, leaving Fin in charge of pouring the Prosecco.

"The girls won't be able to keep this to themselves, they're going to tell everyone in Manhattan," Fin warned but Walker no longer cared.

"Let them. It will save me the trouble of having to put an announcement in the paper. I want us to celebrate this as a family without worrying about what anyone else thinks." He truly didn't feel a lick of concern and it was *liberating*, living just to make his family, Fin, and himself happy for once.

"You're getting married?" Riley yelled as he ran into the kitchen. Fin put down the bottle and spun so he could catch Riley as he flew at him.

"I still can't believe it!" Fin was laughing and they started crying as they jumped up and down. There was a soft laugh as a large man with a full beard joined them. His long, wavy blond hair was wound into a bun, and he was wearing overalls and a faded Led Zeppelin t-shirt. He was also wearing leather flip-flops and Fin cheered as he ran to him. "I'm getting married, Penn!"

"Congratulations! I heard!" The other man said, giving Fin's hair an affectionate ruffle. He immediately reached for Walker's hand and flashed him a warm, openly curious grin. "So you think you're good enough for our Fin?" He asked with an easy laugh. Walker shook his head as he stood and clasped Penn's hand.

"I'm certain I'm not but I intend to work on that every day. Walker Cameron."

"Pennsylvania Tucker. Everyone calls me Penn." He held onto Walker's hand as he searched his eyes. Normally, Walker would have been concerned or taken offense, but he found it calming as Penn peered and hummed faintly. "I think you'll do. Welcome to the family," he said and pulled Walker into a hug. Walker frowned as he patted Penn on the back.

"Thank you. I've always wondered what it was like to join a commune," Walker said dryly. Penn laughed as he released him and gave his shoulder a teasing jab.

"I have a feeling we're going to be friends."

"I don't think I'd mind that," Walker replied and got out of the way when Reid returned with another chair. Gavin scooted along the window seat so Penn could sit in the middle while Reid went to get more champagne flutes.

"Riley brought more Prosecco and Penn brought his famous cinnamon rolls," he announced. Riley cheered as he dropped into the third chair and beat on the tabletop in front of him.

"You can put those right here. I get to be the best man, right?" His eyes were huge as they swung to Fin's. Fin and Reid both nodded.

"Reid and Gavin have each other and I assumed I'd be with you when you found someone. If you ever find someone and decide to get married," Fin said.

"Probably won't." Riley shrugged and threw up a hand. "I'm cursed."

"Too sweet," Fin explained to Walker.

"I can see how that would be a problem..." Walker said, but he shook his head at Reid and Gavin. They shook their heads at him in agreement and Reid gave Riley's back an encouraging pat.

"I don't want to date you but I think you're pretty close to perfect."

"Maybe you could put that in writing for me to show the next guy who friend zones me."

"Have anyone in mind for your best man?" Penn teased Walker, changing the subject. He raised his brows at Walker and gave one of his overall's straps a suggestive tug. "I might be available."

"I won't be having a best man," Walker said. "I'll have Agnes stand with me."

"That's perfect," Fin agreed and sighed happily at him. Walker smiled at Fin over the rim of his cup as he sipped his coffee. "Things tend to turn out that way when I'm with you."

Epilogue

Nine months later, spring, a cottage in Sagaponack, New York...

"He might be the most handsome man I've ever seen."

"I don't think you're supposed to be looking," Reid said but Fin raised a shoulder as he watched the garden from the kitchen window. Walker scooped Charlotte up to waltz with her and Fin sighed dreamily at them.

"It's my wedding and I can do whatever I want. Walker said so."

"Calm down, Groomzilla," Reid chuckled and turned Fin. "Let me fix that." He slapped Fin's hand away when he tried to stop him.

"It's fine."

"It's not perfect. It has to be perfect," Reid said and tugged Fin's tie loose. Fin waited as Reid's fingers flicked and twisted until he was content. Fin took Reid by the shoulders and found his eyes.

"Everything's perfect. You and Agnes did an amazing job with the arrangements. You two could plan weddings as a side hustle."

"Don't you dare put that idea in Agnes's head. Did I tell you that she called me at four this morning to ask if I thought we should have hired a DJ for after the wedding?"

"You did and you were right, we'll be fine with the band. Everything looks amazing," Fin reassured him.

They'd chosen to have the wedding at the Cameron family cottage and to keep it small and private. Fin and Walker wanted the girls to be comfortable and have plenty of room to run and play. Neither wanted a formal ceremony and he fell in love with the cottage as soon as Walker drove his Range Rover through the teak gate for Fin's first Fourth of July with Agnes and the girls. The trees were so much bigger on the park-like estate than the ones Fin was used to in the city and there was so much green. There were four gardens and Fin's favorite was the English garden that sat off the back deck. Agnes had suggested they marry there, under the rose-covered arbor.

"Walker's parents seemed impressed." Fin held up a hand so Reid could slap it. Reid pushed out a relieved breath.

"I didn't think that was possible. They're kind of weird."

"Yeah. They're *really* old and don't like to say a lot or move their faces," Fin said with an apologetic scrunch of his nose. "Maybe they do it to conserve energy." He had a far better understanding of Walker after visiting the family estate in Connecticut.

Walker's parents were like twin glaciers, in wheelchairs that looked more like rolling armchairs with their tufted upholstery and wingbacks. Walker's parents nodded and humphed as they exchanged pleasantries but it was hard for Fin to tell if they liked him. He wasn't even that sure if they knew who he was or understood the purpose of the visit, they barely paid him any attention.

The girls had permitted gentle pats on the head from Walker's father and his mother told them they looked like angels. When it was time to leave, Walker tucked the blankets around his parents' laps as he kissed their cheeks, then declared the visit a resounding success.

"I heard that Walker's mom liked the way you decorated the garden with all those string lights and bows," Fin told Reid but his brother's lips pulled tight as he hissed.

"She asked me if there would be Christmas carols and if I could go heavy on the rum in her cocoa," Reid whispered discreetly but Fin burst into laughter.

"She drinks a lot. Walker said that she can walk and do quite a bit for herself, they just don't trust her not to fall down the stairs or into the pool."

"Well." Reid bit down on his lips so he wouldn't laugh. "Nobody's family is perfect."

"Mine is. And I have the best brother in the world. Thank you for doing this," Fin said as he turned to him. Reid waved it off but his eyes glittered as he brushed an invisible speck of lint off of Fin's shoulder.

"You're the *most* little brother ever but you're also the best and I had to make sure everything was perfect for you. You're my pride and joy, Fin. I practically raised you and I couldn't be prouder of the man you've become."

"I didn't make it easy but you did a pretty decent job." Fin's nose tickled and his eyes stung as Reid coughed softly and cleared his throat. He shook his head and took his time smoothing Fin's lapels.

"There's always been something special about you. I never had to tell you to do the right thing because you always, always,

always did it on your own. You've always put everyone else first and you'll do anything to put a smile on someone's face. You can be such a colossal pain in my ass and there are times I want to strangle you, but then I remember that no one else has a little brother like you and that I'm so damn lucky." Reid stopped Fin when he tried to pull him into a hug. "Your tux!" He grabbed Fin's cheeks and kissed his forehead hard.

"That's weird."

"Shut up. I love you."

"I love you too," Fin said, then held onto Reid's ears and kissed his forehead.

"Don't mess up my hair." He leaned away and tweaked Fin's tie again. "I always knew that you'd be alright because there's nothing you can't do. I did wonder if there was someone out there good enough for you but Walker's a wonderful man and he loves you. I'm really happy for you and it doesn't hurt nearly as much as I thought it would."

"Hurt?" Fin asked weakly. "Why would it hurt?"

"You don't need me anymore. You've got Walker now and he can take better care of you than I can," Reid said, hitting Fin right in the gut. He shook his head and threw his arms around Reid. "Finley!"

"Shut up. I love you." Fin hugged him as tight as he could, the way he'd hugged him when he was afraid of the dark or after a scary movie when they were kids. "I'm always going to need you. I love Walker but I'm still going to come to you when I feel lost. You're my hero and the person I trust the most. I know that Walker loves me but you've loved me longer and you know me better than he does."

"I hope so. I'd miss you and I wouldn't know what to do with myself if I didn't have to worry about you."

"I don't know why you thought it would be that easy to get rid of me." They clapped each other on the back as they parted and Fin nodded at the window. "Mom and Dad seem pretty happy."

"They're not big fans of Walker's parents, but they think he's great. Mom said she was a little worried at first because he's so...reserved. Then, she met the triplets and saw how wonderful he was with them and that settled it. She sees how much he loves the girls and how much he loves you. Dad said he trusted your judgment—for some reason—but he could tell that Walker was nervous when they met and the only reason a man like that would be nervous was if it truly mattered to him."

"Walker was a mess. He thinks Mom and Dad are pretty cool. He read their books and said he learned a lot."

"He told Dad. They're so happy for you and they're madly in love with the girls."

"Isn't that the best thing ever?" Fin said and they both laughed. Fin was proud of a lot of things but nothing compared to the way he felt when he saw how much joy the triplets gave his parents. His parents stopped in at The Killian House whenever they had a reason to cross the bridge and always had little gifts for the triplets.

"It's great and Mom's stopped nagging me about having kids," Reid said. There was a tap at the back door and Fin and Reid smiled when their dad leaned in.

"I'm supposed to send Reid to the garden and to prepare myself to escort the groom," he told them. He stepped inside and pressed his hand against his chest as he shook his head at Fin. "Wow, when did this happen? You were a scrawny theater nerd just the other day. Wasn't I just yelling at you to leave your skateboard on the porch?"

"Oh boy, I gotta go." Reid wiped at his cheeks as he left them.

"You already made me cry this morning," Fin said and held up his hands like his dad had pulled a gun.

"Relax. Mom said I'm not allowed to discuss anything except how handsome you look. I'm not supposed to mention how small you were when you were born or how I used to carry you in the front pocket of my hoodie."

"I won't tell her unless you make me cry."

"I already told you all the important stuff at breakfast. You picked a wonderful man with a beautiful family and you're the happiest I've ever seen you. We couldn't ask for more." The jazz band played the opening of "Somewhere Only We Know" and Fin's stomach did a somersault. "It's time, Fin." His dad offered his arm as Pierce got the door for them.

"Congratulations, Fin." Pierce bowed his head as they passed and Fin heard the faintest sniffle.

"Thank you, Pierce," Fin whispered. "Oh, my God." He should have known it was pointless to think he could get through the rest of the evening without crying.

The sun was setting and the garden looked like a fairy tale as his new family waited along with Fin's "old" family. Walker was breathtakingly handsome in a classic black tuxedo. A pale pink rose was pinned to his lapel. It was from the arbor and matched the girls' poofy princess gowns perfectly. Agnes wore a gorgeously cut tuxedo with a soft pink camisole and an enormous pink diamond brooch. Riley was struggling to hold it together as he held Reid's hand. Reid looked a little annoyed, but he smiled at Fin as their eyes met. Fin's dad coughed and wiped away a tear when they joined Walker under the arbor.

"I guess this is as far as I go. He's yours now. Take care of my little boy. He's special."

"He certainly is and I promise I'll take good care of him."

Walker took Fin's hands in his and there were no more nerves or tears. This was exactly what Fin was meant to do with his life and he couldn't think of anyone more handsome than Walker Cameron III.

"I love you, Fin," Walker began with a shrug when the pastor asked him to share his vows. "I tried my damnedest not to but you make it too easy. You're the smartest, kindest, funniest, most generous person I've ever met. You saved me and gave me a second chance with my girls and you made it easy and you made it fun. I'll never be able to repay you for all the joy you've given me but I promise I'll love you with all of my heart until it stops beating." He slid the hand-hammered platinum band the girls had chosen onto Fin's finger and kissed his knuckle. "'Thank you for giving me another chance and coming back after the girls tried to murder you," he said and everyone laughed. Fin whistled as he shook his head when it was his turn.

"I didn't think we'd be able to work together, but I was wrong. We turned out to be a good team and you were full of so many wonderful surprises. You were nothing like I thought you'd be and I couldn't help myself, I fell madly in love with you and I haven't stopped falling. You surprise me every day and make me fall even more in love. I can't think of anyone I'd rather go on a picnic with and I'm the luckiest man in the world because I get to share all my goodnights with you." Fin's hands were shaking as he slid the band the girls helped him pick onto Walker's ring finger. It had large channel-set emeralds around the platinum band because Fin and the girls were born in May. They were a family and Fin thought of Connor as he kissed Walker's knuckle and vowed to love him and the girls with every bit of his heart and his soul. He promised to protect them and to honor Connor's memory every single day.

"By the power vested in me by the state of New York, I now pronounce you married. You may kiss," the pastor declared.

"Finally!" Fin gasped and grabbed Walker's shoulders. He rose on his toes and everyone whistled and clapped as they kissed.

Walker and Fin gathered the girls in their arms for a weepy ten-armed hug as they were surrounded by their friends and family. Walker's parents clapped sedately and were wheeled away after they congratulated them. Instead of going the traditional route, there were six dazzling tiers of cupcakes. Fin and Walker took a bite out of one at the same time and the girls cut into a super-sized cupcake from the top tier of the tower.

Picnic tables with Mason jar lanterns were arranged on the lawn. The jazz quartet was set up under one of the massive Norwegian oaks and played standards as guests helped themselves to buckets of chilled champagne. The girls chased each other and caught fireflies as the sky grew darker and the moon came out. Fin was tipsy and ecstatic when Walker pulled him into his arms for a dance under the stars.

"Thank you for talking me into having the wedding here," Walker said. Their heads were together as they swayed along with the music.

"It was Agnes's idea but it felt so right. I wanted the girls to be a part of this and for it to be a family celebration."

"I'm glad we didn't get married at a church or in Fiji as I suggested. We can come back here and dance whenever we want and I'll remember how you took my breath away tonight."

"There you go being romantic again," Fin said with a sigh. He rested his chin on Walker's shoulder and marveled at how *right* it felt to lean into this man and relax in his arms. It was second nature now and Walker's hands splayed across Fin's back like they belonged there, like Fin belonged to him.

"Who's that with your brother and that gentleman from the commune?" Walker asked and Fin laughed. He didn't have to look to know which "gentleman" Walker was talking about. They went to Reid's for brunch whenever the girls were with Agnes. Walker and Penn liked to tease each other and Fin could see them becoming good friends over time.

"That's Penn's sister, Penelope. I keep telling you, don't let the beard and the big, messy bun fool you. Penn's an honest-to-God genius and he can fix anything. He's the LeBron James of nannies and the reason Reid wasn't that worried about losing me."

"He's growing on me. And his sister?"

"Penny? She's great. They were a two-for-one deal and Reid got both of them to join the agency."

"So she's a nanny as well... And I assume she's..." Walker cleared his throat and Fin leaned back.

"Obviously, if she's with Reid's agency. Why?" He asked suspiciously. Walker shook his head but his gaze drifted to Agnes. Fin's eyes followed and he pursed his lips. Agnes was staring as Penny laughed at one of her brother's jokes. Fin couldn't blame Agnes. Penny was just as free-spirited and gentle as Penn, but she was much prettier and petite where he was tall and strapping. She reminded Fin of a forest sprite, which was fitting because Penn and Penny were happiest when they were lost in the woods and both were vegan.

"Oh... That's very interesting," Fin agreed hesitantly. "But I'm not sure if they'd be a good fit. Penny's a sunshine-and-granola hippie, like Penn. But she's even purer than he is. I think Penny's last girlfriend was a Buddhist and in the Peace Corps. Penny would definitely think Agnes was hot but I don't think they'd get along all that well..."

"Very interesting..." Walker concurred. "Keep an eye on that and keep me posted."

"Keep you posted?" Fin shook his head. "When would they have a chance to meet again? Agnes doesn't have a child."

"Yet."

"Really? When did Agnes decide she wanted to be a mother?"

"Around six months ago, I imagine. I've been sending her

311

pictures and applications and I think she's ready," Walker replied. Fin's cheeks puffed out as he considered.

"That is *very* interesting but Penny trusts rich people even less than I do. And she'd get on Agnes's last nerve," Fin predicted.

"That's why this is so perfect. Look at us. I'm not down to earth and you don't like rich people. And it's what Agnes deserves." He chuckled deviously. Fin had engaged in his share of little brother fuckery and knew better than to interfere, but he risked a glance at his own brother and grinned.

"You know, Reid isn't running that kind of agency, and he's not going to be happy if he loses *another* nanny to the Camerons."

"I'm sure he'll understand, being a big brother."

"Agnes is sixteen months older than you," Fin observed but Walker waved it off.

"I'm taller and significantly more mature."

"Then that would make you everybody's big brother, except Penn and Gavin," Fin said and Walker snorted.

"It has felt that way lately."

"You love my brother and my friends."

"I do," Walker conceded with a gentle laugh as he pulled Fin closer. "Thank you for sharing them with me. I just wish I had a better family to share with you in return."

"Stop!" Fin stifled a cackle as he swatted him. "The girls are my favorite thing in the whole world. I couldn't love them more if I had given birth to them myself. And Agnes is a treasure."

"I have thought about burying her on the beach several times," Walker murmured, earning another swat from Fin.

"She's the best."

"She is," Walker agreed.

"Her little brother isn't that bad either."

"He isn't?"

"He's kind of perfect, actually. I think he might be the most handsome man I've ever seen," Fin whispered out of the side of his mouth.

"Really?" Walker asked with a warm chuckle and Fin nodded. As far as he was concerned there wasn't a man alive who could hold a candle to Walker Cameron III. But it was so much more than the way he looked, his immaculate suits, or the way he smelled. Fin adored Walker most when he was brave enough to be vulnerable and honest.

"Really. He's not nearly as mean as he wants everyone to think he is, and he's all mine," Fin stated with his usual confidence. Walker hummed in agreement as he captured Fin's chin. He tipped his face back and Walker made Fin's toes curl with a lazy, brain-scattering kiss. Fin sighed dreamily as their lips clung and he held onto Walker. "He's the man of my dreams and I'm going to spend the rest of my life with him."

"I have a feeling you're right. Things have a way of turning out perfectly whenever you're around."

The End

A Day With The Camerons

Grandma's Chicken Noodle Soup

6 Chicken Thighs- bone-in, skin-on
2 onions, just roughly chopped
4 celery ribs with leaves, roughly chopped
6 carrots- 5 roughly chopped, 1 sliced thin for later
2 cloves of garlic
2 bay leaves
1 quart of chicken stock or broth
Fresh herbs of choice, such as parsley, thyme, sage...
Salt
Pepper
Olive Oil
Lemon Juice
Rice, cubed potatoes, or pasta of choice

- Season both sides of chicken and under the skin with plenty of salt and pepper.
- Heat a few tablespoons of olive oil in a stock pot or dutch oven. Brown chicken on both sides, then remove. Discard skin and excess fat and return to pan.
- Add vegetables, smashed garlic cloves, herbs, and bay leaf to the pot. Cover with stock or broth and add more water if needed to cover chicken and vegetables.
- Allow to simmer for 40 minutes, then remove chicken and strain. Let broth cool and skim off fat.
- While the broth is cooling, pick and chop chicken into cubes. You can also shred it.
- Add chicken back to stock along with sliced carrots and more freshly chopped herbs. Season with more salt and pepper to taste. Add pasta, rice, diced potatoes...
- Once the carrots and desired starch are cooked, serve with your patient's favorite crackers.

Chapter Forty-Two

Soft Content Warning: an illness is discussed but the Camerons are coping with a simple, common cold.

He'd grown used to waking up with a smile on his face. They'd been married for almost four months but Walker still felt like he was on his honeymoon when he woke up next to Fin. Those three weeks in the French countryside had been pure bliss but Walker only had to look across the bed to experience the same peace and joy.

Fin's arm was stretched over his head and his lips were curved in a soft grin. He often smiled in his sleep because Fin's soul was as warm and bright as the sunshine slanting across their bed. They had the day off so Walker rolled onto his side and propped his cheek on his palm, enjoying the rare sight of Fin at rest. Walker could tell that he was waking up and knew that Fin wouldn't stop moving until he crashed back into bed at the end of the day.

They took every other Wednesday off and spent the day

out of the house with the girls because both Fin and Walker worked from home. Most of the household had the day off as well. They needed a day outside of The Killian House as much as the family did. Everyone loved their Wednesdays off but Walker cherished them.

At first, he was skeptical when Fin suggested a day without servants, fending for themselves outside of the house. But Walker and the girls loved experiencing the city with Fin as their guide. They did "normal" things like get coffee from Starbucks, and they had bagels for breakfast or stopped in at a bodega for burritos.

Some days, they even took the train or rode in cabs, depending on the destination. Sometimes, there was no particular destination, and Fin and the girls let their whims guide them. It was always an adventure and Walker had a whole new appreciation for the city. He'd spent his entire adult life living in Manhattan but he barely knew it, Walker had learned.

The girls were learning about the city along with Walker, but they were also getting a valuable education about the wider world. They were already better-adjusted than Walker was at their age and their behavior was *phenomenal*.

So phenomenal, that the triplets were looking forward to attending school in the fall. Walker was going to miss having them around during the day, but he was proud of the progress they had made. And they were so *happy*. They were content and ardently in love with Fin. It was touching for Walker, knowing his happiness mattered so much to the girls and that his marriage to Fin had made their lives complete as well.

It was also charming, the way Fin refused to let his marriage to Walker and life inside The Killian House change him. He reveled in every opportunity to do something for himself and teach the girls what he called "basic survival skills" so they weren't too spoiled and out of touch. Walker had already seen a tremendous change in them. They were far more understanding of how privileged their existences were and were far more appreciative of the people who cared for them. It took Walker until his thirties to come to that realization, so he was particularly grateful to Fin for giving the girls a big head start in that respect.

As if he'd heard Walker's thoughts, Fin's eyelids fluttered and lifted. He scratched at his hair as he yawned, then stretched. Walker silently counted, knowing that Fin was only capable of being still for thirty seconds at the most. A wide smile stretched across Fin's face and Walker would swear that the room got even brighter and warmer. He rolled toward Walker and Fin's eyes sparkled with excitement.

"It's *our* Wednesday!" Fin threw an arm around Walker's neck.

"It is."

They kissed and Fin rubbed the end of his nose against Walker's. "You know why I especially love our Wednesday mornings?" His fingers trailed along Walker's jaw as Fin groaned appreciatively.

"We get an extra hour before the girls get up?" Walker guessed. They had a deal: the girls stayed in bed until Walker and Fin came and got them at eight. The girls picked their own outfits and dressed themselves. Walker and Fin did their hair—for better or for worse—before the five of them skipped down the stairs and out the front door.

"I get this to myself for an extra hour." Fin angled his head and sucked on Walker's chin. "And tonight, I'll rub myself all over my husband's beard."

Walker didn't shave on his day off and he wore jeans because Fin wasn't exaggerating. Fin would grab his ass whenever they were alone and would literally rub himself all over Walker's bristly, unshaven face. It was a heavenly way to end a perfect day. But why wait?

"Why don't you climb up and let me taste you now?"

"Walker!" Fin gasped, pretending to be shocked, but he got onto his knees and rose. "I can't believe you'd make such a scandalous suggestion this early in the morning!"

"I don't know what's gotten into me..." Walker murmured, pretending to be concerned.

Fin beamed as he fell forward and pecked at Walker's lips. "I have! *Many* times!" He boasted.

Walker rumbled in agreement. "You certainly have." They often flipped, with Fin pulling out and riding Walker once he was close. "Do you want to...?"

"Always, but we might want to save that for tonight or this weekend. Our extra hour is running out. Nurse Lisa's shift will be ending soon, and we don't want the monkeys loose in the zoo without us."

"Good point." Walker gestured for Fin to hurry and climb aboard.

He happily scrambled up to the head of the bed and turned before Fin threw his leg over Walker's face and sat. Fin cooed encouragingly as he writhed against Walker's lips and tongue. Walker held onto Fin's thighs, keeping him there until he was shaking and begging for relief. Then, Fin crawled back down Walker's body, mounted him, and set a blistering pace. Walker was treated to a magnificent view of Fin's ass as it slapped against his pelvis. Fin planted his hands on the bed between Walker's knees and it didn't take long for them to combust. They laughed breathlessly through a quick shower before pulling on t-shirts, jeans, and sneakers.

"Come on! I'm can't wait!" Fin was bouncing at the bathroom door while Walker fussed with his hair. He had no idea how Pierce made it stand so perfectly. It kept flopping over Walker's brow, making him look like he was trying too hard. "We're going to start at the sea lions and the Delacorte Clock like we always do but after that we're hitting the Literary Walk and visiting all of our favorite statues!"

"The girls do enjoy all the bronzes..."

Fin muffled an excited squeal. "Me too! We're going to see Balto, Alice and the gang from Wonderland, Hans Christian Anderson, Mother Goose, and Beethoven! We're going to swing by the 'Imagine' mosaic and I want to go all the way around to The Belvedere Castle."

"Sounds like you've got a big day planned for us," Walker noted with a grin at the mirror. Fin's and the girls' love of Central Park had rubbed off on him. It truly was a great way to experience the city's history and see its best side. "I enjoy the Minton tiles in the Bethesda Arcade," Walker noted, then grunted as Fin yanked on his wrist, dragging him down the hall.

"The girls are waiting for us!" He scolded, but the room was quiet and the girls were still in bed when they peeked around the door.

"I heard them whispering about fifteen minutes ago and told them to stay put, Mr. Cameron," Nurse Lisa explained.

Beatrice humphed and shook her head at Amelia. "We told her that we had to tell you but she said she was going to hide it so she could go."

"You can't go to the park if you're sick!" Charlotte added.

"Ndo!" Amelia wailed. Her arms were folded over her chest as her feet kicked under her quilt. "I'mb find!"

She clearly wasn't. Her eyes were watery and puffy, and she looked a bit gray. Both Fin and Walker winced. But Fin clicked his teeth as he charged into the room and went to Amelia, thank goodness. Walker was the world's worst patient when he was injured or ill, and he had no idea how to care for a sick child.

"You can go ahead and take off, Lisa. We'll see you on Saturday."

Lisa's face scrunched. "Are you sure?" She asked Fin. "There's no one downstairs. I can call—"

"I promise, I know where the medicine cabinet is and I can find my way around the kitchen," he reassured her. "I doubt Pierce has wandered too far from the house, if there's a crisis."

"We'll be fine," Walker reassured her and gave her a gentle nudge to get her going.

He found it rather touching. It wasn't that long ago that Lisa and other night nurses had threatened to walk out if Walker couldn't retain a decent nanny. And it wasn't lost on Walker that he would have begged on his hands and knees for her to stay before Fin. The idea of being alone with the girls for five minutes would have had Walker in a cold sweat, but alone in The Killian House without any support staff? He would have run screaming. "We'll see you on Saturday," he said with an easy wave. Once she was gone, he raised a brow at Fin, then glanced around the room. "This should be an adventure."

"I wadda go do da park!" Amanda cried. She sneezed, creating snot bubbles as she coughed. Walker reared back but Fin shot him a warning glare before he could run.

"How about a pajama party day with cookies and soup and movies in our room?" Fin suggested. The girls were always happy to pile onto the sofa in the sitting room down the hall and watch movies on the giant television. It was hidden behind a wall of shelves and Fin still got a kick out of watching them slide apart to reveal the screen. All three girls cheered, although Amelia was more subdued. "I think we'll bring the nap time tent with us for our sick princess. OK?" He asked Amelia and bent to kiss her forehead. He pressed his lips against her brow and sighed. "You've got a little bit of a fever but I'll give you something for that and round up some breakfast. Then, I'll take Bea and Charlotte with me and we'll make you some chicken soup and chocolate chip cookies."

"She can help me supervise tent setup and the transfer of all these pillows, stuffies, and quilts," Walker offered. He wouldn't be much help in the kitchen but Walker knew that a decent pajama party required lots of stuffed animals and most of the girls' bedding.

"Perfect!" Fin gave Amelia's hair a kiss and straightened. "You ladies wash up and put on your glamour pajamas while I run downstairs and make us a breakfast basket."

Walker intercepted Fin on his way to the door. "Are you sure you won't need any help? I have a feeling Pierce would be happy to give us a hand and we could let him take tomorrow off."

"Relax!" Fin laughed softly as he kissed Walker's cheek. "I'll be able to find just about anything we could possibly need in that kitchen. It's like being loose in a candy store. And I spent the first twenty-six years of my life surviving without an army of servants, remember?"

"I do but you've never had to care for four other people, including a sick child," Walker argued cautiously, earning an impatient look from Fin.

"She has a cold. It's been going around and I predict we'll all have it before the weekend is through." He shushed when the girls started to protest loudly. Walker shared their concern at Fin's prediction, but he had to set a good example, so he simply hummed and nodded along.

"I will defer to your judgment and experience."

"We're all going to feel yucky, but we'll snuggle a lot and watch all our favorite movies so it won't be that bad," Fin reassured them, immediately putting Walker and the girls at ease.

"You heard the man," Walker said to the girls as he set his hands on his hips. "Let's get your teeth brushed and faces washed while Fin's finding our breakfast."

"Go change into your most glamorous pajamas and prepare to snuggle!" Fin ordered, pointing at the girls' closet as he backed out of the room.

And just like that, Fin had turned what could have been a dreadful day for Walker and the girls into a fun, yet soothing adventure. Walker watched as Beatrice and Charlotte zipped around the room, gathering Amelia's favorite animals, dolls, and blankets. They helped her choose an ensemble and the nursery was filled with their happy chatter. Walker felt unusually capable as he gave the girls lopsided ponytails and messy braids. Each head of hair might have been a shambles but the girls were at their happiest as they marched down the hallway with their arms full of teddy bears and pink bedding. And Walker found that he was at his happiest as well as he looked forward to a rare lazy day with Fin and the girls.

Fin's Ultimate Three C's: Chocolate Chip Cookies

2 1/4 cup flour
5/6 cup oats blended
1/2 tsp baking soda
1 1/2 tsp baking powder
1 1/2 tsp salt
1 cup unsalted butter
1 1/4 cup light brown sugar
1 cup white sugar
2 eggs
2 teaspoons of vanilla
1 tablespoon of molasses
1 cup semi sweet chocolate chips
1 bar bittersweet chocolate, chopped
1 bar of milk chocolate, chopped
Sea Salt for topping

- I run a little less than a cup of old-fashioned oats through a food processor and get it as fine as I can. You can expirament with different flours but you want 3 cups total with All Purpose comprising of at least 3/4 of your flour. Sift with the rest of your dry ingredients.
- Carefully brown the butter, taking it off the heat to cool when it turns golden.
- Add sugars to the butter and the eggs one at a time. Then, add the vanilla and molasses.
- Add chips and chopped-up bars. I like to vary the size of chunks when I'm chopping. The smaller shards will melt into the dough and the larger ones will give you little puddles of chocolate gooeyness.
- Allow dough to rest in the fridge for two hours, then preheat the oven to 350°. Use a scoop and give the cookies just a slight smoosh so they don't roll. Bake time will depend on how big your scoop is but watch carefully! You want the cookies to start to get gold around the edges but they'll look darker sooner because of the brown sugar and molasses. 8-10 minutes is a good starting point, though.
- Sprinkle with coarse sea salt after they come out of the oven.
- Leave to cool on the cookie sheet! They'll finish baking in the middle and be softer.

Chapter Forty-Three

"Get the door, Bea!" Fin gasped. He staggered toward the kitchen, making the girls giggle as they reached for the door. Charlotte was standing on Fin's foot and holding onto his waist while Bea was riding on his back. They were as light as feathers but he pretended he was out of breath as they crashed into the closest counter. He pointed at the sink and trudged on.

It was a little eerie, seeing the kitchen darkened and abandoned when Fin took his first peek earlier. He was hunting for coffee when Pierce materialized behind him, nearly causing Fin to drop a canister of beans.

"What are you doing here? You're supposed to be...off," Fin said. He had no idea what Pierce did when he wasn't working. As far as Fin knew, Pierce never took a day off until Walker made him abide by the new "Free Range Wednesdays" rule. *Everyone* was supposed to get out of the house and enjoy the city or make time for themselves.

"What are *you* doing here? You usually take the family out

for breakfast," Pierce countered, his eyes narrowing as if he sensed a disturbance in the household.

"Amelia's not feeling well so we had to change our plans."

"Oh!" Pierce's eyes swung toward the nursery. "Should I send for the doctor and have the cook return and prepare some soup?" He asked quickly.

"No way! Walker and I can handle this!"

"Are you sure? I would be happy to fetch the thermometer and anything else you might need," Pierce offered but Fin gave the old butler a stern look.

"You had better make yourself scarce before I tell Walker I caught you trying to work on your day off," he threatened playfully, then gasped. "I found this really cool record shop on the way to my parents' place if you're looking for something to do!" That had piqued Pierce's interest so Fin gave him detailed directions and sent him on his way.

Fin had a blast foraging in the colossal pantry and refrigerators. He threw together some scones and found the picnic basket and a fruit salad while they were baking. He packed cheese sticks, little jars of jams and honey, a carafe of coffee, and orange juice boxes into the basket before the scones went in. They were wrapped in a kitchen towel and still warm when Fin strolled into the upstairs sitting room with the basket on his arm, looking like a domestic legend.

The girls were delighted because they loved Fin's scones but Walker was upset. "Nobody told me they were this good," he grumbled around a mouthful. Walker was on his third at the time.

"I can't believe you've never tried them," Fin murmured and shrugged. "I usually make them to cheer the girls up when you're away, but I was sure we've had them while you were home."

"This explains why you don't get upset when I have to go

on a trip," Walker said to Charlotte. "I was beginning to think you didn't miss me anymore."

The girls loudly reassured Walker that they missed him every moment he was away, making him beam and blush. They were so adorable and Fin's heart melted, his family was so perfect and perfectly happy. He wished Amelia wasn't feeling so poorly, but he was rather excited about puttering around in the kitchen with Beatrice and Charlotte and all the movies they planned to watch.

"We're going to start with the cookie dough because that needs to hide out in the fridge for a few hours before we can start baking," he explained, backing up to the counter by the sink. Beatrice let go of his shoulders and dropped with a happy squeak.

"I'll get the chips and chocolate bars!" Charlotte ran for the pantry. She was a blue blur in a Care Bears t-shirt, blue leggings, and blue socks.

Fin bought the girls *a lot* of t-shirts. They had a closet full of beautiful dresses and expensive separates, but they didn't have any *fun* t-shirts. He felt a rush of excitement every time he found the perfect shirt for one of the girls in a thrift shop. Beatrice was sporting a purple t-shirt with Albert Einstein on the front and the quote *"It's not that I'm so smart, it's just that I stay with problems longer."* on the back. It was a men's size medium so Fin turned it into a shirtdress with a few alterations. She had paired it with a purple beanie and tall rainbow socks. Fin thought she looked chic and ready to bake.

"Chocolate chip cookies are my ultimate Three C's and I like to use *three* types of chocolate so they're extra melty," he told the girls and went to get a bowl from the other end of the long worktable. "Riley's stopping by with alphabet noodles for our soup!"

"Can he stay and watch movies with us?" Charlotte asked excitedly.

"Sorry, but he can't today. I asked him to pick some noodles up on his way to work since he's just a few blocks away now. He's dropping them off while he's on his lunch break," Fin explained but the girls were still pouting.

"We never get to see him anymore," Beatrice complained.

"Aren't you glad he's found a cool family to work for?" Fin asked her. "And think of how lucky that kid is. He gets to hang out with Riley now and have lots of fun too."

The girls agreed that it was a good thing and were soon busy, collecting and assembling the ingredients for their cookie dough. Fin didn't tell them that Riley's new boss was also his former childhood nemesis. Or that Fin had received a series of angry texts outlining all of Giles Ashby's many faults while Riley was riding the train to work.

"OK! Let's get started on our soup! We'll make the broth and let it simmer while we're watching *The Princess Bride*," he said, resulting in more cheers and a happily buzzing Bea and Charlotte as they gathered produce and herbs for the soup. The three of them pretended to be Shakespearean witches as they stirred and cackled, then tumbled back upstairs to join Walker and Amelia on the sofa.

The soup and cookies were a hit and everyone was in high spirits despite the sniffles and sore throats that spread through the room, as Fin had predicted. Not that he was surprised at their success. His chicken noodle soup recipe had been perfected by his grandmother. And Fin's chocolate chip cookies worked in any emergency situation. Fin sent six with an extremely grateful Riley when he dropped off the pasta for their soup.

Amelia was already feeling a lot better by the time Fin tucked her in and kissed her forehead to check it. It was cool against his lips and she didn't sound as congested. Beatrice and Charlotte were stopped up but looking forward to a day in the tent with more soup and cookies.

"Goodnight, Sweetheart," Fin whispered and tapped on the end of Amelia's nose. They all took turns reading from *Where The Sidewalk Ends*, laughing when their stuffy noses and scratchy throats made the silly poems sound even sillier. Fin's nose was running like a faucet but his heart felt like it could burst when Amelia kissed his cheek.

"Goodnight, Daddy. I was sad because I didn't want to ruin our day but I had a lot of fun," she said sleepily, then let out a loud yawn.

"Oh, my princess." Fin needed a moment and swallowed loudly to ease the catch in his throat. "Any day I spend with you is magical, even the days that aren't fun. I love you very much and I'll always want to take care of you."

"I love you too," she said before rolling onto her side and tucking her hands under her cheek. Fin made his way around the room, checking each girl's forehead with a kiss.

"We'll see you in the morning," Walker whispered to Amelia, then kissed her goodnight. He turned down the lights before towing Fin from the room. They held hands as they made their way down the hall.

"You should have added pastry chef and baker to your résumé. I would have had far fewer qualms that first morning," Walker teased with a warm wink.

"I didn't need to fluff up my résumé. I had a heartbeat and you were desperate," Fin teased back.

Walker made an exploding sound as he nodded. "A rodeo clown could have walked through the front door and I probably would have hired him," he admitted, but Fin rolled his eyes.

"Any smart clown would have taken one look at those little monsters and ran right back to the rodeo. It's much safer."

That got a frown from Walker "Probably..." He gave his head a shake as they returned to their suite. The sitting room was still buried in pillows and blankets. They'd leave it all for another day or two but Fin was going to introduce his family to the colossal tent fort the next time everyone came down with a bug. "Thank you for making today so special." Walker closed the door behind them and pulled Fin into his arms. "I would have been lost without you, even if I had Pierce and the nurses to back me up. I've never handled it well when the girls are sick," he said with a soft, self-deprecating chuckle. Fin waved it off before checking Walker for a fever. He was a little warm so Fin would give him some Tylenol after they changed for bed.

"I'm the luckiest person in the whole world because you're all mine," Fin said, managing to keep his tone even and almost boastful. But his heart raced as he put his arms around Walker. He hadn't gotten over his crush and still felt a little nervous when they slipped away for a quick kiss or to make out. "It hurt before, having a professional barrier between me and the girls. I couldn't squeeze them and tell them how much I loved them and I could only comfort them so much when they were upset or hurt. Now, I don't have to listen at the door when they're talking about one of our adventures and I can kiss them good-night too. Even days like today feel like a gift because I'm taking care of *my family*."

"I hope you always feel that way because we'd be lost without you now." Walker cradled Fin's jaw and kissed him tenderly. It was lovely and Fin's toes were curling in his socks until Walker drew back and sneezed loudly. Fin almost jumped out of his socks and laughed as he dragged his sleeve over his face.

"Alright! In bed with you," he ordered, turning Walker.

"You had better be coming with me." His arm reached behind him until Walker caught Fin's wrist.

"I'm tucking you in and then I'm running downstairs for tea."

"Do you have to?" Walker grumbled, but he let Fin guide him around the bed and obediently got under the covers. Fin brushed the hair away from his face before kissing him.

"I think we could both use a cup. And a few cookies," he added, making Walker grin as their lips clung.

"I never thought I'd look forward to having a cold but you've gone and made it fun and romantic. Thank you for marrying me and making each day an adventure."

Fin hummed a soft, satisfied sound as he lingered for just a few more minutes before trekking back down to the kitchen. "That's my job and I take it very seriously."

The End

Want more nannies and struggling single fathers?
Giles Ashby Needs A Nanny is coming January '23!

A letter from K. Sterling

Dear Reader,

Thank you so much for your time and for reading *The Last Nanny In Manhattan*. I hope you had fun falling love with Fin and Walker! Before you go, I'd appreciate it if you'd consider leaving a review. Your review would really help me and help other readers find their way to us. And I promise, I read and appreciate every single one of them. Even the negative reviews. I want your honest feedback so I know how to steal your heart.

Please help me out by leaving a review!

K. Sterling writes like a demon and is mother to Alex, Zoe, Stella, and numerous gay superheroes. She's also a history nerd, a *Lord of the Rings* fan, and a former counterintelligence agent. She has self-published dozens of M/M romance novels including the popular *Boys of Lake Cliff* series and *Beautiful Animal*. K. Sterling is known for fast-paced romantic thrillers and touching gay romcoms. There might be goosebumps and some gore but there's always true love and lots of laughter.

A letter from K. Sterling

Once again, thank you from the very bottom of my heart. I love you for sharing your time with us and hope we'll see you again soon.

Love and happy reading,
K.

Before You Go!

Website: https: www.ksterlingbooks.com
Patreon: www.patreon.com/ksterling

Please visit my Amazon Author Page for more K. Sterling titles!

For a complete Lake Cliff reading order, visit us at:
ksterlingbooks.com/lake-cliff

Printed in Great Britain
by Amazon

46117882R00195